C000246100

MY CHRISTMAS NUMBER ONE

LEONIE MACK

Boldwood

First published in Great Britain in 2020 by Boldwood Books Ltd.

Copyright © Leonie Mack, 2020

Cover Design: Alice Moore Design

Cover Photography: Shutterstock

The moral right of Leonie Mack to be identified as the author of this work has been asserted in accordance with the Copyright, Designs and Patents Act 1988.

All rights reserved. No part of this book may be reproduced in any form or by any electronic or mechanical means, including information storage and retrieval systems, without written permission from the author, except for the use of brief quotations in a book review.

This book is a work of fiction and, except in the case of historical fact, any resemblance to actual persons, living or dead, is purely coincidental.

Every effort has been made to obtain the necessary permissions with reference to copyright material, both illustrative and quoted. We apologise for any omissions in this respect and will be pleased to make the appropriate acknowledgements in any future edition.

A CIP catalogue record for this book is available from the British Library.

Paperback ISBN 978-1-80048-119-0

Large Print ISBN 978-1-80048-115-2

Ebook ISBN 978-1-80048-113-8

Kindle ISBN 978-1-80048-114-5

Audio CD ISBN 978-1-80048-120-6

MP3 CD ISBN 978-1-80048-117-6

Digital audio download ISBN 978-1-80048-112-1

Boldwood Books Ltd
23 Bowerdean Street
London SW6 3TN
www.boldwoodbooks.com

For Jill

1

'They want me to do what?' Cara turned from the piano to give her manager her full attention.

'Feature on a Latin Christmas single.'

She blinked. She had heard correctly. 'Is that a thing? A Latin Christmas single? Do you mean like 'In Dulci Jubilo'? That kind of Latin?'

Freddie cleared his throat. 'No. Not that kind of Latin.'

'You mean the record company wants me to appear on some Spanglish version of a Christmas song?'

Freddie pulled up a chair. 'The label contractually requires you to feature on a single written by another of their artists, who happens to be from Colombia, and sings in Spanish.'

Huh. 'Why?' Her hands fell to the keys, smooth and reassuring. She picked out a minor chord and set up a syncopated rhythm.

Freddie smiled. 'I didn't know you could play 'Despacito'.'

She felt her way through a few more chords. 'I didn't know I knew 'Despacito'. I'm just channelling the vibe. It's not my scene, though, is it?'

'No,' Freddie admitted.

Christmas wasn't her scene either. Snow and mistletoe, twinkling lights and tinkling bells were for other people – another life.

'"Contractually required" sounds iron-clad. Does it make any sense professionally?' The ink was barely dry on her record contract. She'd had one UK top ten single. Falling back into obscurity was not only possible but likely.

'I would have argued for you if I thought it would harm your career.'

'I know. It's you and me against the mighty record company. So, tell me why it isn't going to suck? I don't really do 'Feliz Navidad', and 'Heroes and Words' wasn't exactly popular in Latin America,' Cara asked, referring to her break-out pop/rock protest anthem.

'You're the crossover,' Freddie explained. 'The label thinks the song is good enough to chart outside the Latin sphere. They want to make it happen. You have momentum. It makes sense.'

'It doesn't make sense. My influences have more to do with church Latin than Latin America. Am I supposed to shake my hips in front of the camera in the video?' A tickle of concern rose in her throat. Could she even pull that off?

'The video is planned to be a kind of epic love story with a Christmas vibe.'

Cara choked on a laugh. 'An epic love story? Between me and this reggaetón star? Surely there's a way out of this?'

'His music isn't exactly reggaetón, although he did some collaboration years ago when it was first going mainstream,' Freddie said.

'Oh, God. He's a washed-up crooner who wants to get back in the charts?'

'The music's more upbeat than pop ballads. And he had an album out this year. Sort of… tropical party hits.'

She screwed her nose up in dismay. A tropical party hit about Christmas? She pictured dancing pineapples in Santa suits, which was stupid, but at least easier to imagine than herself wearing a bikini in a music video. Could anything be further out of her comfort zone?

'What is Daddy going to say?'

Freddie winced. 'Please tell me that's a rhetorical question.'

She nodded with a forced laugh. 'I'm not going to make you ask him. He only grudgingly enjoyed Orff when he'd been dead for thirty years. The exotic rhythms will give him a migraine.' Like every other risk she took gave him a migraine. There was no hope of impressing her father, but Cara was standing on her own two feet these days – the biological one and the prosthesis.

'Maybe he'll like it. This song – it's called "Nostalgia" – it's good, Cara. It's really good.'

She took a long look at her manager. 'I'm not convinced. What if the song flops and it eclipses the release of the album?' That sounded reasonable – at least more reasonable than the truth. She couldn't exactly ask to get out of it because she and Christmas didn't get along.

Freddie inclined his head. 'I agree the timing isn't great. But the clause in your contract is valid. They can require you to feature on the tracks of other artists when it suits them. And it won't suck. I don't think it'll be Christmas number one, but it's a good song and everyone loves Christmas.'

Cara grimaced. Everyone except Cara and her father. 'Thinking about Christmas in June is just wrong.'

'Shooting the video is planned for London in August, with fake snow and decorations.'

'I hope it's tasteful at least.' Cara turned up her nose, wincing as she saw the dancing pineapples again. 'But we do what we have to do, I suppose.'

'That's the spirit.'

* * *

By the late afternoon, Cara's head was fuzzy and she could no longer tell one version of her own voice from another, so she stowed her headphones with a sigh. She would go for a run and pick it up again tomorrow. The control freak in her had insisted on co-producing the album. She needed to be on top of every detail or she'd succumb to the whispered suggestions from her own mind that she wasn't cut out for a career in pop music.

She could have chosen another career. With her father's unwavering financial support, she could have studied to do anything. But music was as close as she'd come to passion. She'd spent five gruelling years being piddlingly successful on the UK indie scene because she couldn't resist the pull of the songs in her head. After her record deal and her first charting single, she was sometimes nostalgic for those simpler days when less was riding on every song.

Nostalgia... The word had been in the back of her mind since her conversation with Freddie. How could that one word set off the painful memories she subdued every Christmas? The song was probably some frothy jingle with a sappy heart and a bit of Afro-Caribbean drumming. Wasn't everyone who thought Christmas was the season of joy pretending, just a little? But that word, nostalgia, grabbed her by the guts.

She downloaded the demo to her phone and scanned the email. Freddie had sent her the link to the artist's Wikipedia page and website and included a couple of lines of bio. Javi Félix. Was that his real name? He'd won a couple of Latin Grammys, but that was years ago. He'd released a new album entitled *Por el Amor de Ella*, which Freddie had translated as, 'For the love of her – or possibly it. Google translate wasn't very helpful.' She clicked on the Wikipedia link and read while she headed upstairs to change for her run.

Javier Félix Rodríguez Moreno was thirty-seven and enjoyed taking his shirt off in front of a camera. She had to admit he had the abs for it, and a handsome, strong-boned face, but his style was too conspicuous. His musical styles were gobbledegook to Cara – bachata, cumbia, salsa, tropical fusion – but she did see one word to make her nerves wobble – reggaetón. He'd had a good number of hits in the Latin charts, starting when Cara was still in school. He was based in Miami and had an ex-wife and a daughter.

The banner of his promotional website was professional and attractively beach-themed, but Cara wrinkled her nose. She couldn't place herself in any of his promo photos. His smile was too big. His eyes twinkled with the promise of too many mojitos. Perhaps she could hide behind her biggest guitar. And a snowy Christmas video would mean more clothing, right? Did they have snow in Colombia? She had no idea. Could she place Colombia on a map? Somewhere north of Brazil, she was sure. Perhaps next to Venezuela. She was usually good at geography. She spoke bits of French and German from her private school education, but she'd never learned any Spanish. She was going to feel so stupid.

With her running prosthesis on and her earbuds in place, Cara paused outside the dignified Georgian building that housed her flat. Bristol in June was a far cry from the Caribbean at Christmas, but she had to give this song a go. After a few stretches, she switched on the music and headed up the hill.

The first notes made her steps falter. A warm acoustic guitar plucked a few notes from a minor chord and then his voice – powerful and slightly husky – swept through the compelling opening melody. Then a pause. With a muted shout, the rhythm began, at first only a snare drum and hand claps in a pattern that was both elemental and peculiar. She identified the common time signature, but the rhythm was too foreign for her to follow in her internal sheet music. Instead, it went straight to her blood – impossible to resist. The guitar continued its wistful chord progression, the dampening strokes just as important as the strumming. Between the rests in the rhythm and the muted guitar, Cara was struck by what wasn't there. Was that the point? She was reading way too much into this.

After a verse and an unexpected additional bar in duple metre, the song took off with a full drum kit, congas, electric guitar and brass. His voice led the charge, soaring through the chorus and settling back into rough melancholy for the next verse. The Spanish syllables sounded like another rhythm instrument, skipping and rolling through a story which meant nothing to her.

The rhythm would be good for running – good for moving – but Cara was listening too intently to keep up her usual pace. She paused at the top of the hill, blind to the view of the suspension bridge and the sheer drop down to the Avon River which usually lifted her spirits. The instruments dropped away as the song transitioned to a melodic bridge section.

Cara heard a lifetime of music in that section. A renaissance setting of a chant from the Christmas matins tickled at the back of her mind, as well as a section of a Brahms piano concerto she'd perfected after hours of sweat when she should have been studying for her A Levels. It even brought back hints of the piano duet she'd played with her father as a child.

Her obsessive musical brain was processing the new material, but the intensity scared her. The off-beat rhythm should have felt alien, but it invoked a longing – to dance, to wallow and, most worryingly, to remember. She resented her mind – not for the first time – for reacting so powerfully to something she didn't understand.

This was not the time to come to terms with the Christmas she couldn't remember. She should be thankful that this single was so far from the traditional carols that had epitomised the season before her mother had died. But her subconscious was stubbornly searching for them.

The chorus broke back into the song, a layer of joy against the haunting melody of the bridge, and Cara itched to sing. She made do with running. Over the Clifton Bridge, through the deer park and back along the river she ran as she listened to the demo track over and over.

When she arrived back at her building, puffing and pouring with sweat, she felt as though she'd lived a whole life in that song. The shirtless smiler with the mojito eyes had written this? She stumbled down the stairs to her studio, guzzling water, and sat down at the piano. The Brahms concerto was the first thing to come to her fingers.

She hesitated when the Christmas songs began to come, but she couldn't resist. It had been years, but she could still fumble through 'Mary's Boy Child' while choking on memories. When she opened the document with the translation of the lyrics, tears were pricking her eyes and she was cursing the catchy, tropical daylights out of the amazing song and its unnecessarily attractive composer.

Her tears spilled over by the end of the first verse, reading about a season stopped in time and a love that is always looking back. She didn't know what he meant, but she was trapped in the painful memories she usually only faced in December. When she got to the last line of the chorus, her throat was thick. Dance so you don't cry...

That line lodged deeply in her chest as she processed the rest of the words. There were familiar Christmas references: lighting candles, 'The Little Drummer Boy' and the baby in the manger. But there were also evocative images of a Christmas season she didn't recognise: tears of cinnamon, coconut and joy; banging a drum and making a noise and copious references to dancing as the world stood still every Christmas.

She slipped on her headphones, wanting the intimacy of the sound, and listened again.

* * *

Javi stumbled off the stage, swiping the back of his hand across his forehead. Someone handed him a tumbler and he downed it, grimacing when he realised it was rum. He needed water, not rum, but he didn't refuse when the glass was refilled.

'Salud, viejo!'

The backstage crew slapped his shoulders and grasped his hands warmly. 'You can still rock Miami, man!'

Still... He smirked and drained the glass.

'Gracias, chicos,' he rasped and cleared his throat. He tugged his drenched t-shirt off and wiped down his face. He'd sung his last song from behind the drum kit – one of his signature gimmicks – and the drum solo was a killer.

The crowd was still cheering and Javi's blood was still pumping, so he met the eye of the stage manager, shrugged and strode back on. His manager called out and tossed him a bottle of water. He grabbed the microphone and held up a hand to signal the crowd to be quiet.

'Un momento por favor,' he said. He downed half the bottle of water with relief, took a long look at what was left and poured the rest over his head. 'Mucho mejor,' he grinned. 'Uyy, it's hot in here.'

Cheers and whoops wound the atmosphere back up. Women were screaming and hyperventilating as they jostled in the front. He'd been going for two hours now and the audience was getting hazy, but he blew a kiss expansively in their direction.

He had a moment's indecision about what to play. The melody that had been living in his head and his recording software for the past month was burning to be played, but it was the one thing he mustn't give away. For the first time in years the record company was enthusiastic about something he'd written.

'Una más,' he called out and, knowing his band would be in

place by now, he shouted the first line of one of his upbeat party tracks from ten years ago. He held out his hand and someone shoved the neck of a guitar into it. It was the wrong one, but he went with it, holding the microphone to the crowd to sing the chorus and hamming up the racy bridge section.

He stumbled backwards at the end, the guitar sliding on his bare chest, his hair stuck to his face. Another glass of rum made it into his hands and to his mouth. The crowd cheered as he left the stage, knowing this time he had to go.

He was falling-down exhausted, but so pumped he'd never sleep. He slept poorly in Miami anyway. He owned a beautiful condo where he could throw stones at the Bahamas, but all it was good for was lying awake at night remembering how he and Susana had split the assets during the divorce. He'd crash at the studio tonight, or at a hotel.

The studio, he decided. The email he'd been waiting for had arrived as the doors opened at the club. Cara Poignton had uploaded her files to the system and there was no way he'd wait to open them.

He'd never heard of her until the record company had set out its requirements. He now knew her single had charted well in the anglosphere, but he hadn't heard it until a month ago. He didn't know what to make of her or the marriage of convenience they had been forced into. Her single 'Heroes and Words' was a driving anthem with a catchy chorus that had delighted a mainly female audience with its indignant independence. It was a good song, despite being formulaic anglo rock/pop. He was anxious to hear what she'd done to his music.

He changed and took a cab to the studio downtown. Javi was sick of Miami, but at least the taxi drivers didn't recognise him any more. He'd loved this city at first, when Susana had known everyone and the high of selling out gigs was new. Now the gleaming white condos and unrelenting cleanliness reminded him of the times he couldn't see his daughter. At least in Colombia, Beatríz wasn't round the corner and the memories had scarred over. He was spending more and more time at home.

Once inside the building, he pulled out his laptop and plugged it into a workstation. He would have preferred his setup in Barranquilla, but at least he had a pass to enter the studio at three in the morning. He pulled up the email and tried to make sense of the file names she'd uploaded onto the server.

She'd recorded two versions. It seemed professional, but he had to wonder what was different. He'd lay each of them over the demo and compare, but first he had to listen to the raw sound. He was producing the single himself. The song was deeply lodged in him and he would hear it in his mind anyway. What he couldn't imagine was her clear voice joining his – the song in English and in Spanish.

He opened the folder labelled 'alternative version' first and shoved on a pair of headphones. When her voice reached him, he went completely still. It was a fifth higher than what he'd written – soaring and ephemeral. The rhythm was almost completely absent and the sound was raw and vulnerable. She was singing his words as a haunting chant. It worked. Goosebumps spread up his arms to the back of his neck. Sometimes he got the impression that the song had written him, rather than the other way round. Cara Poignton had tapped into that and he was confounded.

Listening to the bare track without the rest of the song was like peering into her mind. He heard every breath. He could taste her uncertainty. It was as though she was right beside him. He couldn't take the headphones off. Her vocals shifted as she sang through the stages of the song. Her interpretation of the bridge section was nothing like what he'd written to mirror his words in Spanish, but his heart pounded as he listened to her sing about mourning elusive memories and the year she didn't even know if the tree had been green. He sat back, stunned by the intimacy of her voice, her reaction to his music.

God, if this was what it felt like to sing about something real, he was glad he usually stuck to parties and drinking and dancing as his subject matter. But for this one song... It was perfect.

When her voice dropped away on the final note, fading to a gasp, Javi sat back, bewildered. He didn't know her. He would never have picked her to feature on his single. But it was perfect. His life had never been perfect and where was the fun in perfection anyway?

He felt strangely exposed, frowning in the aftermath of her incredible recording. Like the rest of the song, she'd crept up on him before he was ready to face any of it. But it was just the music. She couldn't know the chaos of thoughts and feelings that lay behind the track, nor would she be interested. She could never live up to this bizarre affinity in the flesh. It was all in his head.

When he opened the second file to hear a technically faultless recording of the parts he'd sent her, rhythm intact to the last sixteenth, he was able to reassure himself. He could choose this version and bury the spark. It was still a good song.

But the scent of adventure on his tongue told him he wouldn't.

He opened up her email again and hunched over the keyboard.

What, you after writing credit?

He pressed send before he could second-guess his blunt words. He fiddled around on the internet, trying to convince himself that she wasn't going to reply immediately, although she was conceivably awake, over there on the other side of the Atlantic. The laptop pinged and he tabbed back to his email with an uncomfortable grin.

Yes… if you use the alternative version.

That was direct. But he didn't deserve anything more, given the rudeness of his own email.

Okay… if I use the alternative version. Where the hell did that come from?

He tapped his fingers as he waited for her response. Would she be the first to drop the conversation? Why did he care? She put him out of his misery quickly.

It came from Christmas. Wasn't that the assignment?

He smiled crookedly at her word choice. Assignment?

Pretty miserable… mourning and memories and stuff.

Was he trying to offend her? He should have scraped around for some charm – or at least some decent politeness – but his emotional resources were running low.

It's your song. Your bits were pretty miserable, too.

He smiled. She had spunk, and she had a point. But not all of his lyrics were forlorn.

If I use the alternative version, it's our miserable song. Don't you even like Christmas?

She took so long to respond, he almost shut down the computer and succumbed to sleep.

If you don't like it, don't use it. I didn't choose to collaborate on this and to be honest I don't know anything about Latin music. It doesn't sound like Christmas to me. Do what you want.

She hadn't answered the question. He wouldn't have had an answer either. Her voice was still echoing in his mind. He was tired and touched and he should stop chatting to her before it got weirder.

What sounds like Christmas to you, then?

He'd never been good with self-control. Her answer – quicker this time – was a link to a video of a group of singers performing some haunting old song in four-part harmony. It was called 'O Magnum Mysterium' and was entirely in Latin. He chuckled to himself at her old-world traditionalism, even as goose bumps spread up his spine at the crystalline harmonies and timeless feel.

Cool… How do you like this? The title translates as 'I want to sing'.

He sent her a link to Cuban musician Jon Secada's version of 'Rocking Around the Christmas Tree'. He wished he could see her expression. He thought about googling her again to remind himself what she looked like, but this wasn't late-night sexting. It was a professional interaction – as professional as he got.

Christmas with steel drums… I haven't heard that since Boney M.

He paused to grin before reading the last sentence of the email.

But I like your song better.

Something in his chest clogged up. What the hell had he done getting her involved? He'd collaborated with a range of musicians – lots of them women – and blurred the lines of a working relationship, starting inauspiciously with Susana. But there was more riding on this. He was getting old and his chart successes further apart. Perhaps he should have forgotten the whole thing and stuck to what he knew: how to party.

Christmas was one great party anyway – at least in Colombia, the home he'd avoided for too many years. But the nostalgic, miserable themes had crept into his Christmas-inspired song-writing and wouldn't be dislodged.

He grappled for the light, flirtatious tone he excelled at.

Aw shucks. But this one's better. A real salsa party for Christmas. Wanna dance?

He attached a link to a favourite Colombian salsa song called 'Navidad'.

Seriously? That's a Christmas song? This is a Christmas song.

He clicked on the link she sent and watched a bunch of boys in robes singing 'Away in a Manger'. He knew the song – he was pretty sure Bea had been forced to sing it at some school event. But no wonder her Christmas was miserable if she had to listen to that for all of December.

How do you dance to that?

Her reply was almost instantaneous:

You don't.

Now I know why your Christmases suck.

He blinked to force himself to stay awake while he waited for her reply. But exhaustion crept round him with more pull than the warmth of the strange virtual conversation.

Sorry, I'm falling asleep.

He managed to type before crashing onto the sofa. Her reply pinged into his account several minutes too late.

2

Cara closed her eyes and pictured the cortisol draining from her body as she raised her arms in a stretch and took a deep, slow breath. The technique wasn't working as well as it usually did. Her elevated heart rate and roiling stomach gave away that she wasn't as calm about today as she wanted to be.

Exercise was one answer to the anxiety that had been with her since the accident. She would feel better once the instructor turned on the music and led the class through the first dance. She was a hundred miles from her usual class in Bristol, but she hoped the routines were similar. The class was filled with women of all ages and abilities, most of them on their way to work in central London.

She recognised the first song as one of the Zumba classics and found her rhythm. The woman next to her stumbled on one of the salsa-inspired steps, just as Cara had two months before. Infected by the Latin rhythms, she'd replaced her cardio with Zumba. The steps had confounded her at first and she'd had no idea which foot was supposed to be supporting her weight. But the footwork was also a joy. She was physically capable of dancing. She had enough trust in her prosthesis to keep her feet in rhythm.

Covered from her chest to her socks in lycra, it was unlikely anyone would notice she'd been seriously injured. The carbon fibre ankle didn't fill out her leggings properly, but after years of physical therapy and several different prostheses, her movement was barely impaired. The more lasting effects were in her mind.

She joined in with the songs, whether she knew them or not, enjoying the tension draining from her shoulders as she mimicked the beat with her body. She could feel the irony of preparing for a day out of her comfort zone with a Latin pop musician by dancing Zumba. But the song had penetrated her thinking so deeply, she was even beginning to feel the magic of stubbornly dancing in the face of her fears.

Dance when everyone's watching... The line of the song had captured her with its bravery. It probably didn't seem brave to him.

A distinctive tresillo on a high-hat cymbal and a joyful rumble of toms introduced a song that sent a thrill of recognition through her. It was one of his. She'd found herself unable to keep still and had ended up dancing round her flat the first time she'd listened to this old album. But she'd made the mistake of running the lyrics through Google Translate. Catchy as it was, the song was about wanting a woman in a club, but having to resist because he had a girlfriend. Cara didn't find it edifying.

One Spanish word she'd learned was mujer – woman. He sang about a lot of mujeres. 'Nostalgia' was the only song she'd translated that didn't have sex and relationships as a backdrop. Many of his videos featured female dancers inexplicably in their underwear. Sure, it was expected, but, boy, he looked like he enjoyed every minute of it.

Cara was torn about her professional involvement with this guy who wrote fabulous melodies and elemental rhythms, but stuffed his songs full of macho bullshit. Her fanbase was primarily female and she was often asked about the feminist undertone of her single.

She wasn't sure if her reputation would survive the crossover. She was afraid she would seem even more of a fraud than usual.

And she was secretly smarting about that unanswered email. She'd been horrified to send her considered response to his comment about her miserable Christmases, only to find he'd emailed to say he was going to sleep. She was still mortified by the idea that he'd been lying in bed having that awkwardly intimate email conversation.

Then she'd heard nothing from him in over six weeks. Nada. Not even a reply to make her feel less sappy for telling him that Christmas was a difficult time of year for her. Thankfully she hadn't included any details. He couldn't have made it clearer that he wasn't interested. He'd barely been polite, let alone compassionate.

She'd pictured meeting him so many times in an effort to deal with her anxiety about today. She'd tried to tell herself he didn't have to like her and she didn't have to like him. Being honest with herself, she'd planned for an element of unwanted physical attraction. She'd looked up his music videos. He was tall and muscular, with an intriguing face. He moved with innate rhythm and the confidence of an arrogant man. If she planned on being immune to his physical attributes, she would have struggled to deal with it when the little flare was lit in her abdomen.

Instead she'd reminded herself of their different approaches – to music, to life. She was here in London to produce an awesome video. She was not here to be the latest in a long line of broken hearts. Besides, he probably had a girlfriend or a partner. No one was as outrageously single as his music suggested.

She was tired and showing a sheen of sweat as the instructor announced the last song, but she felt much more in control. She was halfway through a Cuban step when a door opened in the far corner to admit Freddie and a dark-haired man in a worn jacket. She tripped and had to throw out her arms for balance. It was him.

His hair was mussed and shaggy and he had a scruffy beard, but it was Javi Félix. Even if he were a household name in England, a casual observer wouldn't recognise this man from his half-naked tropical videos.

Cara froze and forced herself to exhale. She'd come to dance her nerves away, to enjoy the music when no one was watching, but he was here. He studied the instructor critically for a moment, his brow low, but his mouth turned up in a small smile. He leaned against the wall and stuffed his hands in his pockets as he watched.

Freddie exchanged a few words with the instructor, then leaned over and raised a hand to point out Cara. She pulled herself together. It was beyond embarrassing to have him see her sweaty and naïve in her new appreciation for Latin pop music, dressed only in a sports tank and leggings. But she had to show him she had the discipline to make this collaboration professional.

She danced the final stage of the routine with obstinate precision, executing the steps without a stumble. She joined in with the gentle warm-down and then breezed over to where they stood. She took a deep breath. God help him if his eyes strayed anywhere below her chin.

She greeted Freddie without looking at his companion, then summoned some insouciance and met his gaze. Physical attraction – tick. His eyes were dark and twinkled just as much in person as in his promotional photos. Little furrows at the corners hinted at lazy humour. His lips were expressive and smiled easily. But his lopsided smile also showed he knew how awkward this situation was.

Freddie was making the introductions in the background as they eyed each other with tentative interest. Which recording had he used? Why hadn't he answered that email? Could he tell how far out of her comfort zone she was with him? Why did he look so scruffy when he was supposed to be the inveterate charmer of his songs? And what on earth did he think about her exercise class?

'Encantado, Cara,' Javi said and leaned forward. Her breath hitched as he entered her personal space and she chastised herself for the lack of foresight. He was going to kiss her cheek. Her heartrate kicked up. She should have prepared herself for cheek-kissing. She'd been distracted by that disarming smile.

'Will you hold still, woman?' he murmured and grasped her shoulders. She looked indignantly down at his hands and he took the opportunity to plant a kiss on her cheek.

She focused on his scratchy beard on her cheek instead of his lips. Up close he was overpowering with the warmth and vitality of an energetic man. A fresh, sunshine scent filled her nostrils. He pulled back, but before she could enjoy her relief, he was nudging her chin to the other side and repeating the intimate greeting.

'Done,' he said with a satisfied rumble and an amused smile.

His amusement irritated her. 'Now we've painstakingly accomplished the Colombian greeting, how about the English one?' She held out her hand and met his gaze with a toss of her head.

His smile grew. 'Oh, I think we're well past a handshake. I've heard your naked voice.' But he took her hand anyway, which was a good thing because her legs were suddenly jelly. How did he do that? He'd called her 'woman' and still his rasping consonants and lilting intonation made her heart flutter. Her naked voice... Had anyone ever said anything so sexual and yet so lyrical to her before?

She extricated her hand and looked away in an attempt to compose herself. Freddie was guffawing silently. She would deal with him later.

'Cara's been listening to lots of Latin music since you sent over the song,' Freddie began and Cara inwardly cringed. 'And she took up Zumba to pick up some of the dance moves. What did you think?' She gritted her teeth to subdue her embarrassment.

'I think we're going to have a lot of work to do if we're going to turn this... exercise into something fun. And I don't suppose there's any way she can put on twenty pounds by tomorrow? There's not a lot to hang onto.'

His accent wasn't so swoon-worthy now. It was more American than anything else. She lifted her gaze square into his. 'Are you insulting me? Or are you quoting one of your songs? "There wasn't a lot to hang onto" – I'm sure that's a charming description you've used in your lyrics. How do you remember them all? The women, I mean. Not the lyrics.'

He laughed and his eyes crinkled. She'd bet he was more attractive now than he'd been ten years ago in his twenties. There was awareness in his smile that made him grounded and vital. Men had all the luck. 'You translated my lyrics. I'm honoured. I assure you they're much more poetic in Spanish.'

'I'm sure the poetry of sex is pretty much the same in any language.'

'It's love, not sex.'

She smiled condescendingly and crossed her arms over her chest. 'You fall in love with every woman you see across a crowded bar?'

He paused, studying her. The intensity of his gaze sent goose bumps prickling up her arms. He pursed his lips and shrugged. 'There are different kinds of love.'

What a stupid line. 'Oh, for the love of...' she muttered. He grinned and she realised she'd quoted the title of his album.

'I see you're my biggest fan.'

She knew he was joking, but she didn't like being on the back foot. 'Shall we cut the flirting banter and keep it professional?' Was she instructing him or herself? She wanted to grab him and make him explain why he hadn't replied to her email. He wasn't the only one making this personal.

'You think that was flirting?' He looked at her with critical interest. 'If I was flirting with you, you wouldn't be able to think of those saucy comebacks.' His voice was low and it shivered along her skin.

'No flirting required, thank you.' Her breath wasn't quite even. She suspected he noticed.

He waved his open palm in acquiescence and she was distracted by his thick, muscular hands and the shiny calluses on his fingertips. Did he compose obsessively like she did? Or did he just fool around and some Caribbean spirit gifted him with amazing songs?

'A su servicio, señorita,' he smiled.

'I have no idea what that means.'

'You want professional? You got professional.' She didn't believe him. But she was also disappointed by how quickly he had agreed.

* * *

Javi was imagining shards of glass lacerating the soles of his feet. If he wrote a song about Cara, the first line would be something like that. It wasn't his usual subject matter, but Cara clearly wasn't his usual subject.

They opted for silence as they waited for the video production team from the record company to arrive in the conference room. He'd never worked with a woman like Cara – a woman with wary eyes, years older than her age. If he was the eternal boy-child his ex-wife accused him of being, then Cara with her twenty-something-going-on-fifty was going to spend a lot of their time together with that pinched expression on her face.

He risked a glance at his companion. She was sipping tea and pretending to be interested in something on her phone. Although she'd changed into jeans, sneakers and a baggy white top, she still looked tiny and fragile. But he'd seen her muscles that morning at the gym – and her straight hips, her tiny breasts. She was built like a ballet dancer. And he'd said entirely the wrong thing when Freddie had asked what he'd thought of her.

He'd been off-balance since the first moment he'd seen her in person – since much earlier, if he was honest. He hadn't known what to make of her ever since he'd listened to her stunning recording and felt the result of her creativity reacting to his.

She'd looked good that morning, her body following the beat. She executed the steps well. She held herself with straight-backed pride that made a man want to kneel at her feet. But she was so reserved. He knew the song wasn't his usual insta-party track, but he needed it to be fun. If it wasn't, he'd have to face the subject matter as an adult and he didn't want to. That's why he'd wrapped it up into a song.

She turned to him, her expression brisk. 'So, Javier,' she began.

'Javi,' he corrected her.

She hesitated, but then repeated the nickname with a little nod.

A smile unfurled as the familiar little devil crept into his thoughts. 'Javi,' he repeated, stressing the pronunciation of the J as a glottal H and the V closer to a B.

She eyed him. 'I apologise for my terrible pronunciation, but I don't require you to pronounce my name without rolling the R, so I'm sure you can tolerate my accent.'

His smile grew. 'Carrra,' he said. 'Rhymes with barra.'

'Dare I ask what that means?'

'I don't know. Do you dare?'

'It's a figure of speech.'

'I know. But you're cute. Barra means "bar", the place you go to order a drink. I assume you don't dare much.'

She bristled. 'You can assume all you like.'

'And you still won't give me an answer?'

'You didn't answer me,' she muttered.

'Ah,' he said, his smile fading. 'Sorry about that. I was... kinda drunk.'

She looked at him sharply and he found himself unreasonably fascinated by the flecks in her eyes. He took a good look at her: her even, pretty features, long hair that was nearly blonde, blue eyes that were hiding something.

'Forget about it,' she said, looking away. He didn't think either of them would succeed with that. He certainly wasn't going to forget her vulnerable one-liner that he'd been too cowardly to reply to: 'I lost my mother around Christmas.' More than a month later and he still didn't know what to say to that.

All the more reason to keep things light. He crossed his arms over his chest, considering her prickles. 'Is this going to be a problem? We're going to be working – closely – together.'

A ripple ran through her body language and he knew he'd screwed up again. 'I said forget about it. We agreed we'd keep things professional.'

He inclined his head. 'And I'll go further and apologise for not answering your email and commenting on your figure. It was the wrong thing to say. But we're making music together, not doing business.'

She didn't respond immediately. When she did, her voice was flat. 'This whole thing could be a disaster.' He swung his gaze back to her. She wouldn't look at him, but he recognised the shaft of emotion. 'I don't see how I'm the right talent to feature on your song.'

'It could be a disaster,' he shrugged, 'or it could be fun.' She exhaled on a little huff that told him what she thought of fun. He had his work cut out for him. 'But you are definitely the right talent for the song. Want to hear the final master?' That got her interest. 'I've got it on my phone. I'll play it to you after the meeting. I think it's the best song I've ever written. And that's because of you.'

She turned to him in surprise, vulnerability and pleasure flitting across her face. ¡Hurra! He was getting somewhere. 'You wrote it,' she insisted. He grinned at the question in her eyes. She wanted to know if she was getting writing credit or not. He hadn't uploaded the final master to the server because he'd wanted to see her reaction in person when she heard it.

'You made it good,' he hinted, enjoying her sudden eagerness.

'It was good anyway,' she insisted far too graciously.

'I don't need your compliments. I want you to enjoy it. I want your passion.'

The alarm on her face was comical. 'Unfortunately, that's not contracted to the label.'

He laughed and settled a hand on her shoulder. She stiffened slightly, but it felt better having touched her. 'I'll try to earn it.'

'Good luck,' she said tartly and shifted away, although some hostility had left her eyes.

'Do you mean that?'

'Not really,' she muttered.

He fidgeted through the meeting, glad for the production team's enthusiasm, but impatient to play the song for Cara. His career had stalled for five long years where he'd moved back and forth between the US and Colombia, writing songs for other people, arguing with his ex and drifting back into the family fold in Barranquilla. He wanted to show Susana he could be involved with Beatríz, but he struggled to reconcile fatherhood with his career. Writing songs at all hours, throwing everything into gigs had been his life. Now Susana was dangling the carrot of increased visitation, but he didn't know how to write or perform without the temporary insanity of dancing, adrenaline, plentiful sexual advances and alcohol.

'Nostalgia' had come to him last Christmas, spending all of December in Colombia for the first time in years. He'd just moved into the house in Barranquilla. A group of neighbours had arrived to invite him to a novena – an excuse to snoop on their new neighbour. A man had sung a nostalgic Christmas vallenato with an accordion, and he'd all but put a clamp on the man's wrist and dragged him into the studio. By the end of the evening, the whole street was there singing and playing his various guitars and bashing the expensive drum kit and his collection of congas and other traditional drums. His mother had brought her deep fryer and was churning out empanadas. He'd asked his brothers to bring crates of aguardiente, Old Parr whisky, rum and beer. But he hadn't touched a single drink and the cacophony of rhythms which would usually have made him want to break something hadn't bothered him at all. He'd been too busy sampling and scribbling, listening and playing music.

When it was well into the next morning, he'd sat down with his brothers and made toast after toast to the one who was no longer with them. He'd woken up wondering if the whole thing had actually happened, but with a song as pained and passionate as his family – as his complicated relationship with home.

It meant something. And he wasn't sure what to do about it. And now Cara held the key to the song somehow. He'd mindlessly written the thing, but she'd completed it. He had to find a way to open her up and get that whatever-it-was into the video.

The easiest way would be to flirt like hell, tumble into bed and break her heart. The corazón roto wasn't a common element of Latin songs for nothing. Love was fleeting. But it wasn't that kind of song – for once.

When the meeting wrapped up, he leaned down to fetch his headphones from his bag. He wanted to show her now.

She stood to speak to her manager and Javi's eyes drifted. The strong-but-dainty thing was a good look on her. He swept his gaze down her body, glad she wouldn't notice his inspection or the crooked smile on his face. She was an exercising control freak, but it was kind of sweet.

He chuckled to himself. She turned and sent him a questioning look. He brandished the headphones and beckoned her over. When she returned to the chair next to him, he smoothed her hair behind her ears and settled the headphones in place. She didn't move, her back straight, her hands in her lap and her eyes fixed on the table. The one concession to emotion was the corner of a tooth pressing into her bottom lip.

He lined up the track, but he didn't press play until she turned to him, her brows raised. He held her gaze, challenging her not to look away, as she listened to the result of their work together before they'd ever met.

Her body language softened as the first verse played. He pursed his lips in a satisfied smile. She couldn't know the first verse was a feeble nod to his mistakes and he'd kept her out of it. 'El Tamborilero'... 'The Little Drummer Boy'. Except in his version he got lost, stole other people's gifts, followed the wrong stars and left the baby in the manger. Had Cara wondered what it all meant, or did she buy the pithy Christmas references?

She leaned forward, engrossed, as he guessed she had reached the first chorus. He'd brought her recording in at that stage, just hovering round the edges of the sound, promising so much more than his husky mumble of words. He loved how she sang the last line of the chorus: 'Dance so you don't cry'. He'd been so inspired by the brittle power in her voice that he'd rerecorded his, finding the break between his head and chest registers and glorying in feeling like Diomedes Diaz singing a vallenato.

The odd mix of their languages and voices flowed together in that one line and anchored the song outside of time and geography. In other parts, he'd sung in English – for the first time in his life – to emphasise the harmony. But that line just worked.

He noticed the goose bumps on her forearms and felt them, too. She swayed slightly from side to side, her hand unclenching in her lap to tap along with the cow bell in the rhythm of the second verse. He raised his hands and caught her eye, grinning as he clapped along with the movement of her shoulders that was probably unconscious.

Her answering smile sparkled and Javi wanted to beat his chest in triumph. She mouthed the words to one of her lines, her head bobbing from side to side. He mouthed his lines right back, charmed when she mouthed the Spanish along with him. Grinning, they stared at each other for several beats, before inhaling the same breath and mouthing the shout of 'Hey!' that announced the return of the chorus.

He could tell when the bridge started because she closed her eyes and lifted her head. The drama of her words, the perfection of the harmony and the building percussion created a sharp and fitting climax that helped him forget that the words of the bridge were the hardest for him to sing.

Her smile dimmed thoughtfully as the final verse and chorus faded to a minor chord plucked on his father's old concert guitar. As she tentatively removed the headphones, the awkward silence descended again.

'It's incredible,' she said softly, not meeting his gaze.

He nodded slowly. 'That's what we want to match in the video. I hope you're ready to dance with me when everyone's watching.'

Her eyes darted to his and away again. He'd take that as a 'no'. He had her in the music. It would have to be enough for now.

3

'One, two and turn!' And stumble and curse under her breath. Why was there always a pause on the last beat? Although she'd learned the cross-step footwork at Zumba and practised the choreography for the video exhaustively, dancing opposite Javi was different. Everything about being in the same room as Javi was different.

She'd built this up too much. And, yes, he was far too handsome up close. And he smelled kind of earthy and fresh, like she could bury her face in his chest, which was the most bizarre urge, given she barely knew the man.

Their long-distance creative interaction and that one bizarre email exchange shouldn't have counted, but somehow they did. And he'd used her version of the song. She was still recovering from hearing the final result. She'd been certain it wasn't what he wanted. She'd expected to hear the other version when he'd placed the headphones on her ears.

Instead she heard her own soul. He'd changed his vocals to match hers and the result had caused emotion to well up in her throat at the soaring harmony. The beauty of music had been so much a part of her life, more so since the accident. But sharing the

experience? There were too many variables she couldn't control –
least of all her own reactions.

'Keep going!' the choreographer called when Cara would have
stopped. She wobbled through a side-step before finding her
rhythm again. They danced a few bars side by side, but Cara kept
drifting away from him.

'Take it easy. Your steps are too big. It's not your aerobics class
and I don't bite – usually.' His voice was laced with amusement.

She gritted her teeth and took a determined breath, staring
ahead with her brow furrowed in concentration. She fumbled for
his hand for the next set of turns, steeling herself against the intimacy that felt too real.

'Look at me. You're supposed to be a woman in love.'

She looked up sharply. 'And you are an expert on what that
looks like.' Was he single? She was burning to ask him, but her
need to know something that wasn't her business was evidence
itself that their interactions were far too intimate for her state of
mind.

He smiled, his eyes sparking. She always felt he was laughing at
her. Worse, she wanted to laugh at herself with him, because it
might just be easier than worrying. 'I do, on occasion, dance with
women I don't love. Also strange, but true: I have danced with
women who don't love me.'

'But I have to?'

'Yes.' He inclined his head, his grin widening. 'For one song, you
have to love me.'

She slammed her mouth shut and tried to suppress the shiver
that ran through her. It was an amazing song, but he had some
nerve, making her laugh when she was shaking inside... He leaned
towards her and she forced herself to reciprocate, appalled at the
shot of physical pleasure the closeness delivered. Her fingers were
oversensitive as they met the skin of his hands. She was usually

better at separating the physical and psychological, but Javi, with his easy smile and careless words, was messing with her head and her body.

He reached up to stroke the skin under her chin. 'That's not in the choreography,' she protested.

He tugged her close again. 'No, but it looks good. Trust me and play along.'

She suspected trusting Javi would be as big a mistake as playing with him. He didn't look affected by their proximity. She was out of her depth. They had to record the video tomorrow evening and she sucked. She closed her eyes and let out a deep breath. 'I'm sorry,' she said. 'I hate doing videos.'

He nodded slowly. 'Okay, mona. Take your time. Maybe you can imagine you're performing on stage instead.'

She frowned in dismay. 'Even worse. And did you call me a moaner?'

He hesitated. 'No, I called you a monkey, but it's a good thing.'

'Right.'

'Really.' He gave her ponytail a tug and she snatched it back. 'In Colombia, it means you're blonde and you're cute.'

It was irritating how well the line worked on her. 'I'm neither blonde nor cute.'

He grinned. 'You would be if you came to Barranquilla.' The name of his hometown flowed off his tongue like a magic word. 'Sun-bleached hair and a little dress – perfect.'

She eyed him, unimpressed. The line nearly worked. But he didn't know she never wore little dresses any more. 'I get the beach vibe.'

He shrugged. 'It's more of a swamp.'

'You're really selling it. I suppose you prefer Miami these days.'

Although he was smiling, it was a tight, dark sort of smile that was much more dangerous than his shallow charm. 'Not necessarily.'

The choreographer called for them to start again from the top and they moved into their starting positions, facing each other, hands clasped. Javi squeezed her hand or gave her waist a nudge and, although it wreaked havoc with her focus, she followed the lead. She hated the idea of ceding control to him. There was a feeling about him that anything could happen. She had to tell herself it was only a dance. She didn't have to trust him with anything else.

'This is getting better,' he confirmed and twirled her into another turn that wasn't in the choreography, smiling innocently when she eyed him. 'You're good at the steps, but I still don't feel the love.'

'Surely you can love yourself enough for both of us,' she muttered.

He laughed and captured her round her waist. She crashed into him and raised her arms to his chest instinctively. His lopsided grin and the warmth in his eyes held her attention, just as his arm held her body. Her fingers flexed unconsciously and his hold tightened in response. He was so... inconveniently attractive.

'You're cute,' he said with a grin.

'Shut up,' she muttered. 'It's not helping.' His grip loosened and she could breathe again.

'For a gringa – which you are, and there's nothing we can do about that – you're doing great. You just need to loosen up and have some fun – make some mistakes.'

It was her turn to laugh. 'I don't make mistakes.'

'I'm getting that vibe,' he replied, his voice low.

She turned to him with a sigh, relieved he'd backed off a little. 'And I'm not used to channelling my inner Beyoncé.'

He smirked and looked her up and down, making her regret the stupid joke. She wondered if he was going to take the Beyoncé line and comment on her weight again. She would welcome it. If he acted like a macho jerk, she wouldn't have to take him seriously.

But he cocked his head and studied her face with a puzzled expression. 'You don't need your inner Beyoncé. Just be you. We're creating a fantasy world where love conquers all and dancing can fix problems, rather than just helping people forget.'

Cara's stomach dropped. No sign of the macho jerk. But this was worse. Here was the writer of the song. His expression was impassive – almost resigned – but she knew the song too well not to detect an echo of sentiment.

'What does dancing have to do with Christmas anyway?'

'Aside from food, music is Christmas. And dancing is music.'

She completely agreed with his first sentence. But the implied self-evidence of the second flummoxed her. The bleak and slightly ridiculous image of her and her father dancing at Christmas time flashed in her mind.

He broke her reverie with a clap of his hands. She stared as he clapped a sharp rhythm and began a shuffling circle round her, his feet moving in a basic single-double side-step, but nothing looked basic when he danced, his whole body making the beat. He started singing – a playful melody captured perfectly in his mischievous expression – and Cara tried and failed to suppress a puzzled smile.

Reaching what sounded like the chorus, he stopped moving, beat his chest with one palm and reached up for the soaring high notes. Goose bumps ran up her arms and she couldn't take her eyes off him. The song was unfamiliar and didn't sound like any Christmas song she'd heard, and yet, when he performed it, she could feel the tradition – the nostalgia.

He stopped with a chuckle. 'That's "Mensaje de Navidad", one of my family's favourite songs in December. It's not Michael Bublé, but we like it.' He reached for her hand and drew her into the shuffling rhythm, humming the melody.

Without the protection of choreography, Cara had no choice but to feel. After the accident, she'd learned to listen to the signals her body sent her – for balance, for wellbeing and illness – but the signals she was getting weren't the ones she was used to.

Although the dance had an innocent, folky rhythm, Javi was very close, his arm round her back and his legs bumping hers. If she turned her head slightly, her lips would be on his neck. It was mortifying how her mind settled on that possibility and wouldn't let go.

For one song, you have to love me. It shouldn't have been possible to feel so good and yet so confused.

'Music is about enjoyment,' he murmured in her ear.

'I'm not very good at enjoying myself,' she muttered before she could censor herself, 'especially not at Christmas.'

His hand tightened on her back. He surrounded her with his body, his spark and his unpredictable energy. Cara's breath stalled. Her heart rate notched up. It didn't feel like a panic attack, but it was enough for her coping mechanisms to kick in.

She drew away and sucked in a much-needed breath, hastily summoning the comforting visualisations of her piano at home in case her heartbeat raced out of control. 'You're a good teacher.'

He gave her a crooked smile. 'I don't think anyone's ever said that to me before.'

The glint in his eye made her wonder if he was flirting again. She was learning it was his default setting. She had to try to take him less seriously.

She shrugged. 'It was a simple compliment.'

He paused, an idea she didn't imagine was safe written on his face. 'If you really want me to teach you, let's go to a bar.' The low promise in his voice shivered through her and her heartrate jacked right back up.

'What?'

'We've got tomorrow morning to rehearse and you know the steps. Go back to the hotel, have a nap and we'll hit a Latin club tonight. No pressure, let's just soak it up and let go.'

'I don't think so,' she protested weakly.

'Don't you want to get it right?'

How did he know to ask that? She was irritated that he found her so easy to manipulate. 'Of course, but I don't see how a bar is going to help us perfect our choreography.'

He grinned and she saw the mojitos twinkling in his eyes again. She reminded herself that this was the man who sang about picking up lots of different women. 'You need to feel it. I don't want perfect.'

'You want passion.' Her voice was flat. Just because he threw his feelings around like confetti, didn't mean she could learn to do it in a day or two.

He traced his fingertip along her collarbone and, when she pulled away, he reached for her chin. 'It's in there somewhere. I want it. The song needs it.'

She drew herself up, focusing on her irritation at his condescending touch. She took his chin between her thumb and forefinger. His coarse black beard scraped her fingers. 'We're only staying until midnight.'

His lips twitched, but he didn't pull out of her grasp. 'Two. We'll be dancing alone and see nothing if we leave at midnight.'

'One,' she offered and he snatched her hand from his chin to shake it. She stared at his dark hand clutching hers. It was his right hand and the nails were long and groomed into slopes for plucking guitar strings. She wanted to dismiss him as a fun-loving dilettante, but his hands brought the assumption into question. Who was he? And how much would it cost her to get the answer to that question?

* * *

'Where on earth are we?' Cara looked from the boarded-up construction site across the road to the brick arches under the train line beside them. There was a kebab shop down the street and plastic bag tumbleweeds skittering across the road.

The cab had dropped them off at the address Javi had given. She'd expected the club to be in Soho, which had caused apprehension enough. Arriving at Elephant and Castle in the dark was not something she'd prepared herself for. But she'd come so far from the days when she couldn't even get into a cab.

Javi flicked up the collar of his jacket, although Cara found the evening breeze mild. 'This is where the Colombians come.'

'Uh-huh,' she said. His comment didn't reassure her. She looked dubiously at the sign that read 'Nocturno'.

He eyed her with that look that told her he was laughing at her again. 'Go on, ask the question. I can see it in your eyes, gringa.'

She suspected 'gringa' was supposed to be an insult, but he said it with a grin. 'Okay, fine. What kind of Colombians come here? Narcos? FARC?'

He laughed and squeezed her shoulder. She couldn't decide if she wanted him to stop touching her or not. 'You get extra points for knowing about the FARC. You realise there is more to Colombia than what comes on Netflix. But we are currently at peace. The FARC has disarmed.'

'Huh,' Cara said and turned to study him. Was there something behind the flippant tone? When she continued to look at him, he raised his eyebrows in question. 'What's that line from the song? "Longing for the night of peace"?'

His smile was back in an instant. 'Noche de paz,' he quoted with a smile. 'But it's not what you think. That's the name of the song you know as 'Silent Night'. One of my lame Christmas references.'

She eyed him as her cheeks turned pink. 'It was your translation. And why would you be longing for "Silent Night" when the rest of the song is about banging drums and dancing like crazy?'

He shrugged and looped an arm round her shoulders to propel her forward. But she stopped, refusing to let him off the hook. 'What about "Make a noise to drown out the bullets and the sorrow"?'

He frowned slowly. 'Heavy words for a tonto rumbero like me,' he muttered with a dark chuckle. 'Maybe my Christmases are just as miserable as yours. Come on, monita. Let's find you some fun.'

He didn't give her any time to process her stunned surprise at his comment. He pushed open the door of the club and ushered her inside. There was a small restaurant and cloakroom at the front, with few patrons, and music pulsed from the door to the club. 'I tried to find somewhere with live music, but it was too difficult on a Tuesday. My brother recommended this place.'

'Your brother?'

He nodded. 'He lived in London for a few years, but he's back home, now.' He hung their jackets. 'It's a recurring theme, returning to Colombia,' he said as he took her hand and headed for the club. He raised his eyebrows, anticipation lighting his face. 'Are you ready?'

She eyed him. 'No, but I'll manage.'

The music assaulted her ears as the door opened, bass vibrating through her flesh. She recognised the dembow rhythm of reggaetón, with its laid-back Jamaican roots overlaid with urban grit. As much as the Caribbean rhythms had infiltrated her taste, she preferred more melodic music. But the syncopated rhythm with the thrumming four-four heartbeat was a powerful motivator to movement. Javi made no effort to resist and was moving to the beat even as they made their way towards the bar. A handful of couples were on the dance floor. Cara studied them as they pressed their hips against each other.

'Looking for inspiration?'

She turned to him with a straight face. 'Nothing says 'Christmas' like a bit of gratuitous grinding.' She smiled in satisfaction when he guffawed.

Her confidence slipped when he leaned close and said into her ear, 'Happy to help, if you want to perfect your choreography.' His words tingled over her skin, his slight accent adding something spicy to the scent of folly. 'We call it perreo, which comes from the word for dog. Can you see why?' he asked with a smile, as though he hadn't just propositioned her – or was he joking as usual? 'Not a reggaetón fan? I bet you dance to it in your aerobics class.'

'You're laughing at me.'

'Never.' He grinned, scuppering any defence she might have mustered. His smile should have been vacuous. Instead it was disarming. 'What will you have to drink?'

'I'm not sure alcohol is a good idea.'

He blinked. 'How are you going to do this sober?'

'What are you expecting me to do? I was going to sit on one of these stools and take notes.' She wasn't sure if she was joking or not. Could she go out there and just dance with Javi, for no reason but to enjoy herself?

He laughed, his shoulders shaking and his face transforming with mischief. His hand settled on her arm and she wished she could switch off the nerve endings in her skin. 'You're a pretty little gallina.'

'I'm going to pretend that means something capable and sophisticated.'

'You think I'd say something capable and sophisticated?' His smile slid right between her ribs.

'I assume you're calling me a coward,' she muttered through a reluctant smile.

'A chicken, yes. You're capable, sophisticated and smart. And before you leave this bar, you are going to dance with me properly. You'll love it. I promise I'm good.'

She wasn't sure whether to tell him off or kiss him. The latter urge was irritatingly constant. 'I don't need to mimic sex with you on the dance floor for this video to look good.'

He shrugged. 'It would be more interesting than your performance this afternoon.'

'Am I capable, sophisticated, smart and boring?' she said, turning to him in challenge. 'Because I take my work seriously and I don't have enough to hang onto?'

He leaned back, studying her. 'I already apologised for that.'

'I'm not letting you off that easily.'

Her scolding backfired. He sat up straighter and his warm, gripping smile made another appearance to screw with her chest. 'Bueno. You can keep me in line on the dance floor.'

'What line did you think you were going to overstep?'

'I don't know, mona. You've got a lot of lines.'

Cara ran out of banter. She was certain she should be offended. But she felt seen. It was ridiculous, because he'd made it clear she didn't have what he expected – in a dance partner or a... another kind of partner – and he didn't even know half of what made her tick. She blinked to clear her mind. The pounding music and hedonistic crowd were going to her head.

He squeezed her hand. 'Let me get you a drink. I think you're going to need it if you want me to tell you what I think.'

'I need it already,' she muttered. 'All right. What do people drink here? Tequila? I did go to university. I can do tequila shots.'

'What does tequila have to do with university?'

'Students and tequila shots go together.'

He cocked his head. 'Not where I'm from.' He spoke to the barman and then handed her a glass full of crushed ice with agitated mint leaves. 'Mojito.'

Cara failed to keep the grin off her face as she took the glass. He nursed a tumbler of golden liquid over ice. 'I'm waiting,' she prompted, although she wasn't entirely sure what the question was. Were they talking about her dancing or the lines he might cross?

'You can dance. You know that. But you don't have the soul, or the sex.'

She frowned sharply. 'I don't use sex to sell my music.'

'I applaud your principles, but you will if you stay in this business. Why not get happy with it?'

Oh yes, the sexy songstress with the missing leg who could dance seductively on stage despite the obsessive thoughts and intrusive images in her mind. She felt enough of an imposter on stage as it was without adding the expectation of being a sex symbol. She was terrified of the day when she'd have to explain the accident publicly and have it take over her image as it had taken over years of her life.

She watched one woman on the dance floor press her backside into her partner and shake her shoulders while he held her hips. 'You can't truly picture me dancing like that. You do realise I'm British?'

He chuckled. 'Yes, your nationality is hard to miss and no, we don't have to do perreo. Baby steps. But you can't dance with me like a nun. It's messy. It's chaotic – like life.' Javi had leaned close to be heard over the music without speaking too loudly. Messy and chaotic weren't adjectives she wanted to describe her life, but she could sense them in him. He turned back to the bar. Cara hopped up on a stool next to him. Strange that he'd pushed the boundaries of her safe zone all day, but suddenly he was her safe zone in this crazy bar.

'I don't understand the problem. It's not like we're not attracted to each other.'

She sat upright and grabbed for her glass before it toppled. She stared at him. 'Don't say that out loud!'

He shrugged and she saw through his attempt to stifle a smile. 'Why not? It's true.'

'But I don't want to—' She hesitated, feeling like an idiot.

'Did I ask?' He pinned her with a look.

She gritted her teeth. How could he say he found her attractive with one sentence and reject a sexual advance she hadn't even made with the next?

His hand hovered over hers, but he reconsidered and snatched it back. 'Don't beat yourself up. It's clear you'd rather not be attracted to me and I can take a hint. And, would you believe, not every one of these couples will go home together and turn things horizontal.'

That right there was the problem. Attraction for him was an everyday occurrence, whereas she didn't remember ever feeling so flustered.

She gritted her teeth and worked up the courage. She wished she didn't need to know the answer, but he was right about her lines. 'Do you have a girlfriend who might get upset about us dancing for real?'

'It's just dancing.'

'You just helpfully pointed out we're attracted to each other. You might live in a world where you can scope anyone out as long as you look and don't touch, but it will be different for me if you're not single.' God, she hated how stupid she must sound to him. 'But this is not any sort of invitation.'

'I'm single. And I get it. Like I said, this is not some sexual free-for-all. If I was in a serious relationship...' he paused and she sensed an omission in the hesitation. 'Yeah, I'm not in a serious relationship. You don't need to get hot over nothing. I assume I won't have to defend myself to your jealous British boyfriend?'

'I'm not getting hot. And why don't you think I have a boyfriend?'

'Sorry, figure of speech.' His mouth opened as he considered her second question. She already knew the answer and wished she'd never asked. She wasn't easy. Even before the accident, she'd been serious and reserved.

'If you had a boyfriend,' he said slowly, 'you wouldn't be putting up with me.'

She looked at him sharply, but another song started, with brass – and was that accordion – and he smiled broadly. More patrons drifted onto the dance floor. It wasn't only couples. They also danced in groups, although somehow everyone knew the steps. She studied the movements, trying to work out how the music flowed through the entire body in a way that was both sensual and natural.

Javi leaned close with a smile. 'It's a vallenato pop song – based on Colombian folk music. My mom loves to dance to vallenato.'

Cara listened intently, picking out the triplets in the rhythm and enjoying the joyful hum of the accordion. She cocked her head towards the dance floor. 'Go on then.'

'Are you coming?'

4

'Come on,' he wheedled, tugging on her hand. His eagerness was catching. He slipped an arm round her waist and she slid off the barstool before she'd realised. Holding her hands loosely, he shuffled through a few light, rhythmic steps, moving slowly in the direction of the dance floor.

A large group had formed a loose circle, dancing without partners, stepping in time to the languid beat. Javi steered her in that direction with his arm round her.

'There's only one thing you need to know. Repeat after me: ¡Ay hombe!'

'What does that mean?'

He shrugged. 'It kind of sounds like "hey man", but that's not really what it means. Just yell it and see how it feels. Go on. ¡Ay hombe!' He raised his voice and the club erupted in answering shouts.

He pulled her into the circle and started to dance, raising his hands to clap along, while his feet led the sensual flow of movement. He was an effortless showman, rousing the group and charging the air with his high spirits. A couple ventured into the middle of the circle and he whooped and led a switch to a side-step, clapping all the time. He didn't just clap along with the two-four beat, he used his hands as additional percussion. His whole body was the music. Cara stumbled along, too busy staring at him to master the steps.

The couple merged back into the circle and another woman strode in, holding her hand out to Javi. She wore a short, ruffled skirt and heels Cara couldn't have pulled off even before she lost her foot. She moved with the same elemental ease he did. They would look amazing together.

He didn't hesitate. He took the woman's hand and stepped in. Cara swallowed. She wasn't jealous, was she? She and Javi only belonged together professionally, in one song – even if it was the most amazing song she'd ever worked on. She was an interloper with a different way of life. And she would never be able to dance like that.

Their feet moved constantly to the beat, synchronising the movement of their hips. His leg slipped between hers, aligning their bodies. The woman held on to Javi with her arm round his neck. Her movements were delicate and feminine, and Javi's hand on her lower back held her hips a whisper from his. Although their bodies remained an inch apart, it was a sensual courtship dance.

She kissed his cheek as he released her back into the circle and, a few bars later, the song came to an end. Javi turned to take Cara's hand and leave, but the group tugged him back. His smile was broad and showy and, like the rest of him, effortless.

As the next song started, a cheer went up and more people flowed onto the dance floor. Cara recognised the pattern of the snare drum as the opening beat of one of Javi's old singles. He grinned as the dance floor went wild, but he was one of the few patrons who didn't sing along. He danced with the group, but he didn't push himself forward. Didn't he want to be recognised?

It was a fabulous song, perfect for singing and dancing – pure pleasure. She loved the snare drum rumbling along with a lot of rebound. Javi's drummer must be amazing. She was yet to settle on a permanent band – one of the many stresses she still faced. But that glorious rhythm with trumpets and the lazy sweep of his voice singing about some romantic mishap kept her in the moment.

Effortless... Her life wasn't light like that.

Dance when everyone's watching... Somehow, she was enjoying herself. The first part of the bridge of 'Nostalgia' was all about dancing. Dance on the streets, dance on the patio, dance so you don't cry. She hadn't understood what that part had to do with Christmas, but now she could imagine his mother dancing to vallenatos and feel how the crowd stretched out their arms towards their distant home as they danced.

Dance so you don't cry... Perhaps she could face Christmas with a bit more grace if she could dance her way through it. Her mother would have loved it, just as she'd loved singing Christmas carols and shivering in front of the Christmas displays on Regent Street while she quietly shared Cara and Crispin's excitement.

Javi grabbed her hand and tugged her away from the group. 'My turn, mona,' he said with a smile.

The next song was a lively salsa track and she had a decent idea of the footwork. It was the rest of her body she didn't know what to do with – especially with Javi in close proximity.

She pulled back, torn between the freeing mood and her heavy memories. 'Isn't this going to make everything more difficult tomorrow?' She should be worried that she wouldn't get any sleep tonight.

'It will make things easier.' He'd used her distraction to pull her into a loose hold.

He leaned close and she wondered how she had learned to tolerate his disregard for her personal space so quickly. 'What are you afraid of, Cara? I know you believe in the song. If it's me you're worried about, then don't be. I'm just a colombiano screw-up with a good sense of rhythm.'

She scowled at him. She'd watched him for the last twenty minutes. He was a born entertainer with music in his bones. She was the one who might never be able to live up to the expectations of her album. She had a European tour booked after her album launch next year and she still experienced days of hazy, obsessive distraction and stomach upset in the lead-up to a performance.

Javi was flirting with her, but did he even like her? He thought love was cheap and fun. Cara's life – and mind – were more complex than that and she had the awkward relationship history to prove it.

'You said this is about sex. Is that where you see this going?'

He stopped dancing and spent a long moment searching for words. She was satisfied to have regained the upper hand. He rubbed the back of his head. 'It's about having a good time, enjoyment, living in the moment. In Spanish we say lose yourself – or get lost. Perderse. Piérdete conmigo. Get lost with me and let's see what we find.'

She swallowed. She'd been lost. She wouldn't willingly do it again. 'You didn't answer my question.'

'I don't know, Cara. Someone ought to loosen you up. A broken heart would give you something to sing about.'

How did he make it sound like a good thing? She narrowed her eyes at him and smiled caustically. 'And you are willing to make the sacrifice for my benefit?'

He laughed at her challenge and she felt the control of the conversation slipping away. 'I'd be honoured.' He reached a hand up to hover near her face. He studied her face, his mind working.

He closed his hand again and let out a breath.

He met her gaze. 'Just dance with me. Only a dance.'

She wasn't sure if there was such a thing as only a dance between them, but she took a slow breath and stepped back into his waiting arms.

The salsa kept them much further apart than she'd expected. He held her hands only and led her through a cycle of simple steps she knew. The tug of his hands distributed her weight differently from the solo steps in Zumba. But she enjoyed the momentum he created, the approach-and-retreat. His hand brushed her waist lightly to keep her anchored in a turn. She already knew some of his cues from rehearsing that morning. She was smiling before she realised what she was doing.

By the end of the song, her breath was surprisingly short and Javi had been a perfect gentleman. Why was she disappointed? She had to admit he was right. It was fun. It was easy. The attraction wasn't some trap she would fall into never to escape. It was a distraction, but she'd made it into more of a concern than it deserved.

The swell of an accordion announced the next song as a vallenato, although the beat sounded contemporary. Javi drew her closer and she remembered his sensual dance with the woman in the high heels. Her danger gauge slipped up a notch.

One hand pressed into her lower back and the other grasped hers. Her senses went crazy again. This time she recognised the danger: temptation. It had never been so easy to picture falling into intimacy.

He lifted her hand round his neck and she leaned in before she could stop herself.

Lose yourself... The possibility had never sounded so intriguing.

* * *

It had never taken so long to talk a woman into dancing with him.

He'd never been so uncertain whether he was coming or going. And he didn't think he'd ever had a woman ask him straight up if he was angling for sex. It was a poor time to grow a conscience. He should have flirted outrageously with her and enjoyed every minute of the conquest. She may not like him, but there was enough there when they touched to talk her round.

But a saying had been swirling in his head ever since he'd met her: *agua que no has de beber, déjala correr*. He didn't have to drink the water – let it run. The fact that she was making him think about his shallow relationship history warned him not to push it with her. He might sing about love and romance, but he knew just how badly he'd screwed it up in real life.

He was thinking too much. One day with Cara and he needed his head examined. Tomorrow they'd shoot the video, the next day he could fly home and leave Cara to her hard-working, passionless existence. The success of the video was important to him, but not so important he would keep knocking his head against the brick wall of her rebuffs.

Then she softened. Her hand clutched his neck. Her body aligned with his. And he didn't know what to do with her, relaxed and pliant in his arms. Strands of her long hair tickled his fingers. He swung her round just to mess it up. She smiled as she tossed a strand out of her face and reached up to hold onto him again. He felt her smile in his gut. Holding her close was like listening to her voice. From his fingertips right through his chest, he felt something.

Her smile faded when he kept staring at her. Her eyes were the colour of the sea at Barranquilla – a deep blue flecked with brown and green. She had freckles on her nose. He had to focus on her features to ignore her lips.

He was struggling to remember whether he was supposed to kiss her or not. Usually the answer to the question was clear – yes. It was only a kiss. But with Cara it was different. Between the magic of the song and the flaring emotion of the long day, a kiss would not be simple.

He resented the tension in him. Like the cheesy line he'd sung in so many songs, love was a war that he set out to win. He'd thought he'd won when she stopped protesting and enjoyed dancing close. But the conflict in him didn't feel like victory.

The song ended and the opening of a classic reggaetón hit snapped him out of it. The dance floor filled to heaving. Cara took an unconscious step towards him. He had the urge to put his arm round her and pull her to the edge of the crowd where he could shelter her with his body while they danced. But the moments of uncertainty had brought his devil back. He turned her round and pulled her against him.

'Did you want to practise perreo?' he said into her ear and gave her bottom a nudge.

She broke away, her eyes flashing with something that looked awfully like hurt. 'If you need to rub yourself up against something, go find a fire hydrant.' Javi smiled. He liked her snippy comeback. He didn't want to like her.

He didn't respond, silently urging her to walk away so he could screw this up once and for all. She returned to the bar and he finally breathed out.

It didn't take long for him to receive alternative offers. He ignored the lingering presence of Cara, both in the back of his mind and sitting, arms crossed, on a barstool. He returned the smiles of two girls dancing nearby and he beckoned them over.

He'd danced like this hundreds of times in clubs from New York to Buenos Aires. It was fun. It was harmless fun. Or it was supposed to be. It turned out that it wasn't as much fun when he was only trying to prove something.

He danced with both girls, his hands all over them. They were from Spain and gushed over his Colombian accent when they weren't moving against him to the beat. He thought about slinging his arms round them and steering them to the bar for a drink, but Cara still sat there, emitting sparks.

He could feel her, even though he refused to look, which was how he knew immediately when she stood and stalked out of the club. He disentangled himself from the Spanish girls and rushed after her. He was a lousy cabrón, but he wouldn't make her go home by herself.

'Go back and lose yourself, Javi,' she said as she jammed her arms into her coat while walking. 'It's one o'clock and it appears I'm a pumpkin.' Her voice was even. She held her head high. She was so much stronger than he was. 'I've called a taxi. It will be here in ten minutes.'

'Then where are you going? Did you arrange for the cab to pick you up a mile away?'

Her steps slowed. 'I'm getting away from you while I wait.'

'Bueno,' he muttered. 'I'm going to see you into the cab.' He was going to get in that cab with her, but he sensed he should work up to that.

'Fine. Then you can explain to me what the hell happened in there.'

His stomach clenched. Did she want the truth? 'Which part are you talking about?'

'You brought me here to loosen me up and then when I did, you helpfully forgot my existence.' He was such a pelota, a damn idiot.

'It wasn't personal.'

She was too smart for that line, but it took the wind out of her for a moment. 'That's the route you're taking? Tonight was business as usual, dancing in a bar with as many women as possible, including a pity dance for the girl who shared your cab?'

'Relax, Cara. It's a different culture. It's only dancing.'

Her nostrils flared. 'Don't patronise me. I get it that the whole world's a party in Colombia. But I thought you got me! I thought the song... changed something... with us.' Her voice trailed off and she winced, clearly as confused by where they stood as he was.

He looked away and hesitated. 'I don't know where that song came from,' he admitted. 'I don't normally have that sort of depth. I have a good time and I write songs about drinking and dancing and girls. And I don't have serious relationships. That's it. So maybe I just got caught up in the collaborative process.'

She laughed all of a sudden. It was humourless, but proved she was out of his league. 'If you're this charming with all your women, then your reputation has been vastly embellished.' She let out an impatient breath and looked down the street. 'You're lucky I'm desensitised to rejection.'

'I never rejected you.'

'The "I get music and sex confused" line usually works for you?'

'Look, Cara, whatever the hell this is, it's new for me, too. I'm attracted to you. That much I understand. I get that it probably shouldn't happen. But I want something from you and I don't know what it is. I want your soul in the song. I want you mixed up and feeling something. And I can't stand it that you won't give it to me.'

'You're used to women throwing themselves at you.'

'No,' he contradicted. 'It's not the challenge of the chase – I've done that before.'

She raised her eyes skyward and crossed her arms. 'Of course you have.'

'Have you had many boyfriends?' he couldn't resist asking.

'That's none of your business.'

'I know. I'm sorry.'

'What would change if I told you? Would you respect me more if I'd had a few? Would I be more attractive?'

He stared at her, her questions penetrating his habitual world-view to some kind of truth. Music and sex; take the easy way out; let the water run. She saw something – too much – in him. The words tumbled out of him, unpremeditated. 'You couldn't be more attractive than you are right now. The moonlight is showing up the fear in your eyes but you still won't take my shit.'

She sucked in a deep breath and raised her fists to his chest, both making a connection and keeping him away. Her eyes narrowed and he wondered if he was about to get a kick in the balls – he hoped a figurative one.

But instead her palms opened on his chest. Her approach was so slow he had time enjoy the spreading bewilderment at the fact that she was going to kiss him. But that was the last opportunity he had to think.

There was no experimental nibble, no gentle introductory brush. She tilted her head and planted her lips on his. It was a clumsy kiss, more spirit than skill and he adored her for it. He allowed her cool lips to explore his for a long moment, enjoying the lemon scent of her shampoo and the taste of her frustration.

He had the roaring urge to subdue all of her frustration back at their hotel. He wanted to lick his way down her body, taking his time on the curve of her neck and her audaciously tiny breasts. He wanted to sink inside her while she stared at him, demanding his soul – whatever was left of it.

Lost in the feel of her against him, he opened his mouth and kissed her with all his screwed-up longing. Her tongue met his on a sigh of capitulation that he didn't deserve.

This was why the day had turned him upside down. He forgot about the song, about Miami and Colombia and London. This was about a woman who confused him and got under his skin with every word she said and every note she sang.

The cab driver beeping his horn was impossible to ignore. They broke apart.

'Oh, God, please forget I did that.' She turned to the cab, making sure he couldn't see her face.

'That might be difficult,' he muttered. Her embarrassment pricked him.

'I'm not coming onto you,' she said as she pulled open the door of the cab. It was a sign of her agitation that she didn't even notice him following her in.

'I know, mona,' he said. 'I just have that effect on people.'

He enjoyed her sharp look and sat back with a sigh. He wondered if the evening had been a mistake. She sat as far away from him as she could get and he couldn't imagine taking her and her prickly body language into his arms to dance tomorrow. And yet, all the embarrassment and attraction and differences hadn't interfered with the warm amusement and developing... affection?

He stared straight ahead as his thoughts echoed in the silence. He wanted her to invite him to her hotel room. But she wouldn't do it and he wouldn't push it. He didn't want to be the man who seduced Cara Poignton in a day and escaped the next. *Let the water run...*

He'd foolishly said she needed an affair to give her something to write music about. He didn't want to be the subject of that song. He should have left her alone. She was a stray bullet. She was supposed to narrowly miss him.

She cleared her throat. 'I'm sorry to disappoint you if you were after a wild affair and some heartbreak to write a song about.'

Javi grinned and his stomach dropped with a potent mixture of admiration and warmth. 'There's always Easter.'

5

No flirting, no touching and definitely no kissing! Cara was horrified that she had to have this conversation with herself. One insightful comment and she'd forgiven a day of empty flirtation and planted one on him. She'd dodged a bullet when he hadn't pushed it. That he could kiss like that and think of it as just a kiss was proof that getting involved was a bad idea.

Even his rude question about her past boyfriends hadn't dampened the attraction, although it had been enough for her to spend the early hours waiting out the holding pattern of intrusive thoughts about the few short relationships that had quickly gone down the toilet. She was by nature too serious, too fast – losing her mother and brother at eighteen and living with a missing leg and obsessive worries had amplified her natural tendency to be circumspect about sex.

If the serious men she'd dated in the past hadn't been able to handle her, what chance did she have with the man who hadn't even answered her vulnerable email? The answer was a big fat none. They were heading towards nothing, even if it had felt the opposite.

It wasn't a good day to discover her self-discipline was so brittle. She had to spend the day in his arms. At least she had the protection of choreography and she only had to pretend to have fun.

Searching for the upside out of trained habit, there was one blaring advantage to her state of distraction: she'd forgotten about Christmas. But when they met at the rehearsal studio with the key members of the production crew, it all flooded back. She was making a Christmas video – in London. She couldn't hide from the season, trying to feel nothing, as she'd done for nearly ten years.

'We've got Trafalgar Square for a total of four hours this evening, so we have to get this working here – no time for a million takes. The bigger concern of course is the sunset. I need everyone to know exactly what they're doing. I know this is only forty seconds of the clip, but it's the most important part. This is what the fans will remember.'

Cara sucked on her lip and tried not to let the director's words seep into the anxious part of her brain. She would have to treat it like the next level of exposure therapy – let Christmas slap her in the face to prove she could handle it.

When they stood for the first run-through, Javi leaned close, crowding her thoughts just as he dominated her personal space. 'Did I screw up last night?'

She spared him a brief glance. 'You have to ask?'

'How bad?'

She gritted her teeth against the desire to absolve him. This attraction was decidedly dangerous if she could forgive him at the simplest sign of contrition. 'Do you care?'

'Huh,' was all he said at first.

'It's a simple question and you usually have a flirtatious answer ready.'

He grinned. 'You're right. But I thought you didn't want to flirt.'

'I don't,' she said with a huff. 'And I don't want to kiss, either,' she mumbled.

'But—'

She held up a hand. 'I know, I know. I started it. But you participated and we both realise it was a mistake.'

He wasn't doing a good job of suppressing his smile. She wondered if he was remembering the kiss in as much detail as she was. His 'participation' had been devastating. 'So, we're good?' he asked.

She eyed him again. They were a little too good for her peace of mind. 'Yes, I suppose so.'

Putting the day before and all thoughts of sexual tension – sexual anything – behind her should have helped, but she was starting to picture the filming that evening, with the huge Christmas tree the crew would set up on the Square, looking ridiculous in the middle of August. It would be impossible not to remember standing under the tree while a tourist snapped a photo of her family – a family of four. Why did this have to be a Christmas song, on top of everything?

'Come on, guys. Where's the spark?' the director called.

She grimaced and took a moment to centre herself, summoning the languid beat and convivial atmosphere of the club. It was better to hang onto that than think about that Christmas. She threw herself into it.

'Wait a minute,' Javi said and stilled her with a hand on her hip. She wanted to call him out for breaking the rules, but to him the touch wasn't personal – only her reaction was inappropriate. 'Relax, mona.'

'Telling someone to relax never works.' She should know.

He placed his other hand on her hip. It felt proprietary and inappropriately good. Did every woman react to him like this? 'It's not the dancing. You'll be wearing a coat anyway and no one will be able to tell you're throwing your hips around to overcompensate.'

'You're not helping and this isn't even a love song.'

'It's not?' he asked, his tone lighter than his expression. 'Mi corazón sigue latiendo por ti. "My heart keeps beating for you" isn't romantic enough?'

It was the line at the end of the bridge, during which she and Javi would be dancing by the Christmas tree, staring into each other's eyes. It was designed to look like a love story. He was right it sounded like a love story, especially when he sang it with the husky catch in his voice. But there was something about the song that didn't feel like a love song. 'Everything's a love song in some way. Haven't you ever written a love song?'

She pursed her lips. Why did everything he say feel like a challenge? She shook her head.

'Never?' His brow furrowed.

'I have plenty of other things to write about,' she said. 'My life doesn't revolve round men like yours does round women.'

He cocked his head. 'Está bien. Imagine it, then. Imagine we're crazy drunk on love.'

She snorted. 'This is not going to work. I can't suspend disbelief like that.'

He laughed. 'You really know how to cut a guy down.'

'I'm not cutting you down. It's just ridiculous.'

He sighed and leaned slowly closer. 'Take me out of it. It's not ridiculous that you could be in love. You find a guy who falls on his knees when he hears you sing. He writes a song about your freckles and your frowning lips.'

'I'm not going to fall in love with some guy because of a song.'

'What's a guy gotta do?'

She eyed him. It wasn't a serious question. She wouldn't embarrass herself by giving him a serious answer. 'Not everyone wants to live in a love song. Too crazy and... drunk.'

Thank God this would end tonight. Another day and he'd probably make her spill her secrets. 'Pues, I screwed up last night,' he muttered. He turned to her. 'For a couple of songs, you got it.'

She pressed her lips together. 'And then you ruined it.'

He studied her for a long moment. 'Fine. Think about the song, then. Make it mean something. Think about your favourite Christmas memories – the good ones and the bad ones.' She looked up at him in alarm. His expression was grim with that unanswered email.

'That's unfair.' He didn't want to hear about her miserable Christmases, but he wanted her to tap into her emotions for him?

'It's my song and I want your heart in it.'

'On a platter,' she mumbled.

'Just give me something, Cara. Are you or are you not the woman who gave me her soul in the recording?' She hoped that wasn't what she'd done. She couldn't ignore the strain in his voice. It was the tone of the song, so at odds with his lazy flirting. It meant something to him, too, no matter how much he pretended otherwise.

It wasn't a choice. He was right; she'd already thrown herself into his music. She could give him one day and survive it. She gave a single nod and raised her eyes to his, facing the storm. 'Okay. Let's do it again.'

He had a faint smile on his lips as he held out his hand. She allowed him to clutch her hand in his and pull her close. And she faced up to the truth and allowed herself to enjoy it. It wasn't really Christmas. It was August. She was allowed to enjoy it.

She focused on the music, but in her veins and not her synapses. She loved the song. Even more than she'd enjoyed the music in the club, she loved dancing to their song. She discovered

Javi was good at catching her when she whirled too fast and steadying her when she missed a step. She would never be a professional dancer, but this was her song, too, and she wanted to dance so she wouldn't cry.

When they finished the final run-through, she grinned and shook both fists.

Javi whistled. 'Ay, mama! You're on fire!'

She laughed. 'I'm not your mother, you goof.'

He shrugged. 'It's just a—'

'Latin thing. I know. I've heard your songs.'

'Well I'm not your goof,' he said, slinging an arm over her shoulder.

'Are you sure?'

His grin widened. 'I thought we weren't supposed to be flirting.'

'You calling me "mama" and me calling you "goof" is flirting? Maybe you aren't the professional I took you to be.'

His smile didn't falter. 'If I ask you to lunch, will you misconstrue it?'

She laughed. 'I'm meeting my father, sorry.'

His hands flew to his chest. 'You wound me with your rejection. I could come. I can do fathers.'

'Cut it out. I'll see you later anyway. You can't do my father.'

'What's so different about your father?'

'He's a judge at the Central Criminal Court and he likes to be called 'Your Honour'.'

Javi winced. 'Okay, you're right. I'll see you later.' He kissed her cheek and left the room with a wave.

* * *

Uncertainty rose in Cara's throat as she approached the end of the Strand for the filming that evening. She slowed her steps, preparing herself for the view of the Christmas tree. It would be surrounded by a milling film crew and cordoned off to keep out the gawking tourists. Those details, plus the blaring fact that it was still warm from the hot summer day, would stop her from dwelling on the memories of that Christmas – of that night. At least that was the plan.

Lunch with her father hadn't helped. She wondered if he was the only person who didn't like the song. He had been horrified to hear about the love story they were playing out on screen. She wondered how much was a result of his conservative musical taste and how much was because he hated Christmas.

At the first glimpse of Nelson's Column, she stopped, and her legs wouldn't propel her any closer. The air was warm on her skin, but inside she was shivering. Her heart pounded in her ears. She recognised the anxiety for what it was and suspected she wasn't going to tip over into uncontrolled obsession this time, but the niggle of doubt never fully left. Would she really be able to pull this off? What if someone realised the extent of her anxiety and her physical wounds? What if they realised she wasn't a love interest for a handsome charmer like Javi, but a sad, wounded girl who couldn't handle Christmas?

Frustration and force of habit gave her a kick in the direction of her grounding techniques. Visualising home, picturing herself running across the Clifton Bridge with the breeze on her face, taking note of her surroundings, calmed her down, but couldn't unstick her legs.

She'd arrived early because she always did, but also so she wouldn't worry about being late. It might have been better if she'd cut it closer so the pressure could snap her out of it. She didn't want to be standing like a fool on the footpath for twenty minutes, reliving her horrible Christmas in the middle of August, convinced she was an imposter and not a real pop musician.

She turned round and walked back in the opposite direction so at least her feet were moving. Feeling like everyone was staring at her, she hastily took a seat on the bench carved on one side with a bust of Oscar Wilde. The presence of St Martin-in-the-Fields church was palpable behind her.

It was one of the last things she remembered clearly...

Her father's words from their lunch date were still working through her mind – as usual. She didn't have to do this to herself. Self-care was important. She gritted her teeth. She did have to do this, because music was her life. It might be difficult, but she was accustomed to difficult. Her father might be able to avoid the painful memories that came with Christmas, but her mind wouldn't let her – she could only work through them.

She rose and turned to look at the church. It was strange that the end of that evening was a jumble of painful images, whereas the memories of sitting in the pew and hearing her brother's clear soprano fill the church with the first verse of 'Once in Royal David's City' were as clear as her memories of lunch today.

She forced herself inside the church. There was no Christmas tree, no pine boughs, garlands or twinkling lights, but the glowing chandeliers and gold leaf on the column capitals were festive enough to make her chest squeeze tight.

And there was a choir singing. She grabbed for the back of a pew to support herself as the glorious sound of the voices filled her. She stumbled into the pew and held her head in her hands, shutting out the audience and the summer heat and hearing only the transcendent sound, somewhere between the past and the present.

The choir finished and applause startled her out of her deep reverie. They filed off-stage and the moment was gone. Her phone beeped with a message from Freddie to dispel the last of her mood. She should have been relieved. She was usually too afraid to wallow in something that took her thoughts back. Today was about her future and she shouldn't endanger that simply because she had a problem with Christmas. She quickly texted Freddie saying she was in the church and would be right out.

She stood and joined the audience filing out of the church. But she hesitated when the double-doors opened ahead of her and she caught a glimpse of the chaos on the square. She hung back until the church was blissfully empty, staring back at the east window with its warped lead lighting as though it could suck her into the past and she would never have to return. 'Love always looks back' was the recurring line from the song.

Nostalgia... The word alone made her shiver. Javi may not care about her past, but his song – their song – was spanning the divide between those happy Christmases before and the poor shadow of memories she and her father had endured since.

But this year, she would dance. She raised her face into the sunlight slanting through the windows and skipped through a few steps of the choreography. She spun through a turn, grabbing for a pew when she overbalanced. With a chagrined smile, she realised she'd got used to reaching out for Javi. But he would be gone after tonight.

She danced through a few more steps, centring herself again in the present. When she stilled and turned back to the doors, it was to meet Javi's gaze. She stiffened.

It was Javi and yet he didn't quite look like the Javi she'd danced and sparred with over the past two days. He'd shaved off his beard and his thick black hair fell smoothly round his face. His pronounced cheekbones and square jaw were far more prominent without the beard, his lips more expressive. He wore a sharp black coat, which suited London, and a patterned scarf, which didn't. She had to work for her unruffled demeanour. He was gorgeous and she didn't have much left to fight it.

He was watching her with unreadable intensity, as though he

was gathering courage to say something, but she waited for several silent moments and he said nothing. How long had he been watching?

She drew herself together and headed for the doors, steeling herself to brush past him, but he grasped her arm before she could escape. She looked up expectantly. His face was close and unreasonably familiar, entwined with feelings she hadn't wanted to face about her past and future.

But he just looked at her with an odd mix of warmth and bewilderment that both touched her and irritated her. That was Javi. He unsettled her. He made her want to kiss the baffled expression off his face.

'Nice church,' he mumbled.

'That's what you've decided to say?' Cara had to laugh to cover the twist in her chest. 'It's a lovely church. The carol service on Christmas Eve is lovely,' she said, keeping her voice equally indifferent. 'Let's go get Christmas over with.' She fixed her gaze on the doors and strode out of the church.

The blanket of snow glowed silver and blue in the cosy twilight. Shadow and light dappled the pale columns of the National Gallery. The imposing Norwegian spruce kept watch over the square, hushed and still. Thousands of twinkling lights reflected red and silver off baubles and bows, interspersed with flickering candles and wooden stars.

Cara stared at Javi, her arms wound round his neck. His arms were tight round her and his gaze never left hers. Javi's expression was as close as she'd seen him come to solemn as he sang that his heart still beat for her.

'And cut!' They broke apart and Cara burst out laughing, fanning herself and tugging at her scarf.

Javi grinned. 'I'm glad you find this so funny.'

An assistant came at Cara with a cloth to dab at the sweat glistening under her jaw and the make-up crew attacked her with sponges. She fanned herself and hastily unbuttoned the heavy wool coat.

'I see you're in this for the glamour,' Javi teased.

'Let's go again!' called the director and Cara groaned. She was exhausted. Her residual limb ached, her shoulders ached, and she wanted to retreat into her studio and see no one for at least a week. Not even Javi... especially not Javi. She needed a break from the thrill of touching him. She needed to regain her perspective.

The director called for a couple of close-ups while the light was on their side and then announced the final take.

Javi was smiling at her. 'You're nearly home free.'

'It hasn't all been bad,' she insisted.

He laughed and took her hand to draw her into the starting position. 'What are you going to do with yourself tomorrow when I'm on a plane back to Miami?'

Wonder if this really happened. Wonder if we'll ever see each other again. 'Er, I like to run.'

He blinked. 'Okay. Enjoy that.'

She tossed her head. 'I will.'

The light was fading fast after the last take, but the director was pleased. The crew decamped to a pub and Cara sat at the bar staring into a wine spritzer and wondering how and when she'd say goodbye to him. They weren't even friends – were they?

'Are you going to finish that or fall asleep in it?' He leaned his forearms on the bar next to her.

'I'm usually in bed by now,' she explained lamely. He couldn't know that her sleep routine was rigid and necessary.

'Seriously? Sometimes I'm still napping at nine. What about concerts?'

She winced. 'I have to get lots of sleep in the days before.'

He gave her one of his curious looks, but didn't ask. What was the point? He'd be gone tomorrow. 'I'm sorry I kept you out so late last night.'

She spun her glass round from the stem as she considered her words. 'I should probably try to adjust. To be honest, I try to do as few concerts as possible. I picked and chose enough to get a core fanbase, but,' she shrugged, 'my dad was happy to prop me up financially so it was never a necessity.'

'Lucky you,' he chuckled. 'I've been gigging like mad for twenty years.'

She turned to him. 'What happens next?' She felt his discomfort through the few inches of air that separated them. 'With the song, I mean,' she clarified with a dry smile.

'Ah, release date is middle of November, but the record company will organise a bit of hype, so we'll have some sort of critical response and an idea of airplay before then.'

'Ooh, hype. I've never had hype before.' She smiled ruefully.

'It's been a few years for me.'

'Worst-case scenario?'

'People hate it. It dies.'

She frowned into her drink. 'That is one scenario I am unfortunately able to conjure myself. It hasn't escaped me that they would have picked someone more well-known than me if they truly thought we'd chart well.'

'At least your fans won't notice if it tanks. You've got an album coming out.'

'And you? Your fans will notice?'

His expression was somewhere between a wince and a lopsided

smile. 'It wouldn't be the first time for me. Maybe it's time to sink into obscurity. I have a few other things to do.'

Cara watched him sip absently from his tumbler, his fingers splayed on the glass. They'd made music together, but she'd never seen him play, using those fingernails to create the sharp sound she knew from the beginning of 'Nostalgia'. She thought about looking for a live video on YouTube, but dismissed the idea. This was it. They'd made their mark on each other. But it would be a shame if the single failed. She was tempted to reach out a hand to his bare forearm, but he suddenly grinned.

'I'll be thinking of the best-case scenario: we chart so well that you have to come to the US for interviews.' She shuddered at the thought of so many hours on a plane and he hooted with laughter. 'You really don't like me, do you?'

'Don't be silly. I was thinking of the flight.'

He eyed her with scepticism as he lifted the tumbler to his lips again. 'You don't have to like me. I know you like the song.'

'I love the song,' she said, avoiding his gaze. He didn't respond. She took a sip and braved a glance at him. He had that painful smile on his face.

'Do you want me to walk you somewhere? Or wait outside for a cab?'

'Are you trying to get rid of me?'

He glanced at her. 'You've nearly finished your drink. I thought you were so tired you'd want to go.'

She hesitated. Why didn't she want to go? They had to say goodbye tonight. Why not now? Another hour with Javi wasn't going to make any difference, but an extra hour of sleep would set her up for tomorrow.

She drained her wineglass and stood. 'London is very safe. I can walk to the train station by myself.'

'You're taking the train?'

'I'm staying tonight at my dad's, now the filming is finished.'

'I'll walk you to the station.'

'I'm fine. I've done this a hundred times. It's not even ten o'clock and the station is five minutes from here.'

'Then I can take the five minutes to walk you.' He knocked back the rest of his drink and waved a hand in front of him.

He shivered when they stepped out of the pub. 'You're not cold, are you?' she asked.

'I'm enjoying the Christmas vibe. It never gets this cold in Miami, not even in winter.'

'It's always this cold in England.' She zipped her light jacket and they walked briskly to the station. The lights felt too bright when they reached the forecourt. 'That's my train.'

Javi studied the train as though he hadn't expected it, then he glanced back at Cara. She felt the intensity of his look in her gut. 'I might never see you again,' he blurted out.

'It's strange, isn't it?' she murmured.

'It's been...' He cleared his throat and smiled, although his brow was still low and his eyes were sharp. 'It's been fun... working with you.'

'You too.'

He reached up a hand, but let it fall again. 'How about a hug?'

She nodded and a little laugh escaped her chest. He wrapped his arms round her. Her head nestled flawlessly against his shoulder. Her hands splayed on his back. She closed her eyes, thankful he couldn't see her.

Then she let him go. It was only a quirk of fate that had brought Javi Félix and Cara Poignton into an embrace. The return trip to real life awaited.

6

Heathrow airport was glittering with festive cheer as Cara walked to her gate. It wasn't quite December, but the season was firmly set to 'Christmas'. Carols tussled with Mariah Carey and Wham! for the airport soundtrack and her heavy wool coat weighed down her arm as the stifling nostalgia weighed down her spirit. Christmas returned every year, no matter where she was or what she was doing.

Except that this year Christmas had also come in August and stayed for much of the past three months. Cara was on her way to Miami. The looming TV interview was enough to drown out her usually crowded thoughts. She'd been on edge for a couple of weeks, making sure she had enough sleep and playing music for herself and not just rehearsing her professional songs. She'd talked everything through with her therapist and she'd filled a prescription from her GP for new medication she hoped wouldn't turn her stomach.

Flying wasn't always a panic trigger, but the first breath of aeroplane air brought a tickle of misgiving that could easily expand into heart-pounding worry if she allowed herself to imagine a crash, along with the bloody wounds that could launch a panic spiral. If her father knew she was alone, he would probably have his own panic attack. She hadn't told him Freddie's mother had been diagnosed with acute liver failure and Cara had insisted he stay by her side. She was an adult, not a broken teenager or a melodramatic pop diva. Daddy himself couldn't come – his court schedule was packed. As he often repeated, his cases decided people's futures. Her music was 'merely' popular culture.

But it was very popular culture. She was living Javi's best-case scenario. The video had been viewed three million times since the song was released the previous week. Although it was an amazing song that the record company was throwing its weight behind, they were still charting better than expected. 'Nostalgia' hit the UK Top 40 as soon as it was released. It was expected to crack the top twenty this week. Local statistics reported their song as the number five track for streaming in Miami. They were already number fifteen in the US Latin chart. And now in waning November, the bizarre dream of Christmas in August was crossing into reality.

She had watched the final cut of the video over and over, but it had only contributed to the sense of a surreal time-out-of-time. It was sumptuously filmed and subtly edited to create the feeling of continuity, of history. Javi sang his parts outside colourful colonial churches with elaborate, hand-crafted nativity scenes. Juxtaposed over the scenes she assumed were from Colombia were short glimpses of the brown brick Georgian squares of Bristol where the crew had filmed Cara singing.

The production had cut together longing looks the film crew had coaxed from her with Javi's soulful gaze to create the impression that they pined for each other. Then for forty magical seconds, they danced together in the festive twilight. The final moments of the video wrenched them back to their homes, an ocean apart, leaving the viewer wondering what was real – just as Cara wondered about some of the striking moments back in August.

The flight to Miami was uncomfortably real, as was the TV appearance that awaited Cara – to expose her as the anxious pop-fraud she was. Seeing Javi again? That hadn't sunk in. Her memories of laughing with him, dancing with him and that one ill-fated kiss had been separately filed in her mind under a heading somewhere between reality and imagination. The two days with him could not have been as intense as her memory insisted.

She monitored herself carefully for the first hour for signs of a panic spiral. If it had been a night flight, she might have taken a sleeping pill. But jetlag would be difficult enough without sleeping the day away.

Tomorrow she would appear on TV and hope no one noticed she was an anxious little girl dressing up as a sexy pop star. Her stomach clenched and heaved on cue. She'd worked hard with her therapist to ensure her performance anxiety never spiralled, but she was under more pressure than ever. She grabbed for her medication and called for a cup of water.

Her confidence had deserted her already. But the grim knowledge that she'd been here before gave her the thread of hope she clung to. One way or another she'd get off this plane in Miami. She watched the seconds tick by on her phone until the steward brought her the water. She needed to stave off the panic until the medication kicked in.

By the time she swallowed the tablet despite her thick tongue, her forehead was pinching her brain and her jaw was aching. Counting and visualisations evened out her heart rate. There was nothing she could do about the constant clench of her muscles in preparation for a crash. She didn't dare close her eyes.

She slumped in her seat as her symptoms eased. She could do

this. Just because she'd needed pills today, didn't mean she'd end up back in the eye of the storm, where she'd spent years following the accident. Tomorrow was another day.

Seeing past the flight was nearly impossible, and even though she searched the entertainment catalogue for romantic comedies and harmless sit-coms, she struggled to focus. She arrived in Miami a wreck and asked herself again why she did this job.

* * *

Early the next morning, jet-lagged and a little raw, but determined to embrace the day, she dragged herself out for a jog along Miami Beach as the apartment blocks gleamed pink with the sunrise. It was spotlessly clean. The ocean was so clear it glowed turquoise. The air held the familiar tang of the sea that sometimes reached down the Severn and the Avon to Bristol. But the mild air, the coconut palms tottering in the breeze and the rolling breakers glinting in the early morning sun were a jarring change from the damp English November. The natural serotonin gave her a boost.

She stopped for breakfast on Ocean Drive, enjoying the Art Deco facades and the feeling of being in a different place with a different pace of life. Pumpkins, gourds and tropical fruit decorated the tables of the café for Miami's take on Thanksgiving, which had just passed.

There was a new freedom to exploring alone. She wished she could throw on a sundress, like the friendly waitress who brought her coffee, but even her good leg was so scarred it drew pitying glances. Only her high-tech running leggings kept her from overheating in the subtropical November that felt like a Bristol summer.

If it weren't for the extravagant displays in shop windows and picture-perfect Christmas trees in between the palms, she could have forgotten all about Christmas. Why hadn't she and her father thought of this before?

But as she waited for the taxi to take her to the TV studio that afternoon, she was tingling with the memories and the anticipation. It would be the first live performance of 'Nostalgia'. She wished she had a piano to play herself calm, but all she could do was run the song over and over in her mind to banish the hypotheticals.

She pictured Javi at the studio and a different feeling shot through her. It was agitation, but not like panic. She was careful not to pursue fruitless paths of thought and had mostly resisted looking for news of him on the internet. But she had seen that his album had been nominated for a Latin Grammy, although he hadn't won. On the red carpet, clean-shaven and in a tuxedo, he'd been the charmer of the video, instead of the scruffy screw-up who had gotten under her skin. The beautiful woman on his arm completed the image. She was certain he didn't lack for partners to take to awards ceremonies, as he hadn't lacked for partners in the club that night.

But how would he act with her? She expected the meaningless flirting, but what about the undercurrent of curiosity, the wariness of attraction? And how would they sound singing together live for the first time?

When the cab dropped her off amongst the downtown skyscrapers, she gave herself a mental pat on the back for getting there in one piece. With her suit bag over her shoulder, she counted the steps into the marble foyer of the building that housed the TV studio and signed in with a shaking hand. In the elevator, she looked through the reminders on her phone again, refusing to look at her haggard appearance in the mirror. The last reminder made her smile. Last night before she'd collapsed into bed – yesterday afternoon before she'd collapsed into bed at the wrong time – she'd remembered she had to greet Javi with a kiss on both cheeks. He wouldn't catch her by surprise this time.

The elevator doors whisked open. She looked up and her breath escaped her on an 'oof'. He was waiting by the doors for her, his eyes glinting and bottomless. The pull of attraction coiled into a rubber ball and bounced through her torso. She thought she'd prepared herself for the jolt of desire. It was more consuming even than her memory.

He was watching her with eager wariness. He had his hands shoved into the pockets of his shorts. The top few buttons of his shirt were undone. He was clean-shaven, his solid jaw and mischievous lips prominent. His hair had grown so long it was pulled into a ponytail.

Despite the attraction and confusion, she was happy to see him. She grinned and was gratified when his smile matched hers and he leaned closer, his arm resting on the elevator door frame. She took a step towards him and stretched up. He smelled warm and real – not overpowering, just enough to revive that weird desire to bury her face in his chest. But this was Javi and she knew where she stood – a safe distance away.

He closed the rest of the space between them and pressed his lips to her cheek. Her thoughts flew to the devastating kiss.

He kissed her other cheek and drew back, a quirk of his eyebrow a dangerous indication that he knew where her thoughts had escaped to.

'I got my wish. Welcome to Miami, mona.' He took her bag and gestured for her to follow him. 'Rough flight?'

She nodded. 'I wanted to give the make-up crew a challenge. Thank you for noticing.'

'You didn't want me to say anything?'

'Would have greeted your date for the Grammys by commenting on the bags under her eyes?'

He grinned and she regretted saying anything. 'Jealousy suits you. You should have told me you wanted to go.'

'I'm sure you were happy with your date.'

He shrugged and pursed his lips. 'I would have been happier with you.'

She eyed him. 'Thirty seconds to flirting. Is that some kind of record?'

'Took me a while to warm up. I was suckered for a minute because I forgot how cute you are.' He slung his arm round her shoulders and steered her into a rehearsal studio, ignoring her half-hearted scowl.

An hour later she had her answer to how the song sounded live – glorious. Safely sequestered in the rehearsal room with the large, supportive band, she'd dived into the music with relief. The live brass and extensive percussion lifted the buoyant mood. She usually felt naked without a piano or a guitar, but she raised her hands above her head and danced when she wasn't singing.

Armed with a guitar, Javi was compelling. He plucked the strings effortlessly, creating dynamics and colour with flourish that echoed through his body. He leaned into the microphone, capturing the bittersweet character of the chords and the lyrics with his raw voice.

She loved singing the bridge, when the congas transported her mind and body with their syncopated rhythm and she sang her jubilant melody about dancing in the streets and turning on the lights.

The power of the music was in its ability to be both joyful and disconsolate – to make her somehow nostalgic for the future. Was that why the song touched her so deeply? It was honest about the pain and joy of the holiday. It would probably give Javi hives to admit the song was honest and heartfelt, but she felt it and that was enough.

Although when she glanced at him during the bridge, he was leaning into the microphone with his head bowed. When he noticed her gaze, he returned the look with a smile that she imagined was a little forced.

He sang the last line looking straight into her eyes. Telling herself he was performing, she did the same, giving him a smouldering look as she repeated his line in English: 'My heart keeps beating for you.'

The band whooped as the final chord faded. Javi grinned and applauded them, making an exclamation in Spanish as he placed his guitar in the stand. He glanced at her with a twinkle in his eye that unnerved her, then plucked her off the floor in a jubilant bear hug.

'Spectacular,' he rumbled in her ear. His voice rippled through her chest. She melted against him. She loved this song. His heartbeat held the comfort she usually found in the metronome by her piano. But he was much warmer. And the metronome didn't have arms that could clutch her tight.

The band soon intruded, demanding hugs and cheek kisses of their own. Javi didn't stay near her, but stepped away, checking his equipment. When she approached him, at a loose end, he glanced up with a remote smile.

'You'd better get over to make-up. I'll see you in an hour.'

Cara drew back. His sudden dismissal turned something inside her upside down and she realised she'd made a mistake to get so caught up in the music with him. A lurch in her stomach signalled the end of the dreamy period of music-induced calm. It was back to her reality.

She nodded. 'Time to get rid of these bags. I'm surprised the airline let me bring them.' She gave him what she hoped was a sassy smile.

His brow furrowed and he stood and reached for her. She

evaded the touch and turned to go with a weak wave to discourage him from following.

* * *

Railing at Javi's shallowness kept her churning stomach from the forefront of her mind as the make-up artist applied the first layers. Someone else had to have written that damn song. Javi Félix was a libertine who should not have had the ability to produce something so touching. Every time she tripped over her own emotions, he drew back. Typical male.

But it wasn't that she was interested in him. If she ever decided to pursue a relationship, she needed a safe harbour in a storm – not a hurricane of a man.

As the make-up artist performed a miracle on her face, she could no longer ignore that she was putting herself in front of cameras that would broadcast her image across the entirety of this vast country on Thanksgiving weekend. Her mind ran away with the possibilities, from the banal – forgetting the lyrics of the song – to the ridiculous – being assaulted by an armed gunman pulled straight from one of her father's lectures on personal safety. Her logic ran after her thoughts, trying to remind her this was fear talking.

When she retreated into the private changing room, she could feel the distant panic spiral. She removed her dress from the suit bag and retrieved her ballet flats, staring at them both as though they would stab her in the back if she turned round. She'd risked too much. She should have worn tailored trousers and to hell with the expectations of the music industry. She would disappoint them all one day when the truth of her sassy songs came out.

Although it was a floor-length floral maxi, it was still a dress. Underneath, her carved-up legs would be bare and the carbon fibre cylinder of her ankle on display. Even worse, sensible shoes and socks didn't go with a dress. If the high-tech cameras were to zoom in on her feet, they would easily pick up the slight difference in skin tone between her biological foot and the silicone skin covering her prosthetic foot. She wasn't ready for this. She wasn't prepared to become the face of amputees in pop music. She'd fought for so long to simply be herself.

The insistent beat of her heart clamoured for attention among thoughts that had scattered in all directions. She knew she had to fight and this song was worth the struggle. Her breathing exercises came to her with the strength of habit and she was able to dress.

She slipped onto the set as quietly as she could. The presenter – a well-known American personality, she understood – was chatting to Javi in Spanish. He saw her and beckoned her over with a gushed greeting, switching to English. She managed an awkward hand-shake, but she was struggling to concentrate. The familiar weight of Javi's arm fell round her shoulders and the ruckus inside her dimmed.

'Ready for this?' he asked, his lips near her ear. She shook her head furiously. He tut-tutted. 'Careful. You don't want to ruin your hair.' He reached up to smooth a strand back.

As they retreated behind a screen to the side of the shot, it was tenuous, but Cara was in control of her fears. Despite the over-whelming urge to stay and hide, she would be able to force her legs forward. She was going to do it and she was going to make herself proud.

'Cara?' Javi's voice sounded in her ear again.

'Hmm?'

'Are you playing an imaginary piano?'

She looked down at her fingers, which were stretched out as though playing Debussy, then into his eyes. 'Yes.'

He studied her and the lines at the corners of his eyes deepened as he smiled. 'Cool.'

'Not really.'

She wasn't sure what he sensed from her, but he slipped his arm round her waist and gave her a squeeze. She pursed her lips and tried not to read too much into it. Javi just liked hugs.

7

'That's amazing you recorded the whole song without meeting in person. What did you think of him when you did meet?'

Javi felt her glance, but figured it was safer to ignore it. She was nervous. The interview had been stilted and awkward so far. He hoped she'd get in the flow, but suspected it was more likely she'd freeze up. She could say what she liked about him if it would help her get through the interview.

'Uh... I was disappointed, actually. I'd expected him to be charming and well-groomed, but instead he had a horrid beard, messy hair and the first thing he said was that I was too thin.'

'Wow, is that true?'

Javi grimaced. 'Guilty.'

'He apologised afterward. And, to be honest, the song is so amazing I got over it.'

He grinned. She was gripping her hands so tightly she was cutting off the blood flow and her eyes were flashing round the studio in panic, but the sass was so sexy. Grady switched to questions about the song and their fresh enthusiasm sparked easy discussion.

'Yeah, there are more specifically Colombian influences because this is "Nostalgia", you know. But it's not just cumbia or vallenato, although that's what I grew up with. I mean, Cara brought this amazing choir sound and it just worked.'

'I didn't know what any of this was before I heard the demo. But it's basic and complicated at the same time,' Cara added. Javi chuckled when she fell into a technical explanation of the harmonies, using terms he'd never heard. She noticed she was babbling and cut herself off. 'It's... catchy.'

'And we're extremely lucky to have you both here for the first ever live performance of "Nostalgia".'

Cara's sharp intake of breath was so loud it must have been picked up by the microphone. He didn't understand why she was so nervous. The rehearsal had been amazing. The song had success written all over it. She was a high achiever. She should be revelling in the rewards of her talent and hard work. He was the one who was worried about living up to the promise of the damn song.

When she squeezed her hands into such tight fists he was certain she would draw blood, he couldn't stand it any more. He grabbed her hand and forced his fingers between hers. He kept up smooth conversation as he did so, hoping they would use a close shot. She wouldn't appreciate rumours of romantic entanglement, but her tension was killing him.

He kept her hand in his until they stood to move to the stage. She was trembling. She gave their linked hands a perplexed look, as though she hadn't even noticed, and he released her with one last stroke of his thumb.

He wished she could enjoy the performance – as she'd enjoyed dancing in the club before he'd choked on the tension. He could still remember the way the light had played over her painful smile in the church in London. There was something about her that delivered a punch to his gut and made this so much more than it should have been.

He watched her as she took up her position behind the microphone, flicked her hair back over her bare shoulder and raised her head. She held herself like a fighter, but her dress flowed softly round her body. He wanted to dance with her in that dress and make her forget about the cameras. He wanted to knot his fingers in her long hair and mess it up. But she was Cara Poignton and he was... a disappointment. He knew she'd meant the words in jest, but she'd stumbled on the truth. As a musician, a husband, a father – he'd never lived up to expectations. At least this song was a small diversion for Cara. Her career would sparkle into the future without his input.

She noticed him watching her and gave him a nod and a small smile. He wanted to touch her, but the cameras were already trained on them. He settled for blowing her a cheeky kiss. She raised her hand, pretending to catch it and throw it back at him with a sassy shake of her head. He grinned and tugged his guitar strap over his head.

He let the first chord resonate for a pregnant moment. Talking about the song, building up the expectations of the distant audience had given him the urge to turn up the drama. He improvised a couple of bars, picking at the strings with his fingers, and then let the sound fall away. He let the song do the rest. He loved having the adoring attention of the audience – or the cameras, in this case. But this song had never been about him.

Cara's gaze was on the ceiling for the first chorus, where her voice soared above the earthy accompaniment and Javi's own raw melody. Her arms floated unconsciously. She didn't achieve the joy he'd seen in rehearsal – the joy he'd wanted to catch and keep so badly. But she clapped along and he was so used to producing rousing antics that it was a satisfying performance. Only Javi would ever know it was less than it could have been. And he couldn't let that bother him.

Grady returned to congratulate them and make the final plug for the single and then Cara vanished. Javi joked with the band for a few minutes and wound down.

'Cara okay?' the trumpet player asked, and Javi's smile dropped.

'I should check.'

He knocked on the door of her dressing room and she instructed him to wait. When she wrenched the door open a few moments later, she pushed past him and rushed for the elevator. She had changed back into her pants and sneakers. She stabbed the button for the elevator and clenched and unclenched her fists as she waited.

He grasped her shoulders. 'Princesa, what's up?'

She shrugged him off. 'I have to go. I'll see you in Mexico for the next promo.' Her voice trailed off as she gritted her teeth and took a deep breath. She squeezed her eyes shut and sighed with relief when the elevator doors opened.

'I'll see you out.'

'Javi, no!'

He placed himself between Cara and the doors. She wanted to keep fighting, but it was a sign of how desperate she was to get out that she didn't press the button to keep the doors open and make him get out.

'I will be fine. I just need to go and deal with myself.'

'You're not fine, now.'

'No,' she admitted. 'But I can handle it.'

'What's wrong?' She simply shook her head and Javi's alarm notched up. 'Have you called a cab?' She grimaced, a trembling hand flying to her forehead. 'I'll take you to your hotel. My car is in the lot.' He pressed the button for the basement parking level, but when the doors opened on ground, she slipped out and dashed for the exit. Outside the building, she looked around, agitated, before rushing into the neighbouring alley and heaving her guts up.

He scrambled to her side, one arm sliding round her waist to hold her up and the other one fumbling to brush her hair out of her face as she vomited. Something wrenched in his chest as he watched her fall apart, tears streaming down her cheeks. When she was spent and only sobs racked her body, he pulled her away. His pockets were empty, so he searched in her bag for a Kleenex, shoving it into her hand so she could mop her face in embarrassment. Was she seriously ill?

He was relieved and disappointed when she pushed him away. 'I can take care of myself now, thank you.'

'Let me drive you to your hotel.'

* * *

Cara couldn't reasonably refuse, although she was tempted when she saw his car. He drove a sleek black speed machine she didn't care to identify. If she'd had anything left in her stomach, it would have been churning with the mental image of the car wrapping itself round every pole they passed. But it wasn't a long trip and he remained mercifully silent while she trembled in the passenger seat. At least she wouldn't have to worry about him flirting with her any more. Chucking up was the perfect turn-off.

He was familiar with her hotel and parked in the lot instead of dropping her off out the front. 'I can manage on my own,' she pre-empted him.

'Humour me.'

'No. I want to be alone. Thanks for the lift, but I'm not a damsel in distress.'

'Good, because I'm not a hero. But... what the hell is wrong?'

'Trust me. I can take care of myself.'

He sighed. 'That's it?'

'What's it?'

'I don't see you now until we go on stage in Cancún?' His brow was furrowed.

She ignored the warmth in her chest. He only cared because of the music. 'What did you expect?'

He pursed his lips and raised his eyebrows. Was he as confused by their odd friendship as she was? 'I don't know. You don't have to stay alone in a hotel room when I'm here to show you round. When's your flight to Mexico?'

'Tuesday.' She'd been trying not to think about the next stage of their promotion obligations – a live performance on the beach for Mexican television. At least the flight was shorter.

He braced his hand on the steering wheel and leaned towards her. She tried to ignore how handsome he was with his ponytail and strong features. 'Look, Cara, I don't know what's going on with you, but we're not strangers. If you're not up to a tour of Miami, at least come over for dinner tomorrow and we can watch the show when it airs. I promise I'm not trying to get you to have sex with me.'

She almost laughed. 'Because I'm so hot right now.' She made the mistake of looking at him. He was studying her with earnest intensity. 'I don't imagine your addiction to flirting extends to women who've vomited all over you.'

He smiled, his lips crooked. 'You'd be surprised.'

She raised her eyebrows, unimpressed. 'There's something wrong with you, Javi.' He grinned and smoothed her hair, stopping suddenly when he noticed the sick still clinging to a strand. Cara slapped a hand over her eyes. 'Just let me get out of here with some dignity.'

'What time am I picking you up tomorrow? I'm half an hour away – on Key Biscayne.'

'Are you sure it's a good idea?'

'I have a seafront condo. You can watch the waves and ignore me. Then we can coldly critique today's performance. I'll come and get you at 7.30.'

'Fine. I'll see you tomorrow.' She grabbed her things and waved him off, but the escape felt hollow. He wouldn't let her stay cooped up. She wasn't sure if she resented it.

* * *

The sun had set behind the apartment blocks of Miami Beach by the time Javi collected her the following day. The palm trees blinked with thousands of fairy lights. Miami Beach wished the public happy holidays in neon letters. Trying to ignore the tug of jetlag, Cara stared out the window as they skirted downtown and headed out along the causeway.

'The Christmas displays are just... bigger, here.'

'You should see the día de las velitas in Colombia. It's the beginning of the Christmas season for us. Every street, every building downtown is covered in lights and candles. And carnival in Barranquilla in February is crazy. We don't celebrate by halves.'

'I got that impression from the video.' She fell silent again. She was uneasy. Despite the professional reason, going to his home was personal.

The village of Key Biscayne was also festive and glittering. Families were out enjoying the first displays in front gardens as Thanksgiving rolled into Christmas. Cara yawned as she hauled herself out of his car in the underground parking lot.

'Big night last night?'

The withering look would freeze on her face if she spent too much time with him. 'Jetlag – day two,' she explained with a tight smile.

'Come up and eat. Maybe you'll need a nap before the show. It doesn't start until ten-thirty.'

Cara grimaced. She'd gone straight to bed after the puking incident the evening before. For the second morning in a row she'd run along the beach before the sun came up.

He showed her straight out onto the terrace. His condo was on the second floor and looked directly out over the ocean. Glass panelling protected the terrace and an array of tropical plants from the wind.

She glanced back inside, unable to curb her curiosity. What food was he going to serve? She noticed his condo wasn't neat, but it wasn't slovenly, either. He would have to move the jacket and sweater draped over the sofa later when they settled in front of the TV, and probably the guitar left carelessly on the coffee table.

Cara's mind raced ahead, picturing them sitting awkwardly next to each other on the sofa. For once it wasn't her anxiety running away with itself, but some other part of her brain that wondered what it would be like if he lifted his arm and she snuggled under it, pressed against his warm body. Her thoughts took her right back to the kiss she was trying to forget. Javi was far more likely to want to make out on the couch than to snuggle – and it would mean a lot less to him than a cuddle would to her.

He brought out two plates of rice, fish and vegetables and set them unceremoniously on the table. 'I'm not much of a cook, sorry.' He went back through the sliding doors before she had a chance to thank him for going to the effort. He didn't think it was much, but Cara looked with interest at the grilled whole fish, fried plantains and wild rice.

He returned with a bottle of white wine and two glasses. She suppressed her alarm when he poured himself a glass after filling hers. She didn't succeed.

'Take it easy, mona. I'm going to have one glass. I'm not going to drive you home drunk.' She started to apologise, but he waved his hand to stop her. 'Just eat.'

The cool ocean breeze and the stilted conversation didn't encourage lingering after the meal. Cara yawned repeatedly and got sick of Javi's narrow looks. He wanted her to tell him why she'd been ill. She didn't want to see his reaction if she told him. She had no interest in dealing with someone else's shock and pity. Permanent injuries – physical and psychological – weren't a party starter.

They moved indoors and she looked warily at the sofa. She yawned again and started to apologise when Javi laughed. 'I know. This is the worst date I've ever been on, too. Want to make things more interesting?' He winked.

'It's not a date.'

'Tranquila, bonita. I'm trying to behave, but it's not my thing.'

'You only invite women over here when the final destination is the bedroom?'

He pressed his lips together and shrugged apologetically. 'Yes. I don't do small talk.'

'I don't want small talk.' Her voice trailed off.

'What do you want?'

She closed her eyes and raised a weak hand to her forehead. 'To sleep,' she said with a humourless laugh. When she opened her eyes again, he'd crossed his arms over his chest and was regarding her with a furrowed brow. Only the pull of his dark eyes could distract her from helplessly admiring his muscular arms. What kind of weights did he press to get arms like that? It was horrible how attractive he was. She couldn't spare the mental space to resist it.

'Do you want to go back to the hotel?'

She should, but she wouldn't. She sighed. 'I want to watch the programme.'

'Can you stay awake for another hour?'

'Possibly not. Maybe you could wake me.'

A small, indulgent smile touched his lips. 'Pick a spot and nap away.'

Cara made the mistake of checking the time before curling up on Javi's overstuffed armchair with a cushion and a throw blanket. It was two in the morning in Bristol.

8

'I knew I wouldn't get away with that!' Javi winced as he watched himself grasp Cara's hand on national television. 'You were malditamente nervous, mona. Why the hell was that?' He rubbed a hand over his mouth. He was muttering to himself. Cara was dead to the world, slobbering peacefully all over his cushion. Short of picking her up and giving her a shake, he hadn't been able to rouse her beyond a mumbled protest.

After cooking her average food, accidentally coming onto her and then boring her to sleep, he felt satisfied watching her snooze in his armchair. At least he'd finally given her what she needed.

When the spot ended and a commercial started, he flicked off the TV and stared at his guest. Bad idea. He didn't need the reminder that he had a beautiful woman in his apartment – a woman who'd kissed him out of his senses. Why weren't they having an affair? Bringing their chemistry from the rehearsal yesterday into the bedroom would be explosive and miles better than this weirdness.

He didn't understand much about Cara, but he knew she didn't like mistakes. And the thought of being her mistake rankled. Then there was the chemistry itself. It was on a plane with the song – so much higher than his usual mode. Not sleeping with her in London had turned her into a romantic near miss that had messed with his head over the past few months. But she was better as a near miss than a post-affair mess. He would have to keep doing the right thing, as foreign as it was to him. Besides, something was going on with her that he was trying not to be curious about. He'd never dealt well with complicated.

He left her where she was and went to bed. He slept lightly. Whenever she woke up, he'd be ready to take her back to her hotel.

The sounds of someone moving around in the pre-dawn hour woke him. He found her sitting out on the terrace with a steaming mug, one leg propped up on a chair and her shoulders hunched against the cool sea air. He slid open the door to join her, but his gaze snagged on her other leg. He froze and stared. It took him a long moment to accept that her leg just stopped a few inches below her knee and the rest of her trouser leg was empty, flapping in the breeze.

As soon as he'd processed what he saw, he looked back at her face. Her eyes were shuttered, protected by her lashes as she refused to meet his gaze. Her lips were pursed.

'I didn't think you'd be up so early, or I wouldn't have taken my leg off.' He caught the defiant undertone and released the breath he'd been holding. She was okay.

He collapsed into the chair on the opposite side of the table. 'Mi casa es su casa.' He smiled. 'Make yourself comfortable.'

She eyed him. 'Is that all you're going to say?'

'About your leg? Yes.'

'Most people want to know what happened and feel the need to express their sympathy.'

He recognised her dry tone. Why did it feel like he'd missed her since London? 'You know me, Cara. I don't want to know and if I tried to express sympathy, I'm pretty sure I'd screw it up.'

Her lips twitched and she cocked her head in acknowledgement that felt far more significant than the small gesture implied.

'I'm sorry I couldn't wake you last night. Are you mad?'

She gave him a wary look. 'Of course not. It's not your fault I'm —' She cut herself off with a grimace, staring out at the sea as the first glimmer of sunlight broke across the black waves.

'You're what? Tired? Scared? Beautiful?' She ignored him, but a tic in her jaw made him wonder which of his suggestions disturbed her the most. 'Hungry. Are you hungry?'

She met his gaze reluctantly and nodded. 'I should go back to the hotel.'

'Eat something and then I'll take you back.'

He didn't rush, making toast and chopping papaya. He made himself a coffee and when he brought out the fruit, she was standing to press her prosthesis back on. He caught a glimpse of the metal ankle protruding from the convincing fake foot emerging from her sneaker.

'Leave it off if it's more comfortable.'

She frowned as she rolled her trouser leg back down. 'I just wanted to give it some air and change my sock. It's perfectly comfortable. I'm actually very lucky.'

'I'm sure that's a great attitude, mona.'

'But?'

He hesitated. Who was he to be giving her advice? And he definitely didn't want to get involved. 'Here, do you like papaya?' He set the plate down with a clatter and shoved it in her direction.

'What? What were you going to say?'

He sighed and ran his hand through his hair, which hung loose in unruly waves to his shoulders. He thought of her comment about his scruffy beard in London and wondered whether he should have cleaned himself up. 'You're allowed to go easy on yourself, niña.'

'Everyone's a bloody therapist,' she muttered, and her censure felt inexplicably good. 'I didn't get this far by going easy on myself.'

'But what is it costing you? I know you hated every minute of the show yesterday.' Why did he want her to deny that she'd hated every minute? Was he even flirting *for* her now? He was more of a jerk than he thought.

'You think you understand this, understand me?'

'Not even close,' he muttered in immediate reply. 'I just wish… it was different for you.'

'Well it's not and I'm so sorry for putting you through the frustration of futile wishes for other people.'

'You're being sarcastic,' he realised with a smile that felt right and totally inappropriate. 'And I'm being an ass.' He collapsed into the chair opposite her, staring at her face and wondering if he should try to look away.

She sat up straight, that regal posture drawing his eyes down the wiry strength of her.

'I was in an accident, when I was eighteen. It's a long time ago, now,' she said without inflection.

'Some moments last a lifetime. But I thought you didn't want to talk about it.'

She gave him a smile as faint as the pink creeping into the sky. 'I can,' she said with a shrug that held a heavy dose of defiance. 'My leg was crushed. The surgery was mostly successful, but I got sepsis in recovery the following week and they had to amputate.' Her voice was steady, but she hesitated and he sensed the worst was yet to come. 'It happened on Christmas Eve. We were driving home from a carol service where my mother and brother had been singing.'

He winced. 'I'm sorry for insulting your miserable Christmases.'

She laughed. 'Because this is all about you, Javi.'

He loved it when she talked straight like that. He sat up and his hand drifted across the table to hers. He stopped a few inches short. She didn't need his touch anywhere near as much as he wanted to give it. But she lifted her hand and brushed her fingers across the backs of his. It burned somewhere underneath his skin. He perpetually said and did the wrong thing, but she reached out and made it okay again. Unable to resist, he lifted his forefinger and trapped hers. She stilled, but didn't pull away.

'There's more?' he guessed.

She nodded. 'I was trapped in the wreck for a long time. I watched... My mother and brother were in the car, too, and they didn't survive. That and then all the surgery, the constant pain had... other effects.' She sat completely still, her face impassive. He said nothing, barely dared to breathe in case she stopped talking. 'I live with anxiety – in the sense of a disorder, not only your usual nerves – and sometimes panic attacks.' She glanced at him.

'Okay...' he said cautiously, releasing a breath when that paltry response seemed satisfactory and she continued.

'After I was discharged from hospital and physical rehab, even after I got my first temporary prosthesis, I couldn't look after myself for over a year. I was obsessively afraid of the simplest things and I couldn't control it. It wasn't just my leg that had to be reconstructed. I was diagnosed with Post-Traumatic Stress Disorder, and had a lot of exposure therapy, which helped, so I rarely get flashbacks any more. But managing anxiety has become part of my life.'

'You play the piano when you feel anxious? And you exercise.' The puzzle pieces clicked into place with a stab of reproach. He couldn't stop the little rip in his chest at the thought of her fighting for every moment. 'And you pushed yourself to perfect a dance routine that couldn't have been easy.'

Her mouth thinned. 'It was easy, compared to where I've been.

You know what? I lived. Lots of people who develop sepsis don't have a chance. And there's the fact that I survived the crash at all. I might occasionally clam up with fear that my other foot and my hands are going to fall off, but I'm okay.'

Javi's tongue stuck to the roof of his mouth as he stared at her. She lived. She lived with grace and strength and grit. And what had he done with the similar gift of being alive while his brother had died? He was still here, but he wasn't sure he deserved to be.

She sucked on her top lip as her eyes left his. 'At least I'm supposed to be okay. My manager – you remember Freddie – was supposed to come with me on this trip. His mother was taken ill and I insisted he stay behind. I wanted to prove my independence.' She punctuated her comment with a frown and a huff, pulling her hand away from his.

He stared at her hand, picturing himself grabbing it and hanging on because he wasn't finished touching her. 'You have proven it. The only thing you lost on Friday was the contents of your stomach. You did a good job.'

'But I'm at your house being looked after instead of ensconced independently at my lovely hotel in Miami Beach.'

'I'm not the "looking after" type.' He shrugged, moved a few pieces of fruit onto her plate and handed her a fork. 'You just wanted to try my papaya.' He flashed her a smile and stabbed a piece of fruit with his fork.

She gave an unexpected snort and he looked up to see her breaking into laughter. She snorted again and Javi's jaw dropped for a moment before he joined her in laughter. The snort was the cutest thing. It was his new purpose in life to make her snort with laughter.

'That sounded so suggestive,' she said in mock censure. 'Your papaya, indeed.'

He gave her a cheeky grin. 'Giving papaya is Colombian slang, but it's not actually sexual.'

'I don't believe you.'

'It's like inviting crime. If I give papaya, I'm inviting you to take advantage of me.'

'And you're trying to tell me that's not sexual?'

He paused. 'Maybe just between you and me.' He grinned. 'I live for papaya. One reason I never lived in New York. Even LA – too hard to get papaya.'

Her look was quizzical. 'I've never tried it.'

He reacted with mock horror. 'Here.' He held a piece out for her.

She leaned over to take the slippery orange fruit off his fork with dainty lips. The doubtful look she gave him made it more of a challenge than a turn-on, but he was keyed up either way – he wanted to laugh, cry and fight her demons all at once. It was a screwed-up impulse when he'd failed to rise to his own challenges.

'Interesting,' she said.

'That tells me nothing, mona. You can do better than that. Oh, it's amazing, Javi,' he moaned.

She snorted again. 'Why are we talking about papaya? I just told you my sob story.'

'I'm an immature machista. What did you expect me to do?'

She looked at him for so long he wondered if his neck looked as red as it felt. Her expression was sceptical. Was she about to contradict him? The thought that she might spread warmth through his chest.

'I hadn't thought about it, but I suppose flirting is your first response to everything.'

'You've got me.' He inclined his head.

'But why do you do that? It's not the first time I've heard you call yourself something unflattering.'

'It's the truth. I don't do heavy. I'm accepting my limitations. Just like you've accepted you've only got one foot.'

Something flashed in her eyes. Good. She had to remember he was no good or he might get too close and wreck everything. 'I have two feet. But one is artificial. That's the limitation I've accepted.'

'Sorry.' He waved his hand flippantly, feeling like a complete ass as he did so. He often acted like an ass, so why should it matter?

'These limitations you talk about are excuses.'

It was his turn to be indignant. 'I don't make excuses for myself. That would be foolishness. This condo is evidence and I live in it.'

'Evidence of what?'

He had the urge to get up and escape the conversation, but the emotional effects of her confession were riding him. She was strong and beautiful and far too good for him. He had to let the water run. 'It's evidence of failure; lack of follow-through; unreliability; laziness; broken promises.' He petered out on the last one, wondering what she'd make of it and trying not to care.

'You lived here with your wife?'

He nodded. 'You know I'm divorced.'

'Is "Nostalgia" about her?'

He was racked by humourless laughter. 'God, no. It probably should have been about her – it definitely should have been about her. And isn't that the problem?'

She looked at him as though she thought he was crazy. In comparison to her graceful stillness, he probably was. 'You have a daughter, don't you?'

'You really want to see me bleed this morning,' he muttered. 'Yes. I have a daughter I'm rarely allowed to see, and I got this luxury condo in the divorce settlement from my rich and successful wife. I bash a drumkit in the office and piss off the neighbours. I used to smoke and sometimes still do. I drink a lot of whisky and I let my mother wait on me hand and foot when I go home to Colombia. Do you understand now?' He rose from the table and didn't give her an opportunity to answer. 'I left the toast in the kitchen. I'll go make more because it's probably limp and cold by now. I'm sorry I made you eat papaya.'

Part of Cara's mind was occupied wondering whether papaya was supposed to be a euphemism, but mostly she was grinding her teeth in Javi's direction. She wished he wouldn't show those flashes of sensitivity if he was always going to follow up with boorishness.

He left her alone to eat and enjoy the sea breeze and the stunning view, marred only by curiosity about him. She returned to the living room to check her phone, knowing she should ask Javi to drive her back to Miami Beach and get as far away from him as she could. She would see him again in a few days for the promo in Mexico and she hoped the time apart would alleviate his allergy to her serious personality.

But first, the sofa looked inviting – and more comfortable than the armchair that had given her a crick in her neck. The condo was silent. Had he gone back to bed himself? She sank onto the sofa and grabbed the throw blanket.

'Hey, mona,' his gentle voice intruded just before she fell asleep. 'Come here.' She didn't resist the suggestion. When she followed him into a room off the hall, all she noticed was the bed. She sleepily removed her prosthesis and gratefully stretched out on it.

She awoke, her limbs heavy and her mind foggy. The sheets were fresh, the décor was sparse – a guest bedroom. She vaguely remembered Javi showing her in. The sound of voices drifted from the living room. Was he watching TV? she thought dimly. She grabbed for her sleeve and prosthesis and stumbled out of the room and down the hall. She was about to wander into the living room when she heard an urgent whisper.

'I wouldn't go in there, if I was you.'

Cara stopped and stared into a small room which had a

computer and a drumkit in it. Sitting on the stool behind the bass drum, swinging restlessly, was a girl with long, dark hair, familiar bone structure and impassioned resentment on her features. Cara stepped into the room, staring rudely. It was disconcerting to see the evidence that Javi was a father. She was older than Cara had expected, possibly already in her teens.

'I'm his daughter,' she answered the unasked question.

Cara nodded. 'I can see.'

'It's about to get messy. Mom always loses it when we come here. Javi's, like, her kryptonite.' The tone of the sharp conversation in Spanish coming from the next room rose to one step short of shrill and the girl winced.

'What are they arguing about?'

'What do you think? They've been divorced for seven years. I'm the only thing left that they share. Although, if you walk through that door, they might have a fight they haven't had before.'

Cara shook her head. 'Oh, I'm not...' She was so taken aback by the sarcastic antipathy in the girl's expression that she thought she'd better say too little than the wrong thing. 'What's your name?'

'Beatríz.' It was the first time Cara had detected an accent.

'That's a lovely name.'

She turned up her nose. 'Don't suck up to me. It won't get you any points with Javi.'

'You don't call him "Dad"?'

She smirked. 'He's not exactly "Dad" material, is he?' He said something sharply in Spanish in the next room and Beatríz's composure slipped.

'What did he say?'

Beatríz frowned. 'The usual stuff. You should learn Spanish.'

'I don't think I'd get far in such a short time,' she said.

'He gave you an expiry date? He's that terrible?'

'No!' Cara cried, but Beatríz cut her off.

'Shhh, he doesn't know I'm here. Mum got in with her key.'

'What? He doesn't know you can hear him?' Cara turned for the door, but Beatríz zipped out from behind the drumkit and stopped her.

'Why shouldn't I hear what he honestly thinks?'

Cara frowned. The urge to defend Javi was powerful. She didn't like the idea of his ex-wife poisoning their daughter against him, but she didn't imagine he was purely a victim in this mess. Did he want to spend time with his daughter? He'd never voluntarily talked about Beatríz.

'My mom has to dump me on him for a couple of weeks because she's finally landed a decent film role – pretty hard when you're a forty-two-year-old Latina, no matter how awesome her songs are and how famous she is in Mexico. The industry sucks sometimes.'

'But Javi and I are going to Cancún.'

'Awesome. I love Cancún.' Beatríz smiled – a horrid, mocking baring of her teeth – and Cara realised she'd put her foot in it.

'I mean, it's for work. We're not... We produced a single together.'

'I know who you are,' she said.

'Oh... good. That clears that up.'

'Although I'm surprised he shacked up with you. You're not his usual type. But then I suppose he's not discriminating.'

'You don't understand—'

'I'm always being told I don't understand,' Beatríz cut her off. 'I understand more than you think.'

Cara snapped her mouth shut. She wasn't about to explain to a child that she wasn't having sex with her father. 'Don't you have to go to school?'

'My mom has a sweet arrangement with the private school I go to. She makes the nanny go through the stuff with me if I miss it. I have to go with mom pretty much everywhere.'

'Why?'

'So she can keep me away from Javi. I'm the only thing she has left that can make him do what she wants.'

Cara blinked. 'I can't tell whose side you're on.'

Beatríz raised her eyebrows. 'Mom's, of course. But no one's perfect.'

'How old are you?'

'Would you believe me if I said fifteen?'

'Not when you phrase it like that.'

'You could ask Javi.'

'I don't want to interrupt.'

Beatríz almost smiled. Cara inclined her head and prompted her silently. She was intelligent, acerbic and probably as soft inside as her father's favourite fruit. Cara didn't think Beatríz would appreciate the observation. 'I'm twelve,' she admitted.

Cara's brow rose, but she tried not to give away her reaction. 'You're very mature for twelve. And bilingual, too.'

She shrugged. 'This is Miami. Everyone's bilingual.'

'This is my first time here.'

'Is Javi showing you a good time?' Beatríz had the mocking smile back in place. 'He knows every Latin club in Miami.'

'How do you know?'

She rolled her eyes. 'I have the internet. And I go to a private girls' school where most of us have Latino parents. I can't escape the fact that my dad is everyone's crush.' Cara winced. 'It's not too bad,' Beatríz patted her arm condescendingly. 'It's an expensive school. Some of the other girls' parents are narcos.'

'You're not serious,' Cara guessed, but Beatríz didn't have a chance to respond.

'Bea?' her mother called from the next room. She pronounced

the shortened form of her daughter's name less like the buzzing insect and more like 'beya'.

'¿Está aquí?' Javi's voice dropped in shock. His ex-wife snapped something in reply.

'I'm in here with Cara,' Beatríz called out, then turned to Cara. 'Come on. Showtime.'

Cara trailed Beatríz out into the living room, which was crackling with tension. Javi's ex-wife was just as stunning as Cara had expected – huge dark eyes and hair falling in dramatic waves down her back. She had her arms crossed over her chest and stood facing him, statuesque and audacious in her heels. Passion was written all over her features.

Javi rocked back on his heels, his lazy insouciance as incorruptible as ever. He lifted one muscled arm to brush his hair out of his face. She didn't want to find the action, the man with the careless attitude, attractive, but her mouth went dry and she knew the acceleration of her heartbeat had nothing to do with anxiety.

9

Javi summoned all his laid-back fatalism as he watched Cara and Bea emerge from the office. He'd made this mess. Now he had to watch it unfold.

It felt as though Bea had grown again. He never managed to keep track of which stage she was at. He knew with certainty she was well past the stage where she hugged or kissed her father. By the look on her face, she wasn't impressed with what she'd overheard. Some of the blame could be shared with Susana. She always drove a wedge between them. But he was the one who'd said he didn't want to be stuck with her right now.

He approached Bea anyway. Her look was so hostile he didn't draw too close. He tugged on a strand of her long hair and said, 'Hey, ¿qué más, gordita?' with a faint smile.

She tugged her hair free. 'I don't want to be here any more than you want me here. And your buddy doesn't speak Spanish.'

His eyes rose to Cara. She gave him a grim smile.

'Tranquila, Bea. It's not going to be two weeks of suffering.' He looked straight into her eyes. 'I'm sorry I said I didn't want you here right now.' He noticed Cara's muffled exclamation and shrugged off the prick of guilt. 'Any other week I would never have said it.'

'I know. Cara told me you two are off to Cancún.'

'Cancún?' Susana interrupted. 'You can't take Bea on a dirty weekend! You told me you have a promotional thing!'

'It is a promotional thing – in Cancún.'

'But with your—'

'Don't finish that sentence, Susi. It's not what you think.'

'You expect me to believe that?' she scoffed. 'I know you don't usually go for gringas flacas, but she's obviously slept here.' Javi wouldn't usually bother defending himself, but he felt bad for Cara, drawn into his mess. He hesitated. If he protested too strongly, Susana's suspicions would only deepen.

'I don't know what gringas flacas means,' Cara cut in, her voice low and irritated, 'but I'd like a chance to defend myself, if you're accusing me of something. I fell asleep on the sofa and stayed in the guest bed.' She checked her watch. 'It's three in the afternoon in Bristol and jetlag is not my friend.' She strode across the room to the open-plan kitchen and poured herself a glass of water. He admired her even gait – impressed by both the injury she coped so well with and the composure she maintained so elegantly. 'I don't know why everyone keeps thinking he's so irresistible.'

Javi grinned and turned back to Susana. 'A woman after your own heart.'

Susana shook her head. 'You're never serious, Javi. I don't know if I trust you. Perhaps this was a bad idea. Bea should come with me to LA anyway.'

The alarm that knifed through his chest made Javi face up to the truth of how much he wanted this to work, despite the inconvenience. He couldn't pretend he didn't care. The truth tumbled out of his lips. 'I want her with me.' He felt all three sets of eyes on him.

He spared an apologetic glance for Cara, but he didn't dare look at Bea. 'I'll cancel the gig in Mexico. She can go to school.'

'That doesn't sound fair,' his daughter spoke up. She had that calculating look on her face. He wondered what she wanted out of this and how he could get an honest answer out of her. 'Mom gets to go to work but Dad doesn't.'

'She's trying to get out of school,' Cara said and Bea's sharp look confirmed the accusation.

'Who asked you?'

Cara paused to look at all three faces in the room and then shrugged. 'I'm the only one without a vested interest.'

Javi glanced at her, suddenly wishing she had a vested interest in his life. God, he could be so selfish.

'This is none of your business!' Susana spluttered. 'I am her mother and I have custody.'

'I didn't mean to imply otherwise. But I don't think either you or Javi are thinking clearly. She should be at school.' She approached Susana and held out her hand. 'I'm Cara, by the way.' Susana just looked at the outstretched hand.

'I know who you are,' she said after a long pause.

'This is Susana,' Javi mumbled.

When Susana didn't take her hand, Cara deflated and dropped it. 'Okay, I'm interfering and I'm sorry. I thought it might help.'

'Shouldn't you be more worried about your own career? You'll miss out on the publicity if Javi stays here.'

'Don't worry about me. I'm okay with cancelling.' Her eyes darted to his and he recognised the glimmer of relief. It disappointed him. He preferred Cara sparkling with defiance.

'I'm not!' Bea cried. 'It's not about school. I like your song. You should do it. You could get to number one in Mexico. It's already in the top ten.'

'It is?' Cara asked, turning to him like a meerkat.

He nodded. 'Yeah. It debuted at fifteen and now it's number eight.' He couldn't resist adding, 'It's already number three in Colombia.' She clapped her hands over her mouth and he grinned. Resisting the urge to pick her up in a bear hug, he turned to Bea. 'Since when do you care about my music?'

'Since you wrote a half-decent song.'

Feeling pride was a foreign sensation. 'You should still go to school.'

'Mom's already sorted it in case I had to come with her. I've got all the lessons and my grades are fine.' She turned to Susana. 'Mom, even if there is something going on between them, I'll be a cock block.'

He heard Cara splutter at his daughter's language, but decided it was best to ignore it. Bea was no stranger to provocation. 'There's one more thing,' he said and turned to Susana. 'You said two weeks? After Cancún I'm going to Barranquilla for the día de las velitas. I can keep her as long as you need, but I've got a gig in Cali on the seventeenth of December and then we have a TV appearance in Bogotá on the nineteenth, where I can't take her.'

'Hey,' Bea interrupted. 'You said Cancún. You didn't say anything about Colombia.'

'And what's the difference to you?' He wanted to be on her good side, but he didn't like her tone. He already felt bad he hadn't taken her to see his family in years.

'Are you serious? Cancún is beach and fun and lots of people!'

'Sounds like Barranquilla to me!'

'Colombia is... bad roads and... stealing. And muddy streets. That's what I remember.'

He looked out the window and gritted his teeth. 'Since when is my daughter such a gringa?'

'Well my papá is a total naco!' She crossed her arms over her chest.

'I think it's a good idea,' Susana said. 'It always does you good to spend some time with the abuelos.'

'Don't forget all your cousins,' Javi mentioned.

'Is she going to Colombia?' said Bea, looking at Cara.

Javi shook his head. 'She has her own plans.' A slight stiffening of Cara's body language hinted that might not be the case, but Bea was just stirring things up to see if she could get out of coming to Barranquilla.

Bea looked at Cara with a sweet smile that told him she was making trouble. 'Don't you want to see the country where Dad wrote the song?' Cara hesitated, looking from him to Bea.

'I don't think Colombia is on Cara's bucket list,' he answered for her.

'I'm sure it's wonderful,' she said diplomatically.

'If I have to go, she should go, too,' Bea insisted.

Javi shook his head. 'Don't push it. There is always the option of staying in Miami.'

'You don't want to introduce her to your mom,' she taunted. 'She'll get ideas about more grandchildren.'

Javi smiled. Bea was provoking him, but the truth was strangely opposite. The idea of showing Cara Barranquilla held a lot of appeal. But he doubted she shared his enthusiasm.

'Are you doing any promotion for the song while you're there?' Cara asked.

He nodded. 'Of course. But it's local stuff. Your manager thought you didn't need to be there.'

'Well,' she began with a glint in her eye that he recognised as endearing stubbornness. She glanced at Bea. 'If you think I should see it, perhaps you're right. I do have writing credits for the song and I agreed to promote it.'

'You mean you want to stay after your sexpiry date?'

'Bea! ¡Lo estás buscando!' He waited until she looked at him, feeling oddly like a real father – both furious and tempted into immense pride at her smart mouth. He didn't expect that Cara would come to Barranquilla, but having Bea at home with him for the beginning of the Christmas season was an opportunity he wouldn't miss.

He felt a gentle hand on his arm and turned from his belligerent daughter to find Susana studying him with a look he didn't recognise. 'She goes with you,' she said firmly. 'You can deal with the Colombia issue. But, for these two weeks, I'm trusting you.'

Javi swallowed. Had Susana ever said those words to him before? The enormity of what he'd gotten himself into loomed. His gaze swung to Bea, who was losing interest in the fight and tapping patterns on the floor with her foot. He could do this. He had to.

He glanced at Cara. He had two people relying on him. He knew Cara didn't need his help, but he had a responsibility to her. And he knew what she didn't need – his habitual sexual come-ons. If she could survive hell with that amount of dignity, the least he could do was keep his hands off her.

Perhaps it was better to do all his growing up at once.

* * *

'You shouldn't have left her alone.' Cara knew she should keep out of his business, but it was difficult when she'd been singed by the stray shots of emotion that had ricocheted through his living room.

'I'm not going to win any parenting awards,' he said as they cruised along the causeway to return her to Miami. 'And we need to talk about Mexico.'

'I'm truly happy to cancel.'

He paused. 'Because you're scared?'

She bristled. 'That feels manipulative to me. If I need allowances for my anxiety, I'll tell you. You should be thinking about what your daughter needs.'

'You think she needs me to storm into her life and force her to do something she doesn't want to do? In case you hadn't caught on, Bea and I don't have a good relationship – we barely have a relationship.'

She steeled herself against the dip of sympathy. 'Do you want a relationship with her?'

A heated word exploded from his lips. She didn't understand the meaning, but the feeling was obvious. 'How can you ask that?'

'You're the one trying to convince me you're a shallow, womanising libertine.'

'Be careful. If you pity me, I might use it to lure you into bed.'

'I'm not easily lured.' His sharp look shivered through her body, exposing her brave words. 'Or at least you have an effective cock block,' she muttered.

His lips twitched. 'Lightening the mood? That's my job, not yours.' He fell silent. 'Seriously, are you okay with Bea coming to Cancún? It's not going to make... things... more difficult?'

'I'm not fragile. It's a part of who I am, but it's not all of who I am. Don't you dare think less of me now you know. Why do you think I didn't want to say anything in London? I knew you'd look at me funny.'

He glanced at her and she asked herself if she'd ever seen such a serious look on his face. It was a funny look for Javi, but somehow it was even more attractive than his usual smiles. 'If anything has changed, it's that I think more of you, not less. Your music... I get it now. You've made your struggles into art. Now I know why you were always so far out of my league. But Bea smells weakness and she pounces on it. I wouldn't have chosen to put you through it, even without... what you told me this morning.'

She shook her head. 'She's a kitten, Javi.'

Javi smiled and shook his head. 'She's got you already. I'm almost proud.'

'It's not fair to Bea if you're trying to make me dislike her. But since you do that to yourself and it hasn't worked, it must be harmless.'

He paused and his brow furrowed. 'Are you saying you like me, mona?'

She laughed ruefully. 'I suppose I am. Don't let it go to your head.'

'Too late,' he grinned. 'I always get a big head where you're concerned.'

She eyed him. 'Okay, I can see the difficult position you're in about sending Bea to school. We'll stick to the plan. And you don't have to worry about me in Cancún. I'll get through the performance.' He glanced at her meaningfully and she stuck her chin out. 'Without vomiting,' she insisted. 'You worry about Bea.'

'Do you want to fly together?'

'I'd rather not.'

He nodded. 'I wouldn't want to fly with us, either.'

'That's not what I meant. I was thinking of my own issues, not yours.'

'I bet you take forever at airport security. But you don't want me to hand you a barf bag?'

She couldn't help it. She snorted with laughter. She'd never expected to be laughing about her anxiety.

They arrived in the parking lot and her eyes drifted over him as he applied the handbrake and stretched. He smiled ruefully when he caught her watching.

'You do realise I can interpret that look? It's been more than three months since the last kiss. I remember everything, but maybe you'd like a refresher?' His voice was low and inviting, but he stayed completely still. The move was hers to make. The urge to climb over the console and do what he suggested – and more – was powerful. But she hadn't been taking care of her body and mind so carefully for ten years to throw herself into a position of vulnerability with him. At least now she could picture the face of his ex-wife to temper her desires.

'We've established the kiss was a mistake.'

He laughed humourlessly. 'I know, mona. But sometimes it feels like loving you would be redemption.'

His words seeped into her body and she had to grapple for resistance. 'Shut up, Javi. This is life, not a song.'

'It would be a good song.'

She had to remind herself he was talking about sex. This was Javier 'there are different kinds of love' Rodríguez. He might be capable of moments of insight, but he admitted he was a philandering egotist. Unreliable, broken promises... He'd used those words himself. She would do well to take his warning, no matter what protests she felt deep inside.

She pulled herself together. 'Are you saying it would only last three and a half minutes?'

He blinked and then broke out laughing. 'I'm trying not to interpret that as a challenge.' His grin was apologetic and endearing. She winced at her reaction to that smile. 'I'm hopeless, I know.' He grabbed for her hand and brought it to his lips, pressing a kiss onto her knuckles. She inhaled sharply and pulled her hand back.

'I'll see you at the hotel in Cancún on Tuesday. Please bring some self-discipline. Your daughter already thinks we are sleeping together. And don't forget to book an extra room for Bea,' she said, reaching for the door handle.

'We'll meet you at the airport. Text me your flight details.'

'You don't have to—'

'I know. But since I have to learn to be responsible for Bea, let me practise on you. Give me a chance to try that self-discipline.'

She frowned. 'Fine. I'll see you on Tuesday.'

10

The sea beneath was an astonishing shade of turquoise, dappled with darker patches of reef. She caught glimpses of cabanas and windblown palms on the beach, dwarfed by high-rise hotels that glittered with excess. The aircraft passed over golf courses and scrubby wetlands, a stunning deep green.

The flight touched down in tropical paradise to a pleasant twenty-seven degrees Celsius. It wasn't Cara's idea of December weather and she stared doubtfully at the Christmas tree, blazing with lights, that greeted her in the terminal, next to a snowman made of sand. Popular Christmas tunes – in English – piped through the terminal in bizarre affinity with the drab and distant Heathrow. An American café chain was offering the same Christmas sugar hits as in Miami. Only the effusion of sombreros and woven ponchos in the gift shop reminded her she had arrived in Mexico.

The short hop across the Gulf of Mexico had taken barely two hours and she'd kept herself carefully occupied and cautiously fed. She'd downloaded several websites and lost herself in the history of the Mayan civilisation to keep her thoughts off her erratic heartbeat and clenched muscles. She was feeling proud of herself as she strode through the terminal with her suitcase and looked round for Javi. Wondering about how he'd got on with Bea distracted her from their imminent reunion.

She didn't see him at first in the arrivals hall and it was only when he called her name that she recognised him. He was wearing shorts and a shirt with the habitual two top buttons undone. He was also wearing a wide-brimmed hat that was turned up at the sides and intricately woven in black and white with stripes and geometric patterns. It didn't look like the huge sombreros in the gift shop, but he looked more genuine than anything else in the airport. He was also alone.

He took the hat off to kiss her cheeks, but placed it back on again afterwards, his ponytail low beneath. The feel of his lips on her cheek was becoming familiar, like his scent. Familiarity should have led to indifference, but Cara's knees were just as weak as the first time he'd greeted her.

'Where's Bea? Did she chicken out? Or did you?'

He frowned, unimpressed. 'She's getting a drink.' He gestured to the café chain. 'How was your flight?'

'Fine,' she answered quickly. 'It's only two hours – and only one hour's time difference. What's with the sombrero? Are you trying to blend in with the locals?'

He smiled broadly. Thinking he appreciated her wit, she smiled back, until she noticed the mocking gleam. 'This is a sombrero, but you're way off the mark, gringa.'

'For the thousandth time, I apologise for my ignorance,' she grumbled. 'You may have the pleasure of enlightening me.'

His expression warmed and he feathered his fingers under her chin affectionately. She pulled away, partly out of habit and partly to stop the tingle of pleasure from spreading. 'This—' he swept the hat off his head and shook it under her nose, 'is a sombrero vuel-tiao. It is not Mexican. It is Colombian.'

Cara nodded indulgently. 'Okay. We've established your national pride. Are we catching a cab?'

He shoved the hat back on his head. 'Yes, it's waiting outside. If Bea decides to join us—' The flash of a camera flared over his features and he cringed away from the light.

'Is it true you're together? Is it serious this time?' the reporter called out as he approached, camera high. Cara froze. Did her body language with Javi look intimate? What would the headline be? Latin sex God takes pity on awkward Briton? The sound of her own heartbeat drowned out the accusations so she couldn't hear anything else. Even if she'd known what to say, her tongue was so thick in her mouth she doubted she could get a word out.

Her eyes darted to Javi. He stood indolently in that crazy hat and said something to the reporter. She focused on the hat, on the patterns repeating round the crown – squares and triangles in high-contrast symmetry. The airport terminal came slowly back into focus.

Javi's words filtered through her distraction. 'I'm flattered you think my powers of persuasion are so strong, but you'll find Cara has something to say about it, once she's recovered from your rude-ness.' She set her jaw and turned to the reporter. Indignation was her specialty.

Her voice shook more than she liked, but she was just glad she was capable of making her point. 'Our appointment with the press is tomorrow evening at the Playa Marlín. You're more than welcome to take your photos there when we will be much more interesting.' She felt Javi's smile in his body language.

'Did you realise what collaboration with Javi Félix meant when you signed up?' Her brow furrowed and she glanced at Javi. His smile had vanished.

A high-pitched voice interrupted her uneasy hesitation. 'How dare you suggest that she is anything like my mother! ¡Ni siquiera habla español!'

Javi rushed to halt Bea's progress in their direction, but it was too late. They had the attention of everyone within a fifty-metre radius. The reporter turned with interest and raised his camera.

Cara's instincts took over. 'Stop! You are about to photograph a child. Publish that photo on any website that is available in the UK and you will face a lawsuit the size of your behind.' Three incredulous gazes seared her cheeks, but she took a breath when the reporter lowered the camera again. He turned slowly back to her and she clenched her jaw to stop it wobbling. 'Leave us alone – please. You can publish whatever sad rumours you like. Shall we pose in front of the Christmas tree?'

'Are you denying it? Are you claiming you're the only female pop star he's worked with where it hasn't been a combination of business and pleasure? I'm sure your fans will be disappointed.'

'Cara's fans know she's too smart and too independent to fall for my crappy pick-up lines. "The words spew from their empty lips".' The reporter looked questioningly at Javi. 'Haven't you even listened to her damn song? Do your research, man.' He grabbed the handle of her suitcase and stalked off with long strides. She and Bea scrambled to follow.

He handed her suitcase to the cab driver and launched himself moodily into the passenger seat. Cara and Bea sat in the back. Cara gripped her hands in her lap to stop them trembling. She'd dealt with the situation. She was determined to keep her focus and her stomach. But the butterflies weren't helping.

She looked across at Bea. 'Are you okay?' she asked quietly.

Bea sent her a hostile look. 'Of course. Why wouldn't I be? It's not the first time I've shouted at a pap.' Javi said something to her sharply in Spanish and although Cara couldn't understand her response, the sarcasm was obvious. She turned back to Cara. 'If you didn't want to create interest in your relationship, you shouldn't have held hands on national TV.'

'What?'

'Cara didn't watch the programme.'

'Yeah, but she was there.'

'She was... preoccupied.' He met her eyes in the rear-view mirror and realisation dawned. She had a vague recollection of him holding her hand in the studio, but had to stop and ask herself if it had actually happened. 'Sorry,' he said quietly.

She shook her head. 'It's fine. Don't apologise. We'll get through it somehow.'

When she glanced back into the mirror, his eyes were twinkling. 'That's your approach to our promo obligations? Lie back and think of England?'

Cara frowned, self-conscious, but Bea snorted with laughter.

* * *

Javi knew his pattern. No sooner did he make a resolution than he was breaking it again. But that was enough with the flirting. He was determined not to fall into bed with Cara. He wasn't helping either of them, no matter how easily the banter came to him. The reporter's insinuations should have chastened him. It was true he'd slept with all five women he'd collaborated with during his career – starting with Susana all those years ago. He didn't deserve the respect of either woman sitting in the back of the cab.

Cara had been magnificent with the reporter – her trembling only adding to the impression of toughness. She looked like a delicate English rose – especially with her freckles picked up by the glaring tropical sun. But she had some impressive thorns. She didn't even want his apology.

In the hotel lobby, Cara strode up to the reception desk, apologising directly that she didn't speak Spanish and effectively dismissing her companions. Javi glanced uneasily at Bea. His daughter had been staunchly antisocial since he'd returned from Miami Beach on Sunday. She spent most of her time on her phone with headphones in. He'd been relieved to hear the nanny didn't want to travel with them, but if she'd come along perhaps Javi wouldn't have felt like such a glorified babysitter. He wouldn't tolerate another mind-numbing afternoon on the beach like yesterday's, but Bea was gleeful about their glitzy surroundings and threatened to drag him to the mall. It was a far cry from his last trip to Cancún where he'd spent all his time in the water or on a jet ski.

But he forced himself to step away from Cara. She probably had her own itinerary planned out. The thought made him suddenly curious.

'Do you have any plans?'

'Not really. I'm not a beach person, but I don't know what else there is round here.'

'What do you mean?'

She sighed. 'I've never been to Mexico before. I suppose I was hoping for some... culture, but this is just a beach resort, right?'

'I'm sure the receptionist will be able to direct you to some tacos and cactus.'

She narrowed her eyes at him and headed for the elevator. He trailed after her, Bea following with a frown. 'I meant Mayan culture,' she said over her shoulder.

'That's easy. There are some ruins down the beach from here. Shall we go this afternoon?'

'What?' Cara and Bea asked at the same time.

'It's not Chichen Itza, but it's worth a look if you're interested.'

'Definitely!'

'You have to be kidding. You're so whipped, Javi.' He turned to

Bea with a grin. He was a terrible parent. He found sparring with her so much more fun than hanging out.

'I was looking for an excuse to skip the mall. And you know what your mom said. It'll be good for you to spend some time with your ancestors.'

She poked her tongue out at him. 'Ancestors, my butt. Do you know how many times abuelita has told me we're not Mayan? She's descended from the Aztecs, so your ruins can go shove it.'

'In the fine custom of your people you'd prefer to go shopping?'

The elevator dinged and Cara looked between him and Bea. 'Look at you two, bickering like a real father and daughter.' He couldn't tell if her smile was genuine, but it stoked something in his chest which felt oddly like pride. He slung his arm over Bea's shoulder and rejoiced when she didn't shrug it off, although her arms were firmly crossed.

'What time shall we meet?' he asked Cara.

'I can go by myself. It sounds like you two have a date at the mall.'

He reached out his arm to stop the elevator when the doors would have closed. 'Please save me from the mall.'

'Save yourself. Don't drag me into it.'

He glanced at Bea. 'I have an idea. Bea, you come with us to the archaeological zone this afternoon and I'll take you both to the market afterward. You can shop, Cara can get her tacos and we might find some street music, if we're lucky.'

'Huh, lucky,' Bea grumbled. 'You just want to spend more time with her.'

'I live in England,' she pointed out. 'By Christmas you'll have your dear dad all to yourself and we'll never see each other again.'

She was talking to Bea, but everything inside him clammed up with the thought that it applied to him as well. 'We should make the most of your time in Latin America, then,' he managed to say.

'I'm happy to go by myself. I'd be intruding. You need to spend time with each other.'

Bea snorted. 'Because that's going so well so far.' His daughter had inherited far too much from him. 'He's got a point. Maybe it's better if you come along so he's not so bored.'

Cara looked between the two of them with a perplexed smile. 'Er, I'll just put my bag away and we can get some lunch and go, okay?'

Javi let out a breath he hadn't realised he was holding. 'Perfect,' he replied and moved out of the way of the elevator doors. 'Bring a hat!'

He turned away to find Bea watching warily, her arms crossed. His smile dimmed as he remembered he didn't know what the hell he was doing with these women.

'I thought you were trying to get on my good side,' she said with a thrust of her chin that wasn't as belligerent as she'd intended. She'd continued the conversation in English. Was English her heart language now?

Javi hesitated. He thrust his hands in his pockets and shifted his weight as he considered whether he had an excuse to shrug off the question. His shoulders dropped and acceptance settled in his chest. 'You know, gordita, I'm not trying to get on your good side.' He held up a hand when she would have interrupted. 'I want you to be happy – of course I do. But I don't want to follow you around while we ignore each other.'

'You wish I wasn't here. Why can't we just ignore each other?'

He flinched inwardly at her accusation, but the pinch was an oddly pleasant ache. She'd let her sarcastic defences drop. He considered contradicting her, but his instincts warned him she wouldn't buy it. 'Because arguing with you is too much fun.'

Her eyes narrowed and she pursed her lips with a sigh. 'Get a life, Javi.'

He grinned and tugged on her hair. 'That's what I'm trying to do, mija. And you're part of it.'

* * *

'Your mum is Mexican?' Cara asked Bea as they wandered among the crumbling pyramids and columns of the El Rey archaeological zone. It was a small haven of nature and history on the developed island of the hotel zone.

The sun was relentless over the exposed grass. Oleander bushes and a couple of stumpy fan palms were the only plants growing above the ruins. The perimeter was thick with trees and royal palms, with the accompanying chirp of insects and birds. Beyond that, the sea licked the sand in rushing rhythm.

'Half-Mexican,' Bea replied. 'My grandma is from near Acapulco. But my grandpa was Puerto Rican.' Her lips thinned. 'Handy for getting Javi a Green Card.' She kicked a stone, her hands shoved in her pockets, and Cara was struck with the resemblance to Javi. She probably wished she looked more like her mother, but her strong jaw and sharp, dark eyes suited her.

'Is this weather normal for you for Christmas, then?'

She shrugged as though it was a stupid question. 'It's not like many people actually get a white Christmas.'

'Where are you and your mum spending Christmas?'

'Miami. Abuelita – my grandma – is coming from San Juan. She always cooks up a feast and we celebrate, just the three of us. We eat on Christmas Eve – well, on Christmas day, too. And we do presents on Christmas Eve. Actually, sometimes we do presents on both.'

'That reminds me, I need to find something for my dad. He's impossible to buy for and he doesn't really like Christmas anyway.'

'Your dad sounds like the life of the party,' Javi commented.

She smiled wanly. 'We have our quiet, miserable Christmas together at the house I grew up in, in London. We watch a lot of TV and have a low-key dinner á la Marks and Spencer on Christmas day,' she smiled ruefully. 'That's a chain of department stores in the UK.'

'What happened to your mom?' Bea asked.

'She died in a car accident ten years ago.'

'I'm sorry,' Bea mumbled.

'Me too, but don't worry about it.' She felt Javi's eyes on her and glanced at him. He hid his gaze under the hat when she caught him watching. 'What about your Colombian grandparents?' she asked Bea.

'I saw Mamita last year in Miami, but I haven't been to Colombia in years.'

'Six years,' Javi supplied quietly. 'And it was October last time, not December. She's never spent Christmas with my family.'

'Yes, it was October and the whole place was a muddy stink. One little shower of rain and the streets turned into a swamp.'

'Hey, there's no such thing as a little shower of rain in Barranquilla in October,' he protested. 'Just like there's no such thing as a pleasant breeze.' Despite the wild description, he defended his hometown with obvious fondness, his smile wide. 'Now, December,' he raised a hand, pointing at nothing in particular, 'December is the month of pleasant weather. There is dancing and music, family, lights and buñuelos, natilla, pasteles—'

'Is he still speaking English?' Cara asked Bea in a stage whisper.

'Colombians are always writing crappy odes to the homeland.' Bea pursed her lips in a caustic smile.

'Do you think he fancies himself a kind of Gabriel García Márquez?' Cara baited him.

Javi hooted with laughter and roped his arms round both of them, propelling them around a swampy puddle to the next vine-covered stone structure. 'I failed that assignment at school and they nearly revoked my citizenship.'

'Was poetry more your passion?' She grinned.

'At that age I was more interested in experiencing love than writing about it.' He winked unapologetically at her.

'I'll remember that when I turn sixteen.' Bea smiled sweetly and his grin wobbled.

'You're not allowed to turn sixteen,' he said in a low voice, studying the ancient stonework with too much interest. Bea scowled at him.

'Your English is remarkably good,' Cara commented, changing the subject.

He laughed, but it was the humourless laugh. 'I've lived in Miami for more than fifteen years. I should hope it's good. The first five years my English was terrible. I never left the ghetto.' He tugged Bea's hair. 'And my toddler had a Colombian accent.' She shrugged him off and wandered to the next edifice, slipping her headphones in.

'Did you move straight from Bar—Barran... Sorry, how do you pronounce your hometown again?'

'Ba-rrrran-kee-ja,' he said, sounding out the word slowly. She tried to concentrate on the peculiar sound of the rolled R and reminded herself that the 'll' was pronounced like a Y, but in the teeth, almost like a J. Her focus brought her gaze into contact with his lips and then her concentration was shot.

Javi paused and she hoped desperately that he didn't notice the effect he had on her. 'No, I left Colombia when I was nineteen and moved around a bit before settling in Miami. I got my first contract in LA, after doing some recording and lots of gigs based out of Caracas and then Mexico City. The industry was different back then.'

'And then the papaya drew you to Miami?'

His smile was almost a wince. 'No. It's just a reminder of home that I appreciate. Our little joke is closer to the truth.' He paused. 'Susana brought me to Miami and Bea is keeping me there.'

He stopped and faced Cara, no hint of any of his habitual smiles. 'Thank you for standing up to the photographer.'

She waved a hand flippantly. 'You don't need to thank me. It was because of your hat.'

'My hat?'

She shook her head. 'It has a soothing pattern. But you don't want to hear about it. Let's talk about something else.' She took off after Bea, but he grasped her arm to stop her and Cara cursed the warm climate for bringing his palms in contact with the bare skin of her forearms.

'You had an attack?'

'I was anxious, yes. It was an unexpected situation in a new country after two hours of miraculously not falling from the sky.' He muttered something under his breath. 'But it wasn't a panic attack. I know how to deal with my feelings. It wasn't your fault. I absolve you of all responsibility.'

He smiled faintly. 'Fine. I'm not good with responsibility – or feelings.'

She eyed him briefly, not sure if she believed him. When she looked away, her gaze fell on a scaly horror skittering across their path. She shrieked and grabbed frantically at Javi. 'Oh my God, what is that?' His arms came round her as he looked down in confusion. His skin was warm under his soft shirt.

'I thought you weren't a damsel in distress. It's an iguana, sonsa.' He laughed, gave Cara a squeeze and pushed her away from him – too quickly for her senses, but not quickly enough for her dignity.

'It has spikes!' she insisted, shaking her hands wildly in embarrassed defence. It had black stripes and a bulging throat and was several feet long. When she thought of iguanas, she'd pictured little green lizards, not creepy, beady-eyed mini-dinosaurs.

'You two should get on well, then. You can both be prickly.'

'Gee, thanks. I'll buy you a Christmas cactus to remember me by,' she muttered.

11

As the sun set behind the glinting hotels overlooking the Caribbean, a taxi took them onto the mainland. The lagoon was on one side of the road and on the other, between the hotels, a view of the sea and Isla Mujeres in the distance. As soon as the cab turned off the main road, the tangle of power lines, the jumble of colourful blocky buildings, the crumbling concrete and the profusion of iron security grilles proved how far from Miami she'd travelled. Bea had pined as they passed the upmarket mall on the island and turned up her nose when they got out of the taxi.

The market entrance was bursting with colour: a nativity scene and a plastic Christmas tree flanked the door to the covered market and stalls were piled with shiny trinkets, colourful sweets, heaped tropical fruit and cut flowers. It couldn't be further from the wood-and-candlelight cosiness of the Bristol Christmas market.

'This isn't the main market,' Bea grumbled.

'Of course not. If Cara's only in Mexico for three days, she needs real tacos and cactus, not the tourist version. I'll take you to the mall in Barranquilla.'

'Great,' she said with a pinched frown, but once they'd lost themselves inside the extensive market, she didn't bother to hide her enthusiasm. The ladies selling trinkets fussed over her when she admitted her grandmother was Mexican and she was soon wearing two necklaces and carrying a woven bag that Cara rather liked as well.

'Aha,' Javi stopped suddenly and tapped Cara's shoulder with the backs of his fingers. 'Give me your phone.' Cara obeyed with a curious frown. 'Stand there.' He pointed and Cara gave him an indulgent smile.

'A cactus,' she said dryly. 'Or at least parts of one.'

'Prickly pear, no less. Give me your best Speedy Gonzalez.'

'Shhh, these people can understand you!'

'Dad, you're doing it wrong.' Bea strolled up to Cara, leaned in close, held up her phone and opened her mouth in a crazy smile. Cara couldn't help laughing at their image on the screen as Bea snapped the selfie. A few taps later and Bea held up the image, now with a cute filter and '¡cactus! :-o' scrawled along the side.

'Cute,' Javi said in an amused drawl as he peered over her shoulder, but his smile was wide. Cara could see it hadn't escaped him that Bea had called him 'Dad' without a trace of irony.

They strolled by fruit stalls and tables of fresh meat and fish where residents and tourists alike were buying supplies. Javi bought papaya, of course, and bought Cara and Bea each a coconut with the top lopped off and a straw stuck in.

'Mmmm,' she moaned in surprised appreciation as she sipped the fresh, tangy coconut milk.

Tinkling music sounded from the other side of a covered arcade. It wasn't just Javi's ears that pricked up at the sound, it was his whole body. 'Marimba,' he smiled. 'Let's go.'

Two stout old men played the huge instrument, the size of a

table, striking the wooden bars with multiple mallets. They crooned in harmony, one playing a higher melody with two mallets and the other playing the lower accompaniment with four mallets – two in each hand. Another man stood beside them with a basic drumkit – a bass drum, a snare and a cymbal.

Cara placed some money in the hat and drew close to watch. Javi was beside her, coiled with even more energy than usual. The musicians acknowledged their audience with smiles.

'You want to join in?' Javi asked, not looking at her.

She shook her head. 'No way.'

When the song ended, they exchanged more words with Javi, gesturing to his hat. The conversation grew more boisterous and Bea drew close to Cara. 'They've recognised him,' she explained, wrinkling her nose. Stall-holders emerged from behind their wares and produced their mobile phones from their pockets as Javi chatted with the musicians, flashing charming smiles.

The drummer thrust a set of sticks into his hands and he grinned, twirling them between his fingers. He moved behind the drums and bounced a stick on the snare experimentally, flashing Cara a magnetic smile.

'He's such a show-off,' Bea grumbled, but Cara silently disagreed. It was the music that made him, not the other way round.

After a short discussion during which a crowd gathered expectantly, he started up the beat. She'd assumed he'd picked up the drumsticks because he couldn't play marimba, but she was startled to realise that he was a talented drummer – much better than he'd made it sound when he'd bitingly admitted to bashing the drumkit to annoy his neighbours. He rolled the stick across the skin of the snare drum with the lightest touch while driving the vigorous rhythm. As the song went on, his whole body moved. He spun a stick up out of his hands and caught it again in time to clash the tip onto the cymbal in time with the music. The crowd clapped along and broke into couples to dance.

A young man approached Cara and Bea with a smile and said something in Spanish, before clasping Cara's hand and pulling it to his shoulder. Before she could react, he'd pulled her into the throng and was holding her with a firm hand.

He was moving fast, his hips nudging hers as they bounced along. He'd wrapped her arms round his neck and she had to hold on tight to keep up with him. His scent filled her nostrils – not unpleasant, just strange. She looked round to find Bea and was relieved to find her dancing with a middle-aged woman. Then she studied the other couples. All ages were represented and everyone was dancing close, some liberally swapping partners.

Her partner's touch, although firm, was on her back, well above her hips and although his leg was between hers, only their knees touched. He was more interested in dragging her around in rollicking circles than making a move. It reminded her of the night at the club in London, but only because of the contrast. This was impersonal dancing. The way she danced with Javi... not so much.

Her partner asked her something, and she gave him an apologetic smile. 'I'm sorry, I don't speak Spanish.'

'Ay, I got a gringa!' He grinned. 'Welcome to Mexico!'

'Thank you,' she replied politely.

When the song finished, the marimbists tried to convince Javi to keep playing, but he firmly declined and took his leave. He strode directly to Cara. 'Was that okay?'

'Yeah,' she admitted, surprised it was true. 'It was fun.'

He leaned down to study her. 'Fun? Who are you and what have you done with Cara?'

'I'm capable of having fun.'

'Just not with me?' He raised his eyebrows over a lopsided smile. She experienced a tingle of suspicion that he cared more than his smile suggested, but she experienced such a variety of tingles in his presence that she knew better than to trust it.

She pursed her lips. Dancing with the stranger had been simple enjoyment – once she'd worked out she wasn't going to feel overwhelmed. Fun with Javi was... complicated. 'Today has been fun,' she admitted.

He inclined his head in acknowledgement. 'Good. What are we doing tomorrow?'

'Tomorrow? Tomorrow's the filming.'

'We're not expected until 4.30.'

'Yes, but—' She cut herself off. Spending the day sitting in her hotel room trying to stay calm until 4.30 wasn't sounding appealing.

'You're worried if we go somewhere, we won't make it back.'

She sighed. 'Yes, exactly.'

'Okay, I accept your challenge. We can head north – not far. There's some more ruins and a proper beach without the high-rise windbreak. We need to start your iguana therapy if you're going to come to Colombia.'

'Don't joke about therapy. I didn't know if I was coming to Colombia. And you didn't say anything about iguanas.'

'Too scared? The iguanas are bigger – and green.'

'I get the idea: everything's better in Colombia. I believe you. I suppose at least the coffee must be amazing.'

He chuckled. 'Actually, Colombia still exports most of the good stuff. I don't think you're a tinto kind of girl – Colombian black coffee – although you'd probably like the hipster coffee bars opening up in Medellín. But Barranquilla's not so trendy.' He hesitated, watching the marimbists perform an American Christmas carol. 'December eighth is a holiday in Colombia. It's the Feast of the Immaculate Conception and it's a big deal for us. On the evening of December seventh, my family always has a huge jam session at my parents' house. I have four brothers and my dad is a musician, too. The neighbours come and go. We take up our instruments and play everything we can think of. Then in the early hours, everyone in the city spills out into the street to light candles – thousands of them. We light candles on the terrace with the family and the party just keeps going. There are fireworks and music – and dancing, lots of dancing. I dance with my mom, with my sisters-in-law, neighbours, friends, cousins. That's the día de las velitas.'

Cara's skin prickled. She stared at his face, which was pinched with delight and a hint of confusion – nostalgic. Her brow furrowed as she strained her memory. 'Pequeñas luces,' she quoted tentatively from 'Nostalgia'. 'Little lights. That part is about this tradition?' He nodded, but didn't elaborate. She wanted to ask about the end of the bridge, about the line that mentioned forgiveness and cement drying, but, by the look on his face, he'd emotionally checked out again.

'And, as to whether or not you're coming, I already mentioned the possibility to my mother, so you're officially invited and as good as expected.'

She opened her mouth, but was too conflicted to say anything. Who did his mother think Cara was to him? What was she to him? She wanted to go. If she had the choice between staying near Javi or spending the two weeks alone at some beachside hotel, she knew which option she'd prefer. But would it be awkward?

'But it's fine if you want to do something else. We can meet in Bogotá as planned on the nineteenth. No pressure and I should warn you my family can be... a lot. So, feel free to say no.'

She pressed her lips together, the flutter in her chest uncomfortably similar to the thrill of her biggest crush asking her on a date in secondary school. 'Is there a difference between "feel free to say no" and "I'm only asking out of politeness"?' she mumbled.

He dipped his head and she enjoyed the close view of his eyelashes and the little lines at the corner of his eyes. 'You know I never hide behind politeness with you. I've never been able to. I'd love it if you came.' It was the smallest smile she'd ever seen on his lips.

It was an invitation to a lonely friend to spend the holiday together – nothing more. It wouldn't come to anything, but she wanted to enjoy this pull a little longer before consigning it to the realm of memories.

'I'd love to come.'

He straightened immediately. 'Bueno. Text me your passport number and I'll book you onto our flight.'

The intellectual part of her brain kicked belatedly into gear. 'What about the rumours of a relationship? This will pretty much confirm it.'

'It doesn't bother me, mona. But it's understandable if it's a problem for you. Luckily my fanbase expects this sort of thing from me.' He gave her a wry smile. 'My manager emailed to suggest the rumours of a relationship were boosting sales.'

She forced herself to smile in return. 'Anything to make a buck. Okay. I'm in. Maybe I'm getting too good at taking risks.'

'Just don't dance with too many strange guys. I might get jealous,' he said in a light tone.

'And you might be a hypocrite.'

A sudden, insistent beeping made her jump and Javi looked up with a frown.

Bea approached, holding up her phone.

'Look, guys, I gave you five minutes for sexual tension and that five minutes is up. Can we go get some food?'

Cara was laughing too hard to be embarrassed. She nudged Javi out of the way and took Bea's arm.

'I think I'm supposed to have tacos. Can you ask someone where's good?'

'I will,' Javi joined them. He turned to Bea. 'Cara's coming to Colombia. That okay?'

Bea shrugged. 'Sure, whatever. Misery loves company.' Her expression was unimpressed rather than antagonistic, which satisfied Cara. If she truly opposed the idea, she wouldn't keep quiet about it.

* * *

The crowd gathered in front of the stage the next day was larger than expected, even an hour before the performance. Bea grumbled about being dragged off the beach to sit in the fenced-off area to the side of the stage.

'You've been sitting on the beach most of the day,' Javi pointed out.

'Some desolate, windblown beach that was barely Insta-worthy. Me quedé dormida.'

Javi didn't comment on Bea's mix of languages. She would be forced to speak Spanish in Colombia. If she'd rather speak Spanglish with him, he wouldn't complain. 'You should have come into the water.'

She scowled. 'And distracted you from showing off for Cara?'

Javi winced at her tone and spent a moment considering his response. How did he explain that Bea was wrong without setting off her bullshit detector? He had enjoyed Cara's surreptitious appreciation of his semi-naked body in the surf. It made up for her refusal to join him, which had been disappointing, if expected. She preferred to keep her leg covered and he was kidding himself if he'd truly thought she'd get into the water just for him.

'I'm not trying to fool you, gordita. There's nothing going on between me and Cara.'

She flashed up her hands, fingers outstretched. 'Bing! Understatement of the year. She likes you. You like her. I know what that means.'

'Has your mom had any boyfriends?'

'Leave mom out of this.'

'Buen punto,' he conceded. 'You're right, I like Cara. And that means no... It means we can't...'

'Hook up?'

He sighed. Was a twelve-year-old supposed to talk like this? Was a father supposed to tolerate it? He guessed he didn't have much choice. 'Yes. This song is important to both of us. We're working together. We live an ocean apart. Cara takes her career seriously and a relationship with me is too messy. I'm trying to respect that.'

Bea laughed. 'You mean she respects herself too much to get involved with you.'

The truth pricked him more than he was comfortable with. 'Exactly.'

'Sorry I'm late.' Cara emerged from behind a scaffold screen. 'That crowd is crazy. And did you see the Christmas tree on the stage? It's made of sombreros.' Her hair and make-up were already done – her freckles disguised, her long hair washed and styled into loose waves down her back. He missed the sandy plait from Isla Blanca that morning. But her long blue dress with its wide, ruffled neckline that slipped off one shoulder packed a punch. He curled his arm round her waist and kissed her cheeks in greeting, conscious of Bea watching. It was so hard to be good.

'Is the band here? Where are we supposed to rehearse?'

'We don't.'

'What do you mean we don't?'

'These guys are professionals. Most of them toured with me earlier this year. They know the drill.'

Her shoulders sagged. 'But what about me?' she asked in a small voice.

'What about you? You're the most professional of all of us.'

The producer arrived and preparations for the show began in earnest. She rattled off instructions in a mixture of English and Spanish and a technician fitted earpieces and microphones as they ran through the interview questions with the presenter.

'You can have a translation through your earpiece,' the presenter explained to Cara. 'And we will add subtitles to your answers.' Cara nodded, her arms clutched tight across her torso.

'What's up with Cara?' Bea asked just before they were due to go on stage. The shadows were long over the beach and the last rays of the sun were glinting between the hotels. The stage blazed with fairy lights and neon. And Cara had drifted slowly away into some kind of meditation.

'She's just nervous,' Javi explained.

Cara looked up. 'I'm okay,' she said, her voice staccato.

He approached with an easy smile and rested a hand on her shoulder. 'I know. You faced up to all those iguanas today. A little performance on the beach is nothing.' She raised an eyebrow at him, but a little smile curved her lips. 'In fact, in recognition of your achievements since arriving in America, I have something for you.'

He'd seen the necklace at a stall at Isla Blanca while he was fetching their lunch and hoped it might break the ice this evening. He pulled the paper bag out of his back pocket and handed it to her unceremoniously. Her brow furrowed and she looked from the gift up to his face.

'Thank you,' she said, her voice soft.

'You haven't opened it, yet,' he pointed out gruffly. 'You might hate it. But you have to wear it anyway.'

She chuckled and opened the bag delicately. She lifted out the string of wooden beads and, when she saw the rustic pendant, she grinned. His smile stretched wide as she met his gaze, her eyes glinting with humour. 'It's an iguana necklace.'

'The chicken of the trees for the beautiful lady.' She snorted and he joined her in laughing. 'It's a Mayan design, apparently. The TV audience will love it.'

'So do I,' she said, still smiling. She fastened the necklace under her hair.

But he couldn't take any credit beyond an internal 'I told you so' when she sparkled on the stage. Her hands were shaking and her gaze a little wild, but she fought through it with smiles and the glow of enthusiasm. She laughed when her translator made a mistake and she tried some Mexican slang good-naturedly with a horrible accent.

And when she stood behind the microphone and he plucked the first notes of the song she had made magical, she whooped and held her hands above her head, rousing the crowd. She called out 'Feliz Navidad' in her clunky accent and he wanted to drag her off-stage and kiss her senseless. He made do with a smile and a wink that brought a sweet blush to her cheeks.

With her contented presence beside him, he stepped up to the microphone and began to sing. The restive fervour of the audience and the inescapable magnetism of the music flowed in his blood. The guitar was an extension of his fingers, leading him into the past and the future. And when he reached the chorus, Cara's voice travelled with him – high and pure and soaring.

When the audience began singing along with the chorus, the microphone picked up Cara's stunned laugh. He turned to her with a teasing smile. She tugged her microphone from the stand just before the bridge and plucked his sombrero off his head. He grinned as she shoved it on her own head and danced close. At the end of the bridge, where the chorus was supposed to rumble back into the song, he signalled the band to pause.

He dropped to one knee and stared up at her, letting the guitar hang and raising both arms. He made up a few lines about her being the inspiration for a beautiful melody. The crowd screamed, but Javi held her gaze, daring her to smile. She blushed, but recovered quickly with a jerk of her chin and gave the crowd a droll smile. He stood and leaned close, tapping his cheek with his index finger, requesting a kiss. He watched the crowd with a mischievous grin and they cheered.

Her laugh reverberated across the stage through the speakers. She grasped her chin as though thinking. Then she pulled the hat off her head again and shoved it into his face, pushing him away with a smile. He fumbled for the hat, shrugged and placed it back onto his head before counting the band back in. The last chorus was lively with the full effect of their combined voices in harmony and wild cheering from the audience drowned out the final chord.

As soon as they were off-stage, Javi grabbed Cara and squeezed, burying his face in her hair. Thank God Bea was there, or he would have kissed her with every drop of his surging adrenaline, resolutions be damned.

'You were incredible,' he breathed, his voice raw. His blood was pumping as though he'd swum twenty lengths of an Olympic pool. He was holding Cara so tight that he could feel her heartbeat, just below his and just as rapid. She pulled back with a grin, her hands moving from his shoulders to cup his cheeks. The touch seared him with the knowledge that she would have kissed him back.

'You guys, that was awesome!' Bea gushed and another wash of pride surged through him. He let Cara go and pulled Bea into his arms, twirling her round. When he put her down again, she went to

Cara and they wrapped their arms round each other and bounced in jubilation. 'You're going to get to number one. I know it!'

When the haze began to recede, a cough drew their attention to a man standing by the entrance, wearing a linen jacket and holding the handle of a large suitcase. He was red with heat, and agitated.

'Cara, do you mind telling me what is going on?' he asked, his voice strained and his accent clearly English.

Javi's stomach sank with apprehension as Cara confirmed his suspicions. 'Daddy?'

12

'Here, Daddy, sit down. You must be boiling.' He mopped his brow with a handkerchief in a gesture that was in such contrast to their surroundings that Cara had to blink. The tension in the room had shifted so quickly. She'd just given the performance of her life. She'd hit the right notes and remembered the words – that shouldn't have been in question. But she'd also performed like a normal musician. She'd danced and smiled and made stuff up – she'd entertained. The anxiety hadn't magically disappeared, but she'd managed to hold onto the things she loved about performing, rather than the things that worried her. And she'd enjoyed every minute.

She'd especially loved the trembling aftermath, wrapped in Javi's arms, sharing his euphoria. She hadn't realised performing together could have that effect. She could still feel his solid shoulders under her palms, moving with his shaky breaths, and the contrast between the stubble under her fingertips and his smooth lips. She would have kissed him in a heartbeat if they'd been alone. She could see how easily he'd mixed music and pleasure in the past. She didn't dare glance at him now, but warily watched her father.

'Stop fussing, sweetheart. Are you going to introduce us?'

She turned to Javi, her shoulders slumping as she saw everything her father would notice: the unbuttoned shirt, the traditional hat, the messy ponytail. 'Uh, this is Javi and his daughter Beatríz. This is my father, Gordon Poignton, QC.' She added the Queen's Counsel out of habit. She knew her father insisted on it.

Javi hesitated for so long that Cara would have laughed in other circumstances. 'Uh, qué más,' he swallowed, 'Mr Poignton.' Their handshake was short and circumspect.

'Doesn't he speak English?'

'Yes of course he does.' She glanced at Javi, willing him to understand that her father was being protective and not only rude.

'I've never met a judge before,' he explained. His tone was flat with restrained defensiveness.

'I should hope not,' Gordon commented, sparing Javi the briefest of narrow-eyed glances. Cara flushed. She knew her father was conservative and set in his ways, but she'd hoped he would recognise when he was judging something he knew nothing about.

Gordon turned to Cara. 'What happened to Freddie? I was enjoying reading about the success of the single, and then some rumour of an affair ruined it. I telephoned Freddie to ask if it was a publicity stunt gone wrong, only to discover that he was still in London!'

'His mother's ill. I couldn't ask him to come with me. And I'm managing on my own.'

'You call this managing?' He slapped his hand against a glossy magazine, opened to a dog-eared page and showed her a close-up of her hand clasped tightly in Javi's – a still from the programme in Miami.

She gritted her teeth. 'They're just rumours, Daddy.'

'Of course they're just rumours.' He eyed Javi once more. His tone betrayed who he felt was to blame.

'There's no harm done.' Javi's tone was dark, but controlled. 'The performance today was perfect, and sales are strong and increasing.'

'How can you say there's no harm?' Gordon faced Javi with what Cara thought of as his 'evil eye'. He usually reserved it for challenging green barristers to up their game. 'My daughter's reputation is at stake. She is a professional musician – a Cambridge-educated composer. Not one of your women.'

Javi raised his eyebrows and sent her a sidelong glance. She set her jaw and met his gaze. He couldn't think she agreed with her father, could he? If she did, she wouldn't have enjoyed seeing the Mayan ruins with him or coming face-to-face with iguanas or dancing in a street market. The fantasy bubble of contentment and... fun would never have been created. If her father had had his way, it would never have happened.

From the highs of the performance, Cara deflated on a long breath. The fantasy bubble was going to burst prematurely. She resented her father for showing up. She resented the scale of her disappointment.

'She might have some fancy degree and understand about crotchets and time signatures and stuff, but it's Javi who's been teaching her for the past few days,' Bea spoke up with a belligerent frown.

'Teaching her what? About dancing like a primitive? Cara's music doesn't need to be dressed up like that.'

Javi said something gently in Spanish and wrapped his arm round Bea's shoulders. His expression was tight and resigned. He was going to bow out. Cara's discouraged heart raced again when she realised he was ceding to her father and it wasn't right.

'I've learned a lot.' She insisted, trying to find some of Bea's defiant courage. 'Yes, it involved dancing and tacos and iguanas, but I've learned I can look after myself in a new country. I've learned it's more fun to explore a new place with friends who know the language.' Her father was silent, his expression vacillating between blustering disapproval and paternal anguish. 'It's been fun, Daddy.'

She could tell she'd said the wrong thing. 'Fun is choosing to play your favourite song on the piano instead of practising your new piece. This is a distraction. How many Mexicans are going to buy your album?'

'If our song reaches number one,' Javi began quietly, 'the answer is: a whole lot more.'

'Do you even know her music? She made a real effort to understand the musical traditions of your part of the world, but did you look outside of your culture?'

'Of course I listened to her music. And there are 120 million people in this country, many of whom will become fans of the world's newest pop/rock superstar when her album is released.'

'I don't need you to tell me how talented my daughter is.'

'Good. I'm pointing out the business sense of exposure.'

'And exposure is your specialty?' He glanced meaningfully at the inches of bare chest visible between the neglected buttons of his shirt.

'Javi has been in the music business for a long time, Daddy. It's been good experience for me.'

Her father harrumphed and paused for a dramatic moment, but he backed away from the dispute. 'An experience which, it seems, wrapped up on a high,' he said diplomatically. Cara's eyes flew to Javi and found his already on her. What would happen to their plans for Colombia? *I want to go.* The voice inside her was emphatic. 'Is the hotel far, sweetheart? I had an abominable trip and I'm rather overdue some air conditioning and a decent meal.'

His words brought the salty scent of the beach air, fresh with the evening breeze, into focus in Cara's senses. She imagined dinner with her father would be a far cry from the lunch of fresh avocado, shrimp and fish with salad and tortilla crisps that they'd shared on the beach at Isla Blanca.

'It's not far. Here, I can help you with your case.'

'No, no, darling. I've got the case. You watch your feet.'

She stepped urgently back to Javi as her father turned to go. He still had his arm draped lazily round Bea, but his eyes were alert.

'Our plans...'

'The flight leaves at 7.45 on Saturday morning. It's a flight to Panama City with a connection to Barranquilla,' he said quickly, his voice low. 'It's your choice.'

She nodded. 'I'll see you at the airport.' His eyes narrowed. She glanced at her father with an odd mix of emotions: embarrassment, fondness, pity and, the most foreign – rebellion. 'Being realistic, I may not be alone. But I'm going with you.'

* * *

'Did you know that the rate of homicide in this part of Mexico has more than doubled in the past twelve months? Drug gangs are fighting for turf. Drug gangs!'

It wasn't the first time Cara had wished her father wasn't quite so much a judge. What he said was undoubtedly true and she couldn't completely suppress the seed of concern once it had been planted.

'You knew Cancún was on my itinerary,' she said quietly, cutting another morsel of enchilada and wishing she was back at the market eating tacos with her hands. She could feel the stress lines creeping back onto her forehead.

It struck her that Javi liked to live simply. Between the upmarket condo on Biscayne and the house he mentioned in Colombia, plus his jet-setting lifestyle and years of selling records, he could afford to eat at the most expensive restaurants in Cancún.

But Javi and her father didn't inhabit the same worlds. He'd cooked her a simple dinner that night in Miami and was more at home conversing with street vendors than stuffy judges. Gordon Poignton chose his restaurants according to the number of Michelin stars. And her father wasn't rich by London standards – his pride had led him into an austere profession that paid only enough to keep the family comfortably upper middle class.

She wondered what Javi's family was like, what his childhood had been like – obviously filled with music and love and company, if he had four brothers. Music and love she had in common. Her father could play piano, but it was her mother's voice that had provided the accompaniment for a childhood that had been quiet but joyful. Her brother had joined the family when she was seven and had never had the chance to grow into an equal companion.

She glanced at her father, chewing his roulade enthusiastically. Did he realise Crispin would have been twenty-one this year? 'Nostalgia' was playing in loops in her mind. It was supposed to be Javi's story, although he wouldn't own it. But it had become hers, too. Ten years since the accident. Ten Christmases. Love always looks back...

'I knew your itinerary of course, but I expected Freddie to be with you.'

'Because he would be capable of protecting me if I happened to run into El Chapo?'

Gordon didn't appreciate her joke. 'You have mental health problems. You need to take extra care. I know you are stronger now, but this situation is out of our control. They shoot tourists, too, you know. It's not difficult to stray onto the wrong street.'

She pursed her lips. 'It sounds like London.'

'It is nothing like London. The homicide rate in London is less than two per 100,000 inhabitants. In this state of Mexico, it is fifty.'

She should have kept her mouth shut. Her father was a hawk with statistics and always right. 'Fine, but I fail to see how Freddie could have made me any safer.'

'A woman alone is always more vulnerable.'

'Daddy, be honest. The danger you're most worried about is Javi.'

'And my worries were justified. Whether he's just a womaniser or purposefully engineering the rumours, he was the one who started them.'

Cara made a fist in her lap. What could she say? If she explained why he'd grasped her hand, her father would overreact about her anxiety and that would be the end of her freedom. *Freedom...* The word struck her and coloured her interpretation the past week. Her fingers itched to play music. A siren of inspiration called in her mind. She should have brought a guitar. She pictured herself knocking on Javi's door and borrowing one of his, but the fantasy ran away with itself and she pictured him inviting her in, and kissing her until the song was in her body instead of her head.

She couldn't keep the smile off her lips. She was used to her brain running away with itself, but usually it showed her flashes of horrible things that were possible, but unlikely – like being shot by a gangster. A sensual – *okay, sexual* – fantasy was a nice change.

'He's getting to you,' her father accused. 'I can see it. Look, I didn't show you the next page of the article.' He drew the magazine out of his briefcase and set the spread of pictures in front of her. The faces of five women – beautiful, confident women – were set out in a timeline of when they collaborated with Javi, starting with Susana. Paparazzi shots showed each woman on his arm.

She thrust it back to her father. 'I know about this.' She wouldn't admit that having the truth of it before her eyes pinched in her chest. She had witnessed the tension when Susana had been in his living room. And she remembered how he'd described himself as the sun rose over the Atlantic. Her eyes dropped one more time to note the dates. The collaboration with Susana had been sixteen years ago, the next one eight years later, the others clustered in the following four years.

Her heart sank as she asked herself whether she was looking at the reason Javi's marriage had failed. He'd easily admitted he had broken promises. But she'd been too foolishly distracted by the trace of self-disgust in his voice to appreciate what he'd done. Now Susana had been relegated to one of five faces in a glossy magazine and hers would be next.

But her father had told her nothing new: she had mental health challenges; Javi was a compulsive flirt; the fun of the past few days had been a suspension of reality. But she wanted to take home more than a souvenir magnet and her precious iguana necklace. She wanted to take home the stretched horizons. She wanted to take home the knowledge that she didn't need to stay in her comfort zone to be okay.

She'd learned to live with her anxiety, but in Miami, in Mexico she'd lived it up with her anxiety. And now her face would be printed among the famous, beautiful women who had come and gone in Javi's life, as though she were just like them. Maybe he'd been right to suggest she have her heart broken. She wasn't ready for this to end, yet.

'It's good you've arrived, Daddy,' she lied, setting up the next step, 'because the itinerary has changed.'

'What? Freddie didn't mention anything.'

'It's not much, just an extra interview in the city where Javi's from.' She hesitated, but made herself come out with it. 'And his family has invited me to join them for a Colombian celebration for the beginning of the Christmas season.'

Her father choked on some coleslaw and groped for his water. 'You're meeting his family now?' he wheezed, not waiting until the choking subsided before making his objection known.

'They have a candle-lighting tradition on the seventh of December. The song references a lot of the festivities. Javi invited me to come and see it. And there is a radio interview booked. I don't know why Freddie thought I didn't need to attend in the first place. The song is doing really well in Colombia.'

Gordon was still breathing heavily. 'I did not expect to be asking you this, but are you sleeping with him?'

'No,' she answered firmly, resisting the temptation to blurt out that she wanted to. What would her father say to that? 'Javi's not perfect, but you've misjudged him. He flirts a bit and we enjoy making music together, but we both know nothing is going to happen between us.'

'Good. I'm sorry I asked.'

'It's okay,' she said, hiding her smile behind her wine glass. She was glad her father was so eager to accept her assurances. She capitalised on his relief. 'The flight to Colombia is on Saturday morning. Maybe you want to take tomorrow to decide whether you want to come with me? How did you manage to leave your hearings?'

'It was difficult, let me tell you. But I've arranged for my absence until after Christmas. I thought, after the stress of the past few days, you might enjoy a cruise. A reputable liner is leaving from Cozumel tomorrow.'

'I'm not going on a cruise. I'm spending the time in Colombia.'

'It has a stop in Havana for a concert. I don't mind a bit of Cuban jazz.'

'Daddy, I'm not going on a cruise. Perhaps you should go on your own and I can meet you at the end? How long is the cruise?'

'Oh, no, I was thinking of you, sweetheart. A cruise isn't my thing.'

Cara pursed her lips and schooled her features, grasping for something else to deter her father from coming with her. 'Or perhaps you'd like a few days in...' She searched her brain for a nearby location that approximated her father's favourite holiday destination in the south of France, but she came up empty. 'Some place with yachts! You enjoyed that sailing holiday, didn't you?'

He scowled. 'Too much work. You know I've had a stressful year. Perhaps we should return home and recuperate. If the song is already doing well in Colombia, perhaps you won't be required for the TV spot in Bogotá. When was the last time we had father-daughter time?'

'I'm sorry, Daddy, but I'm not going home, yet. I want to see the lights of the candle festival and see Barranquilla.'

'Where?'

Oh, God, he was going to make her say it again? She didn't think she was pronouncing it correctly anyway. 'Barranquilla, Colombia. It's where my flight is headed on Saturday.'

'You do realise—'

'Yes, Daddy,' she groaned. 'I realise that up to seventy per cent of the world's coca is grown in Colombia and that paramilitary groups have terrorised large swathes of territory for most of the past fifty years. I realise it's only been a couple of years since the FARC demobilised and that other groups are still active, and I even know that Colombia has one of the world's worst scores on the Gini index of wealth inequality. I've done my research. I'm your daughter.'

'What's the crime rate of this town?'

'You'll have to tell me. But you can be sure I'm safe with a local host.'

Her father frowned, but the glimmer of resignation signalled that Cara's manipulation had prevailed. 'I'll have the statistics for you by Saturday morning. I can spend the flight lecturing you about personal safety.'

'And I will assure you that I don't give papaya to strange men.' She smiled unrepentantly at her father's blustery confusion.

13

The air conditioning in the airport taxi whined and coughed in an attempt to appease its four passengers in the tropical heat. The driver was listening to a crooning ballad accompanied by accordion. The highway baked in the sun, heaving with hulking pickups, mopeds, ancient compacts, minibuses and converted commercial vehicles.

Gordon sat motionless in one of the back seats, his expression pinched, wincing whenever Bea – squashed in the middle – accidentally nudged him. Javi had insisted on delivering them to their hotel, necessitating the cramped taxi. He'd offered Gordon the passenger seat, but Gordon had reacted to the suggestion with horror and Javi had slipped wordlessly into the SUV beside the driver.

The streets became greener as they approached the city proper, windswept trees spreading their branches from the median strip and palms sticking their heads above the power lines. The atmosphere was fertile. Cara had the impression just about anything would grow in the wild air and hot sun. The city was heavily built-up, with wide roads and concrete. But she still felt the jungle would quickly take over if given the chance.

It was nothing like the bracing cold air that drove families indoors in England in December. But the strings and strings of lights draped between the lamp posts were reminiscent of Christmas at home. Christmas trees were instantly recognisable, despite not being trees at all – just cones of coloured lights with a star on top.

It wasn't just the roads that were busy. The sidewalks were full of pedestrians and street-sellers. The trees provided protection from the sun and a place to eat, drink and converse. From the air, Barranquilla had been a hodgepodge of orange-and-white apartment blocks and irrepressible tropical green. On the ground, the south of the city was a mix of industrial property and gated single-storey houses with tin roofs. The city was full of colour – bright blue sky, pink houses, red sun umbrellas.

'Your hotel is in the north, near the Buenavista mall.' Javi eyed Gordon. 'It's a very safe area.'

'Is it far from the city centre?' Cara asked before her father had a chance to respond. He had researched the city with the zeal of an ambitious junior barrister. 'And where do you live?'

'My house is also in the north, not too far. I'll give you the address. The centro histórico is easy to reach from the hotel by cab, but I'll show you round properly after you've recovered from the noche de las velitas.'

The hotel was a sparkling high-rise decorated with bows, sprigs of fake pine and a balloon Father Christmas swaying in the breeze. Cara stared at the billowing balloon, marvelling at the odd turn the Christmas season had taken. The second verse of 'Nostalgia' made a little more sense when she could feel the cool breeze that, in the song, brought the sons and daughters home. She smiled, remembering the next line about tears of cinnamon, coconut and joy. Now she'd drunk out of a fresh coconut under the Christmas lights of a Cancún market, that line was real, too.

The cab pulled in by the water feature in front of the hotel and Javi and the driver collected their luggage while Gordon critically observed the surroundings.

'Daddy, stop. You're insulting... everyone.' Her gaze slid to Javi, who was holding out the handle of her suitcase. He had his hair down and it blew in the persistent breeze.

'I assume you'd rather check in by yourselves. The festivities tonight are at my parents' place, so let me put the address in your phone.' She approached and placed her phone in his hand, standing close to watch.

'Come around nine and take a nap beforehand,' he advised softly. 'We can put your dad in a cab whenever he wants, but you'll be out until dawn – at least.'

'Should we eat before we come?'

He laughed. 'And insult my mother? Eating is part of the point.'

'Cara,' her father called from the sliding doors to the lobby.

'You go ahead, Daddy. I'm coming in a minute.'

Javi glanced into the taxi, where Bea had made herself more comfortable and was tapping on her phone with headphones in. 'I can't make her wait too long,' he said. His tone should have been apologetic, instead it was low and inviting. Her fingers itched to smooth his hair back. 'Did you see the UK chart yesterday?'

She nodded. 'Number eight, after three weeks. What was it in the Latin chart again?'

'Five,' he grinned. 'And number thirty-eight in the US national last week.'

She clapped her hands together. 'We should celebrate.'

'I'd love to,' he responded immediately. She wondered if he was flirting with her again or if it was her own mind conjuring images from the sound of his voice.

She glanced furtively through the glass doors of the hotel, sighing when she remembered there would be no 'celebration' with her father around. 'I'm sorry for my father,' she grimaced.

Javi's lips pursed in amusement. 'So am I, but you don't need to apologise.'

'I know he's wrong—'

He tore his gaze from hers all of a sudden, and she stopped speaking. 'He's right, Cara. That's the problem. He's right about me, he's right about your reputation. He's even right about Colombia, to a degree.'

'Shh,' she lifted a hand, intending to place her fingertips on his lips, but ran out of steam when she encountered the warning in his eyes. He grasped her hand to force her to drop it, but lingered too long with his fingers on hers. 'Let me make up my own mind about Colombia.'

He inclined his head. 'Fair enough.'

'And about you.'

He shook his head, raising a hand to brush his hair out of his face and shoving the other in the pocket of his shorts. The movement was familiar, the pained expression, too. She discovered that knowing how he moved, recognising his moods only amplified the warm languor of attraction in her belly.

He laughed suddenly, retrieved her hand and pressed his lips to her knuckles in a kiss he'd intended to be perfunctory, but still left her trembling. 'I taught you too well. I said you needed to get out and experience the chaos and the mess of life. I didn't mean my life, when I said it, but I should have realised you're such a star pupil that you'd take up my challenge with enthusiasm.'

'You also told me to get my heart broken.'

He shook his head. 'I was an asshole.'

'You were,' she agreed with a prim nod. 'But perhaps you were an "asshole" with a kernel of inspiration.'

His eyebrows drew together as he struggled to rein in a dark look. 'If you've suddenly decided to go wild, I don't know if I can handle it.'

'Maybe I'm discovering I'm just like every other woman.'

'You're not like any other woman,' his voice dropped and her smile dimmed. 'You're magic.'

'And you're a flirt,' she shoved him in the direction of the taxi, annoyed that touching him felt good. 'You're a flirt who can't distinguish art from life.' His gaze jumped to hers and for once he looked ready to defend himself. But she gave him another push. 'I'll see you tonight with a ravenous hunger.' She belatedly noticed the double meaning, but decided to own it with a satisfied smile.

He gave her one more narrow look and climbed into the cab.

By nine, the evening breeze was cool and scented with salt and life. The hotel receptionist negotiated the cab fare for Cara and her father and they set off for the house. Chunky apartment blocks rose in between squashed single-story houses, broken up by public squares that were full of people and twinkling with lights. Hawkers held out armfuls of coloured lanterns, calling out '¡Faroles, faroles!' She saw an orchestra playing in front of a brightly lit stone monument to a congenial crowd. Lights were strung up in the wide trees with their leaves like shiny green hands.

'This is nothing, now,' their driver spoke up. 'After midnight – that's when we come to light the candles. Barranquilla stays up all night on the noche de las velitas!' Her father made a muttered exclamation he didn't intend the driver to respond to. She hoped he wouldn't last that long. She wanted to dance under the stars with Javi, to celebrate with the rest of the city, and she would stay up as late as necessary to do it.

She was amazed at herself. Her father's extreme warnings of muggings and shootings were barely making a dent in her enthusiasm – perhaps they were cementing her determination. Lying on her bed in the air-conditioned hotel room, she'd run through the evening in her head, preparing herself for the foggy distraction of anxiety as she got tired in an unfamiliar place. But she'd fallen asleep before she could prepare a plan of action. Now her mind was too full of the sights and sounds around her.

They passed a square with a huge nativity scene lit with floodlights, the figures bigger than life-sized. A troupe of dancers in traditional dress was moving through the square, accompanied by drums, traditional flutes and a couple of trumpets. The rhythm dominated the loose, repetitive melody, but Cara felt it strangely suited the nativity.

The shopping centre where Cara had dashed to buy a present for Javi's mother had been full of Santas and snowmen. The contrast between the gleaming mall and the lively streets was striking.

Javi's parents' house was by a small, dusty square with a wooden climbing frame covered in squealing children. The house was a double-storey white block with a glass-brick window spanning both levels. It was squashed in with the rest of the houses on the square and had a small front garden dominated by a glossy tree and a few colourful bromeliads, caladiums and a bird of paradise – indoor plants, in Cara's mind.

Tiled round the patch of garden was a welcoming terrace, covered in lanterns waiting to be lit. Garlands of lights in various colours hung from the roof of the patio and round the doorway.

The security gate on the patio was open in welcome. The commotion inside the house was audible as soon as they stepped out of the cab. Women's voices were raised in what sounded like conflict, but when they broke into laughter, Cara realised she'd misinterpreted the intensity of the discussion. She paused on the terrace, the boxes of gifts balanced in her hands.

'Now is not the best time for second guesses, sweetheart.' Gordon's voice was gruff. 'But I'm sure we don't have to stay long. They won't want the awkward British guests sitting silently in the corner for the whole evening, I'm certain.'

Cara eyed him. Although he would never be classed as 'friendly', he wasn't usually so grim. Could he be nervous? The set of his chin certainly reminded her of the many times she'd had to unstick her own jaw. But her father was wrong. Once they got through the first five minutes and found Javi and Bea, it wouldn't be awkward.

At the sound of her name, followed by a rush of Spanish with a charming nasal lilt, Cara turned to find a woman emerging from the front door. She was wearing a loud apron and had a bandanna tied over her permed grey bob. She waved a cloth urgently for them to come inside.

She gushed and gushed in Spanish, taking Cara's arm and tugging her through the gate and onto the patio. The smell of food – smells, because there was a mixture of sweet and savoury, onions, caramel and cheese – wafted from inside the house. The woman who must be Javi's mother took Cara's face in her hands and pressed an enthusiastic kiss to each cheek, continuing the rush of words Cara didn't understand.

'It's so nice to be here,' Cara managed, stunned. 'Are you Javi's mother?'

'Sí, sí. Soy Mamita.' She held up a finger. 'Mam-i-ta,' she said slowly. She said something else which Cara guessed was her name, but she dismissed it with a wave of her hand and repeated 'Mamita' once more.

Cara smiled. 'Hola, Mamita. ¿Cómo estás?' She didn't reply, but giggled. 'These are for you.'

'No, no, querida,' she said in dismay, but her smile was back in an instant and she took the gifts good-naturedly and set them down to greet Gordon.

She gave no indication that she noticed his stiff manner and leaned up to offer him both cheeks. Cara barely managed to keep a straight face when he recovered from his horror and pinched his lips together to oblige.

Cara glanced through the front door and caught a glimpse of the chaos of the large kitchen. Two women, with aprons and bandannas over sundresses and dark hair, were bustling and joking. Mamita ushered Cara and her father through a set of French doors into the lounge/diner, which was decorated with muslin garlands, candles, tropical fruit, a wooden nativity and a wildly blinking Christmas tree. Three tall men – one older – were talking to Javi, who was holding a snare drum against his thigh. Children were sneaking to the table, shoving little balls in their mouths and dashing back into the square.

Javi excused himself from his conversation as soon as he saw them, put the drum on the sofa and approached with a smile. He grasped Cara's shoulders and pulled her close to kiss her cheeks. He shook Gordon's hand warmly.

'My brothers and sisters-in-law speak some English, my father less and my mother almost none at all – although she's the one who visits me in Miami.'

'She doesn't need to speak English to cook and do your laundry?' Cara teasingly rebuked and he grinned unrepentantly. 'Where's Bea?'

His smile faltered. 'Upstairs. She's... in a bad mood. I don't know if it's the usual or if she's nervous.'

He introduced her to his father Camilo and his two older brothers Juan Andrés and Luis Camilo. 'Their wives are in the kitchen and their kids are running wild round the place. My mother's name is Yuliza, but she probably told you to call her Mamita.'

A harried couple with a baby and a toddler arrived, drawing Mamita and the sisters-in-law into the lounge for cheek-kissing and effusive greetings. 'One of my younger brothers, Sebastián David and his wife Anabel. The youngest hasn't arrived, yet. We'll sit down to eat when he gets here.'

'Is this the house you grew up in?'

He shook his head. 'But it's the same neighbourhood. You won't get Mamita out of her barrio. She knows everyone round here and there are still a lot of familiar faces for me, even though I've been gone a long time.'

'But you don't live in the area?'

He shook his head. 'I'm happy to be nearby, but sometimes I need a bit more... privacy. I don't get that in my old barrio.'

'I see the Félix in your name is for cultural and not promotional purposes,' Cara commented.

'Both. Rodríguez is a common surname, so it made sense to drop it professionally. But we do use our double names – except Jorge. That's my youngest brother. He doesn't have a second name. After five boys, I think my parents ran out of steam with the sixth.'

'Six?' Cara asked, taking another look round.

'One is dead.'

Her eyes flew to his. 'Oh, I'm sorry.'

'You couldn't have known. It's fine.' It clearly wasn't fine.

'My brother would have been twenty-one, this year,' she added quietly, wanting to acknowledge the significance of loss, even if he wouldn't.

He looked at her sharply. 'My brother's been dead that long.' He strode away to greet his brother's family. Cara narrowed her eyes at him.

* * *

When the youngest brother swept in with sweets for the children and lavish kisses for Mamita, and Javi had convinced Bea to come downstairs, they sat down to a dinner of peppery pork stew with rice, wrapped in banana leaves, with thick cornflour pancakes called arepas and green salsa. Cara helplessly attempted a conversation with Mamita, in which neither understood the other, but both kept up the flow of enthusiasm, punctuated by graciously offering and accepting more food and a variety of appropriate mumbles of delight.

At the first tingle of jalapeño on her tongue, Cara glanced at Gordon to see his face mottling slowly. But he cleared his throat and struggled on. He sat by Camilo in a place of honour and only after Javi's father had wordlessly insisted that Gordon try the whisky did his posture relax to something resembling ease.

Cara kept track of Bea's progress at the extra table set up for the children. There was a cousin about her age, another girl, and they were treating each other with such identical haughtiness that Cara was sure they would soon be friends.

After a set milky pudding sprinkled with cinnamon, served incongruously with copious amounts of the cheesy balls called buñuelos, the brothers ran for the pile of instrument cases in the corner and dragged them out onto the patio.

Cara helped Javi move the drums into the corner of the patio and assemble a drumkit with extra congas on one side and bongos set above. 'Papá and Juanito play the trumpet – although papá also plays guitar,' Javi explained. 'Lucho plays bass, Sebas plays guitar and Coque – that's what we call Jorge – plays just about anything, including accordion.'

Cara nodded, then swung to Javi in surprise. 'And you play drums?'

'That's my instrument.'

'It's not your only instrument.' She picked up his hands and turned them over in her own.

Javi chuckled. 'Here,' he wiggled the fingertips of his left hand at her, 'calluses for guitar. And here,' he pointed to the little bumps on the insides of the fingers of both hands, 'from drumsticks.' It took all of Cara's will not to press her lips to his palm.

As a consolation for not kissing him, she kept one hand and stroked it between both of hers. 'Do you play drums for yourself? I mean on your recordings?'

'Usually.'

She smiled faintly, her knees weak. 'You're amazing. I love the drums in your songs.'

'You can reward me by dancing for me when I play.' He traced a finger up her arm and Cara asked herself what on earth they were doing, flirting like this in front of his family. But she didn't want to stop.

'Don't I get to play an instrument? I don't see a keyboard.'

'There's an upright piano in the living room, but the women usually dance.'

'Huh,' she frowned. 'That's sexist.'

'But look, things are changing.' He pointed out his niece, who was opening a violin case.

'Does Bea play an instrument?' He shook his head with a wince. 'What? That's a shame!'

'I think she's had singing lessons.'

'You could teach her.'

He laughed humourlessly. 'I'm sure she would love that.' He dropped his hands from her. 'I'm worried she's going to hate this.' He shrugged and pulled an elastic from his pocket to tie back his hair. 'But you don't need my shit. I hope your dad survives the whisky and the boredom.' He turned to the drumkit, but she grabbed his forearm to turn him back.

'Play some songs she knows. Get her involved. I'll do what I can to help.'

His look was so long and so warm that her breath stuttered. 'If we were alone... I would be trying to work out if I'm allowed to kiss you for that.' His words weren't far from a whisper, but they sent an avalanche of sensation over Cara's nerve endings and she felt like she was trying to breathe through her stomach.

'Kiss me where?' She'd been thinking about cheek kisses and pressing her mouth to his hands and hadn't realised how suggestive the question was until his expression heated with teasing humour and challenge.

'Are you sure you want to know?'

Her heart was beating in her ears, but she wouldn't back away as he seemed to expect. 'Why do you think I asked? I assume you meant my lips and not my cheek.'

He shook his head with a smile burning in his dark eyes. 'Can you be sure I meant your lips, bonita?' He cocked his head and his eyes settled on her ear, then her neck, along her collarbone and lost focus somewhere round her chest. Her hair stood on end. It was hard to believe he hadn't touched her. All he'd done was look and whisper and she was on fire.

'Uyy, ¿es ella tuya?' The youngest brother approached with a teasing smile and punched Javi's arm. Javi said something in reply with a tolerant tone of warning that piqued Cara's curiosity.

'I'm sorry we haven't been properly introduced. You must be the beautiful Cara.' He kissed both her cheeks. 'I'm Jorge, the charming brother with the best English. This lot calls me Coque. Let's let Javi hide behind his drums and you can sit with me.'

Cara perched with Jorge on a bench and watched as he tugged a small white button accordion from a box next to a ukulele. She studied the instrument with interest as he strapped it high on his chest. The cacophony of tuning and warming up filled the square, the accordion squeaking occasionally, accompanied by what sounded like cursing from Jorge.

Neighbours emerged from their houses with raucous greetings. In Cara's English neighbourhood they would have angry grimaces and choice words for their noisy neighbours, but in Barranquilla they brought chairs, greeted each other effusively, shared drinks and settled in for a long party.

All of a sudden, or so it seemed to Cara, the sounds coalesced into a recognisable pattern in four-four time, led from Javi's bass drum. They all knew what the song was, what notes to play. The women were still washing up, but after Javi played an introduction on the toms, they started whistling boisterously from the kitchen, breaking into laughter. Jorge started up on the accordion, and a few bars later, Camilo began to sing a quick, staccato verse, the others joining in for some lines.

'This is a vallenato pop classic from the nineties. We grew up singing this in the old van Mamita used to drive,' Jorge explained, his fingers still moving on the accordion.

The chorus was a catchy call-and-response between Camilo and everyone else – the neighbours and the women in the kitchen included. The song bounced along with Luis' fingers on the bass guitar and the pulse of the bass drum. It was impossible not to move. Cara clapped along, watching the family share their talents.

Her eyes could never stray long from Javi. He moved with effortless perfection. His leg kept the disciplined beat with the bass drum, while the rest of his body flourished with creative energy, flittering over the toms and keeping up the rhythmic interaction of the snare and the hi-hat. It was obvious he'd trained as a professional drummer. She'd never asked him how he'd started his career. She hadn't known he'd also lost a brother.

'The Little Drummer Boy'... It was mentioned in the first verse of 'Nostalgia'. She'd only noticed a series of Christmas references, but she would have to look closely again. It was just like Javi to hide the biographical part of the song.

She felt momentarily guilty for telling him so much about her problems, but never asking about his, until she realised he'd had opportunities to tell her and had purposely withdrawn. That was Javi – hot and cold. But she couldn't resent him for it any more.

14

When the women joined them, the music changed to frenetic beats that demanded dancing. Jorge set a traditional drum between his thighs and complemented the rhythm of the congas. Mamita drew Bea and Cara up to dance. Bea didn't know the steps either, but she learned quickly, unlike Cara, who drew good-natured sniggers.

At the end of the lively set, Javi pulled off his buttoned shirt until he was just wearing a vest. Cara tried not to notice the sweat reflecting the light off his muscular shoulders. His brothers led the neighbours in a round of whistles and catcalls that he laughed off.

The wife with the baby strapped to her was prevailed upon to sing. She had the husky voice and the passion of her varied ancestors and Cara was captivated, even though she couldn't understand the words. Mamita and Camilo led the singing of more nostalgic melodies. Cara thought she recognised the one that Javi had sung lightly in the rehearsal studio in London. When he met her gaze with a small smile, that confirmed it.

One look was enough for her to remember the feel of her hand in his that day as he'd swayed with her to the beat and she'd felt so much more than she'd wanted to. It was its own kind of nostalgia to remember that half-Christmas in August, but now she understood the line of the song about lighting candles and dancing on the patio so you don't fall asleep.

Could he tell how much she wanted to dance with him again?

'What Christmas songs do you like?' Jorge interrupted her spell of distracted longing. His amused look implied she probably shouldn't have been staring at Javi in front of his family anyway.

Most of the Christmas songs she truly loved had been taboo for years. But that night, she was sick of supressing what she did remember, simply because of the horror that came after it.

She glanced at her father, to find him frowning at her already. Couldn't he enjoy the music? Didn't he see this was a safe sort of Christmas, where they could celebrate the season without always thinking about that year? Would he ever let himself enjoy it?

She turned to Jorge, without taking her eyes off her father. 'My favourite is "O Holy Night".'

Mamita asked Jorge to explain and then clapped her hands with approval. '¡Oh Noche Santa! ¡Qué hermosa!'

Gordon was silently grim. Before she could say anything further, someone had picked a key and the brother with the guitar was plucking away an accompaniment. They had to search for the words on their phones, but Camilo started everyone off, singing the first line in his rich tenor.

Cara's skin prickled. The lyrics in Spanish were incomprehensible – jumbled, like her memories. This had been her mother's favourite Christmas song, too, and her father had played the accompaniment on the piano. It hurt to see him sitting across from her, turning as grey as the stone balustrade. But perhaps the hurt was what they both needed. She was sick of the interminable numbness.

When the family had sung it through once, they turned to Cara. 'In English,' Mamita encouraged.

Cara's eyes darted back to Gordon and she hesitated, torn. Before she could make a decision, Bea blurted out the first line in English, her voice clear. Cara glanced between Bea and Javi with a smile, and shifted along the bench until she was sitting next to Bea.

When she reached the second section, Cara joined in at 'Fall on your knees', picking out a harmony a third below. The instruments dropped out, but Cara leaned her shoulder against Bea's and they continued to sing softly to the end of the song.

Cara closed her eyes so she didn't have to see her father and wasn't tempted to look at Javi. She tried to tell herself it wasn't a big deal, but this was the first time she'd sung this song in a decade. It felt surprisingly good, singing a quiet harmony for a grouchy, sensitive pre-teen who didn't know or care what disturbing memories lurked in Cara's head.

Sitting outside under the twinkling lights with the distant sounds of fireworks and music, she was blending the past and the present in the season stopped in time – to steal another line from 'Nostalgia'.

She was scared that if she looked at Javi, she would want to stop time forever.

When they finished singing the song, Cara wrapped an arm round Bea's shoulders and squeezed. 'Thank you,' she murmured.

Bea gave her an awkward smile and disengaged herself from the hug. 'I just like that song,' she mumbled.

'On that note, it's getting late.'

Cara turned to see her father rise from his chair and brush off his trousers. Immediately disproving his statement, salsa music suddenly blasted into the night air from round the corner, followed by convivial shouts and raised voices.

Mamita and Camilo descended on Gordon, understanding his intention, if not his words. Javi joined them and they all talked at once, leaving Gordon frowning disapprovingly in the middle. Cara didn't move. She didn't want to give him a chance to make her question herself. If she was allowed to enjoy Christmas this year, even in this odd form with warm breezes and accordion and 'The Little Drummer Boy' as she'd never seen him before, she was going to embrace it.

It was an indication of how tired, tipsy and disconcerted her father was that he mostly held his tongue when she saw him into a taxi but didn't join him.

'I'll see you at breakfast,' he muttered. It was Cara's turn to hold her tongue.

When she returned to the patio, the musicians were taking a break to pass round more drinks. Cara felt Javi's eyes on her, but she didn't dare look in case he noticed how hard she was trying not to blush. Staying out late with his family felt like she was putting herself in his hands. She liked the feeling more than she should have.

'What's with your dad? Is he racist or something?' Bea asked as soon as Cara sat back down on the bench. She nearly spilled the glass Camilo handed her.

'That's an interesting question,' was all she said at first.

'You're going to fob me off. I can tell.'

She gave Bea a narrow look. 'What do you want me to do? You're either trying to get me to defend him and thereby imply I'm racist, too, or you want me to say something unkind about my own father.'

She snorted. 'It's not that hard. You should try it.'

Cara's mouth slammed shut as she stared at Bea. Then she burst out laughing. 'How do you think up this stuff?'

'I have lots of real-life experience,' she sniffed.

'You're digging yourself a hole, gordita,' came Javi's voice. He leaned against the wall next to the bench and took a sip of his drink. 'Cara's not the spoiled brat you think she is.'

'And I'm not the spoiled brat she thinks I am!'

'I wonder why she might think that?'

Cara tried to stifle her chuckle, but snorted instead. Both gazes swung to her, lit with the same sarcastic spark and stubborn flame. 'Sorry,' she said. 'Do continue.' She mimed eating popcorn out of an imaginary bag until Bea gave her a grudging smile and Javi was shaking with laughter.

Fortified with laughter and the jovial mood of the family gathering, Cara looked Bea in the eye. 'My mother and brother died on Christmas Eve, so it's not my father's favourite time of year. He also likes to think he knows everything, so when something reminds him he doesn't, he can be rude.' Cara cocked her head to watch the familiar response play out in Bea's expression: embarrassment, sympathy, awkwardness. She sighed. 'And he never let me get away with anything when I was your age,' Cara added, letting Bea off the hook. 'Come on, let's have a go on your dad's drumkit.'

She handed the sticks to Bea while she tapped the congas experimentally, enjoying the reverb against her hands and the different tones produced. She could have predicted that Javi would drift closer immediately. He snatched her hands off the skins, holding them still in his.

'If you want to touch my drums, you need to know what you're doing.' Before she could roll her eyes at him, he took one of her hands and placed it flat on the drum on the left. 'This is a quinto. You play it with a palm stroke or an open stroke on the edge.'

She struck the head with her palm and then with her fingers on the rim. He demonstrated a simple bar of alternating strokes and she stared at his hands, enjoying the precise, rhythmic movement and marvelling at the way the gentle touch produced order. When she didn't bring her hands back up to the drums, he shifted on his feet and started playing again, his right hand fluttering between the drums and bringing out the glorious off-beat that made Cara want to shake her hips.

She grinned as warm desire rose in her chest – desire to dance, and maybe something more. She could have laughed with the awareness of how much his hands turned her on.

Bea tapped her on the back and she turned, lamenting the necessity to clear her head. 'Hmm?'

Bea pretended to pick something up off the floor. 'Here, your pride. I think you dropped it.' Even the embarrassment was fun.

'Are you going to give us an actual beat, gordita?'

He squeezed past Cara, nudging her out of the way with a hand on her hip that set her off again. He showed Bea how to put her foot high up on the pedal and strike the bass drum. As soon as she tried adding in the snare, the pulse of the bass drum faltered. Javi leaned down to press his foot on top of hers to keep it going.

'Just feel it. It's hard when you think too much,' Javi said. 'Like life.' He glanced up and shot Cara a grin.

Giving Bea tips on the drums, he suddenly became a monster of a teacher, correcting everything from her hold on the sticks to her persistent delay on the last beat of the bar. Her expression hardened, but so did her determination. Cara wanted to know what would happen if he decided to teach her to play properly. She imagined they'd see sides of each other – and themselves – they hadn't known.

He shooed Bea away when his brothers retrieved their instruments for the next set. Cara took her hand and sat down on the floor by Jorge, where there was a selection of percussion instruments, handing Bea a set of bongos and taking up a pair of claves herself. The rest of the band settled behind their instruments, but Javi stomped over and confiscated the claves.

'What's wrong with you? The percussion fairy won't share his instruments?'

'Bea can have the bongos because she has a feel for it – she just needs practice. You, on the other hand,' he paused, making a belated attempt to soften his tone, 'you don't understand the importance of the claves in Afro-Latin beats.'

Jorge approached as Javi disappeared into the house, his lazy stride like his brother's. 'I think we'd all rather see you dance, bonita.' He earned dark looks from both Cara and Javi, who was returning with a guitar and a frown.

'Here.' He sat her down on the bench, settled the guitar on her lap and handed her a plectrum. 'You play, don't you?' She nodded quickly. 'G major chord,' he instructed, and her fingers settled into the familiar position of the first chord she'd ever learned. Javi leaned close and showed her a strumming pattern with his thumbnail. When she tried it, she found it almost impossible to overwrite the habitual rock rhythm, but when Sebastián and Luis started playing too, she stopped thinking and let her arm lead her through the beat.

The first part of the song was difficult and full of mistakes as she focused on the rhythm while listening out for Javi's shouts telling her what chord came next. But once she'd learned the chord progression, she wallowed in the joyful, syncopated sound and in the intellectual and emotional challenge of making music. Her playing wasn't close to perfect, but she enjoyed every note. She created a stir among the women, who cheered wildly at the end of the song. Cara grinned, her muscles relaxed and her mind quiet.

It was past midnight and the children were starting to wilt when Mamita gathered them round and handed out lighters and matches and sparklers. She sang a song, her voice rough and warm, as she moved from lantern to lantern with the smallest grandchild. The whole family joined in with the song and neighbours retreated across the square to light their own lanterns.

Cara watched Javi, sitting behind his drums, detached, but with his lips moving as though he couldn't help it. Bea stood to the side, her arms crossed, watching her cousins. When nearly half of the lanterns had been lit, Javi's shoulders rose with a deep breath and he stood. He leaned against the house, next to Bea, and nudged her with his shoulder. He fished a box of matches out of his pocket, lit one and passed it to Bea. He fetched a small white candle and held it for her to light, shielding the flame from the breeze with his hand. He gave her the lit candle and motioned her forward with a jerk of his head. He followed her as she hunched down by a purple lantern etched with a butterfly and he lifted the cover so she could light the candle inside.

Cara stared. The square was slowly turning into a glowing meadow of flickering candles, but all she could see was the shadow of nostalgia on Javi's face as he lit the candles with his daughter. When all the lanterns on the terrace were lit, Bea stood. Javi draped an arm round her shoulders and gave her a squeeze. His chin hovered over her head as though he wanted to drop a kiss into her hair, but he hesitated and caught Cara watching him. He gave Bea one more squeeze and approached.

'What do you think of our little tradition?'

'There's nothing little about it. There must be hundreds of candles on this square alone. It's beautiful. Does every street look like this?'

He nodded. 'I'll take you exploring later – if you like.'

'I wouldn't miss it.'

He took a step closer and she lifted her face to his, taking a deep breath. 'You haven't lit a candle.' He wrapped an arm round her waist and shepherded her to the tree, where lanterns were hanging from the branches. He opened the lantern and lit a match, holding it out. She wrapped her hand round his as she took the match, their eyes locked. She looked away reluctantly and stretched up to light the little candle inside.

As she blew out the match, the sound of guitar strings, gently plucked in an immediately recognisable pattern, made Javi freeze.

Sebastián was playing the opening bars of 'Nostalgia'. Cara glanced back to see him staring at Javi as he did so – a challenging look with a tinge of uncertainty. Javi didn't turn round, but he dropped his hand from Cara's waist. Everyone quieted and all eyes were on him. His chest was rising and falling with heavy breaths. Cara's brow furrowed. Why was he hesitating?

He swallowed and turned, stiffly returning to his drumkit with a frown and a shake of his head. Jorge approached with her borrowed guitar and she followed him back to the bench, but her eyes never left Javi. 'He doesn't let us play his songs – ever,' Jorge murmured. 'He doesn't often sing with us. And he never lets us perform on stage with him.'

'Why not?'

Jorge grimaced. 'You'll have to ask him. Probably because of Alejo – our brother who died.'

Sebastián stubbornly played the introductory bars a second time and then silence fell. This was where Javi was supposed to start singing the first verse. The neighbours had drifted back and everyone was waiting expectantly.

Without lifting his head, he glanced at the gathered friends and family on the terrace, at his brothers, his parents, then to Cara. She held the guitar at the ready, wanting to play the chords she knew well but had never performed herself in public. Then his gaze dropped to Bea, sitting on the floor by Cara. She was giving him a wide-eyed hint that he should get started, her hands hovering over the bongos.

He cleared his throat, licked his lips and started to sing. Cara knew his voice, the husky catch when he sang quietly that sounded like tipsy midnight philosophy, the little break in his voice around the E above middle C. But she'd never heard him sing without amplification. She hadn't appreciated the tearing power of his voice.

It was the only time she forgot to come in. He'd started up the rhythm and was singing and drumming at the same time. She was so lost in the hesitant honesty of his performance and her swirling questions that she didn't register that the beginning of the chorus required her to join in. He looked up sharply when she missed her cue and she was startled back into herself. A low cheer went up when her voice joined his. She tuned to him automatically. The harmony was fresh all over again.

She picked up the guitar accompaniment in the next verse. Juan and Camilo raised their trumpets and Mamita led the neighbourhood in singing with Javi. They all knew the words. At the end of the bridge, his mother crossed herself. Cara resolved to look again at the translation, which had never made complete sense to her. Javi's family understood. Whatever 'Nostalgia' meant to him, they understood.

Sebastián left the final chords to her and, although she couldn't pick the strings with Javi's skill, she enjoyed trying. Playing the song had been just as incredible in the square in Javi's barrio as it had been on the beach in Mexico. The audience was smaller, but more appreciative. She and Javi both had to submit to exuberant cheek kisses from Mamita, and she exclaimed something over him with pride.

'You know, I still don't really know what it means,' Cara commented quietly to Jorge.

He glanced at her critically. '"Nostalgia"? It's homesickness.'

She frowned. 'I know what nostalgia means. It's the same in English – longing for the past.'

'But in Spanish, it also means homesickness.'

Cara drew back in surprise. It was a fine distinction, but the realisation settled profoundly in her chest. The 'you' in the English translation of the lyrics wasn't a woman, it was his home country. 'My heart keeps beating for you'. His heart certainly still beat for

Colombia, no matter how many years he had been gone. She remembered the day she'd met him and accused him of liking Miami more than Barranquilla. What a complex set of emotions he'd hidden that day.

But why was he so cagey about the meaning of the song? She understood the more serious subject matter – the bullets and sorrow of a protracted war – was a departure for him, but was the emotion truly so raw that he didn't want to admit to it?

'We Colombians are known for setting out overseas in search of success, but we know home is always better for the soul.'

'Are you the brother who went to London?' Cara asked suddenly.

Jorge smiled, a smile she recognised from Javi – part cocky flirtation. 'That's me. I was there for four years. To think our paths might have crossed before this.'

'I'm not in London very often.' England felt like a world away. Bristol would be hunkering down for long, cosy nights under the twinkling lights and her friends would be heading to the Christmas market. This year she could skip the awkward discussions about why she was so reluctant to join in. Perhaps next year she would go. She'd survived singing her mother's favourite carol. She'd enjoyed the candlelit square and a big family celebration that hadn't constantly reminded her of how small her surviving family was.

But this year, this Christmas was special – a year to suspend normal life and enrich it. This year would be one to look back on, to help her redeem the other good memories. She wanted to lose herself in it, as Javi had told her to do in the music months ago. For once she wanted to lose herself and trust that she'd find her way back.

Her gaze settled on the little accordion at Jorge's feet. 'Can you teach me to play that? Just the basics?'

'Sure. Come here.'

* * *

Thank God Cara was there. He didn't want to dwell on the significance of the song, but he couldn't hide it from his family. They all knew. At least they all knew to back off. Even Mamita had restricted herself to tearful pride. And now he had a distraction to ensure he didn't ruminate on the fact that he'd played one of his songs with his family for the first time – even if that distraction was currently an irritation. Was she flirting with Coque? Of course she wasn't. Cara didn't flirt. Except that she'd started flirting with him.

Javi watched with a frown as Coque strapped the accordion onto her chest and spent too much time adjusting the straps. He nudged her back so her posture supported the weight of the instrument and leaned close to show her how to open the bellows. When he guided her fingers over the bass keys to produce a C chord, she smiled at him and the cramp in Javi's chest tightened uncomfortably. He'd written songs about jealousy before, but never realised it could be just as cutting as he'd described.

He rose restlessly from behind the drumkit, but he had no desire to make small talk with his family, so he grabbed a guitar and fiddled through some improvised bars. He sat on the ground next to Bea, helped her to set up a rhythm on the bongos and continued on the guitar. Whatever they were playing turned into a Beatles song and Bea sang a few lines with a giggle.

'I think Javi's jealous.' Coque's voice reached his ears – which was his brother's intention. 'He's like a puppy sitting down in front of you to get your attention.'

'I don't think so.' Was it disappointment in her voice, or just his wishful thinking? 'Javi has so much love that he doesn't get jealous.'

'Uyy, lady. You have his number.'

Coque and Bea were both looking at him, expecting a response, but he wouldn't defend himself. Yes, the jealousy was screwing with him, but his attraction to Cara was the same old weakness that she had called him on before: sex, music, fooling around – he wasn't supposed to get them confused any more. He ignored their looks, but glanced at Cara. Her brow was pinched and she was avoiding his gaze.

'What do you have to say for yourself, man?'

'Nothing,' he shrugged, studying the guitar strings unnecessarily. He played from touch, not sight. 'Cara knows me well.'

She snorted. 'As if he'd let me know him well.'

He looked up sharply, but she continued to experiment with the accordion as though she hadn't said anything important. From the terrace, Mamita demanded to know what they were talking about. Coque opened his mouth to explain, but Javi silenced him with a look. He turned back to the guitar and struck a chord, strumming a rock music pattern. He looked up at Cara and continued to play.

Her eyes narrowed with suspicion at the familiar chord progression and when he paused and struck the dampened strings in the rhythm at the beginning of 'Heroes and Words', her look was full of wary reprimand. He raised his eyebrows, prompting her in open challenge. Would she sing for his family? He had made it difficult to refuse.

Sensing the tension, the terrace had gone quiet. She pursed her lips, then lifted her chin with a shrug. She took one deep, shaky breath and opened her mouth. 'On the day that the words came,' she began, her voice steady. He strummed the next chord and let it ring as she sang the next line: 'The heroes were dead, but we were survivors.' Her voice flowed lightly through the verse, but the leashed power was evident in her easy melody. He also caught the meaning of a few lines referencing her anxiety. It was a brave song.

By the time she reached the last line of the verse: 'What do you know about okay anyway?' she held the family enthralled. Javi had to remind himself to play. She didn't need the beats, brass and drums to entertain an audience. She only needed her voice and her emotion – honest and vulnerable as it was.

In the chorus, she experimented with bass on the accordion as she sang, a pleased smile lighting her face. He sat at her feet and kept up the accompaniment as something shifted in him. She smiled at him as she reached the angry line he'd quoted to the reporter in Mexico. He couldn't return the smile – his pride and shame were bubbling too much for that. But neither could he look away.

He needed to write a song to get her out of his system. Something sentimental and heart-breaking, about glass piercing his feet and rocks gouging his knees as he hopelessly followed her. It didn't sound very romantic. He was better at that stuff when it wasn't real. He'd only written one song that bled from his heart and look where it had got him – mixed up and at home with a complicated, irresistible woman he didn't want to get rid of.

When she sang the final note, his family erupted into whooping applause and swarmed to congratulate her. He knew she was looking at him, but he refused to return the look until his emotions had settled.

Coque appeared with two shot glasses and Javi stood to join him without thinking, the flavour of the whisky always a powerful reminder of home. 'Es una bomba. You're screwing her, right?' Coque murmured.

The question landed on him like a punch. He should have expected it and he knew Coque wasn't intending an insult. Why wouldn't he think what he was thinking and express it is such terms? It was a conversation they'd had before. But that night it socked him in the teeth. 'Will you believe me if I deny it?'

Coque looked at him critically. 'Hey, I'll be the first to get in line if you're serious.'

Javi's look darkened and he thrust the shot glass into his brother's chest. 'Don't even try.' He wanted to storm away like a moody teenager, but settled for retreating behind the drumkit. He shoved his ear plugs back in and started playing without much thought. His brothers all picked up their instruments and joined in. He scowled at Coque as he helped Cara unbuckle the accordion, but his brother's movements were efficient and apologetic.

They played and danced and sang and drank until there were more children sprawled asleep on the furniture than awake.

Coque strode over. 'Are we heading out?' Javi hesitated, glancing at Cara. 'Ah, you have other plans.' His brother held up his hands. 'Say no more.'

Javi could see Coque's suspicions on his face. He wondered if he should contradict him, but his own thoughts were turning to the one end to the night he couldn't allow to happen. He had to prove to himself he could show a beautiful woman a good time without concluding in the bedroom. It was not the reason he'd asked his mother to take Bea home.

Cara approached with her arms crossed against the breeze. He draped an arm round her without thinking. Coque drifted away with a less-than-subtle salute.

'Does no one sleep?' she asked. 'It's three in the morning and the fireworks and music haven't stopped. I thought this was a pious festival.'

'It's certainly sincere, but the important things in Barranquilla are never quiet.'

'Your neighbours are still dancing.'

'Do you want to keep dancing? Find a party somewhere? Or are you too tired?' he asked, hoping she couldn't tell how much he wanted her answer to be 'no'.

She flashed him a grin. 'Are you kidding? If I'm only going to see this once, you'd better get me straight to the party.' He chuckled and wrapped his other arm round her waist for a brief squeeze.

She wriggled away. 'Your family is watching.'

'At least it will teach Coque to stay away from you,' he grumbled.

She crossed her arms over her chest, but instead of impressing him with her sceptical defiance, it only drew attention to her nipples under her light blouse. For such tiny breasts, they were impossible to ignore. 'My face is up here.' He loved that smart-aleck tone.

'I know – tu linda cara. Did you know that's what "cara" means in Spanish?'

'What? What does it mean?'

'It means "face".'

'Oh, is that all?' She pursed her lips in a wry smile. 'I was expecting something like: "The rhythm of your heartbeat when you first set eyes on the person you're destined to fall in love with".'

He snorted with laughter. 'You've been listening to too many love songs.'

15

They followed the milling crowds headed for a large square closer to the city centre. Cara's wide eyes reflected the flash of fireworks and the neon Christmas decorations. Patrons from a nearby bar spilled out onto the tiled square, dancing in front of a brightly lit monument, to music pumping from a set of huge speakers decorated with intricate, graffiti-style paint.

The mix of warm and cool in the air, the laid-back atmosphere and the beats emerging from the speaker – cumbia, vallenato and the African soukous that were so popular on the Caribbean coast – created a channel directly to Javi's teenage years. As usual, the memory twinged with thoughts of Alejo and the odd combination of defensiveness and buried hurt.

A feeling of unease snaked through Javi as Cara drew him to the bar and declared she wanted a mojito. She drank it quickly and he asked himself how much she'd had to drink at his parents' house. He wasn't sure. If Cara had decided to misbehave, he would have to be extra careful.

'Hey, I recognise that song,' she said with a smile. It was the vallenato favourite they'd played that evening at his parent's house.

She cocked her head to study the dancers and he smiled. She was well and truly loose, but she still wouldn't dance until she'd done her homework.

'Are we going in? Or are you going to make me beg like last time?'

She chuckled, her smile bright and worryingly mischievous. 'I've been waiting all night to dance with you.' His stomach plummeted to his shoes as she grabbed the front of his shirt and tugged him into the crowd.

It was nothing like the first time they'd danced. She was soft and relaxed. She threw her head back and moved her hips with so much enthusiasm it made up for her lack of skill. She clung to him, her body tucked against his. The curve of her back was achingly familiar under his palm. He knew her scent, her vibrant energy, her hidden vulnerability. He was beginning to get used to how everything round them dimmed when he held her in his arms.

Agua que no has de beber, déjala correr. He reminded himself firmly to let the water run. She wasn't for him.

The haze of stars and smoke above them evoked the passing of the year. The dry December breeze brought the gentleness of tropical winter. The crowd celebrated the mild warmth and light, the proud traditions of the best place in the world. And Javi held onto the girl who didn't belong – except in the moment. She didn't belong in the list of women he'd failed.

She was making a good effort to belong in the buoyant crowd. Her hair swung in a wide arc with her hips. She didn't need bare legs and a little dress – her enthusiasm was enthralling enough in pale trousers and a blouse. She danced with vigour that was effervescent, if sometimes charmingly clumsy.

He accepted the inevitability when the couples round them noticed her zeal and laughed and clapped. He encouraged her into a solo turn while he clapped. This was her moment, not theirs. *If*

I'm only going to see this once, she'd said. Another man tugged on her hand and, although her eyes flew to Javi's in question, he didn't protest. The look in her eyes could have been disappointment, but he didn't trust his judgement where Cara was concerned – he didn't trust himself.

If she was disappointed, she got over it quickly. The seed of irritation rose in Javi's throat once more as she was passed from partner to grinning partner. Coque had set him off at home and he still couldn't shake it. He couldn't have her, even if everyone thought he already had, and it would drive him crazy.

With Cara's enthusiasm and obvious inability to speak Spanish, they were soon recognised. A shout went up and phones flashed in their faces. He groped for Cara, holding her tight to his side in the crowd, both irritated and thrilled to have to touch her again.

She had no trouble being friendly and charming, but he knew not to stay long in the crowd after they'd been recognised. After two more songs, he pulled her away, walking in long strides until he could strong-arm his way into a taxi. As soon as he shut the door of the cab behind them, she crumpled into him.

'I've never been so tired,' she mumbled.

'It won't take long to get back to your hotel.'

'Are you coming with me?' The breath hissed out of his lungs and he couldn't reply. 'I want you to.' She fumbled a hand on his shoulder and leaned up to kiss his jaw. Her mouth was hot and her hand adventurous as she explored his chest. The thrill of her touch was sharp and consuming. She wanted him. Was it simply the novelty of resistance that made it feel so much bigger than it should have?

He raised a hand to stop her, but pinned her hand to his chest instead, turning his head helplessly. Their lips found each other with the barest effort. He was awash with attraction too long denied, and the kiss burned.

All his fierce jealousy, the passion of the music, his frustration at how much he wanted her poured into the kiss. A dim voice warned him not to unleash everything; she might draw away. Another part of him wanted her scared off. He groaned – a deep, rough noise that sounded foreign.

She didn't run. She tangled her arms round his neck and held on tight. Her lips were an open invitation. His objections were inadequate. He opened his mouth on hers and urgency flowed between them, communicated with hands and lips in the first furies of exploration. The skin of her cheek was soft and moist under his thumb. Her diaphragm heaved under his splayed fingers. She tasted of joy and life and chances.

At the sound of his name whispered brokenly on her lips, he had to break off and stare at her. How had he let things get this far?

'Cara,' he reproached her gently with a shake of his head and a couple of heaving breaths. 'You're not thinking straight.'

'I'm not thinking at all. It's wonderful. I'm just feeling.' She sighed. Her fingers trailed from his hand up one arm, leaving behind tingles of longing. 'You feel good.'

They'd been on the edge of this conversation all night and Javi was resenting his deep mood, but he couldn't help smiling. 'And you always do what feels good, cariño?' He brushed her hair back from her face. It was knotted and limp from the long night.

'Surely I can do what feels good this once? Or has it all been empty flirting?'

'I'm sorry the kiss got so out of hand. I shouldn't have manhandled you. But you can't challenge me into sex.'

'How am I supposed to talk you into it, then?' She straightened and frowned at him. 'You're not supposed to make this so difficult. That's my job.'

'If it's your job, then do it. Start overthinking. Then tell me you still want to. Picture having breakfast with your father after spending the night with me and tell me you still want to.'

Her lips snapped shut as though he'd shoved a piece of lemon in her mouth. 'Why is your moral compass so different with me? I want to be normal. I want you to treat me how you've treated the beautiful women you've worked with in the past.'

He shook his head in immediate vehemence. He took her face in his hands, holding her still when she would have flinched away. 'You are normal – beautifully normal. And I'm pretty sure sex with you would blow my mind. But you know what I am. You've had my number since the first day we met and you don't want my shit. Nothing's changed.'

Her eyes narrowed. 'Something's changed. You wouldn't be protecting me if you were truly as bad as you say you are. The song... Your family...'

He swore under his breath and let her go. 'Yes, maybe I am trying to gather the shards of my pride so I can face them. All the more reason to behave. Maybe I don't want to be the seducer of innocent musicians any more. I have a twelve-year-old daughter, for God's sake, and a lot of years of selfishness behind me. It's about time I accepted that.'

She didn't respond for a long moment and he refused to look at her. The sound of her breathing told him she was agitated, as did the curse she uttered.

He cradled his head in his hands and laughed. 'You're so cute when you swear.'

'And it's sexy when you're honest. That's why I swore.'

'Lucky I'm not often honest.' She gave him a sceptical look that he deflected with a smile. 'So... are we going to be okay?' He brushed the backs of his fingers down her cheek and tucked her hair over her shoulder.

She nodded slowly as the cab pulled up outside the hotel. She didn't move for a long moment. 'I don't want to go back, yet,' she said, her voice flat.

'You're tired, niña. There'll be plenty of time later.'

'Yeah, with my father in tow,' she muttered. 'The streets are still full of people. Take me somewhere. If you're not coming in, then take me somewhere.'

He pursed his lips against the smile that was dragging at one corner of his mouth. 'You'll fall asleep before we get anywhere.'

She shrugged. 'Nothing to lose, then.'

He inclined his head. 'Okay.' He'd had enough of saying no to her. He gave the driver new directions and they took off again.

* * *

'You're asleep.'

She dragged her eyes open and her hand flew to her mouth as she swallowed sleep dribble and embarrassment. 'I'm not!' she insisted. She hadn't believed she'd fall asleep, not as keyed up as she was from that kiss. But the sleep deprivation was stronger than the rampant attraction. This city was crazy. 'Where are we?'

'Somewhere, as requested,' he said with a teasing smile. 'I love this place.'

She looked eagerly out the window into the dim pre-dawn wilderness. Beyond a group of squat, weathered buildings stretched a narrow strip of rocks, out into the sea. There were fan palms, shrubs and grass growing, but the dirt path was bare and dry. The blue-grey sea and whipping wind gave the place a neglected feel, although there were people about. She was reminded of the sea crashing in front of Javi's apartment in Miami. This spot was wild in a way that couldn't compare to Miami, but the same intimacy she'd felt that morning on his terrace stole over her as she watched him staring out to sea.

'Is that the Caribbean?'

'That side,' he pointed, 'is the Caribbean. On the other side is the river, but the mouth isn't too far.'

'Let's go.'

There were revellers gathered round fire pits on the beach, which stretched out along the Caribbean. Javi spoke to the driver and they continued along the narrow track until it stopped, leaving only a path and a pair of rails, partly buried in the dirt. The path was dusty and dim, but the promise of sunrise was close and music played somewhere in the distance. They got out of the taxi by a second cluster of buildings where a brightly painted restaurant was opening. It was a simple concrete structure with a covered terrace and plastic chairs, but the sea lapped invitingly at the rocks below the terrace.

'We can eat there when we get back. Arepas e' huevo is the best breakfast when you've been up all night and it's good here,' Javi grinned. 'There's a rustic train that takes you to the end, but I doubt it's running.'

'I'm fine to walk. It's so pleasant in the early morning.'

'Everyone here has been up all night.'

They set off along the bumpy track and Cara enjoyed the excuse to reach out for Javi when the terrain was difficult to negotiate in the weak light.

'I don't understand how you do it. I've been awake so long I feel like I'm walking through fog. But then sleep has been a serious matter for me for the past ten years.'

'You have trouble?'

'Not any more – well, sometimes.' She smiled tightly. 'At first I couldn't sleep because everything hurt, especially the part of my leg that isn't there any longer. Then the anxiety took over. It was like being held captive in my own obsessions. I had to be very strict with myself for years after the accident. I could never have done this, even five years ago. I'm used to my strategies now. I have routines and cues and a lot of understanding about the physical and psychological processes of sleep.'

Javi rubbed his face. 'Oh, God, that sounds like toddler sleep training.' She furrowed her brow and looked up at him. 'What? I was still married to Susana until Bea was five.'

'You must have been quite young when she was born.'

He winced. 'That wasn't meant to be an invitation to talk about this.'

'You just rejected my sexual advances. I think a few confessions are in order to alleviate my mortification.'

'If you're so embarrassed, why do you still want to hang with me?'

Didn't he realise that was a dangerous question? 'You could always find me another local guide,' she deflected, smiling in satisfaction when he scowled. 'So, tell me about Susana.'

'Fine,' he grumbled with a shake of his head. 'Yes, I was young when Bea was born. I was even younger when we got married. The mistakes of youth or something.'

'You were married when Bea came along, then?'

He sent her a sidelong smile. 'Nosy, aren't you? Yes, Bea was not an accident. But the separation was already inevitable by then – with the wisdom of hindsight.'

'But you stayed together another five years?'

'Yes and no. We separated a few times. It was... turbulent. We were more apart than together the last year.'

'Did you leave or did she?' She was making him squirm, but if there was ever a time to satisfy her curiosity, it was sunrise at the place where the river met the sea.

He sighed. 'She did. Well, she kicked me out. The last time, she left, so I knew that time it was final.' Cara hesitated, watching his hair in the breeze to avoid the haunted expression on his face. 'Aren't you going to finish what you started? Ask me why?'

Cara's stomach sank as she thought back to the line of faces in the magazine. She didn't want to hear it and she doubted he wanted to say it.

'Perhaps I shouldn't have asked,' she murmured.

He laughed humourlessly. 'Perhaps you shouldn't have. But you're in this now. I was selfish. I never felt I had any responsibility to her and I didn't even try to give her what she needed. I committed to her before the law, but never in my heart, not fully. Maybe I don't have it in me.'

'You didn't love her?'

His answer was an inarticulate choking sound. 'Of course I did...' He muttered something with a grimace.

She took pity on him and didn't point out the flaws in his 'many kinds of love' philosophy. 'But what happened at the end?'

'The end? Oh, nothing much. She'd just had enough. That's the way it goes. You can forgive specific screw-ups, but years of letting someone down is harder.'

Cara ran her tongue along her teeth behind her lips while she decided whether to voice the question. 'It wasn't... another woman?'

'Not really. I mean, yes. When she kicked me out, I would occasionally go and sleep with someone else. There were lots of times I thought it was finally the end – and I celebrated being free.' His tone was cutting and she wasn't sure whether his answer was a relief that he hadn't technically betrayed Susana or more appalling because he'd been so eager to escape. 'Have I fixed some of your mortification?' he asked lightly.

'Now I see why you turned down an offer of sex,' she said quietly. 'I'm not exactly good for making people feel free.'

'Ahh, Cara.' He wrapped his arms round her. She sank into the embrace far too easily. 'I was a moron back then and I haven't always been good to you. I'm starting to think that feeling of freedom is a sham anyway.' His arms tightened and he continued on a murmur. 'You're the water, querida. You're supposed to slip through my fingers. It's better that way.'

They'd reached the river mouth. Waves from the green Caribbean crashed on one side while the alluvial waters of the river rushed on the other. The sun was low over the distant city of Barranquilla and the wilds of swamp and coast. Other couples and groups were taking selfies at the edge of Colombia, but Cara held on to Javi for as long as he would let her. She didn't feel like the water.

'Thank you for bringing me here. It's a special place.'

His shoulders lifted on a huff. 'You're easily impressed. Would you like to see our volcano, too?'

'There's a volcano?'

'About an hour away. If we had time, I'd take you to Cartagena. It's a beautiful, historic city and you'd love it, but it's a bit far. Most of the video was filmed there.'

'Then I've already seen parts of it. We have historic cities in Europe, but we don't have many volcanoes.'

His smile was apologetic. 'I shouldn't get your hopes up. It's not a volcano like you're expecting.'

'I don't care. I want to go.'

'Bea would probably like it, too,' he mused. They turned round for the meander back to civilisation. Javi stopped at the restaurant. 'Let's get something to eat while I call a cab. I hope you're ready to go home, now?'

She yawned. 'Yes, I suppose the night is well and truly over.'

* * *

She fell asleep comically quickly in the cab and he tried not to take it as a compliment. She felt safe with him. She shouldn't, but she did. It made keeping his distance more difficult.

She looked ghostly with exhaustion when he jostled her awake outside the hotel. He ran his thumb along her jaw and studied her. 'Five minutes and you can sleep again. Can you make it up on your own?'

'What will you do if I say no?' she muttered sleepily.

He grinned. 'I won't believe you. If you can tease, you can walk.'

He got out to see her to the door and they stood looking at each other for an awkward moment. 'Your family's pretty amazing. Thanks for sharing the music and the candles with me. And thanks for the sunrise.'

'The music goes both ways.' He brushed a knuckle under her chin. He leaned down to kiss her cheek, but she threw her arms round him. He hugged her back, wondering what on earth this was between them that felt so good, but so impossible. She would never feel like the other women he'd had affairs with over the years. It was the song. It had to be the song. They'd both lost their heads tonight, but at least he was still standing.

He arrived back to a silent house. Mamita was dozing on the sofa. He assumed that meant she would go home when he woke her. A stab of guilt assailed him when he admitted he had hoped she'd stay and help him deal with Bea. It was too quiet, too awkward when it was just the two of them.

'Bea's gone to bed,' his mother murmured as her eyes blinked open. 'She waited up for you for a little while.'

'Sorry I'm so late. I'll call you a taxi.'

She nodded and sat up with a sigh.

'Was Bea okay tonight? Did she talk to you about it? Do you think she had a nice time?'

Her eyes were sharp. 'I think so. She likes to pretend she's not having a nice time.' She paused. 'What about you? And Cara?'

'Cara enjoyed the night.' He purposefully ignored the hint.

'She's talented and passionate.'

He nodded. 'She'll probably be an international superstar one day. You'll be able to tell everyone about the time she spent the noche de las velitas with us.'

'And you will remember the first time a woman broke your heart before you could break hers?'

'Mamá,' he said in a warning tone, 'there aren't going to be any broken hearts. Stop fishing.'

'Then tell me what's going on between you. I've never seen anything like this from you.'

He shrugged her off. 'It's the song.'

She hesitated, then inclined her head. 'You know we are all so proud of "Nostalgia".'

He sighed. 'Yeah, I know.'

'It's not just because it's on the radio all the time. It's because of what you've written – the acceptance, the grace.'

'I don't know if it's true,' he insisted. 'I wish it was true. It's only possible in the music.' Like being with Cara. It was only in the music that they belonged.

His mother was undeterred, as he'd suspected. 'It's a beautiful wish. And I'm proud that it's your wish.'

He said goodbye to his mother when the cab arrived and he opened the sliding door to the garden, restless. The breeze was up again, blowing down the river from the spot where he'd held Cara in his arms and tried to be satisfied with that.

You didn't love her? Cara's question still hurt. If he hadn't loved Susana, who had he loved? His answer should have been 'lots of people'. But he feared the truth was 'no one'.

But he was in the right place to change that – in his house in Barranquilla with Bea asleep upstairs. He wondered what Bea had thought of her first experience of the noche de las velitas. He wondered if she would ever feel as though she belonged with his family. He wondered why she'd waited up for him.

He collapsed into the hammock strung up under the awning and rubbed a hand over his face. If he slept there, he'd hear Bea when she came downstairs. He wanted to see her as soon as he woke up to remind himself of where his head should be.

* * *

'Did you know you snore?'

Javi could believe it when he snorted awake, disoriented, and swung precariously in the hammock as he sat up. He hadn't heard Bea come down. She was sitting at the outdoor table, dressed, with a box in front of her.

'Hey, gordita. Did you find something to eat?' he asked when his voice could function again.

She shrugged. 'Not hungry. I don't want to know how much fat I ate last night.'

He chuckled. 'We don't eat quinoa salad on the día de las velitas.' He swung his legs gingerly out of the hammock and stood. 'You shouldn't worry about it.'

'If I shouldn't worry, you shouldn't call me "fatty".'

'You know it's affectionate and not meant like that. And if I call you flaca you'll think I'm being ironic.'

She looked into the box on the table and pulled out a photo. 'Is this why you call me gordita?'

He sat next to her and took the photo. 'Where'd you find this?'

'Mamita gave me the box last night.'

Javi rubbed a hand over his mouth and resisted biting a finger against the expanding emotion in his chest. The photo showed a chubby, smiling baby with stalks of messy dark hair, strapped into a carrier on his bare chest. Baby Bea was wearing chunky noise-cancelling headphones and he was rehearsing a drum solo. 'Maybe this is where you get your sense of rhythm,' he mumbled and handed the photo back. 'What else you got there?'

'I was still chubby as a toddler.' She handed him a picture of a three-year-old Bea on his shoulders on a sidewalk in Little Havana. Susana wasn't in the picture. She wasn't in many. It pricked him to look at this curated version of that time in his life. The constant arguments, his inability to be the reliable husband she needed dominated his memory.

There had been so many damn decisions. It had been easier to drift away and leave it all to Susi. He'd had some easy times with his cute kid, but full responsibility for his daughter was something he'd avoided – something he'd missed.

'You were damn cute as a toddler – still are.' He nudged her chin with his knuckles.

She gave him a narrow look, but it wasn't hostile. 'There are some pictures of me in Colombia, too. It's nice to see printed pictures instead of everything on a hard drive.'

'Did you see all the pictures of you Mamita has on the walls at her house?' She pursed her lips in what he hoped was an attempt to suppress a smile. 'Was it okay last night? Did you have a good time?'

She cocked her head. 'Yeah,' she said slowly. 'But your family is kind of overwhelming. At least Cara was there to be even more of an outsider than me.'

'You're not an outsider. We're just the Miami branch of the family.'

'But you have a house here, now.'

Javi considered his words for a long moment. He recognised the chance. 'Which means you do, too, mija. But I know it's easier to see each other in Miami. I'm not going anywhere.'

16

Understanding was tantalisingly close, but eluded Cara. She'd written out the words of 'Nostalgia' and compared them with the translation word-by-word, but she was still missing something.

The first verse – the one she didn't sing at all – was a story about himself, she was sure. 'The Little Drummer Boy' was a cute reference to his past, but the rest only proved how little she knew about him. There was something about taking a gift meant for someone else and following the wrong stars. She supposed the line about leaving the baby in the manger was probably Javi tormenting himself about Bea.

She understood the reference to candles in the chorus, and the drums, and she suspected she understood the line about silencing bullets and sorrow, although she couldn't have felt further from the decades of war in the brightly lit courtyard at Javi's parents' house. Homesickness... It had to be about Colombia. She guessed he was extrapolating his own complex bond with the home country he'd left nearly twenty years ago.

The second verse had multiple meanings, cleverly disguised in Christmas nostalgia. La brisa fresca nos reúne todos los años. In performances, he liked to pretend the 'nos' referred to her and Javi, being reunited by the cool breeze. She hated to think how real that would feel when she listened to the song next Christmas, far away in England.

But she suspected he'd originally meant his family – his home. There were evocative references to tears of cinnamon and coconut – and joy. Each verse ended with a line about love looking back.

The bridge began with joyful exhortations to dance without care and she enjoyed the line about lighting candles and dancing to stay awake, now she'd seen it for herself. But the last half of the bridge, where Mamita had crossed herself, was hopelessly cryptic.

She was sure she was missing the point of the line that said: 'There is no end, only sorry'. The Spanish word he'd used was perdón. It also meant forgiveness, mercy or absolution. But it wasn't clear who was in need of mercy and who was giving it. The bridge ended with the puzzling line: 'The cement won't dry until I let it'.

Cara knows me well; he'd said last night. She suspected he barely knew himself. He had to accept that the song had been cut straight from his soul.

She'd managed to sleep until past midday. After a litre of water, she'd felt surprisingly human. She couldn't decide if she was embarrassed or not that she'd propositioned Javi and he'd turned her down. She'd never done anything like that.

With the clear-headedness of morning, she suspected she'd insulted him – not that he'd realised. If he'd asked her to come to his hotel room because he wanted what every other guy she'd slept with had got, she'd have kneed him in the balls.

Instead, he'd taken her to the river mouth to watch the sunrise. He'd told her about Susana. And she'd learned to long for the feeling of his arms round her.

She suspected she'd misjudged him in London, too, accusing him of shallow pursuit of women and hedonism. He hid behind it.

He had been struggling with the depth of the song, with his determination not to let their attraction interfere with the creative results.

They'd again avoided sleeping with each other last night, which was for the best. She ran her palm absently over her residual limb, checking the condition of the skin out of habit. It was a stupid vanity she usually managed to ignore, but there were few people – men or otherwise – who had seen her legs. The few times she tried going out with her prosthesis and scars on show, she got sick of the endless well-meaning questions about how it had happened. She hid it so it wouldn't take over her life again.

Being seriously injured at eighteen had hampered a sexual awakening that was always going to be awkward for the nervous perfectionist in her. She'd been too anxious during her first attempt to lose her virginity during her post-grad years at Cambridge. She still found it difficult to think of the guy's face without feeling nauseous. Since then, sex had been a careful and slow exercise where she had to pause regularly and judge whether her partner could handle the truth of her routines and appearance. It wasn't exactly... fun.

But no matter how much she tried to worry about what Javi would think of her pragmatic approach to sex and her missing lower leg, all she imagined was him lying back with an amused smile and inviting her to take her time.

It was a shame, because he'd been right last night. She'd never had casual sex before and wasn't sure she wanted to. What she'd wanted from him had been so much more. Rested and refreshed, the danger of wanting too much from Javi was clear. They both had enough to worry about. The flirtation was a pleasant distraction and would be a charming memory, but anything more would be a mistake.

* * *

The mornings were heavy with humidity and after the parades and festivities of the weekend the city seemed to wilt. Cara joined Javi for the interview with a local radio station and even enjoyed the impromptu performance. And she purposefully ignored her father's ill humour as Javi showed them the sights of Barranquilla: public squares, colourful, ornate churches, the wide river and the mix of contemporary monuments and historic statues.

Bea was keen to see the volcano, which was also some kind of bizarre public bath, so Javi suggested they go the following day.

'I suppose it will be educational to get out of the city,' Gordon commented as they travelled down in the hotel lift in the morning.

Cara didn't reply. 'Educational' may not have been the word she'd choose, but her father could have picked something worse.

'Did you hear if there was any trouble that night? Nothing burnt down from all the candles?'

'I don't think so,' she muttered.

'No muggings?'

She eyed him. 'I would have told you if I'd seen anything.'

'I don't imagine you saw anything,' he defended. 'I meant if you'd heard reports, or if anyone told you.'

Cara resented the unease that spread from her father's harrumphing disapproval straight to her misfiring neurons. 'I can't speak for the whole city, Daddy, but I've been safe the whole time.'

'You've felt safe.'

'Yes, which was a bloody miracle, so can you give it a rest, please? I'm well aware of what's in my head and what's real.'

'And where does a relationship with Javier fit in with that?'

She turned to face him with a steel gaze. 'In my head – in my dreams, actually.' That shocked him into silence.

They emerged from the hotel into the bright sunlight of another day promising every season except what they knew as winter. Cara looked round for Javi and found him and Bea across the road, sharing a snack on a bench under a spreading poinciana.

She tried not to preen under Javi's warm smile when he saw her, but she was looking forward to him kissing her cheeks and she suspected it showed.

'Ready for operation mud bath?' he murmured as he pulled back from the kiss and Cara belatedly realised that she'd closed her eyes.

She met his gaze warily. 'You said this would work, right?'

'Don't you trust me?' he asked.

'I don't know if I should answer that.'

'Está bien. Let me reword. Are you wearing a swimsuit like I asked?'

She couldn't stop the deep blush at his choice of words, as though she was wearing the swimsuit for him and not for the off chance that she could swim without drawing attention to herself. Not swim – bathe. She still didn't quite understand what kind of volcano it could be.

'I'm wearing a swimsuit,' she muttered.

'Good.' His lips kicked up on one side, as though his thoughts were travelling a similar path. 'I've got a plan. I promise this is a once-in-a-lifetime thing.' Everything felt 'once-in-a-lifetime' this December.

'Wasn't yesterday operation mud bath?' Bea spoke up. Their tour of Barranquilla had started well, but as Cara had been gawping at the enormous statue of Shakira, the downpour had arrived. By the time they made it back to Javi's car, the storm drains were already struggling.

'There's no rain forecast for today. I was thinking we'll head down straightaway and stop for lunch and a swim at the beach on the way back up.'

'Let's get going, then,' Cara agreed and they made their way to Javi's SUV.

'Javi bought fried stuff,' Bea announced, handing Cara a paper bag from the passenger seat.

'Not just any fried stuff. Local delicacies from the fruteria,' Javi said with a smile. 'And juice.' He handed her a cup which she accepted with more enthusiasm. She settled into the back seat with Bea and inspected the little fried zeppelins in her bag to keep her mind off the long drive to come. The starchy dough and garlicky filling settled surprisingly well in her stomach.

Gordon refused the offer of food and eyed Bea as he fastened his seatbelt. 'Is it school holidays for your daughter already?'

'Cara has already chastised me for taking Bea out of school three weeks early. I'm sorry to say we are truanting.'

'Nothing could be more important than education, especially for the next generation of immigrants. This is a poor example to set.' Cara winced at his choice of words. Her father had seen the ups and downs of society, but Britain was a world away from Miami and in a different universe to Barranquilla.

Of course, Javi wasn't offended. He simply started the car and pulled out into the traffic. 'I'm not worried about Bea. Some of us didn't even finish school.'

'You didn't finish school?' Gordon was horrified.

Cara frowned. 'That's not what he said.' *Was it?*

'It's true. I didn't finish high school. I nearly did, but there was too much money to be made.' He glanced at Cara in the rear-view mirror with an easy smile. 'You can close your mouth now, mona.'

'I'm going to go to college in New York with an overseas semester in Barcelona,' Bea announced to three rounds of surprise. 'Unless I change my mind,' she shrugged.

'Wow.' Javi pursed his lips in approval. 'A few years of lessons and I can get you a part time job drumming at the salsa bars in New York.' She gave him a dirty look.

'What are you going to study?' Cara asked.

'I dunno. I'm only twelve.'

Cara looked up as Javi chuckled. She recognised the simple smile he'd worn in Mexico. Lazy and contented suited him. Oh hell, agitated and torn had looked good on him the other night, too. He was wearing an old t-shirt and a baseball cap today, with his hair back in a ponytail and a thick bracelet of wooden beads. The shirt looked soft on his shoulders. It made her imagine wearing that shirt herself – which was a weird fantasy.

Once they cleared the city, the road was a mostly deserted single-carriageway and even Cara was hard-pressed to find anything they could collide with. The landscape was scrubby and flat, houses and villages scarce. And she was going to swim in a volcano.

At least, she hoped she was. The straps of her swimsuit dug into her shoulders – a constant reminder of what she was attempting. She had forced herself to learn to swim again after the accident, but she preferred busy sessions at the pool where she either blended into the crowd or no one had the courage to ask her the questions she hated. She'd not dared go since her single charted, for fear that someone would put her together with the talented pop star who was known for her music and not her missing limb.

She still wasn't sure how she would deal with it today. Bea didn't even know she had a prosthesis. Her eyes were drawn back to Javi, calm and relaxed as he held the wheel. She didn't imagine Bea would hold back from the questions as he had. That morning in Miami when she'd told Javi her full story felt like half a lifetime ago.

You're not like any other woman – you're magic, he'd said when they arrived in Barranquilla. Perhaps today she would be magic enough to bathe in a volcano.

* * *

'What a desolate place!' Gordon's pinched frown deepened as he got out of the car at el Totumo. It was a funny looking patch of baked dirt and stumpy trees at the end of the road, but Javi wasn't about to agree with him.

'I think it's pretty cool. Are you going in?' Bea asked him as they got out of the car.

'Of course not.' Bea caught Javi's eye and he reminded himself to give her a few tips on subtlety. Gordon continued, 'But I brought along a book, so Cara and I can find somewhere to sit overlooking the sea and you and your father can go bathe yourselves in mud.'

'That's not the sea,' Javi said with a smile. 'It's a swamp. The sea is on the other side. You'll get your dose of the Caribbean afterwards.'

He hadn't been to this place in years and there was more evidence of a brisk tourist trade, but that made it easier to wave someone over and discuss the help he needed and was asked to pay embarrassingly little for.

He watched Cara study the stumpy mound of dirt that advertised itself as a volcano. It was the cone of an active volcano and held the record as the smallest in the country, but it was underwhelming at first glance, especially in December, when the surrounding dirt was cracked and some of the trees were bare. Although a minibus of tourists had arrived, the infrastructure was basic – thatched cabanas offered makeshift shelter and simple food.

She noticed him watching her. 'It's even wilder than Isla Blanca.'

'Of course. Outside the cities, that's what you get in Colombia – wilderness. This is comparatively tame.' He took a step closer to her. 'Just tell me if this is not okay,' he murmured.

'What's going on?' Bea asked before she could answer.

'Nothing. Clothes off. Let's go.' He turned to Gordon. 'There is a chair set up for you under that cabana with a drink. It's sugar cane water with lime – I recommend it. We won't be too long. It's difficult to stay in the mud for more than half an hour.'

A woman from the drinks stand took Gordon's arm and led him to the chair with a smile and a flow of words he couldn't understand.

'Thanks,' Cara smiled. 'It was thoughtful of you to take care of him.' He didn't feel particularly deserving of her praise when all his energy was spent lifting his eyes from her body. She'd peeled off her t-shirt and the top of the black one-piece swimsuit she was wearing had sucked all the breath out of him. She had freckles on her shoulders, too. It was a lovely line of them from one shoulder, along her collarbone, across her chest and to the other side.

'Stop staring at the wildlife, Dad.' He blinked and turned to Bea. 'You're so lame.' His face grew hot and he was worried he was blushing. That was a weird part of fatherhood no one had warned him about.

'Don't worry, Bea,' Cara said with a smile. 'I'm sure his next song will be about how he learned not to objectify women.'

He grinned. 'I like the sound of that. I'll call it "You're so Lame". Want to write it with me, gordita?'

She narrowed her eyes at him. 'Er, no.'

'Cara! Are you coming?' Gordon had finally realised Cara wasn't following.

'No, Daddy. I'm taking a mud bath.'

'You're what?'

'Don't worry, I have a plan.' She eyed Javi as she said it, doubt on her features.

He nodded and pulled out the sarong he'd bought yesterday. He thrust it at her. 'Here, put this on.'

She took it with a furrowed brow, but nodded and tied it round her waist before slipping her loose trousers off. He held open the car door and indicated she should sit down. 'Leg off,' he murmured and held out a bag. His chest swelled when she didn't protest, but leaned down to release the catch on her prosthesis. He tried to talk his pride back down. This was everyday stuff. It was the tiniest bit of extra planning. But when her eyes rose to his with tentative excitement, his ego ran rampant. She slipped the leg, several socks and the spongy sleeve into the bag and he clutched it closed.

'And up we go,' he announced as he hefted her into his arms. She gripped the sarong tight to keep her legs covered.

'What are you doing?' Bea asked.

'Come on, gordita,' he called out, ignoring her question and rushing for the steps. He thrust the bag at the waiting attendant with a final instruction to take very good care of it.

'Don't peek,' Cara said, her voice unsteady.

'You're letting me help you. Do you think I'm going to ruin it by peeking?'

'I thought you said you didn't like responsibility.'

His laugh had a grim edge. 'You're carrying all the responsibility. I'm just carrying you. You could have hopped up yourself. Or crawled. I don't doubt your determination.'

'Ah, yes, my determination to have a mud bath is not to be underestimated. But thank you for helping to preserve my dignity. And I feel a bit like a princess, being carried up a volcano – a princess or a human sacrifice.'

He laughed more openly at that, jostling her against him. She grabbed for his neck and he tightened his hold on her. She felt like a princess in his arms – out of his reach. 'For a princess, there should be a less awkward way of getting up,' he said as he negotiated the uneven stairs.

She didn't respond for a long moment, then her hand slid from round his neck to settle on his chest for the briefest moment. 'This isn't awkward.'

He nearly stumbled, but stopped to steady himself and exhale on a long whistle. She packed a punch when he was least expecting it. 'Touch me again and it might get awkward.' He wasn't sure if he was flirting with her or warning her. He was thankful the tiny volcano was only fifteen metres high and they were soon at the top.

'This is insane,' Bea said as she stepped up to the ladder and stared with relish into the crater of congealed sludge.

He set Cara down and she grabbed for him as she found her balance on one foot. He peeled her hand off his chest and wrapped it round the wooden railing. 'Much more reliable,' he murmured, but she looked just as disappointed as he felt.

'I'm going in!' Bea announced and scrunched her face up as her feet submerged. 'It's so creepy!' she squealed. There was barely a ripple as the thick mud closed round her with a squelch. 'I'm floating! Oh my God, I'm just floating!'

He took Cara's laugh as a good sign and descended the ladder himself. 'Whip the thing off and give it to that guy, then get in as quick as you can!'

'That's your great plan?'

'You have a better one?'

'What's under there?'

'I don't know.'

'Well, ask someone!'

'I don't think you'd like the answer.' She pursed her lips and probably would have crossed her arms over her chest if she wasn't gripping the railing so tightly. He leaned back and sank into the mud with a smile. 'Come on. When are you going to get another chance to smear mud all over me?'

There was a warm smack on the back of his head and he turned to find Bea with a predatory smile on her face. 'Your ego is a big target.'

He sank deeper, up to his chin, and struggled over to her. 'Are you sure you want to start this?' He grinned.

'Ugh, how old are you?'

He grabbed Bea round the waist, hauled his arm up out of the mud and smeared a handful all over her cheeks. 'Not too old for a mud fight!' She didn't play fair and his ponytail was soon full of mud. He'd have a hell of a time getting it out, but her giggles were worth the price.

He sat up to flick some mud off his head and felt another splat on his shoulder. He turned sluggishly and grinned to see Cara floating gingerly near the ladder, enveloped in mud, her hair in a topknot.

'It's like swimming in custard. This is the weirdest thing I have ever done.'

'Good. But I said smear, not throw.' He made his way over to her and presented his mud-covered chest to her. 'No? Well, turn round and let me.'

She squealed as she changed position in the muddy suspension. 'How far down does it go?'

'I don't think anyone knows. But you're not going to sink.' He rubbed his hands along her shoulders, massaging gently and trying to keep the touch casual. He was succeeding until she sighed with pleasure and no amount of mud could switch off the desire to pull her closer. The line of mud reached to her neck – just below her ear. That spot was calling to his lips. The delicate cartilage of her ear was looking appetising, too.

'Your mud is drying.' She was peering over her shoulder at him. He forced himself to exhale slowly.

'We'll wash off in the swamp afterward.'

'When you mentioned swamps back in London, I wasn't imagining something so beautiful.' She looked out over the ciénaga with its backdrop of deep green hills, the hazy blue of the unrelenting sky. The glistening water was the domain of birds, not people. 'The hills are so close to the coast and I can't see a single building.'

'You should see the Sierra Nevada de Santa Marta. The highest mountains in Colombia are only fifty kilometres from the coast.'

'Are you serious? I don't suppose that's nearby?'

He smiled. 'Bathing in a volcano isn't enough adventure? It's not too far – two hours north of Barranquilla. But there might be too many iguanas for you in the jungle.'

'It's so close! I can do iguanas.'

'What about insects?'

'I can buy repellent.'

He paused, sliding his fingers once more along her shoulders. He leaned close. 'We'd have to stay overnight. Can you buy repellent that works on me?'

She gave him a longsuffering look. 'I don't need repellent for you.'

He grimaced. 'Keeping my hands off you isn't going so well today.'

'But we both know you're not going to do anything about it. Sexual attraction isn't some kind of battle we're going to lose.'

'There must be a reason why we have so many descriptions of love that involve violence.'

'You mean like cupid's arrow?'

He grinned. 'That's too tame. Here, we worry about love's bullets.'

'I think they bounce off you.'

'Uyy, I'm wounded.'

'No, you're not.' She faced him with that indomitable look on her face that told him she was about to deliver a slap of truth.

'That's exactly the point. You're a moving target. No one can hit you
– except maybe Bea.'

The trapped feeling he'd experienced on the noche de las
velitas crept up his chest again. A moving target... She was right.
But he was running out of energy. He nudged her chin with his
knuckle, leaving behind a smear of mud. 'Where did you learn to
be so good at life?'

She laughed ruefully. 'The school of loss and big girl pants.'

'Big girl pants don't sound very sexy.'

'What do you know?' He inclined his head in acknowledgement. Then her voice dropped with fervour. 'I want to see Santa
Marta, Javi.'

He would do anything she asked in that tone. 'What about your
father? The national park is a bit rustic.'

She grimaced. 'I wonder if I can convince him to stay in
Barranquilla.'

'There is one option. We can camp in hammocks along the
coast in the Tayrona National Park. It's not exactly the Sierra
Nevada but there are hiking trails with views of the mountains.
There's no way he'll want to come along, but he can also be fairly
sure you'll be safe from me.'

'Hammocks? He'll be horrified.' She smiled. 'It sounds great.'

* * *

They drove back up the highway for a late lunch, Cara feeling out
of her own skin in several ways after the morning of mud and
laughter. She was finding it harder to keep her eyes off Javi, no
matter how hard she tried for Bea and her father's sake.

His hair was curling and damp. Scrubbing the mud off him had
been a big undertaking, even for two of them. He'd dunked his hair
into the swamp and rinsed vigorously before flipping it back like a

long-haired dog. She'd sat in the murky water and gawked like a woman in a crappy commercial, even though she'd tried hard to censor her reactions for Bea's sake.

As they drove, he tapped his thumbs against the steering wheel and sang absently along with the American rock song on the radio. His bare arms reminded her of being carried against his chest. The way back down from the crater had been a slippery mess and the ruined sarong had stuck to her residual limb, revealing more than she would have liked, but Javi had delivered her efficiently into the water. After they'd washed off, she'd waited in the water while he set a chair behind some bushes and retrieved her prosthesis. She'd felt Bea's curiosity, but Javi must have warned her not to ask. She didn't want it to be an awkward secret and Bea probably should know, now. But her father's presence bothered her as well. He still found her condition tragic and wouldn't want to witness the conversation that would be like so many Cara had had over the past ten years.

About halfway back, Javi turned off the highway into a township. 'There's a nice restaurant here for lunch and a decent beach, although not quite Cancún.' He smiled at Bea in the rear-view mirror.

He made one more turn, but had to stomp on the brakes, startling a cry out of Gordon, who groped for the dashboard. Cara's stomach flipped, but her attention was snagged by a large group of mourners escorting a coffin across the road to the neat walled cemetery. The sound of wailing carried into the car as the crowd shuffled slowly past, the large, heavy coffin supported on many shoulders.

'I'll see if there's another way through.' Javi pulled out his phone to check the map.

Cara watched the procession with interest, reminded of the memorial service they'd held for her mother and Crispin – delayed by Cara's long recovery. On the day of the service, it had felt like there had been a thousand boxes to tick – customs to observe, wishes to recognise – with no time to feel. She had no doubt the wailing and shuffling was part of the local custom, but it looked cathartic and comforting, too.

Instead of being lowered into the ground, the coffin was taken to an open tomb and shoved inside with some difficulty. A man dressed for labour strode up, looking out of place with his bucket and trowel. She assumed he was trying to make his way through the crowd, but he entered the cemetery, too. Just as Javi was turning the car round, the workman moved a slab over the opening of the tomb and dipped his trowel into his bucket to smear mortar round the stone. It seemed odd to think about a relative quietly decomposing in the tomb. Perhaps the cement gave the mourners the same feeling of finality she'd experienced dropping soil over the urn of her mother's ashes.

With a flash of prickling comprehension, she looked at Javi. The cement won't dry until I let it. It suddenly made sense. The song was about his brother. The cool breeze reunited him with the memories of his brother every year. Love always looked back. Dance so you don't cry.

Did the memory of his brother make the Christmas nostalgia both comforting and painful? And what about homesickness? The poetic references to a Colombian Christmas were also central to the lyrics. The loss of his brother and moving away from his home were wrapped up together in the song and it was so beautifully written her heart wrenched in her chest.

She remembered the dismissive tone he'd used to tell her his brother had been dead twenty-one years. With hindsight, she recognised the tone. It was Javi pretending. It was a long time to pretend something didn't hurt.

He would have been sixteen or seventeen when his brother

died. She wondered about the next line of the song. *Pardon is easy to say, but one day I will mean it.* Did Javi need forgiveness or did he need to forgive? She could understand that the song had bubbled out of him after decades of clinging to feelings he didn't know what to do with. Had the song achieved what he needed?

'I have never seen anything like this,' Cara breathed in awe. Javi had been to the Tayrona National Park before, but he had to agree: he'd never seen anything like the wide-eyed enthusiasm of his companion. He was glad to have organised the few days away – alone, with Cara.

The gentle waves of the Caribbean murmured over the white sand before them, while the jungle rose sharply behind them. Roots and vines tumbled over smooth boulders which joined the jungle to the beach. 'Bea would have liked it,' she said.

'Probably,' he agreed. 'But I didn't have the energy to convince her. And Mamita said she'd take her to the movies with Victoria. I'll bring her back when she's older. We've still got a long way to walk.' He enjoyed the simplicity of being in the jungle with Cara – no career, no family, no past.

'Did you come here a lot as a kid?' she asked as she picked her way along the rocks, steadying herself with her hands.

He shook his head and walked ahead of her on the narrow track. 'Once with my brothers when we were teenagers. We didn't do family holidays like you're thinking.'

'Not enough money?' she asked tentatively.

'We weren't poor,' he said, smiling at her discomfort. 'We just didn't travel, especially not round here. Back then you had to know your way around to be sure you wouldn't stumble into something you shouldn't – right, left, criminal, alphabet soup. The Sierra Nevada is wild. It's much safer now. And Tayrona is tame in comparison.' She didn't say anything in response, and he turned back to find a stricken look on her face. 'I said it's safe, mona. I've been here quite a few times in the past few years.'

'I'm not worried. I'm... sheltered. I can't imagine growing up knowing there were armed groups running free in my country. I'm even too young to remember the Irish Troubles. I don't know how I would deal with it.'

'I didn't deal with it. I left the minute I had the opportunity.'

'And you've been feeling guilty ever since.'

He froze, but forced himself to recover before she noticed the impact of her words. 'What makes you think you know what you're talking about?'

'Because our record company forced you to sing the truth with me.' He stopped this time and turned, clutching the straps of his backpack. For a tiny, sheltered, rich girl, she was shrewd and gutsy. He mustered a half-hearted denial, but she held up a hand. 'I've heard you flippantly deny that the song means anything and I don't need to hear it again. Wait until you're ready to tell me the whole story. But right now, I want to see your jungle. Please find me a monkey and give me as much warning as you can if you see an iguana.'

She swept past him and continued along the track. 'I'll do you a deal,' he called out and she turned with a frown. 'I'll tell you about the song and you show me your leg.'

She inhaled indignantly through her nose. 'Why? You can

assume it's very ugly. My other leg is also badly scarred. Would you like to see that too? You don't need to bully me to cop a look.'

'I don't want to see them. I want you to show me.' Her composure slipped. 'What was your plan after the noche de las velitas? Keep your stockings on?'

'Stop making fun of me.'

He realised too late he was making a mess of this. 'I'm not, querida. I realise it's a big deal for you, but I don't think it is for me.'

'Why does my body have anything to do with you? We're not going to have sex.'

He was starting to forget that. 'It's not just about sex. It's about swimming.'

'Swimming?'

'The Caribbean is right there. It's about twenty-seven degrees in there.'

'I realise you enjoy swimming.' He hoped she meant she'd admired his body as he swam off the beach after lunch yesterday. Swimming was his sport of choice. And he really liked how her eyes had moved over him. 'Fine. If you don't think it's a big issue, there's no need to manipulate me with some deal. I'll show you anyway.'

She marched into the next cove, dumped her backpack onto the sand and started rummaging in it. 'What are you doing?'

'Looking for my swimsuit.' Her movements were stiff. The realisation that he'd hurt her sank in his stomach. He didn't know what he was doing trying to help her. He'd never get this right. And were his motives really so pure? If she insisted on digging around in his wounds, he wanted her to bleed with him.

He dropped to the sand beside her and tugged her hands away. 'Stop. Cara, I'm sorry. You don't have to do anything.'

'It shouldn't be a big deal, you're right. There are lots of high-profile amputees these days who are open about their prostheses.' She wouldn't look at him. 'I should just accept the inevitable. One of these days I'm going to be labelled as the amputee pop singer. I should just get used to it.'

He clutched her hands tighter. 'I shouldn't have pushed you. It's okay that it's a big deal.' He had to touch her. He pulled her hat off and tucked back a strand of hair that had come loose from her plait. It wasn't enough. 'It's just a part of you I don't understand, and... I've got no right to understand it. I get that now.' But he wanted to understand her. He wanted it with a zeal that was foreign.

She swiped at her face with the back of her hand. When she lifted her eyes to his, they were shining with tears, but she had her fighting face on. 'What are we doing, Javi? And what are we going to do when this is all over?'

'Go home,' he said, feeling the wrench already. 'And remember. And maybe write a song about stray bullets and bleeding hearts.'

She jerked the drawstring closed on her backpack and stood. 'I've done enough bleeding for this lifetime. And I hate that metaphor. I hate all your metaphors! Women are only ever metaphors for you!' She slung the backpack back on.

'You're not.' He didn't know if he should have said it or not, but it was different with her.

Her expression slowly softened to rueful acceptance. It pinched more than the accusation that relationships with women didn't mean anything to him. 'I know. And I appreciate that you've treated me differently – for the song, for me, for yourself.' She'd misunderstood. It wasn't simply his attempt to face up to his responsibilities. What he felt with her was something new and he didn't know what to do with it.

He didn't correct her. He laughed instead. 'Are you thanking me for keeping my dick in my pants?'

He loved the steel in her eyes when she scowled at him. 'I cut you far too much slack.'

He settled her hat back on her head. 'You do.' His joke hadn't cleared the shadows from her face. He knew he should leave it alone, but he needed her back. He settled a hand on her shoulder. 'Are we okay? I don't want... I want you to remember this place fondly.'

He couldn't interpret the look she gave him, but it made his heart race with insane hope. 'If there's one thing I've learned on this trip, it's how to make wonderful memories, despite everything.' She reached her hands up to his face and sighed. The sensation of her gentle palms on his skin broke something inside him. The urge to kiss her was impossible to ignore, difficult to resist. Making wonderful memories... He'd lived his life for that. But this was crossing a line. *What are we going to do when this is all over?*

She pressed her lips to his, light, soft, generous and still tasting of distant anger. She pulled quickly away again, but his hand clamped reflexively round her hip. He pulled her hat off again and thrust his other hand into her hair as he followed the retreat of her lips, seeking more. He planted his lips on hers, but the chatter of the jungle was interrupted by the thud of hooves and the sound of voices. She broke away, leaving his hands empty and his mind racing with thoughts of bullets and arrows and happiness just out of reach.

They greeted the mule caravan as it passed on its way to the camping area bearing supplies and the luggage of tourists who followed.

'I'm glad I wasn't getting changed.' She looked at him with that wary, accepting look he would always associate with her.

He retrieved her hat and handed it to her. 'I'm glad I was kissing you.'

'The heavens didn't open to smite you from on high?'

'Not yet.'

'Then let's go. I'm hungry.' He watched her with a halting smile as she returned to the path. He was well out of his depth, but he'd deal with the consequences later. When she looked back for him, he jogged to catch up.

The path turned away from the coast into a marshy area of palms where the mountains rose in the background. They hadn't gone far when he grabbed for her hand and pulled her to a stop. He linked his fingers with hers, enjoying the strange rush and the glow of pleasant surprise in her eyes.

'What?' she asked when he remained still and didn't release her hand.

He tugged her close. 'Just doing what you asked.' He raised his other hand to point at a boulder by the path. An iguana over a metre long was sunning itself.

Instead of cringing in fear, she stepped slowly closer, her eyes wide. He followed, unwilling to give up her hand and laughing inwardly at his disappointment. He should have expected she'd conquer her fear.

She'd reminded him at el Totumo that he wasn't good with responsibility. Even his crude attempts to be there for her fell wide. And what she'd wanted from him – emotional support – he'd screwed up. But realising his mistake wasn't enough to make him let go of her hand.

'That is the most incredible green. He's so pretty!'

The water looked inviting. Rolling affably over the sand of the cove at Cabo San Juan del Guia, the sea was the palest blue. The two-hour hike under the watchful eye of the foothills of the Sierra Nevada de Santa Marta made Cara feel as though they'd left the real world behind and arrived in an impossible paradise of jungle and sea.

There were few buildings. Human life was sheltered in thatched cabanas. They would sleep that night in a shared cabana with twenty hammocks suspended from it, each with its own mosquito net. She was surprised that, far from triggering her anxiety, the wilderness settled it. The world was so big and beautiful beyond her own mind.

She was sweaty and covered with the grime of insect repellent and sunscreen mixed with dirt and perspiration. She was glad she'd brought some gel packs and an extra sleeve for her residual limb. She'd sent Javi straight into the water when he'd dropped his bag on arrival like an excited puppy. She was happy to mind the bags and sit and enjoy the view for a quiet moment – the view of Javi, shirtless and cutting powerfully through the water.

She should be reeling from their earlier conversation. He wouldn't acknowledge his feelings about the past, but demanded she share hers. One minute he was being shallow and avoidant and the next he was chipping away at her heart.

She would miss him terribly when her plane took off from Bogotá in six days' time and returned her to a place where the Christmas season didn't involve iguanas and crazy leaf-marching ants – not to forget shirtless men.

She could imagine how much worse it would be if they'd been more intimate. She could imagine it, but the fear wasn't so good at dampening the temptation. She only had six more days. It was for the best that they had hammocks for the night. Probably.

She understood he wasn't going to make a move. Against the odds, and contrary to his own warnings, she trusted that completely. He was a complicated man who was tired of playing the part of the playboy. But this wasn't casual sex she was contemplating. Could he see that it was different? Could she explain it without him thinking she had starry-eyed notions of forever in her head? Perhaps they had a word in Spanish for 'extreme fondness that can't be love'.

He strode back out of the waves, flicking his hair back. She didn't bother to hide her visual appreciation. He chuckled as he strode up and crouched in front of her, dripping on her trousers. He nudged her jaw shut with one finger under her chin.

'I hope you've been enjoying the landscape.'

She pursed her lips in a smile. 'Very much. I noticed you don't have any tattoos. I thought it was a given these days.'

'I nearly got one a couple times, but... I decided against it.' He sat down next to her, leaning back to dry in the sun. He paused for so long that she wondered if he wasn't going to explain. She hadn't realised the question was controversial. 'I didn't want people to see me as "that" kind of Colombian, you know.'

She couldn't think of anything to say. She could infer well enough what he meant without making him say it. She struggled to picture what his life would have been like before he left home. Despite patches of poverty, Barranquilla was a vibrant and developing city with decent infrastructure. She couldn't imagine the country twenty years ago shrouded in the shadow of chaos. She was working up the courage to ask him about his brother.

'I don't think anyone who doesn't have a tattoo is missing out on much.'

'Said like a – wait, you have a tattoo?' Her smile must have tipped him off. 'Where?'

'Aren't you more interested in what it is?'

'Fifty-fifty,' he grinned. 'I guess it's something to do with music.'

'It's not actually.'

'Go on. Show me.'

She grinned at him and raised the hem of her t-shirt. He sat up as she raised it higher, his smile slipping as he gazed unapologetically at her skin. She lost her nerve at her ribcage, dropped the hem back down and turned over her wrist in front of his face. On the inside of her wrist, in tiny, ornate writing, was a simple date. He grasped her forearm and she wished she had a tattoo on her waist so he would touch her there.

'Why didn't I notice this before?'

'It's purposefully inconspicuous.'

'What's the date? It's more recent than your accident.'

'The last thing I would want tattooed on me is the date of the accident.'

'I get that,' he said quietly.

'This is the date I moved into my own place after the accident. It's nearly three years later.'

'Who looked after you?'

'My dad. He took the first year off work.'

Javi's eyes rose to hers, his brow low and his lips pursed. 'I'm sorry I underestimated him.'

She shook her head, disengaged her arm and reached for his hand instead. If hand-holding was where their relationship was at, she wanted to do as much of it as she could. 'Don't apologise. He is an excellent father, but he's not perfect. And...' She sighed.

'What?' he squeezed her hand.

'He thinks he understands what's going on in my head because he helped with so much of my therapy as I was so young. But he doesn't always.'

'Can you drive?'

She shook her head. 'No, and that's okay, even though I sometimes feel it's a personal failure. It's more because of the anxiety than the physical difficulties. But Bristol has excellent public transport and I can actually ride a bike.'

'Does travelling in a car still make you anxious?'

She grimaced. 'The official answer is yes. But I didn't want to live my life unable to get into a car, so my therapist and I worked a lot on that one and I can usually successfully talk myself out of it when I think I'm having a heart attack in a car. But my biggest trigger is seeing blood.' She shuddered. 'You don't want to be around if I skin my knee,' she forced herself to joke.

'Do you always have anxiety before concerts?'

'With ups and downs, yes. But sometimes I wonder whether it started before the accident. I played in a lot of piano eisteddfods as a child and never managed well before or afterwards. One time I couldn't even walk onto the stage.'

'You played in a lot of what?'

'Competitions.'

'Huh,' was all he said in response and he turned back to the sea. His grip on her hand was barely there.

'Why didn't you finish school?' As she expected, he drew his hand away. But she wouldn't let him retreat. She shuffled closer and tucked herself against him. He gave her a lopsided look, but lifted his arm round her. In the warmth of the sun, with the heat of his skin, she let her muscles go languid.

'Like I said, I was making money.'

'I assume you mean you had gigs as a drummer. You said it that way to provoke my father. Sometimes Bea is so much like you it's shocking.'

He grinned. 'I know. And I can't tell her how much I love her sharp tongue because then she'll work out that she needs to do something worse to push me away.'

'I think she knows that. She's not trying to push you away any more.'

'She stood up for me in front of your father.'

'She calls you "Dad" when she forgets herself.'

'I have to give her back to Susana in two days.'

'I'm sorry this trip is taking you away.'

'Uh uh. No apologies.' His hold on her tightened. 'I have enough confidence now to push it with Susana until I can see Bea more regularly. I have to give you back soon, too.'

'Six days.'

He paused, not moving for the longest moment. He stroked his thumb down her arm. 'Is that how long it is?' His voice was muted.

'Didn't I tell you when my flight was?'

He nodded slowly. 'I didn't want to count the days when I knew I wouldn't like the answer. Are you looking forward to going home?'

'What do you want me to say? No, please don't wrench me from the Caribbean? Yes, I have a hankering for proper tea and mince pies?' *I want to stay with you a bit longer.* He frowned and she grasped the hand curled round her hip to make sure he didn't withdraw it. 'Don't be so moody. I've had an amazing trip and loved every minute of it.'

'It's not over, yet.'

'Yes, I'm looking forward to your concert, the one you mentioned to Susana.'

His expression clouded. 'It's not going to be my best performance.'

'Why not? You're amazing on stage. I want to see your whole show.'

'I don't like performing in Cali.'

'Where is it?'

He waved his hand. 'In the south. Inland from the Pacific coast. It's a big city.'

'None of which explains why you don't like it.'

'Unpleasant memories. It's where my brother died.'

She pulled back to look at him as he stared out at the sea. She hadn't expected a straight answer. 'What happened to him?'

He glanced at her face as though deciding how much to tell her. When he pulled his arm from round her, she let it go. He sighed. 'He was murdered.'

Cara's heart sank, even though it was the answer she'd been expecting. 'That's awful. I'm sorry.'

'It was a long time ago.'

'What was it you said to me? Some moments last a lifetime.'

He laughed humourlessly. 'I hate to think of you remembering everything I say.'

'I hate to think I'll forget.'

'Come here,' he said, his tone tinged with fatalism. He tucked her in front of him, her back to his chest, and closed his arms round her. Her body sighed and hummed. She leaned her head back on his shoulder and inhaled.

'How old were you when he died?'

'Seventeen.'

'I'm guessing it took you two years to save money so you could leave.'

He cocked his head to look at her. 'Yes. I left as soon as I could. How did you know?'

'Drying cement.' She felt him stiffen. 'It's a natural thing to do. You processed an important time in your life into a song. I know you feel exposed, but it's helped too, right? I'm sorry I intruded.'

'I expected you to be an intrusion. But you've stubbornly belonged in that song since the first time I heard your voice.'

'I know losing a brother is terrible, but why is it still a problem for you to go to Cali? You must have been back in twenty-one years.'

'I have been back, but only when I have to. It's not a good story, Cara.'

'Then you'd better spit it out.' He tightened his arms round her, and she held her breath.

'José Alejandro – Alejo – was four years older than me, but we were always close. He played guitar. He was the talent of the family. He won a national song-writing competition when he was sixteen. As soon as he finished school, he was working his ass off for a music career. He had a lot of gigs and released an album, but the music industry back then was entirely geared towards the US and he couldn't get the exposure here. Everything he did was with the aim of getting out of here and getting to the US. He made some dumb choices. I don't know exactly what he got involved in and I don't want to. I mean, how tragic is it that I spend all this time telling you how safe it is and how I've never seen any shit going down and how life is so normal here – at my home – but he screwed it all up?

'A couple of times he couldn't get a drummer for a gig, so I skipped school for a few days to play for him. It started happening too often, and Mamita got mad, but I was determined to keep doing it, especially because I knew Alejo would leave one day. And I didn't believe he'd...'

He paused and the sinking feeling in Cara's stomach fore-warned her. 'You were in Cali with him when he died? Oh, Javi.' She turned so she could wrap her arms round his chest.

'I wasn't with him when he was killed, but, yes, I was in the city. I was too scared to give evidence – not that I knew anything. I just wanted to pretend he'd never brought that shit into my life. And I had to bring him back to Barranquilla in a coffin when his body was barely cold. I hated that city. I hated this country – the empty pride in a screwed-up place that everyone wanted to destroy or escape. They never charged anyone. The only thing that made it manage-able was the thought of leaving the country.'

The lines of the song swam in Cara's mind as she listened to him. Forgiveness... for himself, his brother, for the people who'd committed a terrible crime and never been prosecuted. Had he allowed the cement to dry after more than twenty years?

'But your roots were deeper than you realised and avoiding it still didn't banish the anger. You were hit with nostalgia and the whole country is sharing in it.'

'It took me years to work that out,' he muttered.

'Have you managed it? Have you made peace with it?'

He mumbled something that sounded like, 'Don't ask.'

She settled her head on his shoulder. 'People like the song because of the emotion behind it.'

'You know more about putting your heart into a song than I do. I never even wrote anything about Susana.'

'I can't imagine keeping my life out of my songs, even though it feels like I'm standing in front of the world naked. Are you telling me you didn't love all the woman in your songs in different ways? I'm disappointed. What happened to your lover's soul?'

His laugh was darker than she'd expected and she stared at him curiously. 'I think I threw my soul into the Caribbean on my way to Miami. It kept reminding me that I'd stolen Alejo's dream.'

She shook her head. 'You took the gift meant for another,' she quoted, enjoying his rueful smile. 'You know that's not true. You think you're just "The Little Drummer Boy", but your audience knows better. And besides, your soul washed up again in Barranquilla.' She challenged him with a look. 'And showed you that you've done justice to his dream and made your country proud of you.'

He studied her, his lips pursed. 'I wouldn't go that far.'

'I would.' She picked up his hand, running her fingertips over the calluses.

'Cara.' The way he said her name warned her she wasn't going to like what he said. 'I'm happy for you to know all this, but it doesn't change anything. I'm still... me and you're you.' His hand closed round hers. 'I don't know why we're doing this to ourselves.'

'I really don't get why you have such a reputation as a charmer.'

As she'd hoped, he laughed, jostling her where she was pleasantly curled into him. He leaned in and nuzzled her neck, just below her ear, as though he couldn't help it. 'I've been an obnoxious screw-up with you.' His lips were in her hair and her breath had stalled. 'But at least it's real.'

With his words shivering through her and her heart in tatters for him, she had no chance of resisting the urge to kiss him. She reached up and her lips found his with a little whimper of relief. He answered with a shaky murmured groan as the gentle kiss continued into another and then another. His arms round her grew tighter. She pressed closer, sliding her arms up to cling to his neck.

He swiped his tongue across her bottom lip, making her shiver with the force of the pent-up longing. But he didn't take her invitation to deepen the kiss. He slid his lips across her cheek to her jaw, the spot under her ear.

'Uyy, Cara, this is way too easy.' His gaze dropped. His brow furrowed as he raised a hand slowly to stroke his thumb across her peaked nipple. Her back arched with a heavy gasp. He settled his forehead against hers. 'Sorry, I shouldn't have done that in public. But I love these. Tan pequeñitas.'

She laughed in between gulps of air as their surroundings came back into focus. 'That sounds better in Spanish.'

18

Cara awoke in her little cocoon of cotton and gauze around dawn. Bird calls were a pleasant alarm clock after a quiet night accompanied only by the sound of the waves. She didn't mind being awake early, although she'd clambered into the hammock in exhaustion when they had switched off the electricity the night before.

She spent a long, quiet moment enjoying the chattering jungle noises, reliving the day before. The kisses were front and centre in her memories, but other, smaller things stayed with her, as well: Javi's apologetic smile as he grabbed her hand for the hundredth time; the pair of monkeys they'd found just as they'd given up and were about to return to the beach; propping her sore foot up on Javi's lap and having him massage it through her sock while he teased her with the various Colombian slang terms for foot odour.

His story had coloured her memories and softened her heart. Every little conversation now held hints of the tragedy he'd refused to acknowledge most of his life. It made her wonder about the next steps he'd taken: emigration, career and Susana. By age twenty-five, he'd had a child. He'd never given himself time to heal.

His confession led her back to their argument during the hike.

He'd met his end of the bargain. She still resented the challenge he'd thrown down, although her resentment had cracked when she'd realised he wanted to understand her. But she'd spent ten years telling people to shut up and let her deal with things her own way.

The problem was, she really wanted to swim in the Caribbean. She glanced at Javi's hammock, less than a foot from hers. She'd loved going to sleep next to him, even if they were suspended far enough apart that they couldn't touch. She'd asked him whispered questions that he answered in a sleepy rumble. She'd heard his breathing change as he drifted to sleep. She felt so close to him that it was strange he hadn't seen her residual limb. It didn't define her, but it was part of who she was. She rolled on her sleeve and socks, tugged her prosthesis on and stumbled out of her hammock. She was ready to do it.

She peered in on him as she passed. He was shirtless, with his clothes laid over him like a blanket and his hair spread all over his face. It didn't seem possible that she'd never see him again after she flew out. Surely there was some miracle, some quirk of fate that would bring him back to her – cold and out of place in England. Even in her Bristol comfort zone she wouldn't know what to do with him.

She resisted the urge to lift his mosquito net, neaten his hair and kiss his cheek and instead crept out into the dawn light. The air was cool, which made her smile. It was warmer than some summer days in Bristol, but she'd adapted. The frigid December weather back home was half a world away.

The water retained the heat more readily and was likely to feel warm in comparison. She held her swimsuit in a fist and stared at the deserted surf. She stripped quickly and stacked her clothes in a messy pile next to her towel. The urgent thrill warned her she didn't have much time before she would start to worry. She shimmied into her swimsuit and sat down to take off the prosthesis, stowing it carefully among her clothes.

Hang-ups about dignity forgotten in her mad drive towards adventure, she crawled down the beach and into the sea. She plopped into the shallows, laughing. The waves lapped at her back and the sand flowed softly through her fingers. She sat still as the waves crested against her; she lay back in the water and enjoyed the sun growing warmer on her face. This was the craziest Christmas of her life, and not only because of the weather.

Javi was a dark, sleepy shape on the beach when he approached. She should have got out of the water sooner if she'd wanted to change before he saw her. She wanted him to see her.

'Is everything okay?' he called out, a smile in his voice.

'Yes, fine! Wonderful!'

He yawned and scratched the back of his head. 'I know you're fine, but it's safer not to swim alone. I'll sit here in case you need me. Let me know when you're getting out.'

'I won't be long.'

'Don't get out on my account.'

'I mean I'm hungry.'

'I don't think the guy selling the arepas is going to be here for a while.'

While he was distracted looking at the empty food stand, she crawled out of the water. She could grab her towel and cover up, but she wanted to see his reaction. The angry, independent part of her wanted him to flinch. He was supposed to be a lover of women, the more buxom, the more beautiful the better. But he loved her small breasts and he'd seen her puking and she was afraid her disfigured legs would make no difference to him.

She pushed herself to standing and wobbled in what would be his direct line of sight when he turned back. He would see her legs before he saw any other part of her. And she would have a perfect view of his expression. But he didn't turn round.

'Are you going to get dressed sometime today?' he asked, still looking away.

'You're supposed to turn round and gawk in horror.' Her agitation slowly deflated. She'd missed the chance to catch an unguarded reaction. But his refusal to look made her defiant anger feel unnecessary.

'I made a mistake, yesterday. I don't want to repeat it. I have plans for today which don't involve arguing with you.'

She wobbled and had to grab his shoulder for balance. 'That was yesterday and I accepted your apology. Now take a look so I can sit down.'

'It feels perverted when you say it like that.'

'Only because it's a stupid hang-up between us. I believe you, okay? I believe you don't care what my legs look like. Can we get this over with?'

He turned, but it was to look first into her face. What he saw must have satisfied him and he dropped his gaze with a little nod. He inclined his head and studied her legs dispassionately. His eyes traced the long split on the calf of her good leg. It was raised and purplish. Both legs were pockmarked with gouges where her skin sagged. She had neat little surgery scars round the edge of the mottled stump and a skin graft scar on her thigh. He kept his emotion off his face. But as the inspection lengthened, his jaw tightened and his breath hitched.

'Okay, I'm done,' he said, clearing his throat. He patted the towel next to him and she sat down. He wrapped an arm round her neck as he'd done so many times before. But the tension in him was unmistakable. He didn't feel done.

'Don't just sit there and tremble, Javi. You're allowed a reaction. I know you like a cop-out, but I'd rather you say the wrong thing than nothing right now. A joke will do. Some flirting, maybe? I'm still me.'

He pressed a kiss to her forehead and she could feel his smile on her skin. 'You were right. It's different being confronted directly with what you went through. God, it's heart-breaking, Cara.'

She let his words sink in for a moment. Pity usually made her bristle. She didn't like having responsibility for other people's feelings. But with Javi, it was a relief to have it done. She nodded. 'You pass. B plus.'

'Good.' He pulled her closer to plant another kiss on her cheek.

'Why don't you call me any Spanish endearments any more? I'd even take mona at this point.'

He smiled, but it took him a long moment to answer. 'Your name feels like the word with the most suitable reverence.'

Her lips pursed and she wrinkled her nose. '"Reverence" is a bit much, isn't it? I'm just some girl you want to take to bed.'

He grinned. 'Some girl is sort of right. But I think you belong on a pedestal, rather than in my bed.'

She snorted. 'Urgh, I know those guys Simón Bolívar and Cristóbal Colón – whoever he is – seem to like it, but it looks uncomfortable to me.' She stretched. 'Your bed is sounding much better.'

He was disappointed when she fell asleep in the car on the drive back to Barranquilla, but he wasn't surprised. They'd spent the day hiking and enjoying the views of the sea and the mountains, finishing with an early dinner in the city of Santa Marta. They hadn't set out on the drive back until after nine. But he felt cheated of the last few minutes of fantasy.

He was annoyed by how much he wanted to cling to it. He

should have learned this lesson by now. His life was suspended between Barranquilla and Miami, trying to do his best by his family. The time with Bea had gone more smoothly than he'd hoped. He was at a loss when he thought about putting her back on the plane to Susana. He'd managed to keep his relationship with Cara out of the bedroom, although that achievement was feeling tenuous and hollow.

Feeling disappointment at returning to reality was fruitless and weak. Those words could describe long portions of his life. He was supposed to be breaking free of the pattern of avoidance. But disappointment was what he felt. And desire. The kisses on the beach had driven him crazy. Her lips were astonishingly perfect on his. He was ready to write a whole album of corny love ballads – something he'd never attempted – until he reminded himself that she hated his metaphors. Metaphors were all he had to offer.

At 10.30, his phone rang, jolting Cara from sleep. He saw his mother's name flash up and frowned. Unease swept through his chest. He swiped to connect the call on speaker, his hand not quite steady. His mother was sobbing and it took several moments of dread before he understood what had happened and dragged the car onto the shoulder where he could tremble safely. Bea had disappeared. His hands shook and his chest became concrete.

'Estoy allí tan pronto como pueda, mamá,' he said between heaving breaths and disconnected the call. He gripped the wheel and hollered the most vicious obscenities he could think of in Spanish, shoving the steering wheel with a final yell of, 'Fuck!' Cara was cowering, but he couldn't see beyond getting back to his daughter. He put the car into gear and they jerked back onto the road.

'Bea's gone,' he explained when the animal part of his brain disengaged for a moment. 'Her phone is going to voicemail. My mother doesn't know where she is.' And it was his fault. He didn't bother to listen for Cara's response. He stomped on the accelerator and to hell with the speed limit. He had to find her.

Half an hour later, they were approaching the bridge over the Magdalena river, when Cara cried for him to stop. Startled out of his single-minded urgency, he reacted with instinct and pulled onto the shoulder. She pushed open the passenger door, stumbled to her knees in the footwell and vomited onto the asphalt.

Her hacking retches ripped him open. He'd done this to her. And he would do it again – and again, and again. She didn't deserve to be dragged into this and he couldn't handle the crazy promises he imagined when he was with her. He opened his door to come round and help her, but she grabbed his arm and held him in the driver's seat.

'I'm done. Let's go.' She dragged herself back into the passenger seat and pulled the door shut. Her hands were shaking violently on the clasp of the seatbelt. As soon as he heard the click, he took off again. Once he was comfortably cruising, he reached behind the passenger seat and handed her a bottle of water. 'Thank you,' she said shakily. He didn't say anything. What could possibly help? He barely had the mental space to register her trembling or erratic breathing.

She jumped violently when her phone rang, but fumbled it out of her bag and connected the call. 'Hello, Daddy.' She winced at her father's obvious agitation. 'We're on our way back. Daddy, Bea's gone missing. Perhaps you could meet me at Javi's place in a taxi? I'll text you the address. Yes, I'm fine. Truly.' She disconnected the call as soon as possible and took a deep breath.

'Bea was staying at my parents' place. Maybe you should get him to pick you up from there.'

'Oh, of course.'

His brow furrowed. 'Unless...' He muttered something and grabbed his phone to call his mother back. 'It's across town and Bea doesn't have a key, but Mamá does. And I don't doubt Bea is capable of calling a cab.'

He felt the first glimmer of relief when his mother confirmed that her key to his house was missing. When he pulled up outside his house, he found Gordon already there. He didn't acknowledge Cara's father, but went straight for the gate. It was locked.

'Have you informed the police? I must say it is terribly irresponsible to leave your young daughter unprotected from any number of criminal elements who know how much you are worth. She'd be a prime target for kidnapping even in Miami, I imagine. Here, you're even more well-known and the kidnappers are... very experienced. I don't suppose the police have much of a success rate? I can make some calls for you. Perhaps we can get an investigator from the UK. There was one case I am familiar with—'

Javi forced down the blast of anger and terror and pushed past Gordon with a wordless grunt as soon as he'd got the gate open. The front door was locked, too, but he assured himself it didn't mean anything.

'Bea!' he yelled as soon as he was inside. '¿Estás aquí?' He heard a tap from the studio as soon as he stopped to listen. He burst through the door to find her sitting at the drumkit, sticks in hand, painstakingly beating out the rock pattern he'd shown her. He stumbled and collapsed into a chair. He rubbed a hand down his face and exhaled slowly. '¡Gracias a Dios!' he mumbled.

'What's up with you?'

His head sank against the wall and he laughed from deep in his chest. What was up with him? He was a chaotic mess of horrible emotion. Yes, Bea was okay and partially at fault, but he'd failed his own daughter. And he'd terrified Cara into puking out his car door. And he'd spent two days in a magic fantasy that wasn't real instead of building the foundations of his future.

He phoned his mother first, knowing she would be blaming herself. Then he held his head in his hands.

'Javi?' he heard Cara's voice from the hall. Trust her to still be too polite to enter his house uninvited, even when her voice was thick with strain. 'She's there?'

'Yes, she's here. Gordon can call off the Spec Ops.'

'Cara came home with you?' Bea asked. Her tone made him raise his head.

'We're going to go, now. The cab is waiting.'

'Okay,' he called back lamely. He gave Bea a pointed look until she started to squirm. 'We came straight here instead of taking Cara to her hotel – and I broke a few road rules – because Mamita didn't know what had happened to you.' Anger took its turn in his chest, but his anger was evenly split between himself and his daughter and it didn't remain dominant for long. 'If you didn't want me to go, you should have told me.'

'And make you give up your chance with Cara?'

'There is no chance with Cara. And I'm more concerned about my chance with you.'

'You don't need a chance with me. I can't choose my parents. I'm stuck with you.'

'And I got crazy lucky with you,' he said heatedly. 'I know I was an asshole to your mom for years and a shitty parent. But I want a chance at being more than the lousy guy who fathered you.'

'I didn't think parents were supposed to swear like that.'

'I'm upset, Bea. I shouldn't have left you. Gordon was convinced you were being held for ransom with a gun to your head! I was out of my mind!'

She studied him for a long moment while his heart continued to thud in his ears. He had to take her to the airport tomorrow. Had he been wrong that they'd built something important over the past two weeks?

She pursed her lips and poked out her chin. 'You know, Colombia is pretty safe these days, Dad.' Then she smiled and his emotions spewed in an exhausted heap on the floor. No wonder he'd never done a good job of being a parent. It was horrendous. She looked critically at his sagging form, then shrugged and picked up the sticks. 'I'm shit at this. Can you give me some help?'

He stared at her, a perplexed smile growing wider and wider until it was one stop short of goofy. This sharp, clever, generous girl was his daughter. And she'd asked for his help. It was the biggest day of his life. He picked himself up and walked over. He drew a stool close and reached round her to close his hands on hers. He paused, enjoying the flood of relief and the contentment of sitting behind a drumkit with his daughter.

'First, relax your hands and wrists. You have to dance the sticks off the skins, not bash them.' He helped her strike the snare a couple of times. 'You have to get this at the beginning and then it will come naturally. Now, foot on the pedal and keep the bass drum going. No matter what else you screw up, you have to keep it going.'

She bit her lip in concentration and he winced as she left pauses and struggled through the beat. But she established the pattern. The smile she gave him when she'd managed a few consecutive bars was worth the insult to his sense of rhythm. He would not screw this up.

19

'I'm just tired,' she lied outrageously to her father. Sheer force of will got Cara safely behind the door of her hotel room. Her chest hurt. Her stomach was gnawing on the rest of her body. Even forcing her eyes to stay open wasn't banishing the creeping memories of the crunch of metal and searing pain.

Her hotel room was out of focus. She'd clung to the image of her music studio, the muscle memory of playing the piano and had even resorted to the tedium of reciting times tables in her head as the car had hurtled back to Barranquilla. But she was shaking from the effort. She knew she should feel safe, but she didn't.

She grabbed for her medication with fumbling hands. She started the timer on her phone, impulsively setting it to play 'Nostalgia' instead of her usual piano concerto when the half hour was up. Then she lay down on the bed in a little ball and stared at the numbers ticking away on the screen. The edges of her vision glowed red with the shadowed fear of blood-soaked memories and the taste of a panic spiral, where she worried about the worry, terrified she wouldn't be able to get back out of bed.

Without the familiar safe space of her studio, without a piano, she focused on the numbers on her phone screen until she could force in a deep breath. Muttering 'in' and 'out' through her trembling lips, she reduced her perceptions down to numbers and breaths.

Memories clawed at her, a mush of images that might or might not be real. Her memory of the accident was more of a haunting than a recall, but the images of blood and missing limbs and the faces of her mother and brother felt real, even if they weren't in focus. That night, sending fear shooting right through her chest, was the lurking image of something else: Javi in a car wreck.

Her jaw shook and bile rose up her throat again and she instinctively squeezed her eyes shut, only to force them open again immediately after the image sharpened behind her eyelids. Gripping her phone in a shaking fist, she struggled to maintain her breathing exercises and watched the minutes tick down.

When she had more control of her throat, she started to sing, her voice croaking and weak. Singing forced her to regulate her breathing and cut through the oppressive silence. Favourite Beatles songs usually came to her lips when she couldn't think of anything to sing. Hey Jude came out first, starting with the 'na na' part until she could form words. When she'd sung it through twice, the chorus of 'Nostalgia' spilled out. Her half-lines sounded poignant and broken in the silence of the hotel room.

> *Light the candles*
> *Make a noise*
> *Nothing stays the same*
> *We dance so we don't cry.*

Listening with complete focus to the cracked sound of her voice and thinking about the complex layers of the song, she was startled when her phone lit up and the recording started to play. She took a quick inventory of her vital signs, deciding to embrace the relief as the medication settled over her thoughts.

Her face was dripping with tears and snot and the grime from the day. But it was over. She was okay. She could believe it. As the song played in her heart as well as her ears, it also made her aware of the odd appearance of Javi at her deepest, most difficult time. Perhaps it was because he'd been driving, but she suspected it was because the sense of him had lodged somewhere inside her.

She recorded a video note on the mental health app she used to keep track of her progress, knowing she'd want to remind her future self that she could manage, even without the comforts and routines of home. Then she sat under the shower, washing off sand and dirt in the company of more pleasant memories.

She was puzzled to realise that she wouldn't change anything about the last two days, even though it had led to a traumatic night. She suspected Javi didn't feel the same, but parental responsibility wasn't something she could resent him for.

When she crawled back into her room and pulled herself onto the bed, she noticed she had a text on her phone. It could only be from Javi.

I'm so sorry.

It was all he wrote but was enough to summon the warmth that had burrowed into her stomach at Tayrona.

It's okay.

She was surprised to find it was true. He'd driven erratically without regard for her panic in cars, but it had been the right thing to do. And she was recovering. She had to learn to trust that her world would keep turning even when she feared it wouldn't.

It's not okay. I feel terrible for what I put you through.

You're not responsible for my mental health. You ARE responsible for your daughter.

He didn't reply immediately, so she lay down and composed an 'I'm going to sleep' message. But before she could press send, his reply appeared.

You are always so wise. I miss you. And I know it's the wrong thing to say.

She rolled onto her back and sighed. She'd been trying to ignore the same ache inside her. But it was the wrong thing to say. They shouldn't put anything into words. Her departure would hurt enough as it was. She decided ignoring it was for the best.

Can I come with you to see Bea off at the airport tomorrow?

Of course. I'll pick you up at two.

She hesitated, knowing she should say goodnight and go to sleep. But she couldn't stop herself from asking:

Are YOU okay?

When he took a long time to reply, she smiled to herself. She would normally expect a quick, flippant answer. But she suspected turning into a protective father today was such a profound experience that even Javi couldn't make light of it.

Yeah…

Was all he sent at first.

...?

She prompted.

I can understand why I used to run away from this shit. But yes, I'm okay. Bea is okay. We're okay.

Okay :-). Good night, Javi.

She turned her phone over on the bedside table so she couldn't see the notifications. If she kept texting Javi right now, she would quickly be telling him she missed him, too. Luckily self-discipline was her strong point.

* * *

Cara checked her phone when she woke up after an exhausted stupor of more than eleven hours.

Are you awake? Can I order you some breakfast?

For a second, she thought the message was from Javi and she smiled to herself before her brain kicked into gear and she realised it was from her father. She hadn't decided whether to confront him for his prejudiced behaviour to Javi the night before. Even in the panic, she'd been ashamed of him.

'I'm awake, now. Yes, breakfast would be nice, thanks,' she sent with a sigh. She pulled a brush through her knotted hair while she waited for him to appear. He no doubt had his suspicions about her mental health and wouldn't be far, plus the idea of him leaving the hotel to explore Barranquilla on his own almost made her laugh.

'Sweetheart, how are you this morning?' He enveloped her in a hug that loosened quite a few of the chinks in her resentment.

'I'm doing okay, Daddy. The drive back wasn't great, but I managed it. I'm quite proud of myself.'

'That's wonderful, wonderful.' He pressed his palms together. 'And you've got today to recover before our flight tomorrow, so we'll soon be home.'

'Tomorrow?' She resisted when Gordon tried to lead her to the armchair to sit down.

'I changed our flights this morning in the wake of this horrible debacle. There's no need for you to stay and talk to this TV station in the capital, especially since the song is already number one in this country.'

'It wasn't a horrible debacle. Bea is fine. I'm fine. It's only the worst-case-scenario you imagined that was a debacle. How do you think Javi felt to hear you suggest that Bea had been kidnapped?'

'Chastened, I hope. A father doesn't leave his daughter alone to face unknown dangers.'

'Daddy, he left Bea with her grandparents in his hometown. Almost every parent would do that without a second thought. He was afraid when he heard she was gone – very afraid. And you'll be happy to know I'm sure he blamed himself, too. All you did with your ignorant suggestions was upset him and scare me!'

'I couldn't be happier to be wrong in this case, but I wasn't making up horror stories. My concerns were based in statistics. And I cannot approve of his behaviour.'

'His behaviour has been above reproach, Daddy.'

The long silence was a familiar tactic of her father's. 'I'm not blind, Cara. It's for the best if we leave. Think about it: a few extra days of rest at home, a day together in London to go Christmas shopping. I'll keep the holiday days. You'll have me to spoil you.'

But she wouldn't have Javi. Her heart was protesting so loudly she had to carefully modulate her voice to make sure she didn't betray her agitation. 'I appreciate the thought, but I'm not going home, yet. Friday will be soon enough. We'll have a few days after I get back to spend together before Christmas.'

Gordon's mouth thinned. 'You're worrying me, Cara.'

'That's not my intention.'

'This is not a professional obligation. You're involved with this man.' The way he said 'this man' made her jaw clench. 'As a father, I can't stand here and let him take advantage of you.'

'No one's taking advantage of me. I can stand up for myself. And I want to go to the concert.'

'I, of all people, know how hard you've fought to be your own woman. But don't you see the position you're putting yourself in? He can't be trusted to look after you.'

'In what way do I need looking after?'

He eyed her as though she should know the answer to her own question and her heart sank as her suspicion grew. 'You are extremely lucky to have got through the horrifying experience last night, but I imagine it was a close-run thing. You need to take care of yourself, Cara. What if you have a relapse? What if you can't cope?'

Tears pricked behind her eyes. Her own father didn't trust her ability to cope. The bleakness of the eighteen months after the accident loomed in a dark corner. She could summon the memories easily – the grief, the will to fail, the terror of the future and the lack of control. But it was a familiar enemy and her father didn't know how many times she had defeated it in the past ten years.

'I can't accept that. I won't. Do you know what? Last night, rushing back here in a panic, I thought I would die so many times I

vomited. But in the end, all I lost was the contents of my stomach.'
She had a flash of memory from Javi's terrace on Key Biscayne and
warmth flooded her. More than ever, she wanted to remember
every instant she'd spent in his company.

'He put you through that.'

'He was doing what any parent would do. And I didn't fall off
some kind of psychological cliff edge. It's not always easy, but I'm
not going to miss out on life because I have to manage my mental
health!'

'Listen to yourself. Your infatuation for this man is clouding
your judgement. Your life is in Europe, where you have friends and
family and an album coming out. This isn't life. Do you see your
future in some dingy South American city playing stepmother
because you fancy yourself in love? Let me tell you, that is an illu-
sion that would quickly shatter.'

Cara gaped at her father. She was familiar with his veiled criti-
cism, his indulgent comments that unconsciously belittled her
achievements, his stubborn conviction that he was right. But she
couldn't remember a time he'd so openly criticised her. He was
more afraid than she'd realised. And she accepted with slow understanding that he had reason to be afraid – because she was in love.

The knowledge stole across her heart with silent steps. She
loved Javi. He wasn't perfect, but love obviously didn't care, because
it had grown wild with little encouragement.

The sappy love songs she'd never liked began to make more
sense. But it wasn't the neat strike of a bullet or the stab of cupid's
arrow. It was all of her internal organs rebelling against her brain in
a consuming fever. It was a ghastly metaphor, but how else could
she explain how she felt? It was wonderful and humbling and
awful.

She couldn't stop the laugh when more metaphors flew into her
mind. She wished she could tell Javi, but her father was right about

more than her feelings. Javi had been diligent with his warnings that he didn't take love seriously. Just because he was sorting his life out, it didn't mean that would change. But there was no way she would miss out on her last four days with him. And if she could get up the courage, they would be four days to carry with her through the rest of her life.

'Daddy, please listen. I am not going home until Friday. I am not going to change my mind.'

'Well, I have twenty-four hours to change it for you. I let you go off into the jungle and look what happened.'

'You haven't even asked if I had a nice time.'

'It doesn't matter. I know enough.'

She laughed bitterly. 'You know enough to come to the wrong conclusion. Please, if you can't listen to me, then can I at least have some peace?'

'Do you see what he's done? We don't argue like this, Cara. You and I, we stand together.' *Now your mother and Crispin are gone...* The half of the sentence that went unsaid drained the fight out of her. 'Are you seeing him today?'

She refused to let his words feel like a reprimand. 'Yes. I'm going with them to the airport at two. Bea is going back to Miami today.'

'I'll expect you back for dinner.'

When he turned to go, she didn't resist giving him a dirty look behind his back that reminded her of Bea. Her heart was in deep trouble and leaving was going to hurt. But she couldn't muster any regret.

20

She was waiting outside the hotel at two o'clock and rushed to the car when Javi pulled up, forcing herself inside before she questioned the wisdom of driving again so soon. Bea started to open her door to move into the back, but Cara waved her back in. She was nervous of what Javi might see in her body language.

'I'm happy to sit in the back.'

He turned to look at her as she fastened her seatbelt and she flushed with helpless longing. She loved the way his dark eyes regarded her so intently. He had his hair back in a messy ponytail and he was wearing another soft t-shirt that made her fingers restless with wanting.

'Sleep okay?' he asked so quietly that she realised it was his way of asking if she'd recovered. She nodded.

'Javi said I should apologise to you,' Bea said, turning to her with a piercing look as Javi pulled out of the hotel drive.

Cara took a breath to deny it, but she paused in thought. 'Perhaps I should have told you sooner that I have an anxiety disorder. You couldn't have known that your decision would affect me, so I'll accept the apology.'

'He told me you puked. I am sorry.'

Cara smiled and felt tears behind her eyes again. She liked Bea – too much. 'I puke a lot. The anxiety goes straight to my stomach.'

'Is that why you're so skinny? I thought you starved yourself or something.'

'Bea!' Javi's jaw dropped.

'I suppose that's a reasonable assumption. Bea's lucky she's healthy and eats well, but it's good to be aware of the spirals we can fall into about our body image.' She smiled as Javi looked at Bea in horrified awareness.

'You're old enough to worry about that shit?'

'I'm a girl. Of course I am.'

His eyes met Cara's in the rear-view mirror in helpless dread. She took pity on him and continued her explanation. 'I exercise because it clears my mind. It's a kind of therapy. But skinny has always been my shape. To be honest, since I lost my foot, I haven't thought about it much. Having an amputation and lots of scars defines my appearance more than my weight.'

'Is that why you always wear pants, even when it's ninety degrees?'

'I wasn't keeping it from you on purpose.'

'I get it, Cara. You do everything right.'

Javi looked like he wanted to scold her again, but Cara cut him off. 'She's not saying anything you haven't said to me, Javi.' She turned to Bea. 'You're right, I don't like to make mistakes and struggle to acknowledge it when I do. It runs in the family, unfortunately. Do you want me to go back to the hotel? I'm sorry, I should have thought you'd want some time alone with Javi before you go. I was only thinking of how I wanted to say goodbye.'

Bea lifted her gaze on the last word. *Goodbye. Did it mean forever?* 'I want to say goodbye, too,' she said quietly. She eyed Javi. 'And maybe Dad will need a hug when I get on the plane.' Cara avoided looking in the rear-view mirror in case he caught her blush.

'I'll definitely need a hug before you get on the plane, gordita. So brace yourself.'

'I've been hugging people all day,' she groaned.

'My family came to say goodbye,' Javi explained.

The airport was busy with pre-Christmas traffic – large families with enormous suitcases shuffling through queues, tapping their feet to salsa-style music with festive bells, interspersed with 'Jingle Bells' and Mariah Carey.

Javi was busy arranging for the stewards to escort Bea through security and onto her flight. He was on the phone to Susana much of the time, answering her many questions with more patience than Cara expected. She didn't understand the conversation, but she did understand the emphatic, 'Gracias, Susi. Mil gracias,' at the end and then her heart was doing somersaults in her chest for him all over again.

Her gaze dropped from his dear, familiar form to find Bea studying her curiously. 'You've got it bad.'

Cara started to laugh, but Javi was finishing the call and approaching them. 'Have I ever,' she muttered. 'But...' Her look clouded.

'I get it. You're going home anyway.' The excuse felt unsatisfying, but it was better than Bea leaving with the impression that she and Javi had a relationship.

She hugged Bea tightly goodbye, more upset than she'd expected. A tear escaped, but she wiped it away quickly and Javi didn't see. Bea noticed and gave her one more quick hug, which only encouraged the other tears to continue their mutinous gathering.

She tried her best to look away as Javi and Bea said goodbye.

They, at least, would see each other again after Christmas. But she knew it wouldn't be easy for him to give her up.

'Be good, Dad,' she said.

'I will. You, too, mija.' He said something more in Spanish that made her smile. Cara was concerned that she was the one who would need a hug after this. They were both so precious and she was a wreck.

He came to stand next to her as Bea disappeared through security with a steward. He stared after her, not moving, until long after she'd gone and the awareness of their overlapping emotions grew hard to ignore.

She heard him haltingly exhale. 'So,' he began, his voice a rough rumble, 'about that hug.'

She turned to him comically quickly and threw her arms round him. His arms wound round her and tightened into a warm cocoon. She pressed her cheek to his shoulder and breathed. The sensations were heightened, knowing that she loved him, knowing that cold reality was only a few days away.

'I'm supposed to be sad about putting my daughter on a plane, but now all I can think about is how much I missed touching you.'

'You are sad about putting Bea on a plane. This doesn't change anything between you and her.'

He cocked his head to look at her face. 'You might be right. Beautiful, wise and addictive to touch.'

'And you are still a flirt,' she said, flustered and mixed up. She couldn't deflect his banter so well any more.

'I know. And you probably don't like the addiction metaphor.'

'I hadn't noticed.'

'You're losing touch.'

She nodded ruefully. She was losing touch. She was losing touch with reality and if she wasn't careful, she would let enjoyment drift into hope.

His arms tightened round her and he leaned down slowly. Her breathing went berserk. She was desperate for him to kiss her. She turned her face eagerly up to his. He did kiss her, but it was the briefest press of his lips to hers – a short, affectionate caress that satisfied nothing and left her entirely too worked up.

'If you call that a kiss, then you're the one who's losing touch,' she muttered.

'You want a real kiss?' His voice was breathy and incredulous.

'What does it look like?' She glanced up at him.

'My lucky day,' he murmured and leaned down to improve on the first kiss. It was liquid fire from the moment his lips touched hers a second time. The beguiling pressure of his mouth stole her breath. She felt his silent groan under her hands. He clamped a hand round the back of her neck and opened his mouth against hers.

She was pressed tight to his body, their breath and tongues a desperate tangle, but she wasn't close enough. She grabbed for his neck to pull herself up – and was immediately aware that he was awkwardly aroused and they were making out in the airport.

'Oh, God, I'm sorry,' she whispered. He just laughed, his chest rising and falling under her palms.

'Next move is yours, querida,' he said, his voice low. 'My answer would be different this time.'

His words tingled across her skin, but she remembered her father and grimaced, watching in dismay as his smile faded. 'I have to go back to the hotel. My father is upset with me. I'm upset with him, too, but I am supposed to have dinner with him. He wants to go back to the UK as soon as possible.' She paused, peering up at him through a wince. 'Will you come?'

He laughed again, but it was humourless. 'You want me to come and have dinner with you and your father?'

'Okay, it was stupid of me to ask. I'm sorry. You don't have to deal with him, especially after the way he's treated you.'

'Don't worry about that. He's your father. He's nothing to me.'

Cara wished the words didn't pinch. His daughter had quickly meant a lot to her. She was in over her head, but she couldn't go back, now. 'Either way, what he said was terribly rude and ignorant and it's important to me to apologise for him.'

'Apology accepted. I'll take you back to the hotel.'

Her heart sank when she saw her father emerge from the hotel when they pulled up. So much for working out where she stood with Javi. He looked like he wanted to knock his head against the steering wheel. She'd been so stupid to ask him to have dinner with them. Of course he didn't want to spend time with her father right now.

Javi opened his door with a reluctant jerk and stepped out to greet her father with a handshake.

'Your daughter is headed safely back to her mother, I assume?' Gordon's face was politely blank, as though he thought he was genuinely making small talk and not insulting Javi.

'The flight left without a problem.'

'I think it's best if we take a cab to the airport tomorrow – leave you to get on with things.'

Cara rushed round the car to correct Javi's misconception, but he turned to her with such a dark look that she stopped up short. 'Tomorrow?' he asked, a challenge in his voice.

She shook her head, but her father got in first. 'Yes, our flight back to London is at eleven. I thought it best if we brought forward our departure in light of the situation.'

'What situation is that?'

'Cara has had a panic attack. She should have the opportunity to recover at her own pace rather than being dragged round this country for questionable purposes. Don't you agree that her health is the most important thing to consider?'

'Perhaps you should have considered it before you filled her head with your own fears. You should have seen her. I was driving like a maniac and she just sat there and dealt with it. She puked at the side of the road and then told me to keep driving. That is a woman who can handle whatever she wants. I've been asking myself this whole time whether her brain is in better shape than mine. At least she knows how to cut through the crap and deal with the truth. If she wants to go home then I get that. But she has aced this trip.'

She wished she'd had the chance to pull out her phone and film him for her video diary. She couldn't take him back into real life, but she would take his words, his conviction. Until then she'd never realised it was possible to fall in love all over again with the same person.

She didn't let his angry posture put her off this time. She grasped his hand when he reached for the car door. His nostrils flared as he looked at their clasped hands. She had so much she wanted to say to him, but she had to deal with her father. 'What time is the flight to Cali?'

His brow furrowed. 'Two.'

'Don't cancel my seat.'

'Still deciding?' She could tell he was going to some effort to keep his voice mild.

She shook her head. 'I'm coming with you. Dad just hasn't accepted it, yet.' He exhaled unsteadily and she wanted to raise his hand to her lips and prove herself. But with her father watching, all she could do was will him to see the truth in her eyes. He pursed his lips and nodded. A moment later, he drove away without acknowledging her father.

'Let's go inside. I need a drink. Do you think they have that whisky from the other night?'

'Old Parr,' she said with a faint smile. 'I'm sure they do. Are you very angry?'

'I don't know any more. Javier was angry.'

Cara tucked her arm into his and they walked together to the hotel bar. When he was armed with a whisky and Cara sat behind a mojito, they scrutinised each other silently.

'I'm not going with you tomorrow.'

His shoulders slumped – slightly. The Honourable Gordon Poignton QC did not slouch. 'I realise that, sweetheart. But I'm your father and I cannot happily watch you walk into an affair that will break your heart.'

She took a sip of her drink and smiled ruefully. 'Your warning has come far too late, unfortunately. But I'm going in with my eyes open.'

'You may think that, but life has a way of ripping everything out from under you.'

'Oh, Daddy.'

'Don't "oh Daddy" me, Cara. It's you I'm worried about.'

'As I said, I don't know what could be ripped out from under me except what I already know I've lost.'

'What's that?'

'My heart. Oh, it's a stupid way to word it. I mean I know I can't have him the way I want. I mean I love him anyway.'

'He doesn't deserve it.'

'You've never given him a chance. That's called prejudice, Dad. Didn't you hear him? He's seen all the stages of my anxiety. He's seen the stump and the scars. And he can still say what he said to you. I hope one day I'll find someone else who can say that. But for now, I'm going to take the next few days if that's all I've got.' She swallowed, preparing her next sentence. 'I don't like having to defend myself. And Javi definitely shouldn't have had to defend me. I have a disorder, but I'm not ill. And I'm increasingly confident that I can manage it.'

He didn't look at her for a long moment and when he did, his expression was unexpectedly wobbly. 'You may be recovering from the accident, sweetheart, but I never will. I lost my wife of twenty-three years and my son. I had to watch as the doctors put my daughter back together. Then there was the horror of what was going on in your mind. I couldn't even see what was wrong, let alone help you.'

'You did help me. Without you, I wouldn't have the life I have today. You did everything you could.' She would have leaped off her stool and wrapped her arms round him if she hadn't known very well that her father did not do public displays of affection.

He sighed. 'But you're right. Just because I nursed you back to health, doesn't give me the right to dictate what you do with the life that was saved.' He frowned. 'I suppose even at home you aren't safe from a broken heart.'

'Thank you. I'm sorry we've argued so much. It means a lot to me that you are prepared to trust me. And you can be certain that, when this all goes wrong, I'll run straight back to you.'

'I will be waiting. Just don't expect me to ever forgive him.'

21

What was wrong with him? These were the last few days he had with Cara and he kept screwing up. She had hugged Bea goodbye with genuine affection and trembled beautifully in his arms. She was all grace and honesty, and she kissed like he meant something to her. And he'd recoiled as usual from the difficult part. She'd asked him to come with her to dinner and he'd flaked. When he couldn't avoid meeting Gordon, he'd insulted the man.

Worse than his behaviour were his emotions. He'd reeled from the fantasy happiness of Tayrona to terror and self-recrimination. Then it had been happiness again when she'd asked him to kiss her, then more self-recrimination for not wanting to get involved. Under it all was an emotion he should have named long ago; he knew it so well: fear. He was afraid of how he would feel when she left. He was afraid of how she would feel. And he was afraid he would make everything worse because he didn't know what he was doing. All the songs he knew about cowardice had a different meaning now he had an idea of what was at stake.

At that moment, he was afraid she wasn't coming to the airport. He should have texted her last night. He should have given her the option of pulling out and going home with her father. They were finally travelling alone. The kisses kept getting out of hand. He'd booked two hotel rooms, of course, but they should probably stop pretending that sex wasn't going to happen. He didn't know which of them would regret it the most.

He saw her before she saw him. She was pulling her suitcase behind her – a reminder that she wasn't coming back to Barranquilla. He enjoyed a long moment watching her: the way she flung her plait over her shoulder; the shape of her wrist, turned as she held the handle of the suitcase; her straight back and narrow shoulders that were tirelessly determined.

Impressions of their time together flashed in his memory as he looked at her, taking him right back to the day she'd put him in his place in a fitness studio in London. Now he had three days left and he would not spend them second-guessing this.

'Hey!' He waved her over. She smiled when she saw him, and he enveloped her in a hug. What he'd intended to be a kiss on the cheek turned into an aching kiss on the lips.

'Hey,' she replied, clearing her throat.

He grinned. 'We need to go.'

It was a short flight and took longer to supervise the transport of his three guitars than to take off in Barranquilla and land in Cali.

'You don't travel with a band?'

'Not this time. This concert is a publicity obligation for a radio station and not part of a tour. I tour with a band. But I know these guys and they know me. What about you?'

'I've got band auditions at the beginning of January for my tour.'

'Need a drummer?' he joked, but the flash of dismay in her eyes warned him not to broach the subject of the future, even casually. 'You're just touring Europe, right?'

She nodded. 'We'll have to see how well the next single goes before planning anything transatlantic. Which reminds me,

Freddie called this morning. He was contacted on the outside chance that "Nostalgia" will be Christmas number one – that's a thing in the UK. The song that's number one for the Christmas week gets more airplay and usually more sales. I'm sure they'll contact your manager, too. A UK television station wants a performance of the Christmas number one and an interview for a live variety show on Christmas morning.'

'In London?' She nodded and he wrestled with the pinch of hope in his chest. It wasn't the desire for the song to reach number one in the UK, which should have been his ambition. It was the thought of seeing her again. 'But what are our chances?'

'Low,' she said. 'Getting from number eight to number one would be an unusual jump.'

He nodded. 'Too bad. I like London.' *And I like you.*

Cara had her face glued to the window as the cab drove them to their hotel. 'Cali is a bigger city than Barranquilla, isn't it? It feels bigger.'

'Twice the size,' he nodded. 'And there are more historic buildings. But Cali is mainly famous for music – salsa in particular. I'm sorry we're not going to have time to look round much. I know you like salsa.' He flashed her a grin.

She studied him. 'I wouldn't ask you to show me round a city that makes you uncomfortable.'

He crossed his arms over his chest. 'I wouldn't take you to the hotel where Alejo was killed.'

'Javi,' she scolded, 'stop pretending you don't care.'

He pursed his lips and glanced out the window. 'Maybe I'm sick of holding onto it.'

'Do you... were you planning...?'

'What?'

'Are you going to perform "Nostalgia"? Do you want me to perform with you?'

'I don't think I could avoid it – not that I want to – and yes, perform with me,' he said, qualifying himself immediately, 'if you want to.'

'I want to. We need to perform the song here. Maybe it'll help you let the cement dry.' He gave her a narrow look, but she pressed on. 'Don't be such a sceptic. Music can be truly cathartic and this song...' She waited until he looked her in the eye and he couldn't escape her point. This song had had more of an impact than he'd ever imagined. 'It's made me want to reclaim Christmas. You did that.'

When he would have protested to stop the pride heating inside him, she deflected it by pressing a quick kiss onto his lips and draining the fight out of him. He caught her chin and repeated the kiss.

When he drew back, she opened her eyes and he could see when her brain kicked back into gear. She took a deep breath and licked her lips. 'I assume you booked two hotel rooms,' she said quietly. He nodded. Her gaze slipped from his. 'Well, here's a warning that you won't be sleeping in yours.'

The breath hissed from his lungs. Was that the sexiest thing a woman had ever said to him? It sure felt like it. Images flooded his mind with anticipation: her hair tousled and flowing across the pillow; holding her close without the barrier of clothing. 'You're making me want to blow off the concert.'

'It starts late, doesn't it?'

His ability to think shut down. He gripped her face in his hands and lay his forehead against hers. 'I want you so much, Cara.'

'That's good,' she said, her voice unsteady. 'Because I had no idea how to broach the subject.'

'You did perfectly.'

She smiled and he couldn't resist settling his lips on hers again.

'I didn't realise simply telling a man he was going to sleep with me worked.'

He gave her a wry look. 'It only works on me. I'm a sucker for you.'

* * *

Cara was impatient, but he enjoyed thwarting her attempts to speed things up. Fast and hard was for after the concert when he knew he'd be pumped and desperate for her. This was better. He stilled her hands on her clothes, pulled his t-shirt off and pressed her hands to his chest. They were back at the volcano, back on the beach in Tayrona, together the way they were meant to be.

She was eager and nervous, like that first kiss back in London, and he was charmed all over again. He pressed a hand over her breast, his palm chafing the nipple. She arched her body into his hand, her expression helpless with pleasure.

'I have wanted these since the first time I saw you. It's like they're so small they have to compensate with enthusiasm.' He gripped her ribcage with both hands and teased her nipples with his thumbs. He tugged off her shirt to reveal her small camisole bra and stripped that off, too. He dropped to his knees with a groan and lifted his mouth to her breast. 'So beautiful,' he murmured, unsure if she heard him. She was tottering in his arms, her breathing laboured.

She grasped his shoulders. 'I can't stay standing. And you need to take your jeans off and your ponytail out.' He stood with a grin.

When she turned to the bed, he tugged on her plait. 'Are you leaving this in?' She slipped the elastic from the end and shook it out, her hair falling down the smooth lines of her back. 'Better,' he said with a rumble of approval. She clambered into the middle of the bed and turned expectantly. He held her gaze as he undid his jeans, loving the burn of desire in her eyes.

When he pulled his hair tie out, her smile was laced with affection and he was completely done in. He dived onto the bed and into her arms. He lost himself in kisses that promised the world. He nibbled her neck while she sat up to take off her prosthesis. When she mumbled something about it, he cut her off with a kiss and ran his hand up her toned thigh. His fingertips brushed the bumps of her skin graft scar and his hand tightened. This beautiful, resilient woman trusted him. He had permission to touch her. He appreciated the gift for what it was, touching her with vulnerable reverence. She opened her body to him and he loved her with such slow, aching tenderness he could have wept.

Cara did weep. She sobbed. As soon as it was over, she gasped and sobbed and pressed her hands to her eyes. 'Oh, God, I'm so sorry,' she sniffed. 'That shouldn't have been so easy.'

He awkwardly disposed of the condom and raced back, leaning back on the headboard and hauling her into his arms. He pressed a kiss into her hair. 'Don't apologise. Maybe it was just because we waited so long. I'm just glad you're not puking.'

She eyed him, but there was a smile hidden behind and she slapped his arm in reprimand. 'You might not want to joke about that. The first time I tried to have sex, I puked.' He tightened his arms round her as she paused in thought. 'You get it.'

He shook his head and tangled his fingers fondly in her hair. 'Lucky guess. But I do know you well enough to be sure you'll tell me if I did something wrong to make you cry.'

'Nothing wrong,' she said softly and lay back against his chest. 'Just a bit too right. But I don't suppose you need any compliments.'

'It's not me, Cara. It's us.'

'Do you want me to start blubbering again?'

'Save it for Friday, hmm? I prefer moaning to blubbering.' His hand crept up her torso to settle just below her breast and the little hitch in her breath made him smile.

'Friday...' she repeated, her tone flat.

'Shh, forget I said it,' he murmured, his lips on her neck. 'Wait, are you thinking we shouldn't have done this?'

'No,' she chuckled. 'Although I was worried you might. I don't suppose any of your other... mujeres... cried after sex.'

He grimaced. 'I'm not thinking about anyone else right now.' She accepted his comment and leaned back again. He held her tight. 'We can ditch the concert, right? Stay here all night?'

'I came all this way to see a concert from Javi Félix! It had better be good.'

* * *

Cara caught herself humming as she sat off-stage watching Javi prepare for the show. She was amused and gratified that they'd tumbled into bed the first instant they were alone. She'd never been so relaxed in a concert venue, even on other occasions when she'd only performed one song. She'd never had sex before a concert, either. She was blissfully languid and hopelessly fixated on him. There was nothing heavy about how she felt. If anything, resisting had become the burden. He caught her watching him several times and, as soon as he had the chance, he approached and dropped a lingering kiss on her lips.

One of the band members said something when he returned that made him frown, but she refused to let reality intrude. They would perform this one concert as lovers, and she had the feeling it would be unforgettable.

The band was liberal with the liquor as the support act played. She couldn't avoid sharing one foul-tasting shot with the rest of them and noticed that even Javi gagged as the band hooted with laughter.

'Viche,' he said with a grimace. 'The local liquor. Give me Old Parr any day, or even aguardiente.' The band produced a bottle of rum and Javi accepted a tumbler. He sipped it slowly.

'What is it they keep saying when they talk about me?' she asked. 'Vay-ha or something.'

He smiled and nudged her shoulder with his. 'Vieja. They're teasing me for not drinking and calling you my old lady.'

'This is you not drinking?'

He shrugged apologetically. 'I told you I'm not very professional. Lots of times I've been drunk by the end of a concert.'

'Don't hold back for my sake,' she said with a frown.

He pressed an absent kiss to her forehead and stroked his hand down her arm. 'I'm happy to have the excuse to break my bad habits. And you have given me a very good excuse.' Her cheeks heated and she pushed his hand away.

As she expected the band cat-called and applauded. 'Why are we never alone?' Javi laughed and planted an unapologetic kiss on her lips.

In the buzz after the support act finished, his energy spiked. His preparations were simple in comparison to the psychological hoops Cara had to jump through to force herself on stage. He tuned all three guitars one more time and grasped for one of the acoustics. He played a few bars of something pulsing and rhythmic, his fingers alternately strumming a chord and picking a riff. Then he looked up and flashed her a smile that was full-strength adrenaline.

'Do I get a kiss for luck?'

She laughed and approached slowly. She framed his face in her hands and leaned up to kiss him over the guitar. 'You don't need luck.' He kissed her again and she snuck her hands round his head to steal his hair tie. She grinned mischievously when his hair fell round his shoulders. 'I like the wild look,' she shrugged.

'Good to know,' he said, his voice low. 'See you in a few songs.' And he strode onto the stage without any fanfare. He didn't need it. The crowd cheered and he used the guitar to build up the atmosphere, alternately playing a few chords and calling out to the crowd.

Cara peered out from off-stage, engrossed in the performance. He played and sang, he put the guitar down and danced cumbia to enthusiastic wolf-whistles, pretending to remember where he was and switching to salsa steps for the whooping crowd. His voice alone was enough to fill the venue, low and rasping or soaring powerfully. The crowd sang along with the songs and he enjoyed their enthusiasm. He was so compelling Cara didn't have time to worry about her impending performance. The stage manager reminded her during the song before she was due to go on. But this time there was anticipation running through her veins instead of just dread.

When the song finished, Javi started speaking, but stopped suddenly and said, 'You guys speak English, right?' The crowd cheered. He paused with a cheeky smile. 'You know what's coming, don't you?' The crowd started to cheer before he finished repeating himself in Spanish. He glanced off-stage and held her gaze.

'It is my honour to welcome to the stage the unique, the beautiful and the ass-kicking Cara Poignton!' He raised his hands above his head to clap and she strode onto the stage as steadily as she could. The cheering was wild and piercing and lifted her spirit until she wondered if she could dance on the ceiling.

'Uh, hi guys,' she waved and the cheer rose again. She felt Javi laughing at her, but she was so happily overwhelmed she didn't mind realising what a rookie performer she was. She grinned at Javi and then looked back into the crowd. '¡Te amo Colombia!'

'Woo!' she heard Javi joining in the cheer of the crowd. A moment later, he began the improvisation he used to settle the crowd before the first verse of 'Nostalgia'. His fingers moved effortlessly over the strings. When he started to sing, the enthralling melody of the first verse, the words that admitted mistakes and asked for grace echoed round the venue and reverberated in the crowd.

She pulled her microphone from the stand and moved nearer to him. When the rhythm built, she moved her hips and clapped over the handle of the microphone, watching the crowd do the same. In the last line of the verse, singing about love always looking back, he stared at her, his gaze intent as the instruments built up to the chorus.

It was impossible to interpret the feelings behind his passionate look, but her body responded – her heart responded – and it flowed through her voice in their duet in the chorus. He sang the verse about the brilliance of Christmas reunions directly to the audience. She would not have left his side for anything as he wound up the dynamic to return to the chorus.

Just before the bridge, he swung his guitar behind him and signalled for the band to keep playing. Sensing what he had planned, she pressed her microphone back into the stand and went eagerly into his arms to dance across the stage, slipping into the choreography that had first brought them together and taking his cues to add a dose of spontaneous joy in the music.

The band responded by slipping into salsa music as he swung her round to thrilling cheers from the audience. She grinned and hung on for the ride, dancing close to him the most natural thing.

He drew her close, his arm high round her back and his face inches from hers. Silence descended over the stage and the crowd as the band waited for Javi to lead them back in. But he just stared at her. She thought he might kiss her. She thought she might kiss him and to hell with the awkward questions later.

Instead he pressed his forehead to hers for one gentle moment and returned to the microphone. He spoke slowly, his eyes still on hers and a smile on his face. 'Un beso – one kiss – nunca es suficiente.' The crowd cheered before he could translate the last half for her benefit, but she caught the idea.

He leaned back from the microphone to call out the first line of the bridge: 'Dance in the streets!' And the band came back in with the minimal, rhythmic accompaniment. Cara grabbed for her microphone and took her place next to Javi, grasping his hand as she sang about her interrupted memories and he finally owned up to his mixed feelings about his brother's death.

He threaded his fingers through hers as he took a breath to sing the line that had never been meant for her: 'Mi corazón sigue latiendo por ti.' She knew he meant his heart kept beating for his brother and his country, but the urgent look on his face that night was something new. She clung to his hand and sang the line with him. She knew it so well; she didn't even hesitate over the Spanish.

He swallowed and missed the cue for the last verse about the nostalgic path to the past, the present and the future. His fingers brushed over her cheek and he smiled faintly as he started singing. She joined in with her harmony and they built the dynamic effortlessly, perfectly in tune. They soared through the chorus one last time. Cara revelled in the moment. It was more powerful now they'd been vulnerable in each other's arms. No matter what happened, she would always have this performance. And if she left a part of her heart in this club in Cali, it was worth it.

When the final chord fell away and the cheers of the crowd grew deafening, she pumped a fist in the air and bounced on the spot. Javi swung his guitar round to his back and lifted her high. She wanted to kiss him so badly.

'I want every one of those kisses later,' he murmured in her ear. He put her down and stepped up to his microphone, saying something in Spanish that seemed to be a question. 'What do you think? Should she stay?' The crowd cheered as she crossed her arms and cocked her head indulgently. He produced a set of maracas – another cheer from the audience – and handed them to her. Then he launched into a lively tropical song before she had a chance to refuse.

Cara laughed, enjoying not taking herself seriously, as she danced and shook the maracas. She recognised the song from an early album. It was the story of asking a girl out on a date and being turned down. He looked at her and slapped his hand over his chest as he sang the part about her being so beautiful his feet raced after her – along with his heart. She went along with his performance with a tolerant smile, turning away coyly when he approached to serenade her.

The crowd loved it and she was still laughing at the end when Javi abruptly handed her his guitar and headed for the drumkit. The crowd cheered, but Cara stood dumbly at the side of the stage, holding the neck of the guitar.

He adjusted a microphone on a stand by the drumkit. 'Who wants to hear "Heroes and Words"?' he called out. Cara froze. For half a heartbeat, the audience didn't react and dread pooled in her stomach. But then a cheer went up. Javi said something in Spanish and the cheer grew louder, the crowd beginning to clap in unison.

'What did you say?' she called out to him.

He turned from his microphone with a shrug. 'That you're nervous and you might need a bit of encouragement.' She wrinkled her nose at him, but he grinned and started up a rock beat. 'You can't disappoint the crowd.'

'You'll pay for this,' she said, but her reluctant smile belied her words.

'I'll look forward to it.' He flashed her a suggestive smile and she rolled her eyes at him.

She adjusted the guitar strap and tugged it over her head. The wood was still warm from Javi's body. His guitar felt good in her hands.

He held up a hand to the crowd and stood, fishing around in his pockets. 'You need a pick,' he said to Cara. He came out from behind the drumkit with the plectrum in his fingers and held it out to her. When she reached for it, he pulled it away again. The crowd laughed. He looked to the audience with a cheeky smile and placed it in his teeth.

Cara pursed her lips and placed one fist on her hip. 'Really Javi?'

He raised his eyebrows and nodded, leaning closer to offer her the plectrum from his mouth. She reached for it with her hand and he shook his head with a mumbled, 'Uh uh.'

She turned to the audience and stepped up to her microphone. 'Urgh, men!' she grumbled and the venue erupted in cheers and laughter. But she laughed, too. She approached him and leaned up to daintily extract the pick. Her lips brushed his as an inevitable consequence, and the cheers and wolf-whistles rose.

He winked at the crowd and gave them a thumbs-up before retreating back behind the drums. Cara wiped the plectrum on her trousers, but she was laughing too hard to succeed in pretending she was truly disgusted.

When Javi started up the beat again, her spirit was so light that she didn't think, she just played. She enjoyed the cut of the strings under her fingertips, the vibrations of the guitar responding to her hands. The audience clapped along and the bass player picked up the chord progression and joined in. Her music and passion set free; she enjoyed every sensation.

She didn't know what could ever top the high of that performance, but their heated return to the hotel made a good attempt.

With love and adrenaline and laughter, they pulled at each other in a rush for intimacy.

'You lit up the stage tonight,' he mumbled, his lips on her neck. 'And I couldn't wait to get your clothes off.' His hand snuck under her shirt.

She chuckled through a gasp of pleasure as his hand pressed over her breast. 'Is that a line from a song?'

'If it's not, it soon will be. I'm going to be writing about you for years to come.'

His words sent a twinge of unease through her. 'Your stray bullet?' she murmured as he tugged off her shirt.

'Yep,' he replied, pulling her against his chest where the feel and smell of his skin always enveloped her in contentment. 'The stray bullet that got me in the chest. It will be a long recovery.'

She pulled back to look at him, swallowing. What was he saying? He couldn't know the effect his words had on her. He didn't know how far she'd fallen for him. He didn't know how dangerous it was to give her hope.

But she couldn't stop hoping – or loving. She reached for him and loved him with everything she had.

22

Cara rolled over with a groan when the insistent tinkling of her phone woke her the next morning. She fumbled for it and answered.

'Cara? It's me, Freddie. I'm going to send you a link. You have to see this. Call me back when you've watched it.'

'What?' She propped herself up on an elbow, still groggy. 'Freddie, it's only—' She pulled the phone away from her ear to check the time. 'It's nine in the morning here and we had a late night. Oh.' She turned to Javi, who was stirring next to her, sprawled on his stomach. 'What time's our flight?'

'Plenty of time,' he mumbled and slung a hand over her waist. She brushed his hair out of his face and smiled.

'Oh my God, Cara! Are you in bed with him?'

She froze and Javi's arm tightened round her. His shoulders shook with silent laughter.

'Wow. I missed an interesting trip.'

'How's your mum?'

'She's recovering slowly.'

'I'm so glad to hear it.'

'But I'm serious, Cara. You have to watch this clip I'm sending you. And then call me back. He should probably watch it, too.'

She disconnected the call, puzzled, and tapped on the link he texted her. It was a clip from a music channel, starting with a news anchor.

'The talented pair behind the hit song "Nostalgia" have given us something else to talk about. British pop sensation Cara Poignton surprised the audience at a gig by her co-star Javi Félix in Colombia and the footage shows it was a performance to remember.'

The clip cut to a video of the performance last night, when Javi had sung his own song and she'd had the maracas. He propped himself up on an elbow to watch over her shoulder.

'That's good quality video,' he commented.

'She sang one of her songs and of course they performed "Nostalgia" together and it was all caught on video – including the undeniable chemistry and an almost-kiss that has the music world chattering.' The report finished with a few seconds of their performance of 'Nostalgia', staring at each other as they sang.

The clip ended and Cara was silent, waiting to diagnose what she was feeling. Should she be horrified that an 'almost-kiss' with Javi had made it into the public eye? She wasn't. She was proud of the performance, proud of herself – and of him.

'What are you thinking?' He pressed a kiss to her shoulder and she rolled onto her back. She draped her arms round his neck and pulled him down for a longer kiss. She couldn't get enough of him. She splayed her hands on his back and opened her mouth, her body arching into him as he groaned deep in his chest. His lips were sliding down her neck to her chest, when her phone burst with sound again and they broke apart in surprise.

The auto-play function on the video app had started up another clip and Cara grabbed her phone, intending to stop it and get back to the kissing. But the cacophony quieted, and they heard Javi singing the first verse of 'Nostalgia'.

'It's the video they were talking about. Do you want to watch it?' she asked.

He nuzzled her jaw and mumbled a negative. 'I remember everything about last night.' She inhaled sharply as his lips landed at her solar plexus and swerved to nip at the underside of one breast. She stabbed her thumb over the video to stop it, but before she could turn back to him and participate, her gaze snagged on the little number beneath the video and she froze in shock.

'What?' He sighed and moved back to let her sit up.

'It's been viewed a million times. A million times! Since last night!'

'That news clip must have aired globally and now everyone's searching for the full video.'

Javi's phone rang and they took a long look at each other. 'It's my manager,' he confirmed as he fetched his phone to answer the call. Cara sighed and moved away to call Freddie back.

'It's mad, Cara! Downloads of the song are on the up and this is just the beginning. At the very least you'll probably have some radio obligations over Christmas. Best-case scenario: you'll be busy on Christmas day! I'll keep you posted.'

Cara struggled to share Freddie's enthusiasm. The performance going viral had triggered her unease about the relationship that was supposed to end with a clean, defined exit when she got on the plane on Friday. She wasn't sure how she would react if that changed.

'What's up?' Of course Javi would notice.

'It's unexpected. But, I mean, it's great for sales. And surely it won't be enough to get us to number one.'

'Would that be so bad? To keep this going for a few more days?'

She drew a deep breath through her nose. He could read her far too well and she didn't know how to explain herself without admitting that she loved him and was terrified of getting hurt. 'It's not that I don't want to see you, but this is... neater.'

'You even like your affairs neat.'

'That sounds so awful, but I'm trying not to get hurt.'

He nodded slowly. 'Which is why you stayed away from me in the first place.'

'I don't know if that was ever going to work,' she murmured. She asked herself in dismay if it would have been better if they'd had meaningless, awkward sex at the beginning and then argued until they couldn't stand each other. Instead she'd had time to understand him and to fall in love.

He tucked her hair over her shoulder and ran his finger down her arm, his eyes following its progress with a serious expression. When he reached her hand, he picked it up and clutched it in his. 'I can do neat. If that's what you need, I'll give you neat.'

His words gave her a cold shiver. She didn't doubt his ability to walk away cleanly. At least the vehemence in his voice told her she meant something to him. She would have to be satisfied with that.

* * *

She didn't see much of Bogotá, either – just the impression of a huge city suspended in the mountains. The altitude brought colder temperatures and Cara had to pull out the sweater that had lived in her suitcase since she'd arrived in Miami. She tried to stop herself thinking it signalled the end of her crazy tropical December.

A huge church high up on a hill was illuminated with coloured lights and a blinding angel on top. The Christmas lights of Bogotá were in proportion to the huge nativity scenes in many squares, but instead of the wonder she'd felt experiencing the día de las velitas in Barranquilla, she was thinking of the quiet Christmas she would spend without Javi.

He'd promised her a neat end, but he made clear it wasn't over yet. She could easily get used to falling asleep at night with his fingers in her hair. He kissed her at the smallest occasion. And the cab ride to the TV station was much better with her hand clutched in his.

He leaned over to whisper in her ear, 'Remember Miami?' She looked at him ruefully and his fingers brushed her jaw.

Javi was lively and entertaining in the interview, as far as Cara could tell. She didn't have a live translation and the interview was pre-recorded so her section was in English and would have subtitles added later. Near the end of the interview, she got the impression that the presenter was asking about their romantic relationship and it chafed that she couldn't understand. Javi didn't look at her, which increased her chagrin.

When the cameras stopped rolling after the interview, he grasped her hand and squeezed it, probably out of habit because they'd agreed they shouldn't confirm anything about their relationship. But the presenter noticed.

She approached Cara as they were doing the final checks before the performance. 'How did you like Colombia,' she asked with a meaningful eyebrow raised, 'and Javi?'

Cara fudged some sort of smile and tried not to feel stupid because she didn't understand the subtext. 'I've had a wonderful time.'

She laughed and patted Cara condescendingly on the shoulder. 'He's one of a kind, that man,' she muttered.

'Have you met before?'

'Only professionally. But he certainly lives up to his reputation with women.'

Cara swallowed. 'Did he say something? I didn't understand.'

'Don't worry, he didn't kiss and tell. I asked if you two were involved and he just said he's always in love with women and he'd shown you a good time in our country.'

A good time... That was one way to put it. Cool discomfort rose in her chest to choke off anything else she might have said. He's always in love with women. It was nothing new. She was nothing new – nothing special.

It shouldn't have hurt to be told something she already knew. But it did. Just because she'd changed as a result of their relationship didn't mean he had. Even the TV presenter could see the truth. Only Cara had been foolish enough to hope.

She'd made a mistake. She was one of his women and he was her mistake. It was so wrong – she'd been so wrong to let things go this far. He'd said he was prepared to do 'neat'. She should have realised she wasn't capable of it. She was going to be a big mess by the time she got off the plane at Heathrow.

They gave another heated performance in the studio, but nothing like the way they'd burned up the stage in Cali. Their voices still blended painfully well, but it was the bitterness woven into the song that spoke to her, not the joy. Love always looked back; tears and sorrow; a season stopped in time. She resented that, even now, his song resonated with her emotions. It was so damn Christmas – full of memories and joy and pain.

All she'd achieved this year was to add one more painful memory to the most difficult time of the year. Because it was all over. Whether she stayed one more night in his arms or not, she couldn't go back to pretending that what they had was real.

She tried to escape after the performance, but Javi came after her before she could work out how to call a cab in Bogotá.

'What's going on?'

She stood, rigid, on the kerb and tried to hate him. But she couldn't. He'd only told the truth. He didn't do relationships the way she did. 'A good time' was every day for him, not the life-changing occurrence it was for her.

'I can't do this, Javi,' she murmured.

'Do what?'

'We were a mistake.'

A flash of something crossed his features, but resignation quickly took its place. 'This wasn't how we were supposed to end this,' he said.

'Does it matter? If Tayrona didn't matter, if Cali didn't matter, what difference will tonight make?'

He drew back, breathing heavily. A taxi drew up and they clambered in, looking anywhere but at each other.

To Cara's distress, the feelings grew worse, rather than better, the longer she sat with him. She'd fallen way too far. She didn't do things like risk her heart. Why had she ever stepped off the path she knew?

'Cara,' he said, his voice flat. She almost flinched to hear her name on his lips again. 'Cali mattered to me.'

She gritted her teeth against the urge to grab his lapels and make him take back what he'd said in the interview, but it was pointless. She couldn't change him – wouldn't change him.

'But not enough,' she responded. 'I suppose all the women you've loved have mattered to you,' she forced out.

He shoved a hand through his hair. For a second, she thought he was going to protest, but the words never came, and she should have learned by now to see what was there rather than what she wanted to see. 'Yes, they mattered to me,' he said, his voice rough. 'It's part of who I am. I wasn't supposed to hurt you.'

The words stung. The truth hurt. 'I know,' she muttered. 'We were supposed to have a good time. That's why this was such an awful mistake.' She breathed slowly, gathering herself against a barrage of unwanted tears. 'I'd like to be alone tonight.'

He sat back in his seat with a jerky nod.

She made a run for the hotel room when the cab pulled up, leaving Javi to pay. She burrowed under the covers of the bed, annoyed that they smelled deliciously of him. She stared at the ceiling and listened to her breathing and her heartbeat. Her vital signs were normal. She had no anxiety symptoms to manage. But she had no idea how to deal with the hurt.

She inevitably thought of her father's warnings, hating that he'd been right. A small voice called out inside her that, in the midst of the mess, she and Javi had briefly made something beautiful. But was it worth the price? Lying miserably on the bed, she wasn't certain.

She willed herself to fall asleep, sick of the day, and woke up to the sound of a soft knock and Javi calling through the door. After a long pause and another knock, he came into the room. She pretended she was still asleep as he packed his things. She pretended it didn't hurt to remember him holding her in this bed. She pretended she didn't want to reach out and pull him back in.

She could tell he was finished when he paused for a long moment. He was probably looking at her. He muttered something, his voice harsh, and then left, shutting the door quietly behind him.

She sat up as soon as he left. How was she going to face the farewell at the airport tomorrow? She was upset with herself for wishing away the last look. If her father had been right about Javi, right about where she belonged, did she trust herself enough to be able to handle a messy goodbye?

She pulled out her phone for a quick search and her finger hovered over the screen as the simple answer stared at her. A night flight departed Bogotá for London in five hours' time.

23

She didn't want a welcoming party. The only positive about how awful she looked was that she didn't need to worry about being recognised, despite the uptick in media interest – and she was sure that she could never look as awful as she felt.

Aside from the miserable nap, she hadn't slept since she'd woken up deliciously tangled with Javi to a bright bogotana morning. He was a snuggler, stealing the bed in search of her during the night and mumbling sleepy complaints if she rolled away. His hair was ticklish, especially when he burrowed off the pillow and ended up tucked into her back. She sighed and pulled out her phone. She'd started a list of his faults which she was pretty sure was going to turn into a song. She added bed stealing and ticklish hair to the list. It was a travesty how much she missed the hopeless charmer.

She was going to write a whole album before this was finished and she wouldn't be able to release it because it would prove he was right, and a broken heart was just what she'd needed all along.

And now her father was waiting for her in arrivals – probably with Freddie – and she couldn't let him know how much it hurt. He would have an impression – it couldn't be helped. But she'd prefer to keep the extent of her misery to herself. She scowled at the unrepentant decorations and relentless cosiness that had taken over the airport. So much for reclaiming the Christmas spirit.

She was puzzled when they greeted her energetically. Freddie was bouncing with it and even Gordon was jollier than usual. She should be pleased they weren't concerned about her dog-dragged appearance, but she felt as though she'd missed someone's birthday.

Freddie couldn't hold it in. 'The downloads have been crazy, Cara! The Top 40 has started and you're already the talk of the show. I mean number eight was great, but you have a real chance at the number one! We can listen in the car.'

Oh no... She hadn't thought about the chart success of the single since – oh yes, since another time she'd been naked in bed with Javi. She braced herself for another round of piercing memories.

'I don't have to ask how the flight was, by the look of you,' her father said and patted her shoulder. And there it was – another reminder of Javi. At least Javi had kissed her cheek. Her father was never demonstrative, but, boy, she needed a hug.

'I don't know if I can make it to the end of the Top 40. You'll have to wake me if w-w-we're number one.' *Oh bother, she couldn't even say the word 'we' any more.*

The cold air cut into her skin as they walked to the car. It was sleeting – London's best effort at Christmas snow. Between the concrete carpark and the grey sky, she felt she couldn't see colour any more, but that was more melodramatic nonsense that had to stop.

She stowed her suitcase and was happy to let Freddie sit in the passenger seat next to her father. She leaned her head against the window and closed her eyes, but the speakers blared BBC Radio 1 as soon as her father started the engine. The Top 40 presenters were too lively. The songs were too upbeat. But she was filled with enough dread to stay awake and listen for 'Nostalgia'.

The chart countdown was in the teens as they exited the Heathrow carpark and wound their way to the M4. Traffic was slow on the Friday before Christmas and by the time they pulled up at the house in Dulwich, the countdown was at number five – still no 'Nostalgia'. Gordon rushed out of the car to turn on the radio in the house so they wouldn't miss anything. She should have been touched that her father was excited for her, but she wasn't excited for herself.

The presenters made a big show of announcing the number two. Cara lay her head on the kitchen table – tiredness, twisting emotions and reverse culture shock making her feel as though it was all a dream. She'd only been away three weeks. It shouldn't have been long enough for home to feel so odd. But the Christmas tree in the living room felt perfunctory and she suspected even dancing wouldn't be enough to stem the tears.

'We've been talking about this moment for the whole show. Listeners out there, you won't have missed the absence of our catchy Brit-Latin hit "Nostalgia" from the Top 40 so far. A performance gone viral and some real romance have rocketed this song right up since last week and we're about to find out if it's managed to knock "Good, Good Things" off the top spot this week – just in time for Christmas.'

'Brit-Latin!' Freddie guffawed. 'I love it. That might become a thing.'

Cara's heart sank. It would be a 'thing' she wouldn't be a part of again. She wouldn't be able to hear any of the Latin styles without picturing Javi behind a drumkit, living the beat.

Gordon settled a hand on her shoulder and she covered it with her own. 'We're so proud – I'm so proud of you either way, sweetheart.'

'Thank you, Daddy.' She followed her father's gaze to the photo of her mother amongst the decorative plates on the kitchen shelves. It was one of the few new additions to this kitchen in the past ten years. She wondered if thinking about her made her father happy or sad. The expression on his face was... nostalgic.

She patted his hand, distracted, as the animated BBC presenter announced the number two. 'And this week's Christmas number two is: "Good, Good, Things"!'

Freddie squealed. Gordon gasped. And Cara slowly closed her eyes. Christmas Day with Javi. Too much of her was sagging with relief that she could see him again. But the panicked, hurting part was clenching with fear.

'I can't believe it! Cara, you did it! It's number one! It's Christmas number one!' Freddie babbled.

Gordon kissed the top of her head. 'I'll fetch the champagne. My daughter is number one!'

While they smiled and fussed with the wire and the cork, Cara sat staring out the window, seeing nothing. The presenter announced 'Nostalgia' and she bit her lip to stop the tears. The first chord took her straight back across the Atlantic and over the Caribbean.

She stood, unable to keep a hold of herself, and escaped to her room – her childhood bedroom, the room where she'd spent so much time not sleeping while she came to terms with the mess of her body and the tumult in her head. She shut the door, searching for composure so she could go and have a shower and go to sleep.

'Cara, can I come in?' Her father knocked lightly.

She swiped at her cheeks. 'I suppose so.'

He stopped when he saw her and sighed – a huge, parental sigh. He sat next to her on the bed. 'Things fell apart as we suspected, then?'

She nodded. 'You were right about a lot of things.'

'It doesn't make me feel any better, sweetheart. Is there anything I can do? Chase him out of the country and to hell with the sales? That gets my vote.'

She shook her head. 'I have to face him. Hopefully the prospect will be less awful in the morning.'

'You've always been a serious, professional musician. Nothing has changed, even if you have learned to perform like a real pop star. You'll deal with it the same way you always do.'

'This was never a normal situation, Daddy. Professional never worked.'

'Perhaps it will, now, hmm?'

'I don't think anything will work, now.'

His brow furrowed. 'It isn't like you to be defeatist.'

She scrubbed her hands over her face. 'Yes, well, it's not like me to fall foolishly in love with a notorious heartbreaker,' she mumbled.

'I'm sure it wasn't so deep, sweetheart. You got caught up in the excitement.'

'I wish that were true, Daddy. But I'm screwed.'

He patted her hand. 'You're young. Real love doesn't work like that. It grows over time in a reciprocated relationship. But I can understand this is your first major infatuation.'

His words didn't help. They brought back the image of Javi's dismayed face, telling her all of the women in his life had mattered to him. In his way, he did love her, but he loved easily and differently. That's what had got her into so much trouble.

* * *

'I should have asked Sebas to come out with me,' Coque mumbled as he inspected his beer bottle.

Javi frowned. 'Sebas? He falls asleep on two drinks.'

'And he spends the whole time feeling guilty for leaving his wife and kids, but at least he doesn't sit in moody silence trying to decide whether or not to get drunk.'

'I wasn't planning on getting dr... okay, maybe I was.' He tossed back the rest of his whisky.

Coque laughed and rubbed his eyes. 'Maybe you'd rather be Sebas – at home with the old lady.'

'Shut up, pelota!' His temper spiked, but it wasn't his brother's fault. There was only one woman he thought of when Coque said vieja and he didn't want to be reminded of Cali.

'Look.' Coque gestured to where the patrons of the bar were spilling out onto the street to dance. 'Those two girls. They've made eye contact more than once and I'm pretty sure they want to dance. You don't want to disappoint the lovely quilleras, do you? Just because an inglesa screwed you over?'

'She didn't screw me over.' He'd done that himself. He didn't know why it had gone to hell so quickly. All he knew was that it had hurt so damn much to find her gone. He'd tried to reason with himself and pointed out it had been over anyway. What had he lost by her running? But the truth was he would have done anything for more time with her.

His wish for more time had been granted in a spectacular manner by the listeners in the UK, but her escape had showed him just how much he'd hurt her. She was probably dreading Christmas day – even more than usual.

Coque gave him a sceptical look. 'Where did you leave your balls?'

'You go dance if you're just going to sit here and irritate me.'

'You go and get married if you're not going to dance with girls in bars any more!'

'Yeah, because that worked out so well last time!' He needed another drink.

Coque's expression softened to curiosity, which Javi was even less inclined to indulge. 'Fine. I'll be your loquero and we can talk our balls off. I'll get the drinks.'

'I don't need a shrink,' Javi insisted when Coque returned with two whiskies.

'You don't need a girl; you don't need a shrink. What do you need?'

Cara... Refusing to say it didn't diminish the truth. When had loving a woman ever felt like this?

His brother muttered under his breath. 'Just say it, man. You want the woman back.'

'I never had her – at least, not in the sense of a relationship.'

Coque chuckled. 'Why not? If you had her in another sense, why wasn't it a relationship? She seemed a bit too heavy for casual.'

He cursed. 'Maybe it was a relationship and that's why I screwed it up.'

'You didn't want a relationship?'

Javi paused, his fingertip halfway round the rim of his whisky glass. Did he want a relationship? With Cara? Hell, yes. A relationship with everything: exclusivity, fidelity, responsibility, commitment, love. Was he insane? He didn't do those things, except with Bea. But he wanted to – he really wanted to.

He'd told himself he was bad news for Cara, he didn't have to drink the water – they'd be better off staying away from each other. It had felt like the voice of logic, of sensible restraint. But it had been cowardice. That first kiss had held so much promise it had scared him. He'd been scared of depth, scared he'd fail her, scared he'd gain this kind of love only to throw it away.

He took a deep breath. 'Yes, I want a relationship,' he said with the demeanour of an alcoholic at an AA meeting.

Coque laughed at him. 'Well done, bro. You grew up. Now go

and un-screw your relationship. I don't think it's going to be a problem. She was so into you it was almost too sweet.'

He shook his head. 'She doesn't trust me.'

Coque didn't reply, but sipped thoughtfully on his drink. 'Susana did a number on you, man.'

'What?!'

'I know you think you messed it all up, but give yourself a break. She blackmailed you into having a kid when you weren't ready.'

'She didn't blackmail me.'

'She put on the pressure.'

'And I could have pushed back.'

'Could you? She made you, Javi, and you know it. It's not surprising it went to shit and it's her fault as much as it is yours. Plus, you're still protecting her, however many years after the divorce. That's the behaviour of someone trustworthy.'

'You're making me out to be some kind of saint – which will never be believable.'

'You think you're some kind of serial heartbreaker, which is pretty egotistical. Do you think you'd cheat on Cara?'

'Of course not.'

Coque looked skywards in exasperation. 'Exactly, you big cabrón! So, you made a few mistakes. That was then. What are you doing now? Are you going to be drunk and miserable? Are you going to come with me and try to have a bit of fun with some beautiful women? Or are you going to get your culo onto a plane to England and shack yourself up?'

He remained frozen. Since when did Jorge know what he was talking about? He wasn't sure if he had any right to it, but the insidious seed of hope had been planted. He had to be sure he could do this before he approached Cara. There was too much at stake to stuff up a second time.

He stood, taking a final sip of the unfinished drink. 'I'm going home. And tomorrow, I'm going to Miami.'

'What?'

'I need to talk to Susana.'

'Buena suerte, bro. Hang onto your balls.'

* * *

'Javi? I thought you were spending Christmas in Colombia?'

He should have expected she'd be shocked to see him. He'd never arrived on her doorstep unannounced. The only times he'd been to her house were the rare times he'd collected Bea or had to sign something unpleasant. On previous occasions he'd found the house too big, the columns too imposing, but he was in a different frame of mind that day. He appreciated the nativity in the window, the wreath of pine and tropical flowers on the front door, the paper cut-outs and the candles.

'How'd it go in LA?'

'Good,' she said, still staring at him.

'Can I come in?'

Her eyes grew wary. 'What for?'

'If... if it's okay, I need to talk to you.'

'About Bea?'

'No... Can I just come in?' She eyed him critically before stepping away from the door so he could enter. 'I'm glad your filming went well,' he mumbled as she led him into the living room. A voice called from elsewhere in the house and the smell of garlic and onion wafted from the kitchen.

Susana nodded. 'Thank you for taking care of Bea.'

He shook his head. 'Nothing to thank.'

'I think she had a nice time, although you always have to read between the lines.'

He smiled. That was his daughter. And he loved her to pieces. Maybe he was succeeding at this parent thing at last. 'It was hard to send her back. We should talk sometime about... that.'

'You want to talk about custody?' She was instantly on the defensive.

'No, Susi. I mean, yes, but not now. That's not what I came here for.' He paused and she prompted him with an expectant look. He opened his mouth, but it was so damn hard. 'Do you think...?' He cut himself off. 'Do you think I've changed?' *Sounded crazy.*

'What are you going on about, Javi? It's four days until Christmas and I don't want to deal with this right now. I've had a busy couple of weeks, and I want some peace with Bea and my mother.'

'I'm sorry,' he apologised immediately. 'I didn't think of this from your side – as usual.'

'What is this? You're not making any sense.'

'He's in love with Cara and he doesn't know what to do.' He looked up to see Bea in the door, the familiar, narrow expression on her face. He grinned.

'Hey, gordita.' He wrapped his arms round her, belatedly realising that they hadn't hugged in Miami before. But she slipped her arms round him and squeezed back. He kissed the top of her head. 'Missed you.'

When he turned back to Susana, she had her arms crossed and a perplexed expression. 'Is that true? You came here to talk to me about a woman?'

'Is that okay? I need to... put some things to rest.'

Susana sighed, a huge heartfelt exhale. 'It's okay,' she said, her lips pursed. 'I've been waiting years to have this conversation with you, but it's not how I expected.'

'When is life ever how we expect? I'm sorry – for disrupting your life, for the crazy arguments. For what it's worth, I'm sorry.'

'You've apologised to me a hundred times, Javi. That's not what I'm talking about.' She turned to Bea. 'Mija, can you go and help abuelita in the kitchen?'

Bea smirked and saluted. Javi hid his grin. 'I'm sorry she's so much like me,' he said in a low voice once she'd left.

'She wants lessons on the drumkit. I assume that was your doing.'

'Great! I may have had something do with that.'

'This is different,' she commented, her brow low.

He straightened and blinked at her. 'It is, isn't it?' And he suspected he already had the answer to whatever question he was asking with his heart. He wouldn't run any more – not from Susana and his past, not from his future. He'd wandered aimlessly into his music career, haunted by Alejo. He'd stumbled into the relationship with Susana. How had he not known what he wanted? It seemed so clear to him now: Bea and Cara. He wanted a life that involved both of them, whatever the impracticalities.

Susana gave him a small smile which he returned warmly. He was lucky to have strong women in his life as he fumbled through. 'You're different,' she said.

He nodded slowly. 'It's strange, but... yes.'

She patted his arm with a sigh. 'It's not strange. It's life. You've been building up to this. The struggle about going home? That was part of it. You've been asking more and more to deepen your relationship with Bea. I wouldn't have left her with you if I hadn't noticed. And, Javi,' she smiled, a bittersweet, generous smile that tugged him into the past, 'the man I married and divorced would never have written "Nostalgia".'

He blew out a long breath. 'It took me long enough to own the words.'

'Your heart realised faster than your brain.'

'That's poetic. Have you been writing songs, Susi?' he grinned.

She ignored his teasing question. 'What did you need to put to rest? If it's something to do with me, then I should apologise, too. I sensed as well as you did that there was something about us that wouldn't last, and instead of accepting it, I hung on too tight.'

He shook his head, 'No. You put your heart into it and I didn't. Don't apologise.'

'Stop it, Javi. If you want to put things to rest, then you have to accept grace as well as culpability. If you want it to be different with this woman, stop being afraid of the end and look at the beginning.'

He swallowed, riding out the wave of emotion brought on by her words. He was struck by the thought that he didn't deserve her overtures of reconciliation, but he corrected the unhelpful impulse. He would make sure he did deserve it. Cara had accused him of clinging to excuses. She'd been right. Blaming his own limitations was just one more way he'd run from responsibility.

He wasn't only going to react. He was going to act. No matter how Cara responded, he needed to tell her how much he wanted to be with her and what kind of relationship he pictured – a permanent one. He'd tried so hard to convince her he didn't do permanence; it might take a while. But he had a couple of days to formulate a strategy.

'Are you okay?'

He nodded with an amused smile. 'Yeah, yeah. Uyy, you gave me more than I bargained for. But it's good. It's what I needed to hear.'

She smiled and cocked her head. 'Do you want to stay for dinner?'

'Your mom might kill me.'

'Bea won't let her.'

He grinned. 'Thanks for the invitation. I'd love to. I need to work out how to talk to Bea about this without her realising what I'm doing.'

Around the dinner table, the topic of Javi's next destination came up in conversation.

'I have to go. The song reached number one there and there's a live TV thing on Christmas Day.'

'I always wanted to go to London,' Bea said with a smile that hid something.

'Are you hinting, mija?' he asked her. 'I don't think your mom can do without you. It's Christmas.'

'Please, mom? It'll just be this once. I really want to see Javi make a mess of this.'

'Bea!' Susana scolded. 'He hasn't invited you to come. Do you think he's likely to now?'

'Yes,' Bea smiled innocently. 'Cara likes me, and he'll need all the help he can get.'

'You'd help me?' he asked incredulously.

Bea shrugged. 'I like her, too, and if she's crazy enough to love you back, then I'd better fall into line.'

'You don't have to fall into line.'

'It's okay, Dad. I'm okay with it. Chill out.'

'Did she just call you—'

Bea interrupted Susana's observation. 'Yeah, so what? Don't read too much into it. I'm still going to call him Javi when I want to. So, can I come?'

He glanced at Susana. She pursed her lips for a moment, but nodded. 'Yeah, you can come, gordita.' She jumped up with a squeal to hug first her mother and then Javi.

'My friends are going to be so jealous.'

24

She'd heard nothing from Javi. It had been two days since 'Nostalgia' had been revealed as the Christmas number one and he hadn't even texted her. She hadn't texted him either, but the ball was in his court – at least that's the excuse she used.

Her jetlag was passing quickly this time, but she wasn't sleeping well. Perhaps she'd robbed herself of closure by escaping Bogotá without telling him. Her departure was going to be a source of awkwardness on Christmas Day. She should have faced up to the consequences of her decisions then, rather than living with these days of apprehension now.

The electric piano was still set up in her room, where it had been for nearly ten years. But it had been years since she'd needed to slip on the headphones and play herself calm in the middle of the night. She was writing songs. It seemed to be her response to both anxiety and heartbreak. And if some of the songs – who was she kidding – all of the songs – were about Javi, she forced herself not to care.

She was up at two in the morning for the second night in a row, her fingers drifting across the keys, when her phone screen flashed up. She froze. Barranquilla was five hours behind London. He was the only person she could imagine texting her right now. She bit her lip and reached for her phone.

Can I see you when I get to London? My flight lands at eight tomorrow night.

Her brow furrowed. He meant tonight her time. Tonight! Oh, God it was actually happening. She would have to face him with all her hurt, her fear and her longing.

I don't think that's a good idea.

She texted back.

Did you celebrate the number one?

Not really. Did you?

Jorge tried, but I wasn't very good company.

She resisted the urge to apologise and refused to enjoy the confused thrill of hearing he shared her turmoil.

How's Jorge? And your mum?

Good, but I'm in Miami.

Cara frowned, wondering what had taken him back to Miami. The messaging app showed that he was typing for a long time. When his response appeared, it was one short line. Perhaps he'd drafted and deleted more.

I'm bringing Bea to London.

A smile touched her lips. Their relationship was one area where the crazy December trip had been a success. She started typing an enthusiastic response, but realised that would imply she wanted to see them before Christmas Day. Why did he want to see her? Was he angry with her for escaping without saying goodbye?

That's nice.

She sent, wincing at the inadequacy. She could imagine what Bea would say if she saw the message. She did want to see Bea. If she was honest, she wanted to see both of them.

Are you sure we can't take you out for lunch? We'll be sightseeing for two days before the filming – soaking up some Christmas spirit.

She considered her response for a long time. She needed to be disciplined, repeat her sleep routine and go back to bed. The warmth and confusion of texting with Javi wasn't helping.

Maybe after the interview. I need to get through one thing at a time.

Signalling an ominous wobble in her emotions, she couldn't resist adding:

Are you angry with me for leaving without saying goodbye?

Not at all. I understand more than you think, mona. I was angrier with myself.

Cara smiled bleakly. Of course he was angry with himself. Oh God, she loved him so much.

Damn, I've just realised what time it is in England. Why are you awake?

Sleeping poorly. I'll go back to bed as soon as you let me.

There was a long pause and she wondered if she should go to bed. She pursed her lips at the delay and then the message dropped in.

I'm trying to be good, but that sentence was practically an invitation.

You see everything as an invitation. Good night, Javi.

Good night, corazón.

Great, she'd never sleep now that Javi had flirted with her and called her 'heart'. But she repeated her sleep routine, brushing her teeth again, reading a few pages of something boring and covering her clock so she couldn't see the time and get anxious about lack of sleep.

Then she woke up to sunlight peering round the curtains. The texting had settled something inside her. She knew how to deal with Javi. It was dealing without Javi that was the problem.

It struck her that she had been trying to forget everything amazing that had happened over the past three weeks. Could she afford to lose the memories of lighting candles in the warm night breeze? What about how it had felt to dance in the street? Or the achievement of singing her Christmas heartache until she could finally look back with love and not fear?

She opened up the video diary app on her phone, intending to record another reassurance that life goes on and no misery lasted forever, but her gaze snagged on the date just as she hit record.

'It's been nine years and 364 days since Mum and Crispin died,' she blurted out, instead of her usual self-conscious greeting to her future self. 'And today I want to look back with love. I want to make a noise to drown out the sorrow and I want to dance so I don't cry.'

She hastily stopped the video as her eyes welled up with tears. They were the usual salty kind, not Javi's fanciful tears of cinnamon and coconut. But she needed them to be okay, today. She wanted to find the joy. She couldn't keep Javi, but she wanted her Christmases back.

She started small, putting on Christmas carols at breakfast and moving photos of Crispin and her mother onto the mantlepiece near the tree. She bought mince pies and made mulled cider. Her father didn't react beyond wary thanks. One advantage of the mess she'd been in since she got back was that he was probably too relieved to see her up and dressed to challenge her.

She wasn't surprised to see her phone light up at nine that evening as they were watching a Christmas special. She snatched it up as though he could see who was sending her a message.

We're here, in case you changed your mind.

Nope, sorry. I'm glad you arrived safely. Enjoy London.

IT'S FREEZING. What do you suggest we see? Bea's first time (but she's freezing).

She experienced a sudden pang to join them. It felt like a part of her had run away to tour London without her. She wanted to take Bea on the London Eye and to the waxworks' museum and through a few rooms of the National Gallery to see her critical, childish eye on the artworks. She wanted to laugh about the difference between tacos, arepas and... sandwiches. She'd bet they'd never tasted a turkey, cranberry and stuffing Christmas sandwich.

She took her time composing a list of things they should see and impulsively ended it with:

Send me pics.

It was torture the following day. Every hour or so pictures would drop into her phone, either from Bea or Javi. Bea sent a selfie of the two of them in the queue for the Eye with bored expressions. Forty-five minutes later was the photo of them in the capsule high above the city. Javi sent her a picture of Bea with the waxwork of Bob Marley. She sent a picture of Javi talking to some street performers on Oxford Street and then another of him performing with them – then one final picture of him breathing on his frozen hands with a grimace. She couldn't bring herself to reply, but the photos kept coming.

They visited a Christmas market, but didn't think much of the punch. Javi stood behind a carolling choir in Victorian dress with a goofy smile. Bea's expression of joy under the lights of Regent Street made Cara laugh – Bea was just as excited about the shops as she was about the decorations.

The following day – Christmas Eve – she saw pictures of the two of them with Santa at the sumptuous Christmas grotto at Hamley's toy store, then wrapped in a fleece blanket on the top floor of an open-topped bus, and another of them pretending to kiss a Yeoman Warder on the cheek. When she received the photo of Tower Bridge framed by their hands forming a heart, her lips wobbled and tears threatened. She tried desperately to convince herself that he was trying to re-establish their friendship, nothing more. But the stubborn flame of hope wouldn't be extinguished.

'Are you quite all right, Cara?'

She closed the app quickly as though caught doing something she shouldn't. 'I'm fine.'

Her father watched her for a long moment – too long. 'Is he sending you messages?' She didn't reply, but her father saw confirmation in her features. 'Don't put yourself through this, sweetheart. You need to be strong.'

She set her jaw, seeing the pictures again in her memory. She might be hurting, but she wasn't weak. Even though she had to say goodbye to Javi again tomorrow, knowing him, loving him had been worth something to her. Her father might never understand, but she wouldn't ignore it.

'Don't worry, Daddy. I am stronger than you think.'

'Of course you are, Cara.' He patted her hand and scowled at her phone.

She took a deep breath. 'Are you okay? About today, I mean?'

'Cara, why are you asking?'

'Why not?' she challenged. She grabbed the remote and turned off the TV. She wanted a real Christmas, and not just the cosy TV specials. 'Ten years. Don't you want to do anything? Don't you want to remember?'

Gordon's face lost its colour. Cara swallowed, but stood her ground, just as she had the last time he'd looked at her like this: when she'd sung 'O Holy Night'.

'Do you think I've forgotten anything about your mother?'

The shock of emotion swooped across her nerve endings and she stared at him, both of them horrified by the gathering tears.

'I can't forget and I can't make it stop hurting.'

Cara broke first, slamming her hand over her mouth. 'I don't want to hurt you, but I want to remember.'

'But what if... What if all we remember is the end?'

He sounded so lost, echoing a fear she knew well. She sat on the arm of his chair and wrapped her arms round him, experiencing the odd sense of the passage of time and continuity that was unique to the season. A season stopped in time, as Javi had put it. Nothing changes much, nothing stays the same. Life had whirled round her family in a frightening storm, but she was determined to hold onto the things of value.

'We have to remember the end,' she said softly. 'That's part of it. But I don't want to lose the rest. Mum loved Christmas. Can't we go to the carol service? I remember it. I remember Crispin singing. It was beautiful.'

'Cara,' he continued and something in his tone betrayed his stark fear. 'I can't.'

Her spine tingled with recognition. Perhaps he understood her better than she'd thought. 'What do you mean?'

'It's Christmas Eve. I can't leave the house. I don't know what I'll see. And I don't want to enjoy it.'

His words painted the last nine Christmases in a new light and she tightened her arms round him. Miserable Christmases... It had taken this bizarre clash of Christmases to show her the truth. She hadn't been celebrating the season. She and her father had been punishing themselves and shutting themselves away in fear.

She grasped his shoulders. 'Dad, we can do this. We won't drive. If you get stuck seeing the past, it will go away again – trust me. And if you don't feel like you deserve to enjoy Christmas, then you're condemning me to the same fate. I survived, too.'

He lifted a hesitant hand to her cheek and she grabbed it in both of hers. 'You did more than survive, sweetheart. You thrived. Your mother would have been so proud.'

'She would be proud of both of us,' she murmured. She glanced up at the mantlepiece. 'We're muddling through.' She stood and headed for the door. 'Come on. We've still got time to make it to the five o'clock service.'

* * *

A few flakes of snow stopped them on the way to the train station. They paused and stared, before warily glancing at each other.

Gordon licked his lips. 'Well, the Met Office might be announcing an official white Christmas,' he said gruffly, before tucking her hand into his elbow and forcing his feet forward.

'We're not driving, so it's fine,' Cara added, not sure if it was for her benefit or Gordon's. They were all in on this reclaiming Christmas business. If it snowed again, like it had that year, it would be all the more effective – she hoped.

'Best not to mention it,' Gordon muttered.

They clung to each other as they emerged from the station. The wind had picked up and more snowflakes were swirling. Cara was struck by memories, but not the ones she'd expected. As they came round to the main entrance of St Martin's, she stared at the huge Norwegian spruce dominating Trafalgar Square, in between the fountains glowing with coloured lights.

The elaborate August farce had become its own odd Christmas memory. She would always remember Javi and the one Christmas where their lives briefly tangled.

And the photos he and Bea had sent her? She tried to tell herself they boded well for an amicable goodbye, but her hope was frustratingly stubborn.

She couldn't help it. She was going to love Javi for a long time. At least she was learning how to treasure the good memories.

Bolstered by acceptance, she turned to her father with a bright smile. 'We made it.'

He nodded. 'We did.'

'We'll get through this, Daddy.'

He studied her as though he could tell she wasn't only talking about the memories of her mother and Crispin. 'We will, sweet-heart. Shall we go in?'

Cara tucked her arm back into his and they turned to take the steps up to the door of the church, glowing with candles inside. But about halfway up, they heard voices and froze. Cara's newfound acceptance lurched and stumbled. Who else would be speaking Spanish in his low, lazy voice outside St Martin-in-the-Fields on Christmas Eve?

If there had been any doubt, the response removed it. 'But, Dad, we're Catholic!' The 'duh' was implied.

Cara's throat closed and her hand tightened on Gordon's arm. But it wasn't with worry. Without stopping to soothe her father's chagrin, she let go of his arm and bounded up the steps.

He was hunched against a column, a ridiculously colourful scarf round his neck and his hair poking out from beneath a beanie. His hands were shoved in his pockets and his head was cocked, regarding Bea with an expression of exasperated humour that was deeply familiar.

She came to a sudden stop, staring at him, and he looked up. His smile fell away and he straightened, taking half a step in her direction before hesitating. His eyes were asking questions, but she didn't dare guess what those questions were.

'Cara.' His voice was breathless with the same bewildered wonder that she felt.

'You remembered the church,' she murmured.

He took a step towards her. 'I remember a lot of things from round here.' Her breath hitched. She remembered, too.

'How about we remember our manners,' Gordon interrupted. 'The service is about to start. As it is, I'm not sure if we'll get seats... together.'

Javi's lips twitched at the less-than-subtle hint. He raised an eyebrow at Bea, but her protests had fled.

'You guys didn't say "hello",' she pointed out.

Cara's cheeks warmed and she turned to Bea. 'Hello, Bea. I'm glad you could come.' Her arms rose of their own accord, just a little, but it was enough for Bea. She launched herself at Cara for a hug that sent Cara's heart tumbling a little further.

Javi and Gordon shook hands and then he turned to Cara expectantly. Her blush deepened. He took slow steps in her direction and raised a hand to rest it on her shoulder. She struggled to keep her eyes open. She loved how he touched her.

'Hello,' he murmured as he leaned down to kiss her cheeks. She leaned up to him helplessly. How did he do this to her? She knew how. She loved him.

He studied her for a long moment, his thumb brushing her jaw. And he leaned down again, his eyes drifting shut. Cara sucked in one last desperate breath. She didn't care where they were. She wanted this kiss more than she'd ever wanted any Christmas present.

But a loud clap startled them. Cara opened her eyes in a daze to see her father rubbing his hands together. 'Oh, look, the snow is getting heavier. Let's get inside.'

The flakes were a little fatter, but it wasn't as inconvenient as Gordon's interruption had been. Javi drew back and Cara wasn't sure whether she was more annoyed with her father for interrupting or Javi for letting him interrupt. But Bea's sly smile reminded her that it probably wasn't the best moment to rekindle their passion.

They found a pew with just enough room to squash in. Bea ushered Javi in first, but then hung back, giving Cara a meaningful look. But Gordon grabbed for her arm. 'Look at the lovely amaryllis! I don't remember the amaryllis. Do you think the flower arrangements are different?'

Cara suppressed a sigh, but she turned to her father and made a perfunctory comment about the flowers while Bea followed Javi into the pew. Cara took her seat next to Bea, aware of Javi's eyes on her. She took off her gloves and stared at her hands to stop her gaze rising to his.

The organ sounded and the congregation stood. Javi and Bea fidgeted as the choir filed in, holding candles and singing 'O Come All Ye Faithful'. Gordon eyed them. Cara belted out the carol, ignoring them all, but inwardly joyous to be sitting among this odd tribe on Christmas Eve, among memories of her family.

Her odd tribe... How she wished it could be real, despite all of her attempts at pragmatism. She glanced at Javi, who looked up from the order of service immediately to meet her gaze. What was he thinking?

She spent the service either blushing under his gaze, sneaking peeks at his handsome, familiar features or getting lost in the swirl of hope when their eyes did meet. And all the while the choir sang well-known carols and the congregation murmured the familiar words of the Christmas liturgy. Cara's memories were a warm travelling companion, from the nostalgic past into an unknown future.

'Thanks for coming, Daddy,' she whispered to Gordon.

His look was strained. 'Did you plan this?'

She shook her head. 'Sometimes the plan writes us.'

'You know I'm not a "go with the flow" kind of person,' he muttered.

'I know. And I love you regardless.'

He eyed her with as much warmth as he could muster. She understood. Between the thrill of hope for the future and the freeing defiance of reclaiming Christmas Eve, Cara was incapable of feeling anything but generosity towards him.

As they filed out of the church in the milling crowd, Javi snagged her hand. She couldn't stifle her smile as he came up behind her and leaned down to whisper in her ear. Whatever was going on between them, she wanted it. She was ready to listen. In the warm light of the chandeliers with the snow falling and the wind blowing in the darkness outside, anything was possible.

She took a deep breath, feeling his warm presence behind her, wondering what he was going to say.

'Can you ice skate?'

Laughter bubbled up inside her. Could she reply 'I love you' to that question? She glanced back at him and their eyes resumed their conversation.

'Yes, I can ice skate.'

'Good.' His grip on her hand tightened and he pulled her through the crowd.

25

Javi's mind raced as he wobbled round the ice rink in the courtyard of an imposing building of honey-coloured stone. The wonder of a snowy Christmas was happening round him, but inside he was charting new territory. Her sweet smiles and long looks were more than he'd hoped for, but he had a complicated apology and a deep promise to deliver and he had to get it right.

His feelings weren't simply part of this Christmas spirit – to come out once a year to warm the heart with memories. He planned to take this magic into the rest of his life – their lives. If only he could forget how far out of his depth he'd ventured and work out how to do it convincingly.

Seeing her had caught him by surprise. He couldn't believe he'd nearly given in and kissed her. He had to remember that his mind was further down this path than hers. She didn't know that anything had changed.

His head swirling with urgency, he missed a gouge in the ice and overbalanced, crashing onto his backside. Why had he thought this was a good idea? He'd only ice skated about three times in his life.

Bea sailed gracefully past and poked her tongue out at him. He gave her a dirty look, but she glanced pointedly behind him. Javi followed her look to see Cara had made it out onto the ice after sending them ahead with the explanation that it took her a while to get skates on with her prosthesis.

She favoured her leg while she skated but God, she looked beautiful while she did – beautiful and elegant. She smiled as she skated up.

'Need a hand?'

He grinned up at her, blindsided by how much he loved her. She was supposed to be hurt and angry – as he deserved. There was a wary glint in her eye that he hoped to banish, but otherwise she was showing him enough grace that he felt giddy. He gripped her hand and she helped him up.

'Thanks,' he muttered.

'You're not very good,' she grinned.

He shrugged. 'I'm a tropical kind of guy.'

'I know. I've tried your papaya.' She snorted at her own joke and he couldn't resist. He dipped his head again.

But he forgot to compensate for the change in his centre of gravity and slipped forward, grabbing for her shoulder. He found himself on his knees with his face shoved into her stomach and her hands holding him up. She was shaking with laughter.

He cursed his second abortive attempt to kiss her. That wasn't the plan. Apology first, kiss second. Actually, the plan had been apology first, promise second, kiss third, but at this rate he wasn't going to be able to wait.

'Cara! Are you okay?'

Javi looked up with a frown to see Gordon fretting from the other side of the barrier.

'I'm fine,' she called back with a dry smile.

'Perhaps I should come out there,' Gordon called out again.

'No, Daddy!' she called back and Javi struggled to suppress a smile. Bea swept past again, making frantic gestures at him to get up and get on with it.

Cara helped him up again and he clamped his arm round her shoulders. If he ever made anything of this, it would be all because of her astounding grace.

They skated side by side, bumping into each other because of mismatched strides and utterly silent, despite the words hanging between them like a garland of lights. He could feel Gordon's gaze on them from behind the glass. He wished he could wait for a time when he'd have her alone, but between Gordon and Bea, when would that be?

He figured starting some kind of conversation was better than nothing. 'Wasn't the carol service a bit too much Christmas spirit for you and your father? Not that I'm complaining about running into you.' He backtracked carefully. 'I mean, I wasn't stalking places—'

'Shut up, Javi,' she muttered. She glanced at him. 'I decided I wanted a bit more... nostalgia this year.' She paused and he stared at her as she grappled for the right words. 'I'm glad we ran into you, too.'

This was it. He had to say something. But what? 'Cara...' he muttered helplessly. She looked up; her expression clear in the glow of the cosy lights. His chest expanded.

But the music suddenly stopped and the skaters slowed in confusion. Javi had to throw his arms out for balance as he nearly ran into a little kid while Cara came to a neat stop and waited for him.

'Um, time to change direction!' came an announcement through the loud speaker. The other patrons looked at each other in confusion. Cara was frowning at the glass hut where Gordon was standing near the office.

'Unbelievable,' she muttered. 'What were you saying?' She looked up.

He took a deep breath, 'I missed—'

The music started up again – a jaunty, blaring version of 'Jingle Bells' played much too loudly – and he slipped backward in surprise. Finding himself on his backside again, he rubbed a hand over his face. But his gloves were wet.

'It's kind of nice to see you're not good at everything,' Cara smiled as she held her hands out again.

'You have no idea,' he mumbled.

'How come you went back to Miami?' she asked over the music as they set off again.

He nodded in acknowledgement and launched into the first part of his important explanation. 'I went to see Susana.'

'To collect Bea?'

He smiled. 'Bea collected herself, but I'm glad to have her along. I was thinking a lot about things... you know.'

She slowly pursed her lips. 'No, I don't really know.'

He inwardly cursed and his eyes flitted between Gordon's glower and Bea's wide-eyed expectation. 'I... You... Bogotá...' His words petered out. His skin prickled with more than just cold. God, this was difficult.

'I thought you were supposed to be a poet,' she said sweetly.

Laughter erupted inside him, expressing the tension and surreal ridiculousness of the evening. His shoulders shook with it and then he was stumbling again, grappling at Cara for balance. She grabbed him and he stabilised.

They came to a stop by the Christmas tree at one end of the rink. He grabbed her hands. 'I didn't want to hurt you. I don't want to hurt you,' he blurted out.

'I know,' she said gently, a shadow of regret crossing her features. That wasn't the reaction he'd intended.

Bea slowed as she skated past. 'Gordon says they have to take the last train and it's coming in about half an hour!' she called out.

Frustration struck Javi first. How was he supposed to calmly set out his feelings if he had two disapproving eyes on him and only half an hour to make sure she understood? But a spark of inspiration shot up amidst the chagrin. He was supposed to be a poet. 'Nostalgia' had brought them together – both literally and figuratively. Could another song ripped right from his heart communicate everything he needed to say to her?

He liked the idea – a lot. He was no good at this heart-to-heart stuff, but if he'd managed it in a song once, then he could again. He'd always thought a song about Cara would be unlike anything he'd ever written. He was going to write that song.

They both looked back to see Gordon approaching with purpose. Javi grasped her shoulder and turned her to him.

'Give me a chance,' he said urgently.

'What do you mean? Dad's right, the trains don't run late on Christmas Eve.'

He nodded. 'I don't mean now. I mean always. I know you have to go, and God knows I can't say what I need to say in front of your father. But don't give up. I'll have a Christmas present for you tomorrow.'

'A Christmas present?'

Gordon wasn't far away, now, and Javi didn't want to leave her with the little wrinkle of confusion between her brows. 'I wasn't supposed to do this until after the apology, but screw it.'

He pulled off his gloves, thrust a hand into her hair and kissed her. It felt as though it had been months instead of days. His sense of time was screwed up by how much he missed her. He wished the heat of her mouth would slow down time and allow him to sink into the intimacy that was now so important to him. But all it managed was to shock Gordon into hesitating.

Javi pulled back, conscious of their witnesses, but the dazed disappointment on Cara's face heated him enough to forget the snow was falling.

'Cara,' Gordon said, his voice stony.

She blinked and looked up at Javi in confusion.

'Tomorrow, I'll explain everything,' he promised.

It was difficult to wave her off, but the twinkling lights on the tree and the warm stone buildings surrounding the courtyard reminded him that Christmas wasn't over yet – especially not in this country, where the main celebration waited until tomorrow.

'Well, you screwed that up,' Bea said as she skated up.

'It's harder than you think,' he said flatly. 'But I have a plan, at least. Let's go back to the hotel. We have a song to write.'

'We?'

He smiled. 'We. You have to help me with the English.'

She wrinkled her nose. 'Is it going to be sappy?'

'It might be sappy.'

'Urgh, Dad, this is so not normal.'

'Maybe not, but I don't want to do this without you, mija.'

* * *

He wasn't surprised when the song flowed much better than the damn water he had tried not to drink. He and Bea bickered and joked and made music until late in the evening until he was satisfied with the result.

They called Susana so she could hear the chimes of Big Ben at midnight and then he tugged Bea in for a hug.

'Thanks for coming, gordita. It's the best Christmas present.'

She looked up at him, her nose wrinkled. 'That had better not mean you forgot to get me something.'

He chuckled and pinched her shoulder affectionately. 'I'm not that bad a dad.' He turned to his suitcase and pulled out two wrapped packages. She opened the larger one first to find a pair of drumsticks and some professional-quality headphones. In the smaller box was a pair of earrings.

'How'd I do?' he asked as she attacked the packaging of the headphones.

'Pretty good,' she said with a nonchalant smile that didn't quite hide her happiness. 'Merry Christmas, Dad.'

* * *

'I still can't believe the nerve of him!' Gordon muttered as they got out of the taxi into the still, glittering frost of Christmas morning in a deserted central London. 'I'll make sure he leaves you alone today.'

Cara couldn't believe the nerve of him, either. He'd kissed her right in front of her father. It had felt amazing. Ever since he'd asked her in his husky, impassioned voice to give him a chance, her heart had been floating among the snowflakes. And she was counting on him not leaving her alone today. He had a mysterious Christmas present for her. When she thought about it, she felt like a child sitting by the tree, yearning to open the bright packages.

Her rational mind was trying to tell her that nothing had changed between them. He was still the slippery lover who didn't want responsibility. But this time she didn't want to listen to reason over her fevered instinct. She wanted to enjoy the surreal hope that had taken hold of her. It had already been a Christmas like no other – a bridge between the painful past and a future that didn't scare her as much any more.

'The hopes and fears of all the years are met in thee tonight.' Gordon had been too distracted the night before to protest when she put on the old vinyl record her mother had always played at

Christmas. She'd mellowed him with wine and mince pies and eventually he'd settled into his armchair with a final mutter about it all being over tomorrow.

Cara suspected – hoped – he might be wrong, but weren't family arguments a proper part of Christmas, too?

'It'll be fine, Daddy. You'll see.'

He studied her, his expression slowly softening to bewildered admiration. 'That's what I'm supposed to tell you.'

'And I appreciate it every time you do,' she smiled.

Freddie greeted them enthusiastically as they arrived at Trafalgar Square and Cara stood for a moment to stare at the tree and enjoy the stillness of the cold morning. It was twenty-five degrees colder than that evening four months ago when she and Javi had created a dream.

The TV crew was preparing in a heated marquee at the side of the square.

'Has... he arrived, yet?' Gordon asked as they went inside.

'Javier's not here, yet,' Freddie replied and Cara stifled a laugh. Javi's full name sounded odd and distant to her and Freddie's pronunciation was atrocious.

'Good,' Gordon said, so emphatically that Freddie glanced at him, startled. Cara greeted the production crew distractedly and watched the entrance with anticipation.

She didn't have to wait long. Bea came through first, making a beeline for Cara and giving her a hug and a 'Merry Christmas' that made her grin.

'Happy Christmas to you, too.'

'Do I get a hug, as well?'

Cara gave her heart firm instructions to stay where it was, but it disobeyed deplorably when she lifted her eyes to his. He was wearing his Colombian hat and a grin that made her knees weak. His guitar was strapped onto his back like the extension of him she suspected it was. And he had a glint in his eye that promised everything.

She managed some kind of mumbling response in the positive and then melted into his arms. If the embrace was her Christmas present, it was the best one she'd received in her memory.

Then he leaned down to whisper in her ear. 'Merry—'

'We're due at make-up,' Gordon boomed from across the marquee and he approached with quick steps.

Javi rolled his eyes, but he didn't seem disturbed by her father's machinations. He released her with slow reluctance.

She twisted round to stare at Javi as she was propelled away. Follow, damn it! She needed to hear what he had to say. But he didn't move. He cocked his head in chagrin and stuffed his hands in his pockets. Had she been wrong?

'What about my Christmas present?' she called out.

'Cara!' her father reprimanded with surprised bluster.

But Javi looked up and met her gaze. He smiled slowly and gave a nod. As she settled in the chair behind a curtain for make-up, her phone vibrated and she fished it out of her pocket.

This is for you…

A moment later, a video thumbnail appeared. It was a still of Javi with his guitar in what looked like a hotel room. She bit back a thrilled gasp. For her… No matter what the song said, she was touched that he'd written it. But which direction had he taken? Was it a song about lost bullets and bleeding hearts? Or did that glint in his eye mean this wasn't just another song about a woman he'd loved? She stared at the screen as the video loaded.

The make-up artist asked her to lift her head and she deactivated her phone screen with a frustrated sigh. Her father hovered. She stared in the mirror at her poor attempt at a straight face as she submitted to the make-up. Her phone burned in her pocket – at least that's how it felt.

When she was done, she emerged to find Javi waiting on the other side of the curtain for his turn. He gave her a mysterious smile and handed her a pair of headphones before disappearing behind the curtain.

She found a seat and turned away from her father, slipping the headphones on. At least she usually had a similar routine before performances and Gordon would think she was just preparing for the show.

With a last, choppy breath, she tapped on the video. The first thing she saw was his hand with the long fingernails, retreating before the camera, and then his face came into focus, his expression grave. He tucked his hair behind his ear and mumbled, 'Un, dos, tres, cuatro.' He strummed the guitar in a whimsical pattern on the off-beat, while a basic percussion accompaniment sounded from off-camera. Bea? His head beat subtly in time and his hand flew over the frets.

Her eyes narrowed when Javi started singing.

> *I thought promises were hard to keep*
> *And if I failed the price was steep.*

She wasn't used to hearing him sing in English. She suspected he wasn't used to singing in English. The words struck her in the chest.

> *So I made none, even when I should*
> *I didn't tell the truth, even when I could.*

He looked into the camera.

But then I learned...

With a flourish, his strumming built into the chorus, starting with a line of soaring melody that stole her breath.

This is not a love song.

Goose bumps stole up her arms and she swallowed the bubble of emotion. Her throat closed and her heart was racing, but it was elation flowing through her body. It wasn't just some love song. Javi was singing his heart and soul – for her.

He smiled into the camera, a rueful, open smile that she felt through her whole body.

> *I've handed in my rifle and made cupid give up his bow*
> *I only want to be with you and watch love softly grow.*

Her eyes stung as he returned to the strumming pattern for the verse. She blinked as fast as she could. She didn't want to ruin the make-up artist's hard work.

> *It's so sexy when you tell me the truth,*
> *When you see and you care and you make the first move.*
> *My stupid weapons of love don't exist,*
> *You neutralised them the first time that we kissed.*
> *Everything changed...*

She gave up the battle with the tears, holding a hand to her mouth as the first drops stained her cheeks. He repeated the chorus, his voice reaching out to her heart as his image blurred with her tears.

Was this real? She didn't dare doubt him when the song was so simple, so heartfelt and nothing like anything he'd written before. She'd known who he was inside – she'd felt it. Now he was willing to embrace it, to embrace what they could have if they stopped believing in their own limitations.

The music paused and she dabbed at her eyes to see him giving the camera a grin. She smiled back, unable to do anything else, even though it was stupid.

> *With you it's not a conquest or a struggle,*
> *I just want to hold your hand in the jungle.*
> *I want every tomorrow – cada mañana,*
> *I'll hold you and watch you face life's iguanas.*
> *You're so brave...*

He shrugged, his hands falling from the guitar. 'Bea thought that was silly, but I like it,' he said through a smile. *I like it, too*, she grinned. His smile took her back to Tayrona, to the time their relationship had progressed to hand-holding and honesty, and everything between them had changed.

He started up the chorus again. This time, the last line was slightly different: 'I only want to stay with you and watch love softly grow.' He dealt the final blow in the bridge, with sudden minor chords and a voice quiet with emotion.

> *I know nothing's perfect, least of all me,*
> *I know now what I fool I was, thinking love was free,*
> *I know you're scared to trust me, but you don't need*
> *   to be.*
> *I know what I'm working for – it's a future with you*
> *   and me.*

She breathed a huge sigh of relief. She hadn't been wrong.

Loving Javi was not a mistake. Trusting him, trusting her feelings had been a brave accident, but a life-changing one.

The song trailed off as he repeated this is not a love song a few times and finished with a husky, 'It's much, much more.' He pursed his lips and reached into the picture again, switching off the video.

Cara took a shuddering breath. Then she ripped off her headphones and ran. He'd given her everything. Now it was her turn.

* * *

She's not watching it. There's no time. Stop fidgeting. Javi pursed his lips and breathed out slowly. Hope was torture.

He was finished in the make-up chair mercifully quickly and, when he stood, Bea rushed in, her eyes bright. 'Dad, quick!' She pulled on his arm and he followed her without question. 'It's Cara. I think she's heard the song!' He did his best to ignore the fireworks in his chest. This was it.

When he pushed aside the curtain, she had his guitar strapped over her shoulder and was checking the tuning. He halted, loving how she looked with his favourite guitar. His mind went back to Cali, to the best concert of his life.

She strummed experimentally, the fingers of her left hand strong and delicate on the strings. 'There's a pick in the case,' he said and her eyes flew up. He stared at her, his mouth forming some kind of giddy smile. She bit her lip and he knew her mind was in Cali as well. She stooped to fetch the plectrum and stood with a deep breath.

'What is going on?' Gordon thundered from the doorway. 'You're supposed to be out there in five minutes!' Javi's anticipation wavered.

Cara's eyes lifted briefly to his, then she turned to her father. 'This is more important than the show, Daddy.'

'What is?' He glared at Javi. 'Is this your doing? I can't stand by and watch you upsetting her.'

'He's not upsetting me,' she said firmly. 'You've always been there for me, Daddy. But this is my move to make.' She glanced at Javi. 'And I'm making a move.' A grin pulled on his mouth. He didn't dare take his eyes off her. His chest was swelling and his breath ragged, but the blast of mad hope was exhilarating.

She swiped her hair out of her face and turned to him, her head high. 'I wrote this the other night. It's not finished...' she muttered. He nodded and held her gaze. There were silent eyes on them and rustling in the background as the TV crew gathered in curiosity, but he could only see Cara. He'd recorded his video so she could dissect his heart in private and react without embarrassment. She was standing before the whole TV crew with a guitar – for him.

Her song started with a dramatic riff that she fumbled slightly, but played defiantly. When she started singing, her voice was low and clear and strong.

> *Of all the things that weren't meant to be, we weren't*
> *meant to be the most.*
> *It wasn't meant to be so good; I wasn't meant to get so*
> *hurt.*
> *You weren't meant to be so kind, so funny, so brilliant, so*
> *real.*
> *You weren't meant to ever know how much you made me*
> *feel.*
>
> *I hate to say I love you*
> *I hate that you're the first*
> *But I'll carry you with my broken heart*
> *Because that's what love deserves.*

She stopped all of a sudden. 'That's all I've got so far. I couldn't get any further.'

Javi's smile widened with dizzy pride. She was stunning and courageous, and he would make this work for the rest of their lives. He sprang into action, rushing to her and thrusting his fingers into her hair. He brought his face close and murmured. 'I love you so much, Cara. I don't want to let you go – ever. I'm so sorry I didn't understand in time. Tell me I can fix it.'

'You already have,' she whispered. 'I'm sorry I ran without giving you a chance. I couldn't finish the song because I knew it couldn't be the end – I mean, I didn't know, I felt.' She lifted her head to close the distance between them and kiss him. He closed his eyes and allowed himself to be blown away. He pressed into the kiss, wanting to fall deeper, responding to the relief arcing between them.

'I love you,' he repeated between kisses. 'Let's finish that song together – with a different ending.'

She opened her mouth, kissing him deeply until a groan rose up from his chest. 'I had a whole list of your faults that are ready to go into that song,' she said against his lips.

He chuckled, leaning his forehead against hers. 'At least you know what you're getting. Save it for our tenth anniversary.' He grinned. She lifted her chin and he pressed another kiss to her expectant lips. 'Take the guitar off, corazón. I want to hold you.'

She tucked perfectly into his arms – warm, familiar, belonging.

'Thank you for writing the song. It was beautiful,' she said.

'I'm relieved you liked it. The Colombian way would have been to serenade you at your window, but I imagine you would have thrown something at me if I'd embarrassed you in front of your father's neighbours.'

'Mm-hmm,' she confirmed with a smile. 'I don't want a grand gesture. I just want you – and your brilliant music.'

'Our brilliant music,' he murmured.

* * *

It was a delicious feeling of déjà vu to dance with him again under the Christmas tree on Trafalgar Square. It was difficult to sing because she wanted to laugh. Javi's broad grin and twinkling eyes didn't help. She'd known in August that this song had the power to change her life and this man would disrupt everything. She hadn't realised how wonderful the disruption would be. Life with Javi would be gloriously messy – even as they held each other safe.

At the end of the bridge, Javi ditched the choreography and lifted her high against him as he sang, 'Mi corazón sigue latiendo por ti.'

'And my heart keeps beating for you,' she murmured in the pause. Javi's arms tightened round her and his smile was lopsided and glimmering with approval.

She threw her arms round him when the song finished, not caring that the cameras were still rolling. She swiped her microphone and his to the side and gave him a quick, hard kiss. She felt his laugh under her palms.

'What happened to professionalism?'

She grinned. 'That kiss would have been much longer if I wasn't such a professional.'

'Er, I take it the rumours of a relationship can be confirmed?' the presenter asked as she approached awkwardly to keep the show moving. They cut to a pre-recorded section and a cheer rose. Cara turned to find Bea and the TV crew clapping and whistling. Gordon stood frowning next to her, but he dropped his shoulders with a turbulent sigh that told her he'd come round.

Bea glanced at him and then turned, her hands on her hips. 'Look, if I'm okay with this – and I might point out I'm the one getting a wannabe step-mom – you'd better get with the programme.'

He scowled. 'And I'm supposed to be your step-grandfather?'

She shuddered. 'Oh, please. Just don't say nasty shit to Javi. All he's done is love her stupidly.'

'Stupidly is it?' Gordon muttered.

'What have we done?' Javi murmured with a smile.

'It's going to be an interesting Christmas lunch.'

'I have the feeling all our Christmases are going to be interesting from now on.'

'Is that a promise?'

He chuckled. 'No, but this is: I love you.' He kissed her again, stealing her breath before she could respond. 'I love you for all our Christmases – for a whole lot longer than the three and a half minutes it takes to hear a love song.'

'I love you for longer than your fans will remember your love songs – even the one that's not a love song. Shall we put it on the internet?'

His smile was rueful and indulgent. 'You think it would be popular?'

She grinned. 'That and I want everyone to know how crazy drunk in love you are.'

He laughed. 'Me? A victim of cupid's arrow?'

She stretched up to look him in the eye. 'Careful, I might start appreciating your metaphors.'

'They're all for you, now.'

Her heart beat wildly at the tender words. It may be corny and passionate, but that was Javi and she didn't care because it was truly Christmas and he was truly hers.

EPILOGUE

'Oh, this one's bad, but Javi will love it!' Bea squealed. 'Why did the turkey join the band?'

'I don't know. Why?' Cara joined in with mock anticipation.

'Because it had the drumsticks!' she giggled.

'I'm not sure it's a compliment if you think I'd find that funny,' Javi drawled, straightening his bright pink paper crown.

'Let's do another one!' Bea suggested, holding out eager hands for the end of Cara's Christmas cracker. When she'd bought them on impulse in her determination to reclaim Christmas, she never expected to get through the whole pack and with such an enthusiastic partner.

They pulled – popped the cracker – and this time Cara ended up with the middle. She unrolled the paper hat and set it on her head with a grin at Javi. She pulled out the joke on the little slip of paper. 'This one's appropriate too: what do you call Father Christmas on the beach?'

'What?'

'Sandy Claus.' She grinned as Javi and Bea groaned in true

British Christmas spirit. She flicked the little plastic frog from inside the cracker at Javi and he caught it and flicked it back. Unable to resist, she leaned over and gave him a kiss.

'Ugh, guys. We've witnessed enough for today.'

Javi grabbed her hand as she moved sheepishly away and whispered in her ear, 'I haven't.'

Cara grabbed a cracker and held it out to Gordon. 'Dad?'

He inclined his head and grasped one end. She thought she saw a hint of a smile, but she suspected her father was so full of conflicting emotions that she wouldn't detect much. They'd always had Christmas crackers when her mother had been alive.

Cara won the middle, but she handed it to him. 'You have to put the hat on.'

He eyed her and set the paper crown on the table. But he unrolled the joke and cleared his throat. 'What do you get if you cross Santa with a duck?'

'What?' asked Bea.

Gordon frowned. 'A Christmas quacker. I can't believe someone gets paid to write these.'

A timer sounded in the kitchen and Cara stood, but Gordon was quicker. 'I'll get it.' He waved her back into her seat and she watched him go thoughtfully.

'Are you sure he's okay with us joining you?' Javi asked quietly.

Cara wrinkled her nose thoughtfully. 'I don't know, but it's not just you. We haven't had this much laughter at Christmas for a long time.'

'I'm sorry if you wanted to be miserable.'

She grinned and squeezed his hand. 'Sometimes you need a few miserable Christmases to really appreciate the joyful ones.'

'Um, I'll go help in the kitchen.' Bea stood and disappeared before Cara could even look up.

'Alone at last,' Javi rumbled and pulled her close, planting his mouth on hers for a proper kiss. She grabbed for him and the paper hat fell to the floor. 'It's awkward how much I want to be alone with you,' he murmured and kissed her again.

'Wow, that pudding looks great!' Bea called out artificially loudly and they sprang apart.

Cara smiled wryly at him and nodded, mouthing the word 'awkward' with equal conviction. He mouthed back 'later', and she giggled.

Bea held the door open for Gordon who was wearing an apron and carrying the pudding on a tray, along with four champagne glasses. Cara's mouth opened in surprise to see the apron. 'That's Mum's!'

Gordon set the pudding down steadily and gave her a grim look. 'Is that okay?'

She just looked at him for a long moment. 'Yes. It's okay.'

He nodded stiffly and held his hand out to Bea. She handed him the bottle of champagne she'd carried out from the kitchen. Gordon wrestled with it for a moment before the cork popped and he poured three glasses. He filled the fourth with juice and handed them round.

He looked at each of their faces in turn, lingering on Cara's with wistful nostalgia before swerving to Javi's with grim challenge. 'I hope you'll all know what I mean if I make a toast to being okay this Christmas.'

Javi smiled slowly, meeting Gordon's gaze with a warm nod. They clinked glasses, and Gordon cut the pudding while Cara added brandy sauce and handed round the bowls.

'Umm, well that's weird,' Bea commented, chewing slowly.

Gordon looked up sharply, but Cara put a hand on his arm. 'Remember the jalapeños,' she muttered.

They cleared up the dishes and moved into the kitchen as the album of carols from the choir of King's College, Cambridge finished the final, triumphal verse of 'O Come, All Ye Faithful' that was only to be sung on Christmas day.

Before Cara could line up another song, Javi grabbed her phone with a mischievous smile. A moment later, a rousing conga beat and syncopated salsa piano filled the kitchen. He grabbed Bea's hand and twirled her round.

Cara glanced at Gordon, whose frown looked decidedly half-hearted. 'No,' he said drily.

'How about Cara and I wash up,' Javi suggested as the next song started. 'Gordon, thanks so much for lunch. But you deserve to sit down and have a rest. Bea, you like napping, don't you?'

Bea rolled her eyes, but took the hint. Even Gordon decided to play along. When they were finally alone, he pulled Cara close and they danced for a few joyful minutes before it descended into more kissing.

'I would applaud your ingenuity, except that we have to wash up,' she murmured, her lips on his jaw.

'It's all part of the plan,' he muttered back. He backed her up to the sink and reached round her to turn on the tap. When the sink was full and sudsy, he turned her round and rolled up her sleeves. 'There,' he whispered in her ear.

She couldn't have said how many flecks remained on the dishes because she had so much trouble concentrating with his soapy hands moving with hers and his lips straying to her neck.

'I think I love Christmas,' she sighed with a chuckle.

'I love you. And just think: there's a lot more to come than just Christmas. There's año nuevo and carnaval, Easter and Colombian Independence Day in July.'

She wiped off her hands and turned, looping her arms round his neck. 'Do you know day what I look forward to most?'

'What?'

She grinned. 'Tomorrow. And then tomorrow. And then tomorrow.'

ACKNOWLEDGMENTS

There are so many people who have joined me for different parts of this journey to the publication of my first novel. I am forever thankful to Caroline at Boldwood Books for believing in this story enough to take a chance on a rookie author. Also to my editor, Sarah, for sharing the weighty responsibility of putting my words out there and helping to make sure the book is deserving of its lovely readers.

I need to specifically thank my mental health sensitivity reader, Laura McKendrick, who helped me analyse the story, characters, scenes and words for their impact on and representation of people with mental illness. She did an amazing job. I'd also like to thank the lovely scientist Dr Jimena Barrero Canosa, who test-read the book, representing her beautiful country, Colombia.

Anyone curious about the video diary app Cara uses can check out Mental Snapp and the mental health artists community, started by the inspiring Hannah Chamberlain.

Credit also goes to my two usual readers, RB Owen and Lucy Flatman, without whom this book would definitely not be here. You two have been a source of professional growth, confidence and community on my writing journey and I don't know what I would do without you.

I would also like to make special mention of my Zumba instructors Cornelia and Carina who, unbeknownst to them, provided the mental space to run through the scenes of this book!

Lastly, I'd like to thank the people who turned me into a writer. My mum and dad, with their unique combination of encouragement and humour, and my sister, who always believed in my writing, even when I didn't really myself. Thanks to my husband and kids for putting up with a dirty house and basic dinners when I'm in drafting mode, but mostly for appreciating me for me. And I can't finish without mentioning Jessie Klug and Sarah Radcliffe, my oldest and dearest friends, who I forced to read the first novel I ever wrote back when I was twenty and who have been with me this whole way, even when we live countries and continents apart.

MORE FROM LEONIE MACK

We hope you enjoyed reading *My Christmas Number One*. If you did, please leave a review.

If you'd like to gift a copy, this book is also available as an ebook, digital audio download and audiobook CD.

Sign up to Leonie Mack's mailing list for news, competitions and updates on future books.

https://bit.ly/LeonieMackNewsletter

ABOUT THE AUTHOR

Leonie Mack is a debut romantic novelist. Having lived in London for many years her home is now in Germany with her husband and three children. Leonie loves train travel, medieval towns, hiking and happy endings!

Visit Leonie's website: https://leoniemack.com/

Follow Leonie on social media:

 twitter.com/LeonieMAuthor

 instagram.com/leoniejmack

 facebook.com/LeonieJMack

ABOUT BOLDWOOD BOOKS

Boldwood Books is a fiction publishing company seeking out the best stories from around the world.

Find out more at www.boldwoodbooks.com

Sign up to the Book and Tonic newsletter for news, offers and competitions from Boldwood Books!

http://www.bit.ly/bookandtonic

We'd love to hear from you, follow us on social media:

facebook.com/BookandTonic

twitter.com/BoldwoodBooks

instagram.com/BookandTonic

Printed in Great Britain
by Amazon

26713810R00185